HEREWARD

www.transworldbooks.co.uk

HEREWARD

James Wilde

TRANSWORLD PUBLISHERS
61–63 Uxbridge Road, London W5 5SA
A Random House Company
www.transworldbooks.co.uk

First published in Great Britain
in 2011 by Bantam Press
an imprint of Transworld Publishers

A CIP catalogue record for this book
is available from the British Library.

ISBNs 9780593064887 (cased)
9780593064894 (tpb)

Addresses for Random House Group Ltd companies outside the UK
can be found at: www.randomhouse.co.uk
The Random House Group Ltd Reg. No. 954009

The Random House Group Limited supports the Forest Stewardship
Council® (FSC®), the leading international forest certification organization.
All our titles that are printed on Greenpeace approved FSC® certified
paper carry the FSC® logo. Our paper procurement policy can be
found at www.randomhouse.co.uk/environment

Typeset in 11½/14pt Sabon by
Kestrel Data, Exeter, Devon.
Printed and bound in Great Britain by
Clays Ltd, Bungay, Suffolk.

2 4 6 8 10 9 7 5 3 1

ACKNOWLEDGEMENTS

For help and guidance, Dr Richard Hall, Director of Archaeology, York Archaeological Trust for Excavation and Research, and York Visitor Information Centre.

CHAPTER ONE

29 November 1062

It was the beginning of the End-Times.

Black snow stung the face of the young man. Skidding knee-deep down the white-blanketed slope, he squinted in the face of the blizzard as he struggled to discern a path through the wild countryside of high hills and dense forest. On his tongue, the bitter taste confirmed his fears: ashes, caught up in the swirling white flakes. He was too late. Beneath the howl of the gale, he could hear the roar of the fires ahead and he glimpsed the billowing dark cloud just above the ridge, while at his back came the bestial call and response of the hunting party, drawing closer as he tired. From hell into hell.

With numb fingers, Alric pulled his coarse woollen cloak tightly over his black cowled habit, but his teeth still rattled, as much from fear as from cold. He was barely into his eighteenth year, his face as yet unlined by life's strife. Hazel-coloured hair hung wet and lank against his thin face, his tonsure already growing out, and black rings lay under his hollow eyes. At that moment, the security and peace of the monastery at Jarrow seemed to belong in the memory of another, more innocent person, one uncorrupted by searing despair. He thought of his mother and father who had sent him to the monastery as a child for a life in service to God. What would they think if they knew how badly he had let them down?

Shrieking like lost souls, the ravens rose in one jet-black cloud from the spindly trees as he staggered up the next slope. His breath burned in his chest and his joints ached, but he drove himself on, grabbing on to branches to drag himself through the drifts. As the blizzard eased, he saw there was no way to hide his path. Across the desolate white landscape, his footprints trailed behind him for three miles, leading the raiders directly to him.

At the top of the ridge, he made the mistake of glancing back. Silhouetted against the lowering grey sky on the hilltop a half-mile behind him was Death, the battleaxe Grim gripped in his right hand, a spear in his left. Harald Redteeth paused only briefly, the wind whipping his cloak, before plunging down the hillside into the trees. Like a pack of wolves, his men swept over the hilltop behind him, silent now, sensing their prey was close.

Frantically, Alric crested the ridge, only to fall to his knees in the snow in shock when he saw the devastation heaped upon the village he had made his home.

A black pall covered the clearing in the forest as scarlet and gold flames blazed from every timber-and-thatch dwelling in Gedley. Only the crackle of the fire and the hungry cawing of the birds could be heard; no pleas for help, no cries from mothers searching for children, or defiant men raging against their suffering. Nor was there any sign of the ones Harald Redteeth had sent on ahead.

My fault, Alric thought, before angry self-loathing overwhelmed his guilt. *All my fault!*

Throwing himself down the incline, he picked up speed, his weary legs pumping out of control until he stumbled and fell, crashing against the boundary post next to the stream.

Hair, clothes and eyelashes white, he hauled himself to his

feet and ran into the trees, calling the names of every inhabitant of Gedley one after the other. There was no response.

He might as well have set fire to the houses himself, plunged a spear into the chest of every man, woman and child. Could God forgive him? Could he ever forgive himself? Lost in the choking smoke, he wondered if he should stop running, let Harald Redteeth kill him too. He deserved his fate.

The monk cried out in shock as the floating figure of a man loomed out of the acrid fog, arms outstretched like the Lord upon the cross, eyes wide and staring. A moment later, Alric realized the man was dead, and one stumbling step forward revealed that the body was suspended in the thorny branches of a hawthorn tree. Wild hair and beard, both stained a deep blue, formed a fierce halo above a rusted hauberk that bore the marks of many strikes. Pink scars from battles past criss-crossed the arms and face. Alric's gaze skittered to a vision of butchery and he reeled backwards, sickened: the carcass had been ripped from sternum to groin and the throat slashed, as if one killing had not been enough. Blood spattered the snow at the foot of the tree.

The slaughtered man was not one of the Gedley villagers, the monk saw. For six months, Alric had broken bread with every one of them while ministering to their needs, and this was a fighting man, not a farmer. He could only guess it was one of Harald Redteeth's raiders.

But who had taken his life? The men of Gedley were not warriors.

Baffled, he fought to order his thoughts, and stumbled on through the smoke. Fifty paces further on, he cried out again. A severed head had been rammed on to the top of a boundary post, the neck cut clean across. A raven gripped the thick brown hair and pecked at one of the white eyes. Alric felt his throat tighten in mounting panic. Could this be another of the Viking's men? Northumbria was a lawless place, but never had he witnessed such brutality. Dizzy, he recalled the villagers' hearthside tales of the wicked *wuduwasa* that roamed the haunted woods gnawing on raw bones, and the shadow-spirits that waited among the trees for the unwary traveller. The monk crossed himself to ward off any watching evil.

But then the roar of the inferno wrenched him back to Gedley, and he blinked back hot tears of shame. Let the Viking and his men come; his own life no longer mattered if he could save just one survivor. But even though he shielded his face, the inferno seared his throat and drove him back. Falling to his knees in frustration, he began to sob.

When the racking had subsided, he raised his eyes to heaven and began to mutter a prayer for forgiveness. He caught a flash of movement on the periphery of his vision, but the smoke swallowed up whatever was there almost as quickly as it had appeared. His heart pattered. Another fleeting movement followed, and then another.

The instinct for self-preservation finally overcame him. Scrambling to his feet, he staggered away from the fire towards, he hoped, the path that led deep into the shadowy safety of the forest.

A cry rang out, followed by a response further away.

Alric blanched. They had found him.

Running wildly, he tripped over a tree root and sprawled across the frozen ground, cracking his head and grazing his cheek. He knew he did not deserve to live, but he did not want to die. The conundrum brought another bout of sobs, but they died in his throat when he raised himself up from the snow.

The dew-pond on the edge of the village was now a lake of blood.

On the far side of the hollow lay the bodies of the villagers, hacked to death and heaped high as if they were firewood, their blood draining into the churned-up slush. Appalled, Alric gazed at the hellish scene until a sound behind him made him spin round; too late. Brandishing a bloodstained spear, one of the hunting band loomed out of the smoke, his wiry hair and thick beard frosted with snow. His hate-filled eyes blazed.

'Who are you?' Alric croaked.

'You know,' the Viking said with a broken-toothed grin.

Alric did: the one the ravens followed, the bony figure with the scythe who cut down all men; his own personal end.

Thrusting his hand into the monk's cloak, the warrior hauled him up and cuffed him so hard that Alric saw stars. When his head cleared, he found himself back on the frozen ground staring into the lake of blood.

Something moved just beneath the surface.

At first he thought it was just ripples caused by the icy wind, but then a bubble broke the sticky surface and then another. A wild-eyed figure rose from the depths, slaked red from head to toe.

'The Devil!' Alric gasped.

CHAPTER TWO

'No devil.' The bloody apparition grinned at the monk, who recoiled from whatever he saw in the gore-stained face. 'I am Hereward.'

As he emerged from his hiding place, the warrior swept his sword in an arc that sent scarlet droplets showering across the snow. The Viking hesitated, his lips curling back from his teeth, and raised his own weapon. Hereward felt a rush of euphoria. Too slow, he thought. He could see the questions turning over in the other warrior's face, the hint of unease in his eyes. Still trying to make sense of what he was seeing, the Northman swayed off balance, awkwardly preparing to thrust his spear.

Stepping over the whimpering monk, Hereward cleaved the haft in two, and followed through with another two-handed slice. At the last moment, the Viking lurched back a step so that the sword merely raised a trail of golden sparks from his mail shirt instead of carving him open. Losing his balance, he crashed down to one knee.

'He is defenceless,' the monk stuttered.

'Good.' Hereward angled his sword above the mail shirt and drove it into the man's chest until the tip protruded from his back. The Northman gurgled, eyes frozen wide in shock. When

Hereward withdrew the blade, hot blood trailed from the body where it had been opened to the air.

'You did not have to kill him,' the monk said, aghast.

'He would have killed you without a second thought. And he helped slaughter all of them.' Hereward nodded to the pile of villagers' bodies.

Croaking, the dying warrior tried to call out to his comrades. Hereward hacked off his head with one blow and picked it up by the hair, studying it with contempt for a moment before hurling it deep into the forest.

'What are you?' the monk said in disgust.

'Your saviour.' Hereward felt the ecstasy of the kill already begin to ebb, and the resonant voice inside him called out for more blood. It throbbed in his head, in his very bones, the hungry urging of the thing that had lived with him since he was a boy. For a moment, he listened for the sound of approaching feet. They were hard and cold like their northern home, these mercenaries, he thought, and seasoned by battle. They would not be deterred by sentiment or fear. He had ghosted out of the trees to kill the stragglers when they put the village to the torch, glimpsed by the others only in passing, and he knew that one on one was no contest. But if they came in force he would be at a disadvantage. 'They'll find us soon,' he murmured, trying to pierce the dense smoke. 'I counted another four here. Probably more on the way.'

'Yes . . . there are.'

'Then you have a choice: stay here and be food for the ravens, or come with me.' He could see that the monk thought both options equally abhorrent, and with a shrug he prowled into the frozen wood. He hadn't gone far when he heard the sound of the monk scrambling to catch up.

'Tell me you did not murder any of the villagers.' Anger laced the monk's voice, but he was fighting back tears of grief.

'I did not.'

'You are not from Gedley. What fight do you have with Redteeth's band?'

'Redteeth? That is their leader's name?' Hereward shrugged, wiping the sticky drips from his brow. 'I am a man of Mercia. I was resting here in the village on my journey to Eoferwic. When the Northmen started their slaughtering, they made the error of trying to kill me too.' Hereward thought back to the moment when, bleary-eyed from sleep, he had emerged from the house into the din of the attack. The raiding party roamed among the blazing houses, cutting down anyone who crossed their path. His first thought had been that the men who had pursued him from the court in London had finally caught up with him. Then, as he prepared to run, he had glimpsed a sight that turned a knife in the open wounds in his heart. A woman crying out as an axe split her skull, a small child sobbing at her side. The warrior winced. The vision had disinterred memories of two other women lying at his feet, their dead eyes staring blankly up at him. In an instant, his murderous rage had boiled up and after that he remembered only the iron scent of blood, the crack of bone and the throat-rending screams that followed the dance of his sword.

Away in the fog of burning echoed the sound of running feet and a cry of alarm, quickly answered. The Viking's headless body had been discovered, Hereward surmised. He grabbed the monk by the arm and hauled him on. 'Battle with your conscience when you are not in danger of having your head removed.'

The man stumbled along behind Hereward on weary legs. 'They will not give up until they find us. Harald Redteeth can track a man through woodland far thicker than this—'

'Quiet,' Hereward snapped. 'If you are planning to babble all the time, I will leave you behind.'

The monk glared at him. 'Harald Redteeth will not rest until we are dead.'

'And I will not rest until he is dead. Choose your side now. Only one of us will be left standing when this business is done.'

With the angry bellows of the raiders drawing closer, Hereward darted among the tangle of oaks and ash trees without waiting for a response. Cutting round a rocky outcrop that would hide them from their pursuers for a while, he plunged down a bank into a freezing stream, the exhausted monk struggling along close behind. The warrior felt his feet turn to ice in his leather shoes, but the discomfort was a small price to pay to ensure that no trail would be left to mark their passage.

As they splashed along, the monk gasped, 'My name is Alric. My home is the monastery at Jarrow, but I have journeyed far and wide to spread God's word.'

'God seems to have forsaken this place.' Hereward could see that the monk would be a burden in the coming battle. And his chatter was as irritating as the incessant drone of a horsefly. Hereward weighed the advantages of clouting the cleric un- conscious and leaving him for the hunting party to find.

'What are you thinking?' Alric wheezed.

'Ask me in a little while.'

Where the stream cascaded down a tumble of rocks, the warrior grasped a branch to lever himself out of the water. He hesitated, studying Alric for a moment before reaching out to help the monk. Stooping to cup his hands in the icy water, he swilled some of the blood away to reveal streaks of long blond hair, and a strong jaw. His eyes were a piercing pale blue. As the caked gore sluiced off, the blue-black marks of the warrior were uncovered on his upper arms, spirals and circles made by punching ashes into the skin with an awl. He saw the monk eyeing the gold rings of a man of status round his forearms and biceps, but he was not about to satisfy the curiosity he discerned in his companion's eyes.

The monk relaxed a little when he could see that Hereward was not the devil he had first perceived. 'You are not a common thief. You have had some tutoring,' he remarked. 'I can hear it in your voice.'

'No questions.'

'I would know what monster I accompany,' Alric said defiantly.

Hereward turned and pressed his blade against the monk's neck. 'Any more and I will gut you with my sword Brainbiter.'

'You would kill a man of God?'

'I would kill anyone.' The Mercian fixed his pale eyes on Alric, and saw something that surprised him: a deep, dark part of the monk wanted to die.

'You do not scare me,' Alric said, blinking away tears.

Ignoring him, Hereward glanced back along the stream. He absorbed the thinning light and the intensifying blizzard and knew that without shelter they would soon freeze to death. 'They will be here soon,' he said, turning to look into the darkening depths of the forest ahead. 'How far to the next village?'

'Half a day, at least. We will never survive the night.'

'Is there any other shelter?'

Alric hesitated. 'There is a woman who lives alone near here. She is *wicce*.'

'Which way?'

'No!' Alric protested. 'She carries out necromancies and enchantments and divinations. She is a heathen who denies the Paternoster and the Creed.'

As the shouts of their pursuers began to follow the path of the stream, Hereward grabbed Alric's shoulders and shook him. 'We do what we do to survive. You would rather die than break bread with a heathen?'

Snapping from the strain, Alric launched himself at the warrior, punching and kicking, spittle flying from his mouth as he raged. 'None of this matters. They will pursue us until we drop from exhaustion! We are already dead!'

'Yes. We are. All of us.' Hereward swung his fist into the monk's jaw and knocked him cold.

Dragging his companion across the snow and rocks to a broad oak tree, the warrior stripped off his own blood-sodden woollen tunic and leggings and used them to bind the monk to the bole. Once he was done, he tucked his leather pouch containing coin and a knife behind a rock. Naked, he flexed his muscles so that the blue whorls that covered his torso rippled in the fading light, and then he bellowed. A moment of silence ended in an abrupt crashing in the frozen undergrowth as Redteeth's men raced towards the sound.

Hereward bounded off into the growing gloom.

The monk must have come round in time to see him disappear into the trees, for the warrior heard Alric roar, 'Monster! You *are* the Devil!'

From his hiding place, Hereward watched two of the Viking mercenaries skid down the snowy bank to arrive beside Alric, one clutching an axe, the other a spear. Two more followed, wearing helmets and well-worn mail. 'It is only the monk,' the one with the axe said. 'The other has fled.'

'He left me here to slow you down!' Alric shouted. 'Pursue him! He is only a moment or two ahead!'

Hereward spied the two helmeted raiders following his trail; their time would come first. The Viking with the spear turned to Alric. 'Your debt can only be repaid with blood.'

'Harald will want to take that payment himself!' Alric replied bitterly.

'I will take your head back to him. He will be pleased with that . . . and reward me fully.'

Hereward saw Alric close his eyes and call on the Lord to save his soul. As the prayer whispered out on the wind, the Mercian was already circling round the two men trudging along his trail. When they separated to widen their search, he struck, allowing one blood-chilling scream to echo among the trees.

The monk's two remaining tormentors laughed. 'Your friend is dead,' one of them said.

'He is not my friend!' Alric snapped. 'He is nothing but a beast.'

Nearby, the dead man's companion crashed through the undergrowth, each guttural curse a testament to the fear he now felt. Once again Hereward struck with the speed and efficiency of a wolf, delaying the killing blow just enough to draw out another cry. It rang above the gale whipping through the branches.

Slipping back to where he could observe the monk and the two remaining raiders, Hereward saw that the Vikings' faces were drawn; their humour had drained away. The mercenary with the axe made to venture into the trees, but his comrade caught his arm to hold him back.

Letting his chin fall on to his chest, Alric whispered, 'He is the Devil.'

Ignoring the cold, Hereward waited, watching the fear rise in the two warriors. They raised their weapons as they circled the monk, searching for an attack from any direction. Long moments passed with only the howl of the wind and the blast of the snow. The darkness slipped among the trees and enveloped them.

Finally, Hereward moved from his hiding place. Knotted together by their long hair, the two heads arced from the shadows, twisting and turning to crash into the snow at the feet of the raiders with a splatter of blood.

Overcome with rage at the slaughter of his comrades, the warrior with the axe roared his battle cry and raced forwards. The warning from the other Northman came too late.

Spectral in the gloom, Hereward stepped from behind a spreading oak and swung his sword into the back of the raider's neck. Before the Viking had even hit the ground, the naked, blood-streaked man bounded towards the final mercenary. Hereward felt the rush of his bloodlust engulf him. The world diminished to his opponent's eyes and the dance of blades.

The Northman ducked the first strike though it drove him back. A storm of iron, Hereward's sword hacked right and left, high, for the shoulder blade, horizontally towards the ribcage. Struggling to stand his ground, the wild-haired mercenary dodged each blow and tried to bring his own weapon to bear.

For several minutes, the two men battled around Alric, fighting to keep their feet on the treacherous ground. Lost to his wild passion, Hereward failed to account for the deepening snow. Cursing, he went down on one knee. The mercenary saw his opening and thrust his spear.

Hereward threw himself to one side, bringing up his left fist into the warrior's groin. As the Viking doubled over in agony, the English warrior jumped up and rammed his knee into his opponent's face. The mercenary crashed backwards, unconscious.

Hereward heaved in a deep breath. As his vision cleared, the whispers in his head fell silent and his rage subsided. He moved to release the monk.

'They could have killed me! You did not know I would still be alive when you returned!' Alric shouted.

'No, I did not.' With irritation, the warrior waved a dismissive hand as if swatting a fly. 'You seem to believe that I care whether you live or die.'

Once Alric was free, Hereward stripped off the unconscious warrior's mail shirt, tunic and breeches and dressed in them. His arms and legs felt numb from the cold, but the feeling would return soon enough. Using the blood-soaked garments that had secured the monk, he tied the naked mercenary to the tree.

Alric slumped on to a fallen trunk, head in hands, repeating a short prayer in a tone of wrenching desolation.

'Do not pray for me. I am long since damned,' Hereward muttered as he checked the knots were tight.

'I am not praying for you.' With red-rimmed eyes, the monk levelled a haunted look in the direction of Gedley.

The Mercian could see that his companion was troubled by more than the deaths of the villagers. 'Who pays the Northmen? And why do they hunt for you?'

The young monk wiped the snot from his nose with the back of his hand. 'No questions,' he parroted.

Hereward shrugged. 'Then we both have our secrets.'

Shuddering from the cold, the mercenary started to come round. The English warrior reclaimed his leather pouch from behind the rock and removed his bone-handled knife. With his thumb, he checked the edge for sharpness.

Uneasily, Alric looked up from his prayers. 'What are you going to do?'

'I am going to flay the skin from him as I would a deer. And either his cries will draw Harald Redteeth towards us where I can butcher him too, or they will drive him away,' Hereward said.

In horror, Alric jumped up. 'You cannot do such a thing.'

'Fear is what drives all men in this world. Those who wield it, win.'

'No,' the monk urged. 'Love.'

Hereward laughed. 'When the Northmen first sailed to England in their dragon ships, they defeated us by instilling fear, so we are told. They sacked your monasteries and raped our women and we English ran like whipped dogs. The good Christian folk frighten the heathens to drive them from the land. And your own God threatens you with the Devil and the burning fires of hell if you stray from the path of righteousness.'

'What has made you like this?'

The mercenary moaned as he came to his senses. When Hereward leaned over him with the knife, the scream tore from his throat before the cold metal had even been pressed to his skin.

Alric shouted over the din, 'You rise from the blood of innocents. You kill, without guilt, as if you have no soul. I ask you again – what made you like this?'

'God made me like this.'

CHAPTER THREE

The blood-chilling scream ripped through the night-shrouded forest, growing shriller and more intense with each passing moment until it no longer sounded human. For that, Harald Redteeth's men gave thanks, for they could pretend it was some wild animal or fearsome monster hunting among the trees. But when it rolled on as though it would never end, they bowed their heads and clutched at their ears, unable to extinguish their visions of the suffering their comrade endured.

Harald Redteeth listened impassively to the agonized sound. He was a mercenary who took the coin of any man, be he merchant, thegn or king, who wanted death dealt quickly and harshly, and his appearance underscored his fearsome reputation. From the eyeholes of his axe-dented helmet, his black, distended pupils reflected the dancing flames of Gedley. His wild hair and beard were stained red by the dyes his people made from the hedgerow berries, his coarse woollen cloak hanging over furs greased with lamb fat that kept out the cold. And underneath those he wore his battle-scarred mail, rusted and bloodstained, and a sweat-reeking tunic. The skulls of birds and woodland animals swung from the hauberk on leather strips. At his side hung his axe, Grim.

'There is still time to save him,' Ivar, his second in command, muttered.

'He died long ago,' Redteeth replied. 'What you hear are the echoes as his spirit leaves his body.'

Ivar wrapped his woollen cloak around him against the blizzard as he sifted through every brutal campaign and bloody raid he had experienced for something that sickened him more. 'Why doesn't the bastard just slit his throat and be done with it?'

'He is trying to draw us out, into the forest, at night, where he has the advantage.'

'And the monk?'

'The tracks show he went with the stranger. If that is true, he could be dead by now, or he will be soon. We will search for his body at first light.'

The scream continued to plumb the depths of agony. Listening intently, Harald Redteeth noted a melody that no others heard, the song of life that throbbed behind the surface of everything, with a heartbeat for a drum to keep the steady pace until the song came to its end. He began to whistle along. Ivar gave a troubled sideways glance, and took an unconscious step away.

The monk was business, easily dealt with for the handful of coin, but the stranger was intriguing, Harald ruminated. Who was this warrior who fought with such brutality and passion? And why had he decided to involve himself in a matter that did not concern him?

We are the law here, Redteeth said to himself. *We decide who survives and who dies. The stranger will not leave Northumbria alive.*

Absently, he held out an open hand. Ivar delved into his pouch and handed over a small number of the dried toadstools. Carefully, Redteeth examined the scarlet caps dotted with white, and the large creamy gills.

'It is the Blod-Monath,' he said thoughtfully. 'We have made our sacrifices as our forefathers did, but the Blood-Month demands more. This winter is earlier and harder than most, and now this stranger . . . I would know what it all means.' He paused. 'There is talk among the seers of an ending. Omens . . . portents . . .'

'Is this the Fimbulwinter before the great battle that heralds Ragnarok and the end of everything?' Ivar asked, unsettled.

'Perhaps. Even the Christians see the omens too.'

'They say a raven spoke to Earl Tostig, and he blanched and hid himself away in his hall, and refused to tell anyone what the bird said,' Ivar remembered with a shudder.

Redteeth popped one large and one small toadstool into his mouth. 'We will make camp here where there will be warmth to see us through the night. Leave me now, for I journey far beyond Midgard to the shores of the great black sea. If I die before I return, you will take the lead.'

Nodding, Ivar walked away, bellowing to the others to set up camp. They all knew the dangers of the ritual Redteeth had embarked on. Sometimes the spirits did not allow the traveller to return with the knowledge he had gained along the shores of that vast sea, or in the dense, endless forest of the night. But Redteeth had wrestled with the powers before on more than one occasion, and he had always returned unscathed, with the words of the *vaettir* still ringing in his ears.

The ritual was important, Redteeth thought with fervent passion. The old ways were dying out. The Christians now dominated his homeland, praying in the churches and proclaiming the way of their One True God. But his father had taken him into the woods when he was a boy and told him the meaning of the silver hammer charm he wore on a thong round his neck. The man had cut young Harald's thumb with his knife and they had shared blood, and then, together, they had butchered a wild-eyed pony with their axes and smeared its essence on their faces. As they sat beside the campfire the boy had learned that the same ritual had been conducted by his father's father and *his* father and so on back to when the first man and woman were birthed from the armpit of the frost giant

Ymir. The Viking spat. The past was who you were – you could not trade it for a new life.

Leaving the others behind, he made his way to the rim of the blood-filled dew-pond. While he waited for his journey to begin, he squatted on the edge of the pool and peered into the depths.

Time passed. The roaring of the fire diminished, and the screaming ended suddenly and starkly. Even the wind dropped so that there was only a comforting silence with the snow falling all around. It was a sign. The guides had heard him.

Nausea came first, but passed quickly, followed by a sweat that froze upon his forehead. When it cleared, a deep, abiding peace descended.

Turning to the flickering flames on the embers of what had been the village he saw faces watching him. The *vaettir* were stirring.

'I will never let the past die,' he told them.

Through the stark branches of the swaying trees, he glimpsed the *alfar*, moving out from their homes in the deep wood. Their eyes glowed with an inner light that spoke of the land across the sea.

'Through blood and fire, I will keep the dreams of my ancestors alive,' he told them.

A moment of tension fell across the area, and Redteeth felt that a presence had arrived, although he could not see it. A voice rang out, clear and loud in the depths of his head: 'Come with me to the shores of the great black sea and I will tell you many secrets. I will tell you of the End-Times that are coming, and the stranger, and the part he will play in it.'

The Viking mercenary looked round until his gaze alighted on a raven squatting on one of the corpses on the other side of the bloody dew-pond. For a moment, the carrion bird fixed a beady black eye upon him, and then it took wing high into the falling snow and the night.

Redteeth's head filled with blood and fire, and he joined it.

CHAPTER FOUR

'Run!' Hereward barked as he propelled Alric through the white forest. Their hot breath clouded in the bitter night air and the crunch of their footsteps matched the pounding of their hearts.

A howl rolled out away to their left, echoed by another off to their right. The wolf pack closed.

Weaving among the oaks and ash trees, the two men slid down banks, leapt rocks and stumbled through patches of brown fern. In places the forest path lay hidden beneath a thick covering of snow and Alric appeared too dazed to search for landmarks.

'He was a man,' he whispered as they ran, his puffy, tear-stained face filled with an abiding horror. 'One of God's creations. What you did to him was an abomination.'

'It saved your life.'

'My life is no more valuable than his.' Wild-eyed, Alric grabbed his companion's arm and dragged him to a halt. 'How could you see such agony and still continue?'

Glancing into the gloom, Hereward glimpsed grey ghosts, the only sound the soft patter of their paws when the wind dropped. He thrust the monk into a clear channel among the trees, only to find their way barred by another stream. 'You are right – your life is no more valuable than his,' he snapped. 'If I did not need you to lead me to shelter, I would leave you out here to fend for yourself.'

Alric levelled a determined eye. 'You must pay for your crimes.'

'And what will you do? Strike me with a Bible?' A flash of grey against the white; low, circling. Another. 'Now, find the path to the *wicce* house or we both will die.'

'Perhaps that is for the best. I earn my redemption by keeping a monster like you from the world.'

Hereward felt his anger rise. He should have left the whining man for dead and been done with it. Drawing his sword, he backed against an oak. 'Pray for yourself, then. I will not go so easily.'

Alric hesitated. Hereward watched conflicting emotions play out across the other man's face. With an anguished cry, the monk whirled until he located a tree that he recognized. He jabbed a trembling finger. 'That way!' he said with fury. 'And may God forgive me for my weakness!'

Hereward ran alongside the stream towards the tree, but he already knew it was futile. He couldn't see the house anywhere in the forest dark, and the wolves would be close, following the meaty stink of the blood that caked him.

He leapt a fallen trunk and found himself skidding down a bank into a hollow clogged with brambles and the remnants of another tree that had been struck by lightning. By the time he realized it was the worst possible position, the wolves had lined the edge of the hollow, their silhouettes stark against the snow.

'Damn them!' he snarled at Alric as the monk rolled down the bank into a deep drift. 'It appears that God has granted your prayers!'

Hacking his way through the vegetation into the centre of the hollow, he began a slow turn, watching for the first attack. He suspected that at least ten beasts moved around the rim; there could be more beyond.

Alric cried out as the first wolf leapt. An instant later, all the predators surged forward. As fast as the snarling beasts, Hereward flashed his sword back and forth, chopping down two before he was engulfed in a mass of snapping jaws. He fought with fist and elbow, slashing with his sword whenever he managed to free himself enough to swing. Blood smeared his torn flesh as he reeled from the ferocity of the attack.

Three more wolves fell in quick succession, disembowelled. Before Hereward could catch his breath, another leapt for his throat. Throwing himself to one side, he felt its jaws latch on to his upper arm. He ignored the pain and lunged for the beast's neck. Clamping his teeth on the wet fur, he tore out its throat. A gush of arterial blood soaked his face as the wolf fell away, thrashing and turning across the hollow in its death throes.

He glimpsed the terrified monk crammed into a space beneath the roots of the fallen tree, but then the remaining wolves attacked as one. He sliced through two with rapid slashes of Brainbiter, and shattered the skull of the third, but the final wolf caught him wrong-footed. The force of its attack propelled him backwards into the brambles, and as he hit the icy ground his sword flew from his hand.

The wolf fell on him in an instant. Straining, he managed to hold its snapping jaws an inch away from his throat, but he felt his strength ebbing.

From the corner of his eye, he caught sight of Alric scrambling from his hiding place and bounding up the side of the hollow. At the top, the monk paused to look back, his expression dark, and then he hurled himself over the rim and away.

The wolf drove its jaws closer and closer to Hereward's face. Hot breath blasted against him, gouts of saliva splashing his flesh. His arms trembled. All he could see were those cold, jewelled eyes moving nearer, until they filled his entire vision.

A sudden impact smashed the wolf's head to one side. Hereward recoiled in shock. When he had gathered himself, he saw the beast lying on the bloodstained snow, its skull caved in. A large bloody rock lay beside it.

Alric stood nearby, hands on his knees as he caught his breath. He exchanged a glance with Hereward, but all he could manage was a nod.

'Why?' Hereward asked as he levered himself up, searching for his sword in the snow.

'Because I am better than you,' Alric gasped. 'And because I rise to the purpose God gave me.'

Hereward reached out a hand to be helped to his feet, but the monk only looked at it before pulling himself back up the side of the hollow. 'I am not your keeper,' he said.

Using his sword to help him, Hereward levered himself up the slope. Blood flowed from numerous tears in his flesh, but none of them appeared so serious that he would not be able to survive until they reached shelter. Deep in troubled thought, Alric waited for him beyond the edge of the hollow.

'Do not think that because you saved my life I am now in debt to you,' Hereward said.

'No, you would sacrifice me in a moment if it served your purpose. I am not blind.' Alric glanced at the red splatters trailing in the other man's wake. 'You are providing a clear path for any other wolves out there. We should move quickly now.'

They continued their journey in silence, Alric searching for landmarks, Hereward using his sword to support him. The blizzard whipped up until they could barely see more than three feet in front of them. The warrior felt it grow colder still, and he knew it would only be a matter of time before the warm-sleep took them.

'Have I put my trust in a fool only to pay for it with my life?' he said.

'Your life is mine now to do with as I please,' Alric snapped. He came to a sudden halt, peering through the lashing branches. 'There – is that a house?'

As Hereward followed the monk's pointing finger, more howling rose up at their backs. Shoving Alric forward, Hereward limped behind him as fast as he could manage. He had not fled the dogs of the king's court and fought his way across half England to die in the snow as food for wolves. The two men clambered over rocks and fallen trees, mounds of snow drifting on them from the branches they disturbed. The crashing of the wolves in the undergrowth drew steadily nearer.

Just when Hereward was convinced Alric had been mistaken, a low wattle-and-daub-walled house with a thatched roof loomed out of the night, so ramshackle it appeared on the point of collapse. Set as it was deep in the surrounding trees and rocky outcrops, it almost appeared a natural part of the forest.

The monk pounded frantically on the wooden door until he heard a voice on the other side. 'Go away.'

'Please,' he begged. 'The wolves are coming.'

After a moment, the door swung open a few inches and Alric and Hereward barged into the smoky interior. Hereward slammed the door with his shoulder and dropped the latch. Resting his forehead against the rough timber, he felt the last of his strength draining away.

'Go now! I will have no churchman in my house!' From the gloom of the single room, a woman lashed out at Alric with a broom made from hazel switches. Her cheeks were hollow and her hair hung lank and grey, but she struck with such a fierce strength that the monk fell to the mud floor.

Hereward lurched forward and stopped the next swing of the broom with one hand. 'Hold.'

Eyes blazing, the woman looked the blood-smeared warrior up and down.

'We will pay you well for shelter,' he said, jangling the pouch. 'Till sunrise, and then we will be away.'

'Not him.' She pointed a quavering finger at Alric. 'His kind have tormented us for generation upon generation. First they come with smiles, then they come with scowls, finally they come with sticks and spears.'

'If he troubles you, I will clout him myself.' Hereward rested against the door for support. He regretted becoming involved in this business. It was a distraction, and now here he was, weakened and wounded, with miles still to go to Eoferwic. He knew he would never reach the town on his own.

'Who are you, coming here like a butcher?' the woman said.

'My name is Hereward, and I thank you for your help. The monk goes by the name Alric. Let us sleep on your floor till dawn and we will be gone.'

'How do I know you won't kill me and steal all I own?'

Hereward looked round at the almost bare room, at the bed of straw next to the fire, and the few meagre cooking pots. Bunches of dried herbs were stacked along one wall. He smelled the sweet aroma of lavender and sorrel. His gaze shifted to dangling skulls large and small – badger, rabbit, mouse, sheep – suspended on fibre strips.

'Because you are a witch and you will curse us!' Alric shouted, scrambling to his feet.

'Yes!' The woman pointed her bony finger at him again; he backed away a step.

Sighing, Hereward grabbed Alric and manhandled him against the grubby wall. 'We are seeking shelter for the night,' he hissed. 'Do not ruin it with your stupid ways. Or would you rather I killed her and be done with it?'

Alric looked from Hereward to the woman, his brow furrowing with concern. 'Very well,' he whispered.

From his pouch, Hereward plucked a silver penny which he tossed to the woman. 'Payment for one night. Fair?'

The woman took it eagerly and nodded. 'There is bread,' she said. 'And water. I have herbs which will help your wounds heal.' She indicated a corner of the room away from the hearth. 'Make your bed there, but know I sleep with one eye open.'

The two men gathered some filthy straw from a pile and scattered it against the wall. The bitter cold still reached through the hard-packed floor and the thin wattle wall, but the fire offered some comfort, and at least they were out of the biting wind. After Hereward had rinsed his wounds with water, the woman ground up some herbs in a crucible and mixed them with a handful of pig fat for him to apply to the gashes. It stung at first, but soon all his injuries felt pleasingly numb.

During the application of the balm, Alric sat in a daze, hands hugged around his knees. Once the woman had lain down and was snoring loudly, he asked, 'Where do we go from here?'

'I know where I go,' Hereward replied. 'To Eoferwic.'

'I could return to the monastery and seek sanctuary, but . . .' The monk's words tailed off.

'You will have to confess your sins.'

Alric glared at the warrior until he saw that Hereward was not making a point, and then his shoulders sagged. 'I cannot go back. I cannot stay here. Harald Redteeth will not cease in his endeavours until he finds me.'

Clutching his bloodstained knife tightly against him, Hereward laid down his head. Exhaustion filled him, and it would be several days' hard journeying through the snow to Eoferwic. 'Sleep,' he said. 'We are safe for now. And the world will not seem so bad at first light.'

The raven flew back to earth, and Harald Redteeth returned with it.

For a few moments, he gathered his thoughts, still immersed in the sensation of flying. When the memories of his walk along the shores of that great black sea had receded, he marched towards the makeshift camp, and bellowed, 'Ho! To me now!'

Crawling out of their shelters into the gently drifting snow, his bleary-eyed men gathered around him.

'Break up the camp. We set off in pursuit of the stranger,' Redteeth growled.

Clapping his arms around him for warmth, Ivar replied, 'It is not first light for many hours.'

'Our plans have changed.' Pulling down his breeches, he urinated into a vessel from one of the burning houses. 'Drink,' he said. 'Let the juices of the toadstool fill you with the passion of our ancestors.'

He passed the vessel of steaming urine to Ivar, and then to the other men. The power of the toadstools lived on within it, but his journey had removed the poison that could trap them on the shores of the great black sea.

'Hear your ancestors call to you,' he said. 'Feel the pull of the tides, and the rising fire in your belly. Now is the time we track the stranger. Now is the time to strike.'

CHAPTER FIVE

The hooded man rode into the teeth of the blizzard, his unlined face numb from the cold. His grey woollen cloak lay beneath a thick covering of snowflakes, as did his horse's brown mane, and the packhorse behind him, laden with one of the secrets of God. He felt unable even to turn his head to search for the two armed guards who had accompanied him on the long journey from the small village near Winchester.

The white curtain obscured London's filthy streets, but occasionally he glimpsed torches away in the dark. Deaf from the howling gale, he didn't hear the guard yelling at him until the man rode alongside, slapped a hand on his shoulder and pointed ahead. The high timber palisade surrounding the king's palace loomed out of the storm. A cloaked and hooded sentry stood on a platform above the great gates, holding a lantern aloft to see who was approaching.

'It is I, Redwald,' he called through numb lips, 'on the queen's business.'

The gates opened in jerks as the sentry and another man wrenched them back against the drifting snow.

'Hell's teeth, she had better reward you well for being out in this weather,' the sentry called as the young man rode by.

In the enclosure, the wind dropped a little, but the bitter cold still ate into Redwald's bones. At least he had done good work, and he *would* be rewarded, if not now, later. Barely suppressing a grin, he threw back his hood to reveal a face that still had many childlike qualities. The curly brown hair, the apple cheeks and full pink lips suggested an innocence which he used to his advantage around the court. He had seen at first hand what a hard place it was, filled with strong, cunning men all seeking their own advantage in a constant shadow-game. But he would not be broken by it. He would survive.

Clambering down from his horse, the young man stamped the snow from his leather shoes, and clapped his hands together and blew on them. The guards had already slipped away in search of fire and mead. Their footprints joined the tramped paths leading to the doors of the newly built timber-framed houses jumbled tightly together across the enclosure, every thatch and wooden roof creaking under a thick white blanket. The Palace of Westminster, King Edward's new home and the culmination of years of devout dreams, sprawled across most of Thorney Island on the banks of the Thames to the west of the City of London. The earls and the king's thegns complained about the bitter wind blowing off the river in winter, but Redwald had heard that Edward had been directed to build there by God.

And looking at the vast silhouette looming up beyond the palace buildings, the young man could almost believe it. The stories burned in his head: that a fisherman had had a vision of St Peter at the site, that the ageing king had heard angels and had set about the building of a monument to God with an energy that dwarfed that of much younger men. Redwald recalled the gossip that the monarch had never lain between the thighs of his wife and the new abbey was all that the old man cared about in life. Studying the outline, he thought he understood the king's mind. Every day Redwald had watched the best stonemasons in all Europe raise up the grandest church in the world to replace the one used by the Benedictine monks, and Edward had been there, overseeing the construction arch by arch, column by column. Following the lines, even in the dark he could see it was almost complete; only the roof and part of the tower remained unfinished.

The hairs on Redwald's neck tingled erect; it was more than a sacrament, it was a sign of power, earthly power, for if you could build such a thing you could do anything.

'Do you have it?' The excited woman's voice cut through the howl of the wind.

Redwald turned to see the queen stumbling eagerly through the snow, a thick woollen cloak of madder-red protecting her from the elements. Though Edith had passed her thirtieth year, the young man still saw the beauty of her youth that had enticed many a male. Some would say the king, almost twice her age, was a lucky man, he thought. But he would not wish it for himself: though she stood behind the throne, she might as well have been seated upon it. He recalled hearing the lash of her tongue as she chastised her attendants, and sometimes, in her quieter moments, he remembered seeing the cold determination in her face. But then Edith was a Godwin, of Wessex, and many believed that family *was* England, in essence.

'I do,' Redwald replied with a quick smile, eager for praise, 'but it did not come easily.'

'Quickly, then. Bring it into the warm.' The queen turned on her heel and marched back towards the king's hall.

Calling for one of the boys to take the mounts to stable, Redwald fumbled with frozen fingers to remove the small oaken chest from the back of the weary packhorse. He half expected it to glow, or to feel warm to the touch, but the iron hinges were unbearably cold. Holding the box tight to his chest, he navigated the slippery paths to the hall.

He eased through the doorway and sighed in gratitude as warmth washed over him. Flames blazed high in the great circular hearth in the centre of the lofty room. Two slaves continually fed the fire with logs to keep the winter at bay. The orange glow washed over the tapestries hanging on the walls, the Opus Anglicanum unmatched anywhere in Europe, but the

35

illumination did not reach the shadows that clung to the broad rafters. After the hardship of his journey, Redwald relaxed at the sight of the works of art on display: the breathtaking fresco painted on the eastern wall depicting the Stations of the Cross, the casket carved from whalebone, the gold plates studded with jewels and intricately engraved, the ivory cross filled with carved angels. Surely, as the king's guests said when they saw them, there was no place grander than England in all the world.

Throwing off her cloak, the queen beckoned to Redwald and pointed to the long table where he should lay the casket. As he put the box down, a booming voice rang through the hall: 'More old bones?'

Redwald beamed as Edith's brother, Harold Godwinson, strode across the room; a stablehand had once suggested to him that Harold never walked slowly anywhere. Powerfully built, with a strong jaw and a handsome face, his jet-black hair gleaming in the firelight, the Earl of Wessex flipped open the lid of the box to reveal a yellowing tibia. 'As I thought. What is it this time?'

Redwald hung on the older man's words. Harold was everything he dreamed of being: confident, wealthy, powerful, charismatic; safe.

'The shankbone of St John the Baptist, brought from far Byzantium by a good Christian merchant,' the queen replied, clapping her hands together with excitement. 'It is said it can bring a dead man back to life.'

'And you are winning?'

'Of course. Do I not always? My husband's search for relics stutters and starts. When his abbey is consecrated, it will be Edith of Wessex who will fill it with the glory of God, and it will be the name of Godwin that will be on all lips.' She flashed her brother a sly smile.

The earl laughed. 'What do you say, Redwald? The queen is a playful sprite. She loves her mischief.'

'As do we all,' the young man replied. They all laughed.

Harold clapped a hand on Redwald's shoulder. 'And what do you say now, Edith? I told you this lad was reliable. I see great things ahead for him.'

'He has served me well, where others failed. Perhaps you should take him into your employ.'

'Perhaps I should.'

Redwald felt a swell of pride; to escape the miseries, the doubts, the fears and the insecurity of his life was all he wanted. In Harold's employ, he would be privy to great things; he would be a part of something that mattered.

While Edith examined her relic with hungry fingers, the earl led Redwald away, his mood darkening with each step into the shadows that clustered at the far end of the long hall. 'I know you can be trusted,' he said, 'and you have proved it to me in times past, but I have to take care. Plots and deceits whirl around the throne like the deep currents around the bridge across the Thames. I have to be sure.'

'I understand.'

'I know you do, which is why I have invested so much faith in you.' The earl fixed a sharp eye on the young man. 'The king nears the end of his days, yet he has no appointed heir. That is a dangerous concoction. If we wish all that we have achieved in England to endure, we must work to ensure the throne does not fall into the wrong hands.'

'I only wish to serve.'

'Very well. I will think on this matter more.' Harold took Redwald through an annexe to the door of another room where men sat drinking from wooden cups along both sides of an oak table. Several slumped drunkenly in pools of ale. Staying out of sight by the door, the earl pointed to two men locked in quiet, intense conversation at the far end of the table. Redwald recognized the blond-haired Edwin, Earl of Mercia, as handsome and vital as Harold, but quieter, and the man's brother Morcar, almost the opposite of his kin, hollow-cheeked and long-faced like a horse, his hair already thinning.

'I do not trust those Mercians,' Harold whispered. 'They are always plotting in dark corners and I fear they know more than they let on. Watch them for me.'

Pleased to be given responsibility so soon, Redwald agreed.

When they returned to the hall, the younger man voiced the question that had been on his mind for some time. 'Is there any news of Hereward?'

Harold shook his head sadly. 'I know he is your brother in all but name, but you must put him out of your head. He is both traitor and murderer. He will never be allowed to return to London. With the blood of innocents on his hands, it is only a matter of time before his punishment catches up with him.'

Redwald nodded, but he couldn't put the blood out of his mind, and the woman's body lying within it, her eyes wide and accusing. The picture haunted him, in his sleep, in the quiet moments when he was going about his chores. 'I would not see harm come to him.'

Harold turned his piercing gaze on the lad for a long moment and then nodded. 'Understood. You have grown up alongside him, friends beneath the same roof. Your loyalty is impressive. Now, go. Try to give some comfort to Asketil. His life has been made miserable over the years by his son's violent and wayward behaviour, but since Hereward brought slaughter to the Palace of Westminster it is as though the thegn is drowning in deep water.'

Redwald said goodbye and hurried out into the night, his mood sobering as he neared his house. Inside, his vision adjusted slowly to the near-dark. Only a few embers glowed in the hearth. On a stool, Asketil stared into the remnants of the fire with heavy-lidded eyes, a cup of ale held loosely in his right hand. Redwald thought how old the thegn looked in the half-light, as if many years had eaten away at his skin and greyed his hair in the short time since Hereward had fled.

'You're back,' Asketil slurred, his gaze wavering towards the young man.

'Yes. It was a long journey from Winchester in the snow.'

Asketil beckoned Redwald to draw nearer, leaning forward

to scrutinize the young man's face with his bleary eyes. 'I wish you had been my son,' he said finally. 'You were always a good boy, even in those days after they brought you to me when your mother and father died.'

'Do not think badly of Hereward.'

'Do not think badly? He murdered a gentle woman who held only love in her heart for him. He has destroyed this family with the shame he has heaped upon us. Look what he has done to me.' The thegn slurped the last of his ale, then threw the cup into the corner of the room. Redwald was surprised to see Hereward's younger brother Beric slumped in the shadows there, his arms wrapped around his knees. The boy stared at the boards as if no one else was present. He had not spoken since he had learned of the murder and the accusations against his brother. Redwald recalled the girls in the kitchen whispering to him, 'Beric is broken.'

Broken. A terrible legacy had indeed been left by the blood spilled that night.

'Since we took you in, you have always been loyal to Hereward,' Asketil continued. 'And that does you credit.'

'He was . . . he *is* . . . my friend.'

'He is, and always has been, unworthy of your friendship. Since his mother died when he was young, Hereward could never be tamed. In Mercia, his name is despised for the crimes he committed as boy and man. Robbery. Drunkenness. Violence against any who crossed his path. Wilful destruction of the property of his neighbours. I did all I could to teach him how to be a man, and I failed.'

'Do not blame yourself . . . Father.' Redwald felt unworthy to use that word, even though he had lived in Asketil's home since he was a boy.

His eyes glistening, Asketil looked away. 'My business with the king is done, for now; I go home as soon as the snows melt. You must stay here, and work for Harold Godwinson, if he will have you. He is a great man. He . . . he should be king one day, and you will be well cared for, as you deserve.' He choked on his words for a moment. 'It was Harold who asked the king to declare Hereward exile so we would not be forced to go before the Witan and make the case for all to hear and debate across the land.'

'And . . . and what of Hereward?' Redwald whispered.

Asketil glared into the embers. 'He will be made to pay for his crime, and soon. He has betrayed me . . . you and Beric . . . his mother's name . . . and the king too. Only blood will set that right. And when he is finally gone I will not mourn him.'

CHAPTER SIX

Black glassy eyes glistered in the gloom. Silent and watchful, the ravens brooded in the branches of the lightning-blasted oak, the darkly gleaming canopy of their wings mirroring the churning clouds above. Hereward felt unable to look at those solemn sentinels. Their gaze spoke to him of terrors long gone and worse yet to come. And as a deep-rooted dread chilled his bones to the core, he turned and ran along the track towards his father's hall. He was a man and yet he was also a boy, and there, waiting outside the door, was his mother. Shadows spun by the gathering storm fell across her face, but her golden hair shone beneath her white headdress. Behind her, just inside the hall, a figure loomed, silhouetted against the ruddy glow from the hearth. Hereward's heart began to pound.

What have you done? What have you done? The words swirled around him, the ravens cawing their accusations.

His hands felt wet, but he dared not look down at them. 'Do not worry,' he whispered, 'Redwald will avenge us.'

The Mercian's eyes snapped open. Fingers of early morning light reached under the door. He lay on the thinly spread straw, his bones aching from the cold radiating through the beaten-mud floor. By the glowing embers in the hearth, the old woman snored under her filthy woollen blanket, but Alric was gone, probably to empty his bladder, the warrior guessed.

Redwald will avenge us, he thought, as the last of the troubling dream drifted away.

Rising, he stretched. Though his wounds still ached, the witch's balm had stripped the edge off the pain, and his limbs felt stronger after the night's sound sleep. Would he be well enough to reach Eoferwic? The woods were rife with wolves and outlaws stalked the old straight tracks, if they were even passable after the heavy snows. He fought back his doubts, knowing that the king's life, and his own, depended on his flight reaching its end.

Thoughts of the court reminded him of Tidhild, dead at his feet, her black eyes looking up at him, and in a surge of grief and guilt he swept out into the cold morning. The glare of the sun off the dense white snow blinded him. When his vision began to clear, a shape among the trees a stone's throw from the house coalesced into the form of the young monk. Yet the man was naked, Hereward saw with shock, with a noose round his neck, a gag across his mouth, and his hands tied behind his back. Precariously, Alric balanced on the tips of his toes on a wobbling chopping block. His eyes were wide with fear. Another rope ran from the block across the frozen ground and into the trees.

Redteeth, Hereward thought. A trap to lure him out into the open. He silently cursed himself: Brainbiter still lay on the straw where he had been sleeping. And then he cursed the monk for failing to keep his wits about him. 'Kill him! I care not!' he shouted.

With a snap, the rope across the snow was yanked taut and the block flew out from beneath Alric's feet. He kicked and flailed as his full weight dragged the noose tight round his neck.

Defiance forgotten, Hereward raced from the house and flung his arms round the monk's waist, raising him up so the noose loosened. Supporting him with one arm, he tore the rope from Alric's neck, and together they collapsed into a drift. Hereward yanked away the monk's gag and bonds. 'You are a fool,' he snapped.

'They took me unawares—' Alric's words died as the shadows fell across them.

Standing up, Hereward looked deep into the wind-lashed face of Harald Redteeth, the Viking's pupils so dilated his eyes appeared all black. Hereward saw a hint of madness there. Wrapped in furs over their mail, bristling with axes and spears, the band of six warriors clustered around their leader.

'Stranger,' Redteeth said with a whimsical wave of his hand, 'you have caused me no little trouble.'

'I have given you a taste of hell. There is more to come.'

Redteeth laughed without humour. 'Your time is over.' He held Hereward's gaze for a long moment, sifting what he saw there, and then he nodded to his men.

While two Vikings grabbed an arm each and dragged Hereward back to the house, a third tossed Alric his clothes and bundled the monk along behind. The rest of the mercenaries drove the old woman outside at spear-point. Her shrieked protests and curses rang out until Redteeth snatched a spear from the nearest warrior and drove the blade through her stomach. Alric cried out in horror. It was clear to Hereward that the young monk blamed himself for this death as he did for all the ones in Gedley.

'Kill us and be done with it,' he said, in a voice cracking with passion.

Redteeth turned on him. 'Your time will come, monk. I wish to savour your demise before we cut off your head and take it back to the man you have wronged.' To Hereward, he continued, 'I would know your secrets, stranger. You are clearly a warrior of no little skill, yet you put your own life at risk for those you do not know. What gain is there for you in interfering in my business?'

Held tight between the two mercenaries, Hereward showed a cold face. 'Lean closer. I will whisper it to you.'

Seeing the contempt in those eyes, Redteeth nodded to Ivar.

Without warning, the second in command crashed a giant fist into Hereward's face, splitting his lip. Once the ringing in his head had cleared, the Mercian tasted iron on his tongue, and spat a mouthful of blood into the embers.

'Let us begin with questions you can answer easily. What is your name?' Redteeth asked.

Hereward did not respond, and Redteeth nodded to Ivar once more. The second punch sent a jolt of pain through Hereward's head and neck.

'What is your name?' Redteeth repeated calmly.

Hereward said nothing. Savage blows rained down on him, but he took it as he had taken every beating in his life, and there had been many. His left eye swelled shut, his lips turned to a pulp, blood streamed from his nose and his left ear throbbed so much he could hear nothing on that side. Redteeth asked again.

'Why do you not tell him your name?' Alric cried incredulously. 'You told it to me in an instant. It is not a secret! You are only buying yourself more pain!'

'My name . . .' Hereward mumbled through his torn lips. 'My name . . . is mine. It is what I have.'

Redteeth nodded to Ivar once more.

'His name is Hereward!' Alric shouted. 'There! You do not need to hurt him more!'

'Hereward,' Redteeth repeated. 'That means nothing to me. Now . . . where are you from?'

Unable to watch the punishment inflicted upon his companion, the young monk turned his head away, but he flinched with the sound of every blow. Hereward felt puzzled by his reaction. Why would anyone care?

After a while, he floated free of the shackles of the world. The voices around him receded and he was in the fens, a boy, catching fish on a sun-drenched afternoon. He was stealing a gold cup from the abbot's room to sell to buy mead with his friends. He was looking down on the torn body of Tidhild, her hand so pale against the blood.

Icy water crashed against his face, shocking him alert.

'Look at him,' Alric said. 'He is not human to suffer in silence so.'

'We have only just begun,' Redteeth replied. The Viking paced the house, flashing glances into the corners as if things waited there that no one else could see.

When two of the men had stoked the hot embers in the hearth, Ivar placed a pair of iron tongs, a poker and his long knife in the flames. While they absorbed the heat, Redteeth addressed Alric, who was slumped in one corner, his head in his hands. 'Christian man. You have converted many of my people to the Creed. They no longer talk of Odin hanging on Yggdrasil, but of Jesus on the Cross. You build churches in the old stone circles and in the sacred groves, and by the wells and the springs. That is how you lure them. I have heard your kind say your God is better than mine. Is that so?'

Alric nodded.

'Your ways are better?'

'Yes.'

Redteeth nodded slowly. 'So a Christian man should not break a vow sworn in his God's name?'

Alric bowed his head.

'Will your God forgive such a transgression? Will he wash away the stain of blood caused by such a crime? So many innocent deaths?' Redteeth stepped forward and kicked the monk hard in the stomach. 'If you had not run like a coward I would not have had to slaughter the people who sheltered you. Think on this in your final moments.'

'Leave him,' Hereward croaked.

'You would prefer your own pain to his?' Redteeth said. 'Why, you must be a Christian too.' The warriors all laughed loudly.

At the Viking commander's order, Ivar removed the poker from the fire and held it close to Hereward's ribs. The Mercian gritted his teeth as his flesh bloomed under the searing heat. When Redteeth leaned in to whisper, Hereward could smell his enemy's meaty breath and the vinegar reek of his sweat.

'Why would you dare to risk offending me? What lies in your head?'

Hereward looked Redteeth in the eye and grinned. 'You will never know.'

Responding to a nod from his leader, Ivar pressed the hot poker to Hereward's side. Pain lanced through him, and the stink of his own sizzling flesh rose up to his nose. His roar tore his throat, but it was the sound of triumph, not defeat.

'Look at his eyes!' Alric shouted. 'You waste your time! I tell you, he is not a man – he is the Devil!'

'He is a man,' Redteeth replied with a shrug. 'And we will find his humanity, given time. Perhaps when we cut his skin from him, as he did to my own man Askold.' He pointed to the blade in the embers.

Wrapping his woollen cloak around his fingers, Ivar plucked the glowing knife from the fire, its heat so intense the mercenary flinched even through the covering.

'Begin with his right arm,' the Viking commander ordered. 'Start with the skin. Then remove the flesh and muscle down to the bone.' He added to Hereward, 'We will carve you like the wild boar at our Yule feast.'

As the Northmen jeered and laughed, Hereward hid his thoughts behind a blank expression. He had noticed that Ivar had leaned in close when he brandished the poker, closer than he would ever have risked if the Mercian's arms were not pinned. As the second in command approached with the red-tipped knife, Hereward waited for the opening to materialize and then lunged forward. Clamping his teeth on Ivar's cheek, the English warrior bit down to the bone and ripped away the chunk of flesh with a twist of his head.

Howling, Ivar lurched back, dropping the knife on to the old woman's bed. Amid the crackle of straw, grey smoke curled up. When the Mercian felt his two captors loosen their grip in the confusion, he wrenched his arms free, jabbing his right elbow into one throat and driving his forehead into the face of the second man.

He felt the thing inside him rise up, the other Hereward, born of rage and bloodlust, unconstrained by human values, and he welcomed it. The pain of his wounds vanished. As strength flooded into his weary limbs, he reacted with a speed that made the mercenaries seem lead-footed in comparison. Snatching up the poker, he lashed it across Redteeth's face. From the corner of his eye, he saw the monk wriggle out from among their captors and wrench open the door. Good, Hereward thought. He planted one leather sole in the Viking commander's gut and propelled him out into the snowy morning.

The mercenary band began to gather their wits; too late. As flames licked up from the hearthside bed, Hereward snatched up his sword, hacking one man in the face, then whirling to lop off the right hand of another. With a flick of his shoe, he kicked the burning straw across the room to the other straw at the back. The fire rushed up the timber frame to the thatched roof.

As a sheet of flame spread over their heads, panic erupted in the dense smoke. Hereward darted outside before the Vikings could react. Grabbing Redteeth's axe from where the mercenary sprawled in a daze, he slammed the door and embedded the weapon in the splintering jamb to seal it shut. The roaring of the fire drowned out the terrified shouts from within, which turned to screams as the burning roof began to fall in.

Through the throbbing of the blood in his head, Hereward heard Alric cry out. The Viking commander was struggling to his feet. Whirling, Hereward kicked Redteeth in the face with such brutal force that the mercenary pitched backwards, unconscious. His fury spent, Hereward's euphoria faded. The world suddenly looked too brittle, cold and bright. Lurching from the pain seeping back into his battered body, he attempted to lift Redteeth. 'Help me,' he croaked.

'You are badly injured,' Alric said as he shouldered the Viking's bulk. 'You will not reach Eoferwic alone.'

'I have survived worse.'

'Sooner or later your luck will run out.'

47

The screams of the trapped warriors died amid the roar of the fire as the walls caught light and the flames soared up high into the sky. Hereward thought of Gedley and felt proud.

When Redteeth came round, confusion flickered across his face, then uneasy awareness, then simmering rage. Hereward watched the play of emotions with cold satisfaction. The noose was tight round the Viking's neck and his hands were bound as he wavered precariously on the chopping block. Alric turned away as the mercenary fought to keep his balance, no doubt remembering his own ordeal.

'This is not an ending,' Redteeth growled.

'It is the end of your story,' Hereward replied. 'Except for the part where the ravens feast on your remains.'

'You should have left well alone,' Alric added.

'Good Christian man,' Redteeth spat.

The monk was a strange man, Hereward thought, but he might have his uses. Turning his back on the glowering Viking, he said, 'You are a free man now. What will you do? Return to your monastery?'

Alric hung his head. 'I am not free. If Harald Redteeth does not return with my head, another will come in his place, and another after that, until this matter is done.' His eyes flickered in the direction of Gedley. 'I will never be free.'

'I have business in Eoferwic . . . grim business,' Hereward said, searching the other's face for even the barest hint that betrayal lay ahead, 'and I cannot risk becoming food for the wolves.'

The monk's eyes narrowed. 'What manner of business?'

Hereward hesitated. How could he tell the younger man that it involved murder, conspiracy and the security of the very throne of England itself when he had no idea who could be trusted or how far the plot reached? 'There are lives at stake,' he said. 'More, perhaps, than died in Gedley.'

'You butcher without thought for God's work. Why would you be concerned with saving lives?'

'We all wrestle with our devils, monk. Can any man truly say he is wholly saint or wholly sinner?'

Alric's eyes brightened as if he had alighted on some great notion. Waving a finger, he said, 'And you would have me accompany you?'

'If I can be sure you will not pass judgement on me on the road, as it seems in your nature to do.' He could feel his legs growing weaker by the moment. They would need to find new shelter, and a chance to recover. 'These wounds drag me down. You are right: I will never reach Eoferwic on my own.'

The monk pondered.

'I will pay you well,' the warrior added, jangling the pouch at his hip.

'Very well,' Alric said, setting his jaw. 'You need me now, and I, God help me, need you for protection, at least until we reach Eoferwic.'

Hereward clapped a weak hand on his companion's shoulder. 'You are a whining little shit, monk, with a miserable disposition that makes for poor company. But if we can survive the hardships of this wild land, I will shoulder the burden.'

While Alric cast one tormented backward glance at the Viking balancing on the block, Hereward felt the weight of the secret he carried with him. With a heavy heart, he peered among the clustering oaks and ash trees, but saw no sign of the pursuit that had dogged him for so long. Perhaps there was some hope after all, he thought.

As Hereward lurched away with Alric supporting him, Redteeth roared his defiance: 'This is not an ending!'

If Hereward had searched the depths of the Viking's eyes at that moment, he would have seen that Redteeth was right. It was not an ending. The red-bearded Northman would not give in to death.

He *was* Death.

CHAPTER SEVEN

'Harald Redteeth is dead. Why do you waste so much time watching for pursuers?' Alric struggled to keep the crack out of his voice, but he felt irritable from exhaustion and hunger and the bitter wind burrowing deep into his bones.

Hereward crouched on the granite outcropping, one hand shielding his eyes from the midday sun. Now his wounds had healed, the sinewy warrior showed no sign of feeling the cold as he searched the bleak, white landscape tumbling away from the foot of the hillside below them. There were times when the young monk thought his companion more beast than man, at home in the wild countryside, perceiving scents that Alric could never smell on the knife-sharp wind, identifying spoor, detecting the merest hint of movement a day's march away or more, hearing notes of warning in the cawing of the rooks, and, for all he knew, the voice of God in the soughing in the branches.

'Men move through the forest below.' The warrior rose on to the balls of his feet and for a moment the monk lost him in the glare from the thick snow lying across the hillside. 'Five, I think. Tracking us or collecting wood?'

The monk narrowed his eyes in suspicion. 'Do you fear that they are hunting me . . . or you?'

Hereward laughed. 'Would you wait and ask them yourself?' Bounding down from the rock, he scanned the way ahead over the windswept hilltops. 'If we are caught out here in the open, we will soon be enjoying the sleep of the sword.'

Alric had watched the warrior's mood improve by the day as they neared Eoferwic. At times a robust humour had emerged, almost as if the Mercian sensed an opportunity to slough off whatever burden weighed him down, the monk mused. He saw learning in that face, most surely, and even some warmth. He had to accept that his wild-eyed companion was more of a puzzle than he had first believed. 'It would be a blessed relief. I get little other sleep these days,' he muttered.

'You are free to leave at any time.'

'Then who would pray for your black soul? I am all that prevents the Devil from rising up to offer you a throne beside him.'

'The Devil on one hand and a monk wittering and whinging and whining all day and all night on the other. A hard choice.' The warrior leapt to the monk's side, landing gracefully.

Alric shrugged and walked ahead. 'The meek are blessed.'

'Dead. The meek are dead, because they leave their spears under their beds.'

'And blessed.' Alric ducked when he heard rapid movement at his back. A large stone flew over his head and crashed into a drift. He whirled, jabbing a finger. 'That could have staved in my skull.'

'I must practise my aim,' the warrior said, his tone wry. 'But let us move on. There will be sharper stones in the valley.'

Grumbling, Alric stalked ahead. He cast one look down into the black woods and saw nothing, so he picked up his step, stumbling through the knee-deep snow. The two men slipped and skidded down the steep slope, sometimes turning head over heels so that their eyelashes and hair became crusted with ice. As his chest began to burn from his exertions, Alric asked, 'You have kin?'

'Two brothers.' Hereward paused. 'One I call brother, but he is not blood.'

'How so?'

'When I was a boy, my father took him in. Redwald.' The warrior's eyes took on a faraway look. A hint of tenderness, Alric wondered? 'His father was killed, by outlaws, I think. And his mother died too. The sickness.' He shrugged. 'He was alone, and my father welcomed him to our hall and treated him like a son.'

'And does he share your love for blood?'

Hereward laughed quietly. 'Redwald is the better man.' Tapping his head, he added, 'He has sharp wits and cunning ways. He is wise beyond his years, and his plots and plans would make Harold Godwinson proud. Even as we speak, he will be putting all his skills to good use on my behalf.'

'And what plans and plots does he weave?' Alric spoke lightly, to draw out more of the warrior's hidden side.

'Ones that lead to revenge.' The monk saw the hard look that flashed across the other man's face. 'Though we are not joined by blood, there is no more loyal brother than Redwald. He will take his time, and work hard, over days and weeks . . . years, if need be . . . and when the hour is right he will destroy the one who wronged me. This is his vow.'

Alric was troubled by Hereward's harsh tone, but also surprised by the first confidences he had heard in the ten days they had been travelling together. 'You and your brother have a strong bond.'

The warrior looked to the far horizon as he remembered. 'When I was old enough to skin a deer, my father gave me his knife, as fathers do to eldest sons, and as his own father did to him. It had a short blade, old even then, but kept sharp on the whetstone, and a handle of whalebone carved into the shape of an angel. Soon after, it disappeared. I knew that Redwald had stolen it. I could see it in the cast of his features and his quick glances. He felt guilt. And he knew that I knew. But I said naught.'

'Why?' The monk's brow furrowed.

'Because he had nothing of his own. Not for him a knife

handed down from his father, or land, or gold. And more . . . who we are' – the warrior pressed his right hand on his heart – 'comes from the ones who forged us. When he lost his mother and father, Redwald lost the knowledge of who he was.'

Alric was touched. 'So you allowed him to keep the gift your own father gave to you, because it was the only thing he had in all the world.'

'And in that moment we were bound together as true brothers.'

Alric's thoughts turned to the many friends who had died in Gedley, men and women who had trusted him, whom he had betrayed through his own weakness. And above all the one death that haunted him more than all others. Tears burned his eyes. Redemption would come hard, he thought, if at all. Could he ever clear the stain on his soul?

Reluctantly, the monk lurched up the next hillside. He watched the broad shoulders of the man ahead of him, the erect back that defied the savage cold, and he imagined Hereward's past. A fighting man who betrayed his thegn. A woodcutter's son who killed in an argument over food, or a woman. From what depths did the inhuman brutality surface? What had driven the Mercian into this cold, inhospitable place in the cruel heart of winter? What business did he have in Eoferwic and how could it prevent many deaths? His crime must have been terrible indeed. He had little faith in God, less in his fellow man. Alric was his final chance.

At the summit, the monk was blinded by the snow-glare. When his eyes cleared, he saw the sun flashing off two meandering rivers and, in the distance, trails of black smoke against the clear blue sky. He could discern the regular pattern of many houses against the white, and the tower of a great stone church.

'Eoferwic,' Hereward said.

Alric's stomach complained at the fading memory of their last meal, two days gone. 'And will we stay until the feasting at Christmastime?'

The warrior chuckled. 'If your fellow churchmen can endure your whining voice, you can stay until Judgement Day.' The monk flashed a questioning glance. 'In Eoferwic, we go our separate ways.'

Alric felt wrong-footed, just at the point where he had started to entertain hope. 'These last ten nights, you would have frozen to death in the woods if not for me,' he floundered.

'True. A small gift of food and a place next to the fire on a cold night are more readily given to a churchman.' The warrior looked baffled by the other man's hesitancy. 'What ails you now? Since we left Gedley you have been cursing every moment you have spent with me. Now you wish to be friends?'

'I wish . . .' Alric shook his head, the words dying. What did he wish?

'Besides, we are even. Two nights ago, when we took shelter at the farm, our host crept in, to harm you, I think. I imagine he still prays to the old gods and feared you would discover it and bring the wrath of your fellow Christians around his ears. I sent him away with the flat of my blade.'

'I do not want you to save my life,' Alric said sharply. 'I am here to save you.' And there it was, he realized. But Hereward merely laughed, a rich, full sound rolling over the snowy waste.

For the rest of the day, they walked on down the hillside and across the wind-blasted plain. Alric struggled through the deep drifts, his face and fingers numb, but his nimble mind turning with a precise gyre.

The warrior followed the trail of a raven across the sky, the one point of black in the entire vista. 'The night I was born, there was a great storm,' he said, speaking almost to himself, 'and the lightning cleaved in two the great old oak tree beside the hall. My mother said it was a prophecy, of what I was never sure. But from that night on, I was told, all the ravens would gather there, filling the dead branches, like black leaves.' He watched the bird disappear, and then bowed his head in thought as he trudged on.

As the sun slid down towards the western hills, the sky ignited in pink and gold. The mournful honking of geese echoed across the plain and wintering swans rose in one white cloud, the beating of their wings like thunder. The snow seethed with sinuous shadows. Though the ground was frozen hard, treacherous pools lurked among the long yellow grass rising out of the white covering, their glassy surfaces ready to shatter at the first footfall, pulling the unwary traveller beneath the ice. Hereward appeared to have an almost mystical sense of their location, and picked a path through the increasingly dangerous terrain with ease.

'I am a son of the fens,' he explained. 'To foreign eyes my home appears green and pleasant, but it conceals hidden bogs and water courses that can steal a life in the blink of an eye. As children we are taught to respect the land, and watch and listen for the secret signs. Those who learn the lessons live. Those who do not are lost to the black waters.'

Soon the monk could smell woodsmoke on the wind, and behind it the fruity stink of human waste. Eoferwic lowered at the confluence of the two grey rivers, a dark smudge under the winter sky. Beyond the defensive ditches, Alric could see the line of the tall palisade that had been stained by so much blood during the waves of attacks that had made the city such a dangerous place over the years.

'Surely your pursuers will find you here? If they have tracked you across England, what safety is there anywhere?' Unable to feel his feet, the monk stumbled on to the rutted track leading to the gate.

Hereward's hand fell to the hilt of his sword. 'I carry my safety with me.'

'And how long do you think you can keep killing before death catches up with you?'

'I have learned my lessons well, monk. Life is hard. No one can be trusted, not even those joined to you by blood. The only truth in life is the edge of my blade. It cuts through all lies.'

'This winter chill has reached into your heart.'

'You arc too soft, monk. You find comfort in your prayers, but traps lurk all around, and they will kill you eventually.' He clapped a friendly hand on Alric's shoulder. 'If you learn one thing from our time together, it should be that. I would not see you throw your life away.'

The two men stepped cautiously on to the wooden bridge leading across the defences. Wide enough for one cart, the timber gleamed with ice. The first ditch was empty. The second was filled with frozen stagnant water, smelling of rotting vegetation. Helmets gleamed in the dying sunlight along the fence, and Alric could feel hard eyes scrutinizing him.

'Speak your God-words at the gate,' Hereward whispered. 'They will more easily admit us.'

'Why should I when you are to abandon me the moment we step within?'

'Then stay out here for the night.'

Complaining under his breath, Alric strode forward to speak to the men at the gate. Cold and keen to close the barrier for the night so they could return to their fires, they nodded distractedly at his lies. The monk was to meet the archbishop at the church, and he had hired the warrior to protect him on the journey through the lawless countryside. With a grunt and the wave of a spear-point, Alric and Hereward were admitted.

Eoferwic still echoed with the sounds of the day's business. The thatched, timber-framed wattle-and-daub houses were set gable end to the rutted street, each one upon a regular, narrow, tightly packed plot. Through the open doors, Alric saw the floors were bare earth, scattered with discarded rubbish that had been trodden in by the inhabitants. At the backs of the rows were yards where stinking cesspits and piles of rotting rubbish stood beside the wells where the people drew up their water.

Noisy workshops hummed with the activity of craftsmen, or rang with the hammers of metalworkers. Despite the chill, many worked in the open air in front of their places of business, out of the smoke and the reek. Alric had heard that ten thousand souls lived here now, and if that were true it would be amazing, for could there be any more in all of England?

When the wind changed direction, he inhaled the dank

odours of the wharves along the Fosse, which were filled with the creak of wood and the slap of sailcloth from the great vessels moored along the frozen banks. At Jarrow, he had heard of the wonders that were brought to Eoferwic by the trade ships: silk from Byzantium and fine gold jewellery from the Low Countries, colourful seashells from the hot lands far to the south, soapstone from the Northlands, and wine and pottery from the Frankish kingdoms.

After so long in the wilderness, Alric was happy to see the men and women bustling along the street, and the children running at play. The chatter and the shouts sounded like music to his ears. He breathed deeply of the comforting woodsmoke and wished he could live in a city all his days, where life was easier and learning and discourse thrived. Emerging from his reverie, he realized the warrior was striding off along the street.

'Wait,' he called, hurrying alongside. 'Where do you go?'

Hereward stopped and turned, his pale eyes catching the fiery gleam of the setting sun. 'Our time together is done. I saved your life, but I do not own it.'

'I paid you back in kind. Your journey here would have been harder without me.'

'I give thanks for the aid you gave me, but now I travel alone.' Pausing, he looked to the crimson horizon. 'In my dreams, I see the path ahead littered with corpses. I must cross rivers of blood beneath a sky lit by fire. No peace for me, churchman, and peace is all your kind speak of. Our ways lead in different directions. I go to the setting sun, where the dead wait. You face the dawn. Understand?'

'No man should walk through life alone.'

Hereward leaned in, his stare unwavering. 'Are you listening? Death waits for any who walk by my side. I did not save your life only to see it wasted on some godly whim. I can only offer you hell. Go now, or I will take my sword to you.' He held the monk's gaze for a moment longer and then turned and marched away without a backward glance.

Alric took a deep breath to steady himself. God had offered

this warrior to him. Saving Hereward was the reason why he had been placed upon this earth, he had decided, and he could not allow himself to be deterred so easily. Yet he knew he would not sway the warrior with words alone. He watched him walk away into the twilight and then he followed, keeping close to the houses where the men gossiped away from the worst of the wind and he would not easily be seen. Hereward strode on, pausing every now and then to exchange a few words with passers-by, perhaps asking for directions.

A small crowd of men and women had gathered outside a metalworker's hut where the drifting acrid smoke caught the back of the throat. Perched on a pile of logs, a man with only one eye and one hand complained in a loud voice and shook his good right fist in the air. Caught up in the speaker's passion, the attentive audience shouted words of encouragement. Distracted, Alric heard only snippets, enough to know that the group was unhappy about someone or something. He was watching Hereward, who had stepped aside to avoid five wild-bearded Viking warriors brandishing spears who stormed into the crowd, barking demands that the listeners go home. Clearly afraid, the men and women scattered. By the time the last one had gone, the one-eyed man was nowhere to be seen, and the gruff warriors were roaming among the huts, searching for him. The leader of the group paused to study Alric. A jagged scar ran from above his left eye across his nose to his right cheek. His stare was cold and unwavering, the look of a man who saw enemies everywhere.

The night was coming in hard. Only a sliver of red and gold lay in the western sky. Alric shivered in his woollen habit as the temperature plunged. All around him men began to vacate their workshops, abandoning their hammers or their looms to make their way back to their hearths for the evening meal of bread, bean stew and ale. The monk slipped through the steady stream of weary workers until he saw Hereward turn left into a street echoing with the calling of swine, where the smell of rotten apples hung thick in the icy air.

Near the pen where the fat black and pink pigs were kept, four youths taunted a smaller lad. Tears streaked the boy's pale cheeks and he lumbered around with a limp, trying to avoid their swipes. Hereward paused to watch. Alric waited too, studying the warrior, wondering what thoughts were passing through his head. The four bigger boys grew rougher, finally knocking the weaker one to the frozen mud. Hereward flinched.

The monk smiled, a tingle of expectation running down his spine. This was it, he thought, the moment when the warrior revealed his true nature, that deeply buried goodness that Alric had sensed during their long journey. His soul.

As the four bullies launched sharp kicks at the whimpering lad, Hereward roughly pulled them back, flinging one of them so hard that he fell on to his behind. The monk broke into a grin.

He lies to himself about who he is, he thought with a nod. *My task, then, is to bring him to awareness of the good inside him.*

Hereward hooked his large left hand into the smallest boy's tunic and yanked him upright. Silently, he cuffed the lad across the ear, whispered a few words to him and threw the now sobbing child back to the ground. While Alric tried to make sense of what he had seen, Hereward disappeared into the growing gloom and the monk had to hurry to catch up.

The street was deserted and icy stars were glittering in the black sky when he saw the warrior reach an enclosure. Hereward paused at the gate, surveying the dark bulk looming ahead of him, and then strode towards the golden glow falling through the open door on to the snowy ground.

Alric's breath caught in his throat. The thatched hall was the largest building in all of Eoferwic, dwarfing five nearby houses. There was no doubt in his mind. It had to be the hall of Tostig, the earl of all Northumbria. What connection could Hereward have with one of the highest in the land?

CHAPTER EIGHT

The sun was setting over London in a crimson blaze. A knife of shadow slashed through the heart of the white-blanketed Palace of Westminster from the stark silhouette of the new abbey's unfinished tower. Torches sizzled in the crisp air as the Master of the Flame brought light to the enclosure and in the king's hall slaves stoked the fire for the night to come.

Redwald crept through the gloom against the church's western wall. With his hood pulled up to mask his identity, the young man eased past the shaky wooden ladders soaring up to the timber platforms on their vast pillars of elm. All around, the clatter of the stonecutters' hammers rang out, the masons labouring in the dying light under the direct instructions of the king, who could not bear to see his great work lying unfinished for a day longer than necessary. Redwald could smell the earthy tang of the stone dust and the woodsmoke from the fires the workmen used to keep warm.

Low voices echoed from the abbey's shadowy interior. He edged to the arch where the west door would eventually be fixed and peered inside. Ruddy light falling through the window-holes tinged the drifting snow on the floor, and he could see the moon and first stars through the open roof. Two silhouettes stood in quiet conversation in the centre of the nave. When they walked a few paces towards where the altar would be located, Redwald saw that one was the king. The young man had never seen the monarch looking so frail; his skin was almost the colour of the slush at his feet, his head bowed, his limbs thin. Sweeping his right arm towards the sky, Edward was saying in a faint voice, 'All things are in truth two things. This church, this great stone building, is a testament of our devotion to God. But it is also a man.'

Puzzled silence hung in the air for a moment. The second figure shifted uncomfortably. It was the man Redwald had come to spy upon, Edwin of Mercia, brimming with vitality next to his fragile companion. The earl's red woollen cloak shone in stark contrast to the king's bloodless appearance.

'Unformed rocks are hewn from the earth, rough and purposeless,' Edward croaked. 'And then the stones are shaped by the weight of wisdom and the quiet reflection of others, and they take form, and rise up, and gather meaning, and purpose, and become something filled with God's will. Become a testament to God and his plan.'

'You say . . . every church . . . is a man.' Redwald heard Edwin struggling to mask his baffled contempt.

'And every man is a church.' The king nodded, smiling. The earl continued to shuffle, looking around the soaring walls.

Redwald started at the sound of running feet at his back. A young messenger barged past him to whisper to the king, who gave a curt nod, bid farewell to the Mercian earl and followed the messenger out of the church. Pressing back into the deep shadows so he would not be seen, Redwald watched the monarch pass by and thought he saw a faint smile play on Edward's face. He struggled to understand. The king had a young, attractive wife, and wealth and power, but his servants said he had become obsessed with prophecies and omens, and was building this monument as if it was in some way protection against what he feared was to come. Perhaps it was just vanity, Redwald thought, for the monarch knew his name would last

61

as long as the great stone church stood, and that would be until Judgement Day.

Rough hands grabbed his cloak, tearing him from his reflection. Before he could cry out, his unseen assailant bundled him along the cold wall and hurled him through the doorway into the church. Sprawling in the snow, he looked up into the horselike face of Morcar, the Earl of Mercia's brother. 'It is Harold's pup.'

Edwin drew his sword and planted the tip firmly on Redwald's chest. 'I know you. The brother of the murderer.' Redwald's cheeks flushed.

'He was eavesdropping.' Morcar's lips pulled back from his teeth like a cornered animal's. 'No doubt to report back to his master.' He spat a hand's width from the young man's face.

'You are a Mercian. You march under the banner of blue and gold.' Edwin pressed the tip of the sword deeper into Redwald's flesh. The point burned, but the young man forced himself not to cry out. 'How can you be in the employ of that Wessex bastard?'

'You know the Godwins would have crushed Mercia if they could,' Morcar continued. 'They plotted against our kin, and worked to see our own father killed. His final days were a struggle to survive. But Harold Godwinson will not win.' He snarled the final words.

Edwin grinned, but coldly. 'What does Harold fear? That I gain favour with the king? That I will finally prevent his own ascent to power?'

'He does not fear you,' Redwald retorted, red-faced with anger. 'You are too young and untested to be Earl of Mercia. And you would not be there now if not for the death of your father.'

Fury flared in Edwin's features at the insolence. He whipped up his blade to slash it across the young man's face.

'Hold.' The voice echoed across the cold, empty nave. Redwald recognized the confident humour lacing the word. Harold Godwinson strode in, his cloak thrown back so all could see his hand upon the golden hilt of his sword. 'Has my lad slipped under your sword, Edwin?' the Earl of Wessex continued. 'He is a clumsy oaf at the best of times, but that is a mistake that could have cost him an eye.'

Edwin hesitated for a moment, and then sheathed his sword, stepping back. 'You play a dangerous game.'

'And the king wastes his final days building monuments to God, when he should be protecting this realm . . . and ensuring the throne is passed to an Englishman,' Harold snapped.

'To you?' Edwin turned away to hide his sneer.

'Or you.' The Earl of Wessex stuck out his hand to help Redwald to his feet. 'In Normandy, William the Bastard has already laid claim to our throne, and he plots, and he waits. And King Harald in Norway thinks he should have it too. So why do we two fight when we know our true enemies?'

'Why?' Edwin's eyes blazed. 'You know why.' He shoved Morcar towards the door and the two Mercians walked out into the dark.

'I am sorry,' Redwald said. 'I was a clumsy fool. I put you at risk.'

'You are a bright lad, with great days ahead of you, but you still have much to learn. Heed me and you will gain all that you dream of.' But the young man could see that the earl was distracted, and after a moment he realized that Harold was listening to approaching hoofbeats on the frozen mud of the road beyond the enclosure. Beckoning Redwald to walk with him, Harold strode out of the church. The bonfires cast an orange glow up the stone walls of the church, but the masons had packed up their tools and gone for the night.

'It is within your power to make amends for the stain placed on your kin by Hereward's actions,' the earl continued. 'You can set poor Asketil's heart at rest. He deserves more than the blow his wayward son has dealt him.'

'I want to serve England in any way I can.' Afraid of the answer he might receive, the young man nevertheless summoned up his courage. 'Does this mean you will take me into your employ?'

'You have proved yourself.'

Redwald's heart leapt. Harold Godwinson's patronage was all that he had dreamed of since Asketil had first introduced him to the earl. He felt he almost had his hands round the rope that would drag him out of the slough of his early days, and he would not let go whatever happened.

'You have worked hard to gain my trust,' the earl continued. 'I like that. I remember when I was your age, and the dreams I had then. I learned from my father that life is a struggle, but the prize is always worth it.'

In the gloom, Redwald noticed Harold's huscarls waiting around the enclosure, battle-hardened Wessex men who carried their spears as if they were a part of them; clearly, the earl would not have risked confronting Edwin and Morcar in such an isolated place without his own protection assured.

'There is much I can teach you, and much you can do for me.' Harold fixed his attention on the torchlit gate where the sound of hooves had come to a halt. The sentries were calling to someone outside the palace. 'You saw today the threat Edwin and Morcar present. Once Edward has died, they want the throne for themselves. They whisper and plot. Power is all that concerns them, not England.'

'I will keep watch upon them, as you asked. And whatever I hear I will bring straight to your hall.'

'Good. I fear the worst. If the prophecies and omens that fill Edward's head are true, we all face dark times ahead.' Holding up his hand, Harold brought Redwald to a halt. The gate hung open and five men in charcoal woollen cloaks were leading their horses into the enclosure. In the flickering light of the sentries' torches, Redwald saw sallow, foreign features and darting, suspicious glances. But all the men walked with confidence, he noted, as if they felt they stood on their own territory.

'Normans.' Harold's face darkened. Steadily, his huscarls gathered at his back. 'They covet everything we have. Our land, our wealth, our laws, our art. We live and breathe fire here. We drink and feast and fight and sing. But the Normans are like cold stone. Taxes and ledgers and vast, grim churches, that is the Norman.'

One of the men, the leader of the group, Redwald guessed, held Harold's gaze for a long moment before following a sentry towards the king's hall.

'What do they want here?' he asked.

'Sometimes I think Edward is losing his wits. At other times I think he is more cunning than a fox,' the Earl of Wessex mused. 'Would he truly dare offer England's throne to his mother's people?'

Redwald watched the black-cloaked men disappear into the warm glow of Edward's hall. Everything was changing, as the prophecies foretold. What did the future hold?

CHAPTER NINE

Hereward warmed his hands against the fire roaring in the hearth of the vast hall. Relieved to be out of the harsh Northumbrian night, he watched the flames making the gold plate shine like beacons in the half-light. Jewels of red, blue and green sparkled in the sumptuous tapestries covering the walls. Looking round, he saw the hall was the finest he had seen; the earl was clearly enjoying the riches to be had in the north. Newly built in the latest two-floored style, the timber of the frame still smelled fresh. The sunken floor comprised boards suspended over a straw-stuffed vault to keep the building warm in the winter months. Two feasting tables and benches ran the length of the hall, and at the far end, on a raised platform, was the earl's seat, carved with dragons on the arm rests. When he listened, the warrior heard the cracked, dark wood of the throne speak to him of the old days, when men were great heroes filled with fire and vengeance, not weak, sickly things who used shadow-words to achieve their aims.

Yet for all the comfort, his thoughts swept out across the frozen flood-plain into the suffocating dark. He saw burnished helmets, and eyes glowing with fire, spear-points stabbing towards the stars with each relentless step, and he knew there would be no peace for him in this life. Soon his enemies would be at the gates of Eoferwic and he would be forced to take a stand. But here it would be on his terms, perhaps even with good men at his back. He felt relieved that there would be no more running, and that he could finally be true to himself. Survival was nothing without truth.

The messenger darted in from the cold, his ruddy cheeks and curly hair making him appear boyish. Hereward was reminded of Redwald and felt a pang of regret that he might never see his brother again. 'Fear not,' the messenger gasped. 'No enemies will reach you this night. Earl Tostig will join you shortly, but he has ordered men to watch the gates and to refuse entry to any strangers approaching during the hours of darkness.'

When the young man had departed, the warrior basked in the warmth slowly returning to his frozen fingers and toes. He could smell the resin of the wood becoming sweeter as it sizzled in the flames, but then his nostrils flared as another scent reached him on the draught. Spices brought in from the great hot lands beyond the sea and mixed in a paste made from tallow and herbs, which the women used to make themselves more appealing.

'Why do you hide?' he called. 'Am I so fearsome?'

A shape separated from the deep shadows at the rear of the hall. With hair as black as raven-wing and creamy skin, the woman was clearly not a Dane, nor English, Hereward would wager, though he could not place her homeland. She was, perhaps, a year or two younger than him, wearing a plain forest-green dress held by an oval brooch.

'You are not fearsome.' Holding her chin up brazenly, she strode to the hearth and flung a handful of dried leaves into the flames. A sweet scent filled the air. The earl was welcoming him, as he had hoped.

'You have never met any man like me,' he said in a wry voice. He watched her dress fold around the body beneath and realized how long it had been since he had been with a woman.

Perhaps glimpsing his lingering stare, she paused, teasing

with her lips but eyeing him from a position of strength. 'I see fresh scars, like those on the arms of any of the huscarls. I hear boasting, like the easy, empty words that echo from the mouths of the boys who dream of being heroes, but know in their hearts they will never achieve that height. I see . . .' she made a noise in the back of her throat, 'nothing I have not seen before.'

'And yet you waste your breath talking to me.'

'When I hear of a new arrival, who has braved the lawless lands beyond the fence, on foot, in the middle of winter, I would see for myself if this is a fool, or one of the signs.'

'Signs?' Hereward circled the hearth, watching the woman through the smoke. He saw a flicker of apprehension cross her face.

'Of the End-Times.'

The warrior shook his head.

'At the minster, I heard talk that Archbishop Ealdred has sent word out for all men to watch for signs that this is the End of Days. And across Eoferwic everyone whispers of some wise woman's dream that Doomsday draws near.' The slave searched Hereward's face for anything that he might be hiding.

He laughed. 'These are winter stories, to frighten in the long nights. Every age believes it has been chosen to be the last. And if these are the End-Times, then so be it. There is little of value in this world.'

Puzzled, the black-haired woman remained silent for a moment. 'You are not afraid?' But at that moment the hall echoed with the approaching clatter of metal and tramp of leather on wood, and the slave retreated into the shadows. From the gloom at the far end of the hall emerged Earl Tostig Godwinson and his wife Judith, accompanied by five of his huscarls in hauberks and furs. Eyes gleaming beneath their helmets, the bodyguard were tall and lean, fierce of expression and heavily scarred. They were wild-bearded Vikings in the main and carried their axes as if Hereward was to be cornered and killed. The Mercian recognized the jagged facial scar and implacable stare of the one at the head of the band. He had led the dispersal of the crowd gathered outside the metalworker's hut earlier that evening.

But Tostig held his arms wide and boomed a greeting. Dressed in a ruddy-dyed linen tunic under a thick woollen cloak, the earl stood a hand shorter than Hereward, his brown hair curling into ringlets and still sprinkled with the snow that must have started falling outside. He moved with a wolfish lope, his body strong and battle-hardened. But Hereward knew the man's face hid secrets easily and it was difficult to know what he truly thought. In contrast, Judith's face was open and smiling. A heavy-featured but not unattractive woman, she had gained some weight around her middle, but hid it beneath a beautiful linen dress dyed the colour of the sun. Tostig had married well, Hereward thought. As the daughter of Baldwin, Count of Flanders, the Bruges-born woman had powerful connections. Judith smiled at the new arrival. She had always been kind to him on the few occasions they had met at court, when every other noble had treated him with suspicion, contempt or fear.

'I thought my servant was mistaken,' the earl said, warming his hands in front of the fire. 'Hereward of Mercia, here, so far from his home?'

'You have not been to court in recent times?'

Tostig grunted. 'Between repelling the raids from the north and trying to instil order among the unruly herd here in Northumbria, all my attention has been needed in Eoferwic. Let me tell you, my young friend, every night I dream of my old home in the south. This is the most lawless place on earth, and even the so-called civilized men are quick to rise up in violent protest if they feel they are not getting their due.' With a weary shake of his head, he drew up a stool beside Hereward. 'But I expected no more from a people fired by the blood of Viking pirates,' he added with a note of bitterness.

Hereward saw the toll the heavy burden of office was taking upon the earl. His shoulders were hunched, his brow continually knitted. There were many in London who said Tostig was not up to the task of bringing order to Northumbria. He had lived all his life in the shadow of his brother Harold Godwinson, a strong and clever man, who had earned his power at court. But when Earl Siward had died, Harold had fought hard to have Tostig sent north, to ensure the Godwins controlled most of England. Only Hereward's own home, Mercia, remained free of their influence, and there the newly appointed earl, Edwin, was inexperienced and no threat. *Or perhaps no obvious threat*, he thought.

'What news do you have from the south?' the earl enquired, shaking off his mood.

'Edward's court is a mess of plotting and deceit.'

Tostig laughed. 'That is news?'

Judith joined them, resting one hand on her husband's shoulder. 'You are troubled,' she said, her brow furrowing in concern. 'What has driven you here to the cold north?'

'My enemies have pursued me from London, determined to take my life.'

'You always were skilled at finding adversaries,' Judith said with a sad smile.

'I am cursed with a difficult nature.' Hereward returned the smile, remembering how she had once slipped him a honey cake when he had been left supperless in the cold outside the king's hall after a fight.

'Pursued you?' The earl tossed a log on to the fire. Golden sparks soared up in the fragrant smoke. 'Why would they risk their lives in the middle of winter?'

'They are afraid that I learned dark secrets.'

'Did you?'

His face impassive, the warrior said nothing.

Judith laughed. 'He has learned to play the game of kings and earls.'

'The king is ailing. His time on this earth may well be short, and as he has no issue the question of who wears the crown will, as you well know, be a matter of earnest debate.' Hereward dangled his bait lightly. 'I would think the Godwins would wish to have their say.'

Tostig's eyes glittered. After a moment's reflection, he turned to Judith and said quietly, 'Leave us to discuss this matter.' Once she had departed with the huscarls, the earl demanded, 'What do you know?'

Hereward paused, searching for the correct words to describe the event that had changed the course of his life and possibly heralded his death. In his mind's eye, the warrior saw himself stumbling drunkenly through the palace enclosure towards his home and his bed. He smelled the smoke of the hearths and the stone dust from the masons' work on the king's great folly, his new abbey. He heard the owls hooting in the trees on the far side of the wide, grey river, and the singing reverberating from the royal hall. He could still taste the sweet mead on his tongue and feel the night breeze caressing his skin as if every aspect of that night had been locked into his head for all time.

When he heard the echoing cry he raced to investigate. Where the vast stone blocks and timbers for the abbey's construction were piled high, he glimpsed fierce movement on the edge of a circle of flickering torchlight. Two men, hooded and swathed in dark woollen cloaks, were plunging spears into a third man sprawled on the hard-packed earth. A pool of glistening blood was growing around him.

When Hereward yelled an alarm, the two murderers darted into the night. The warrior knelt beside the victim, but could see instantly that there was no saving him. The man's face was unfamiliar; his beard and lank hair were turning white, his cheeks were hollow and his eyes were sunk deep in their sockets as if he had not eaten for many days.

'Do not leave me!' the man gasped, grabbing hold of Hereward's wrist with a desperate strength.

'I am here. Tell me who did this to you. I will see that you are avenged.'

'I do not know their names.' He dragged the warrior in closer. 'Six summers gone I killed Edward Aetheling, the son of old King Edmund Ironside. Poisoned him. In Oxford.'

Hereward felt his drunkenness vanish in an instant. He was

still being tutored by the monks at Burgh Abbey when he had heard of the death of the man who had been chosen to succeed England's childless monarch. Edward Aetheling, the son of the present king's half-brother, was in his forty-first year when he was brought back from exile in Hungary with the sole intent of being groomed to inherit the throne. No culprit had ever been found.

'I wanted more gold,' the man croaked. Tears leaked from his eyes. 'To buy my silence. And they told me they would pay me here tonight . . .'

Hereward's mind raced. 'Who told you?' But the victim would never answer anyone again, silenced in a more bloody manner than he had anticipated before he could implicate others in his terrible crime.

Querying calls rang across the palace grounds, answering the warrior's earlier cry of alarm. After a moment's hesitation, Hereward realized he could not risk being found with the victim. Someone would suspect he had learned too much.

Back at the house he shared with Asketil, Beric and Redwald, he found his adopted brother snoring in his sleep and woke him roughly to recount what he had witnessed. Perched on the edge of his bed, Redwald had sat with his head in his hands, more aware than Hereward how grave was the situation. After a moment's hesitation, he said, 'I overheard Earl Edwin instructing two men in the shadows of the abbey earlier today. I did not recognize them, and they stopped talking when I neared and glared at me until I departed.'

'Edwin? His kin have always rivalled the Godwins in their lust for power. But could the Earl of Mercia really seek the throne for himself? He has no claim. The Pope would not sanction it. William the Bastard . . . Harold Godwinson himself . . . surely they would all resist?'

'It is a grand prize,' Redwald said. 'Worth a grand risk.'

His head still spinning, Hereward said, 'If there is a plot here, the king's own life could be at risk. Poison, the man said. We must raise the alarm . . .'

'Wait.' Redwald jumped from the bed and grasped his friend's shoulders. 'Did anyone witness you hear that last confession?'

'No . . .'

'Are you certain? The two murderers could have watched from afar, and if they thought you privy to such a terrible secret, your own life could be at risk.'

'Nevertheless, the king must be informed.'

'Of course. Let me think.' Redwald paced around the hearth, scrubbing his fingers through his brown hair. 'I have it. No one will suspect me. I will go to raise the alarm. You go to Aedilred's house. He is with his kin in Wessex. Edwin's men will not think to look for you there.'

Grinning, the warrior clapped a hand on his friend's shoulder. 'This is like those summer days in the fens, saving each other from trouble.'

Redwald grinned in return. 'Drink some ale to steady yourself, brother. I will be back soon. But not too much – you are a foul drunk.'

He had drunk too much, and the rest of the night had spun away into confusion. But he recalled with clarity the moment when his life fell into the dark. He remembered the blood, gleaming in the firelight, the hot-iron smell of it. He remembered Tidhild's eyes staring up at him, through him, into that everlasting night-world. His love's eyes. And he remembered fleeing, shortly before his own father had asked the king to declare him outlaw.

Shaking his head to dispel the memory, he eyed Tostig through the curtain of grey smoke and the whirl of scarlet sparks. 'The court has the appearance of a still summer pool,' he said. 'But sharp-toothed predators swim beneath the surface. I now know for certain that the king's chosen heir was murdered, and I fear Edward's own life is at risk from plotters.'

Shock flared in the earl's face, then disbelief, as the warrior had expected. Calmly, he explained what he had seen and heard that night, and expressed his growing concern that Edwin of Mercia, his own earl, was preparing to move for the throne once Edward had died. But he did not tell Tostig of Redwald's mission or what happened after Redwald had left, only that he had left London that night. And he hid the fact that he was outlaw, mistrusted by the king and despised by his own father, for fear it would damage his case.

Tostig listened with rapt attention, growing more troubled with each word. 'And these enemies who pursue you. They are the plotters?'

'Or in their employ. I need to be silenced. They know I cannot stay quiet on these matters. To ensure I should not be believed, they have tried to implicate me in the shame of that night's murder.' *Murders*, he thought. 'But they know they must have me killed, quietly, before the truth comes out.'

'It would have been easier for you to flee abroad.' The earl rose and strode around the hearth in thought. 'I must send word to London. While the snows are heavy, by ship is our best course. But it must be secret. Too forward and Edwin will be alerted – plotters have eyes and ears everywhere and we do not know whom we can trust. And if we speak too loudly too soon, Edwin may be forced to move quickly, before we are ready. Our actions may even bring about the king's murder.'

'I agree. Caution is the only way. If word can be got to the king himself, he can prepare his defences and strike back while Edwin is unguarded.'

'Very well, Asketilson, I will send a man on one of the trading vessels. With luck, we may hear back before Christmas.'

Hereward felt relief that his burden had finally been shared, but, studying Tostig through the smoke, he wondered if he had made the right decision. In the fog of shifting alliances that swirled around the court during these wintry days surely near the end of Edward's reign, no man could have a clear view of the path ahead. But his options were few. To run for ever, like a frightened hare, or to escape, recover, prepare and return to claim the vengeance that set his heart beating like the drums on the galleys.

Tostig allowed himself a tight smile. 'A great game unfolds

around us, and we barely see the pieces, never mind the moves.'
He held a hand out to Hereward. 'You have done a great thing
this day, at risk to your own life. The king will for ever be in
your debt. There is a place for you to lay your head here in my
hall and I will do whatever is in my power to protect you from
your enemies. For now, my huscarls could benefit from your
sword-arm. Join them, and help me bring order to Eoferwic.
And let us both pray that we can stave off disaster on every
front.'

CHAPTER TEN

Black smoke billowed. Hereward stood stark against a wall of flame, his body streaked with blood. Light glinted off axes slicing the air, and the clamour of battle thundered all around, and the screams of dying men, and futile prayers rattling in Christian throats, and he knew he was the cause of it. And he laughed loudly, his voice cracking with madness, as if his only joy came from the suffering of others.

'Where is the God I was promised?' he bellowed into the howling wind.

And then all sound and fury drained away, and he was lying by his own hearth, in the fenland, and his mother was stroking his head. But, as always, he could not discern her face, and her voice came as if from the depths of a dark cave, and he felt unbearably alone. He asked her when he would find peace, but she didn't answer. She never answered.

Hereward woke with a start. New logs crackled on the fire and servants bustled into Tostig's hall with ale and bread, and wooden and clay bowls for the night's feast. The dreams tormented him. Would they ever fade away, he wondered?

Easing into the shadows along the edge of the hall, he watched the guests arrive. In the mill of bodies, he glimpsed many he recognized from court, among them Archbishop Ealdred, a longtime ally of the Godwins and adviser to the king, in his grey linen tunic, and several thegns with gold rings on their arms and gold on the hilts of their swords. Once the most important guests were seated, the commanders of the huscarls blew in, a whirl of coarse laughter and glowering looks and loud demands for mead. It was always wise to indulge the ones who were your strong right arm, Hereward knew. Finally, the earl and Judith took the seats on the small dais at the head of the tables.

As the echoes of the dream faded, he felt his stomach rumble, and prowled to a seat at the end of the bench. All eyes turned towards him.

'Bid welcome to my guest, Hereward of Mercia,' Tostig boomed.

'I thank you for your hospitality,' the warrior called back. 'I will try not to sup all your ale, but I have a fierce thirst.'

Laughter rippled around the hall, but Hereward could feel their scrutiny as they sized him up: threat, rival, fool, ally? He expected suspicion at first, but he had no quarrel with any of them and they would soon understand that. After the hard journey, he felt only the desire to fill his belly and lose himself in drink.

As he anticipated, the men around him soon joined him in laughter and tall tales. He devoured bowls of fish and pork, cheese, bread and honey cakes, rarely loosening his grip on the wooden cup that was always kept brimful with ale. In the hot, smoky confines, the shouted conversation throbbed to the rafters, growing louder with each cup that was swilled. A man with dyed red and yellow scarves tied to his head and wrists juggled with balls of linen stuffed with straw. Scops played the harp and sang of battles and blood and the sea, and in the lull between entertainment the wisest men weaved riddles that all around the table competed to answer first.

'My nose is downward. I go on my belly and dig into the ground, moving as directed by the grey enemy of the forest and my master and protector who walks stooping at my tail.'

'A plough. And that grey enemy is the ox. An old one, but good.'

After a while, Hereward felt the words become the low, constant drone of a wasp in the back of his head. He weighed every face he glimpsed, studying the subtle shift of shadows, the curve of mouth and squint of eye, the adjustment of head and arm. As in the wild, he saw faint hints that could mean life or death to him: who was a potential threat, where danger might lie, who might betray him, who held power and who desired it. The warrior watched the easy relationship between Tostig and the archbishop. There was an alliance there. He expected no less, for they both wielded power in Eoferwic, and they had travelled together to Rome to see Pope Nicholas only two years earlier.

But time and again Hereward found his attention coming back to the scarred leader of the huscarls. His name, Hereward had learned, was Kraki, another of the many Viking mercenaries offering brutal services to anyone wishing to hire them. As the man gnawed on a goose leg, his gaze flickered back to Hereward, suspicious, cautioning.

'Hereward. Will you play the harp for us?' On the low dais, Judith leaned forward in her chair, smiling. All eyes in the hall turned towards the warrior. 'Our guest revealed his great skill at one of the king's feasts. His look may be fierce, but he has the soul of an angel,' she added warmly.

With a grin, Hereward pushed away from the table and strode to the centre of the hall to take the harp. The first note he plucked propelled him back through the years. A moment of peace, caught in the pale light reflected off the still waters of the fens, his mother listening to his early attempts at making music, nodding appreciatively. Drifting in that rarely visited place, Hereward played by instinct. He summoned an achingly beautiful melody, and sang a wistful lyric of a time before dissent, when all was peaceful and hope and joy held firm. Many of the battle-hardened men developed moist eyes, and lowered their heads to hide them.

Embarrassed by the emotion he had accidentally revealed, Hereward ended his song. A long moment of silence was broken by applause. 'To wield a sword with one hand and music with the other is a sign of greatness indeed,' Judith proclaimed. 'You hide your talents well.'

'I am rarely accused of such a crime,' he said, raising more laughter.

When he returned to the bench, most of the guests' attention was upon the juggler who performed by the glow from the hearth, but Hereward noticed several pairs of eyes remaining on him. Archbishop Ealdred watched slyly. Judith smiled at him, like a mother to a son, he thought. Kraki glowered from behind the remnants of his goose leg. And one other cast brooding looks coloured with resentment, one of the huscarls, a squat man with thick lips and flaring nostrils.

The raven-haired woman who had greeted him in the hall carried in a large wooden pitcher of beer and deferentially refilled Tostig's cup before moving along the table in his direction. Although she did not look up, Hereward sensed she knew where he was and was pretending disinterest. He grinned to himself, and nudged the drunken Dane beside him. 'Who is she?'

'Acha,' the Dane slurred when his eyes finally settled on the woman. 'Take no interest in her. She is filled with fire and poison, and will cut you with her tongue if she has no blade to hand.'

'She is not from Eoferwic?'

'She is Cymri. Tostig brought her back with his other slaves from his battles in the west. Acha is not her true name, but she will tell no one what her father named her. She has found some favour here, from the earl's wife, mainly, though what Judith sees in her I cannot tell.'

From the corner of his eye, Hereward glimpsed the squat huscarl shift his gaze towards Acha; the man had noted the warrior's attention. Sensing trouble, Hereward was not surprised when the Viking grasped Acha roughly round the waist and dragged her into his lap. The woman fought back, but her captor cuffed her hard around the head.

'Leave her,' Hereward called, and the drunken man at his side became instantly sober.

'Do not anger Thangbrand. He fights like a cornered stoat. And Earl Tostig values his sword-arm,' he whispered.

Thangbrand grinned, gap-toothed. Hereward knew he was being provoked, a familiar ritual that followed him wherever he went. Positions in the hierarchy of strength needed to be defined. But he felt the blood begin to beat steadily in his head at the violence the other man had shown towards a woman.

'I need no protector,' Acha spat, her eyes flashing towards Hereward. Thangbrand laughed and cuffed her again for good measure.

Hereward rose from the bench. His head throbbed with a powerful beat that stripped away his awareness of Judith's troubled expression or Tostig's intense scrutiny. 'Only cowards harm women.' He heard his own words as if they were spoken by another. His full attention was riveted upon Thangbrand, seeing in the Viking's eyes contempt for both Acha and himself. The cold loathing he felt was lost beneath the thunderous pulse now filling his skull. His devil was riding him, as it had since he had first picked up a sword and felt the edge bite through flesh and bone and gristle, when he had first seen the light die in an opponent's eyes, and heard the whisper of the escaping soul. 'Do not raise your hand to her again.'

Dimly, he heard a roar run along the great tables, urging the two of them on to battle. He half glimpsed the fists shaking in the air and the cups raised high. More entertainment for a cold night. They did not know what terrible thing they were wishing upon that hall.

Thangbrand stepped away from the table. His eyes flared in the firelight, and his lips moved. The sound that issued forth was the dull drone of lazy summer bees, but it mattered little; the words would be familiar. Of slights, imagined or created, of honour, of glory and hurt and blood.

Hereward rounded the end of the table and faced his opponent. 'I wish you no harm,' he said, the words ringing clearly
in his head, though the expressions on the faces all around held
a startled look, as if he had made an animal noise. 'Return to
your bench and apologize to the one you have injured and there
will be an end to this.'

The Viking's shoulders dropped, his stout legs braced.
Fingers twitched towards his axe, but he would not dare raise
his weapon in the earl's hall, Hereward knew. His mouth torn
wide in a battle cry, the huscarl thundered forward, broad arms
wide and fingers crooked.

The warrior met his opponent like an oak resisting a gale.
Bone and muscle clashed like hammers. Digging his filthy,
broken nails deep into Hereward's upper arms, the huscarl attempted to fling the warrior towards the hearth and was surprised when his rival, taller but slighter, resisted. The two men
threw each other around the hall in a wild dance. Thangbrand
was strong, but in his blood-driven state Hereward felt no pain,
only burning rage; no exhaustion, only a single-minded will to
crush the man before him.

Attempting to cripple, the Viking kicked at the tendons at the
back of Hereward's ankles. The Mercian shifted his weight to
avoid the strikes and butted his head into Thangbrand's face.
The huscarl's nose exploded. Hereward scented blood, and his
head thrummed in response. He butted again, shattering teeth.

As the Viking reeled back, he raked his nails across Hereward's
face, attempting to hook out an eye. The Mercian caught a
finger and snapped it. Howling, Thangbrand crashed into the
bench, grasped a cup and flung mead at his opponent's head.
Blinded, Hereward staggered back. The cup rammed against
his skull. Stars flashed behind his eyes.

Spitting like a wildcat, Acha threw herself on to Thangbrand.
The Viking shook her off, punching her in the jaw for good
measure, and Hereward felt the last of his control drain from
him. With a roar, he leapt.

Impressions flashed through his mind, like the sun through

branches on a woodland gallop. Thangbrand's face torn in horror. Blood spraying, blows raining down. Hereward's silent world spun, for how long he did not know, flashes of fists whipping through his head in a blur until the stink of searing flesh in his nose brought him to his senses.

One hand was gripping Thangbrand's throat, while the other was holding the Viking's face side on in the blazing fire. Screams were tearing out through shattered teeth and ragged lips, sounding, Hereward thought, almost like a gull's cry. The huscarl's features were almost unrecognizable, so badly beaten were they. And now the right side of his face sizzled and charred.

Rough hands dragged Hereward back. The reedy screams died to a whimper as the Viking mercifully lost consciousness in the arms of his rescuers.

Whatever had transpired during the time that was lost to him, Hereward could see it had affected every man and woman in the room. Eyes flashed towards him, filled with fear or loathing, but those gazes never lay upon him for more than a fleeting moment for fear they would draw his attention. Nothing he saw there surprised him. Such looks had followed him since he was a child. Alone as ever, he had survived, and that was all that counted.

'Animal.'

'Devil.'

The same words repeated, as they always had been, as they always would be. The pulse of blood in Hereward's head faded away. He didn't struggle against the strong arms holding him fast, or flinch when axes rose to his chest. He ignored the curses and the threats and the hate-filled stares. Raising his head, he looked for Acha, but she was nowhere to be seen, and Judith too appeared to have fled the hall. Even those he wanted to please could not bear to see him. As always.

No matter. He had survived.

'Wait.'

The bodies surrounding Hereward parted. Tostig strode up to the warrior, his sharp blue eyes searching his guest's face.

In a low, emotionless voice, he said, 'You have stained my hall with blood. You came here seeking my aid, yet you have done all within your power to give offence. What do you truly wish, Hereward Asketilson? To destroy yourself? If so, the road you have chosen leads that way.'

'He must be punished for what he has done to Thangbrand,' someone muttered.

Tostig searched for the speaker. All heads bowed, and the earl returned his attention to Hereward. 'These are hard times, and there are harder times ahead. Everywhere I turn, I hear talk of portents and omens. You have deprived me of one of my strongest men when my huscarls are pressed to their limits. Here is your punishment, man of Mercia. You will replace Thangbrand in my warband and we will see how you survive in the simmering cauldron that is Eoferwic. Pay back your debt, with your life if need be.'

The earl turned on his heel and strode away. Hereward looked round at the faces of the scarred, bearded men surrounding him, every eye burning like an ember. They were brothers, and he had wounded one of their own. For every moment he spent in their midst, death would never be far away.

CHAPTER ELEVEN

In the bright of the new day, the circle of huscarls shook their fists towards the blue sky and roared their approval. Their wooden shields rattled against their hauberks to the rhythm of their cheers. As they pawed the snow of the hall's enclosure with their leather shoes, they released blasts of clouding breath with every contemptuous guffaw.

On hands and knees at the centre of the ring, Hereward kept his head down so that his blond hair fell across his swollen cheek. His mind flashed back to the first time his father had struck him after the death of his mother, and his rage burned. When he was ready, he stood up and let the icy wind cool him. Wiping the back of his hand across his bleeding nose, he shook the last of the din from his skull and turned to face his new brothers of the shield. Looking around the dense circle of weather-beaten faces, he saw contempt, but also a hint of fear. That was all he needed.

'A cowardly blow,' he said.

'*You* speak of honour?' Kraki circled the Mercian, bear-like in his thick furs, leather and chain mail, his silvery helmet casting pools of shadow round his eyes. 'You fight like a cornered animal.' The commander of Tostig's huscarls was a veteran of battles across the frozen river valleys of the Varangians and of the Byzantine campaigns in the hot lands to the south, Hereward had learned. That the Viking still lived was proof enough of his prowess, but his heavily scarred skin had become a map of his successes. Brutal and cold, loyal and fair, he seemed a stew of contradictions.

'I fight to win.' Hereward spat a mouthful of blood on to the snow. From the moment he had joined the huscarls that morning, they had made it plain that he was to be punished for his savage attack on Thangbrand. As he stepped up to them with his new shield and axe, he had been tripped, then kicked and punched repeatedly. It would do little good to express the remorse he felt for the extent of the Viking's wounds, he knew. Reparation had to be made, a balance struck, and the admission that he could not control his inner devil would carry little weight.

Kraki pressed his face close. 'This is Northumbria and we are huscarls. We do not send a man before the Witan to account for his crimes. We have our own rules. Here we follow the old ways, of blood and fire. Honour is all.' He glanced around the circle. 'A man of honour has firm principles. A man of honour fights for his friends in time of need. For his people, his land.' The huscarl leader looked the warrior up and down with unconcealed contempt. 'You have no honour. You are nothing.'

Hereward bit his tongue.

Jeers ran through the ranks. From the edge of the hall ground, a large brown bear rose up on to its hind legs and bellowed in response to the sound it heard. Tostig had had the beast brought over from the Northlands, for entertainment and as a symbol of his own untamed power. Though it was shackled in its own enclosure, its roar chilled all who heard it, the warrior saw.

Kraki glanced towards the bear and nodded. 'There, the sound of your kin calling to you. But brutish strength and a beast's ferocity and cunning will not keep you alive for long. That rage that burns so hot in you will be your end.'

Hereward feared the commander's words were true. 'I will prove my value, with my sword and my axe.'

The Viking snorted. 'Not this day. There is too much bad feeling towards you. Who here would want a wild animal at his side, as likely to attack him as the enemy? If you would be trusted, we must see you have been tamed.' He turned his back on the warrior and walked away. 'You will toil with the slaves until I summon you, fetching water and cutting wood for the hearth. Even that work is too good for you.'

Hereward's cheeks burned, but he would endure. He had suffered worse, and at least he had found respite from pursuit. It was even possible that Tostig would aid him in his struggle for justice.

As the huscarls surged out of the gate into Eoferwic, he suppressed his pride and joined the slaves. For most of the morning, he hacked logs from the trees dragged in from the woods to the south. A constant supply of fuel was needed to keep the winter fires burning, and fast though he worked the wood pile never seemed to grow any larger. The other woodmen eyed him with sullen suspicion, but he kept his head down, allowing the rhythm of his labour to still his troubled thoughts. Only when the sun was at its highest and his arm muscles burned did he wipe the sweat from his brow and go in search of food.

Gnawing on a hunk of bread, he rested in the lee of the hall, watching the bear prowl its enclosure. The sweet smell of woodsmoke hung in the air, barely masking the choking odours drifting in from the filthy streets. As he looked idly round, a figure moving stealthily through the deep snow caught his eye. Though her cloak was pulled tight, he saw it was Acha. Something about her cold expression and determined step drew his attention, and his puzzlement turned to unease when he noticed she was approaching the house where the injured Thangbrand lay.

With a rush of realization, he threw the bread aside and raced between the huts. He caught up with Acha at the door to Thangbrand's dwelling and grabbed her wrist as she half turned at the sound of his shoes in the snow. A knife flew from her hand into a drift. Her eyes blazed. With her free hand, she lashed out, raking her nails across his cheek. 'Leave me be,' she snarled.

Hereward dragged her out of sight round the side of the hut and pressed her against the wall until she calmed down. 'You planned to kill Thangbrand? Has he not suffered enough?'

'No. He laid hands upon me . . . he shamed me . . . he deserves death.'

'Have you lost your wits? You would not escape punishment. At the least, you would suffer the agonies of an ordeal. At worst, death.'

'He shamed me!'

Hereward was struck by the murderous fury in Acha's eyes. 'I cannot allow you to risk your own life—'

'Allow me?' she snapped. 'You have no say in what I do. I am no little rabbit, weak and frightened and needing a man to fight my battles. In my homeland men bowed before me—'

She caught herself, and in that moment Hereward understood she had been a woman of some standing before Tostig had taken her prisoner. She looked away, her jaw set.

'Heed me. I know full well the curse of uncontrollable passions. We need no enemies – we destroy ourselves,' he said. 'This is a mistake. I will not let you sacrifice yourself to gain revenge.'

'I do not need your protection.'

'You think I can help myself? I could not turn away and see you or any woman destroyed.'

'Then you are a fool.' She threw off his grip and pushed by him. He felt relieved to see her ignore the knife as she walked back towards the hall. Following in her wake, he recognized that he had done some good that day, a small recompense for the trail of misery he had left behind him over the years. Perhaps Acha understood that too, deep beneath her anger, for she glanced back at him once she reached the hall. Her expression looked curious, but before he could wonder what it meant, she disappeared inside.

CHAPTER TWELVE

Terror haunted every part of Eoferwic. As the cold days passed in the slow march towards the Christmas feast, Hereward had grown to realize that this place was no London or Mercia, where the rule of law held sway. Northumbria truly was wild and untamed. Though the age of the Vikings had passed, their spirit of fire and rock had been embedded in the land, he found, and the people here were of an independent nature. They felt aggrieved that Tostig, a man of the south, had been imposed upon them and they caused trouble on a daily basis. Even the earl's decision to hire Northmen for his huscarls had done little to placate the people. Those loyal to Tostig were beaten, their houses burned. Open talk of rebellion rustled in the marketplace and along the wharves and in the tavern.

Hereward cared little. He had his own plans for revenge and they consumed him. But he knew he had to bide his time until he learned whether the earl's messenger had successfully convinced the king, or Harold Godwinson, of Edwin of Mercia's crimes. At least there had been no sign of the enemies who had pursued him so relentlessly across moor and hill. Perhaps they had fallen to the wolves or the cold, he hoped.

Yet in the quiet moments during his hard labours alongside

the slaves, he found himself watching for Acha. They had exchanged looks across the smoky hall, but her dark features always kept her feelings locked away. Three times he had tried to speak to her, but she had spurned him as if he was not there, and he had no way of knowing if this was some game she was playing or if she truly did hold him in contempt. Beside the waters of their Mercian home, his brother Redwald had once warned that some woman would be the death of him, and when he looked into Acha's cold gaze he wondered if that might be true.

A week after the brawl with Thangbrand, a grey pall blew across the south of Eoferwic and he was at last summoned from his menial tasks to join the earl's men. The familiar feel of his sword in his hand soothed him. As Kraki waved the huscarls out of the enclosure and over the frozen ruts into the wall of smoke rolling across the tightly packed houses, Hereward knew he should keep one eye on his companions. They loped like a pack of wolves on each side, clutching axes that could easily be turned on him in the confusion.

Wind-whipped flakes of charred wood and smouldering straw mingled with the falling snow. Out of the billowing cloud, frantic men, women and children jostled along the narrow street. The fire's roar drowned out their frightened cries. 'Keep your wits about you,' Kraki called. 'These bastards are like ghosts. You'll have a face full of blood from a split head before you even know anyone's there.'

Thrusting fleeing men and women aside, he strode up to Hereward, his eyes lost to the shadows beneath his helmet. 'The rabble-rouser is in there,' he growled, jabbing his axe towards the smoke. Through the folding grey, red and gold glowed dimly. 'Find him before he escapes again.'

'What about the fire?'

'You weren't scared of the flames when you burned Thangbrand,' the Northman sneered, his ragged scar flexing above his beard. 'Ravenswart is rounding up enough of these frightened mice to carry water so we can stop the fire spreading.

Get in there, and don't come back until you have that bastard.'

His mail clanking, Kraki ran back towards the milling huscarls. He barked orders at his men to save cattle and corn while Ravenswart attempted to bring the conflagration under control, and then directed twenty of the troops to surround the burning area so their prey could not escape when Hereward flushed him out.

His throat stinging, Hereward plunged into the smoke. The sound of the fire and his footsteps became muffled. When he broke through to the other side, he saw that the jumble of workshops, stores and houses was devoid of life. Hammers, augers, axes, spades and rakes lay where their owners had discarded them when the alarm had been raised. A fallen butter churn spilled its sticky contents on to the dirt. The roar of the fire was louder here, and he could see the flames leaping up above the thatched roofs.

Eyes stinging, Hereward watched the dark entrances to the shacks. He had learned that the 'rabble-rouser' was Wulfhere, the one-eyed, one-handed man he had seen on his arrival in Eoferwic, a woodworker who had grown more outspoken about Tostig's rule since the summer had waned. Now the man was openly calling for the earl's overthrow. Peering towards the blaze, Hereward saw that this time the troublemakers had targeted the home of one of the earl's wealthy merchant supporters. The fire had been lit with care, taking into account the direction of the wind, so it would not spread into the heart of Eoferwic.

The snow was falling faster now. Hereward found his vision reduced to the width of the icy road. Choking and coughing, he searched hut after hut, moving steadily closer to the burning house. When the rafters collapsed, a loud crash echoed over the roofs and golden sparks swirled up to greet the white flakes. The warrior could hear the shouts of Kraki's men circling the burning street. If Wulfhere was still within the smoke-filled area, there would be nowhere for him to run.

Sensing movement on the edge of his vision, he darted into

a weaver's shop where a blackened cauldron bubbled over hot embers, ready to make the colours fast. The air was heavy with the sweet fragrance of woad leaves, dried weld and madder roots. Wool and flax were piled in one corner and a warp-weighted loom leaned against the wall, a sheet of linen half complete where it had been abandoned by the weaver. Turning slowly, Hereward looked around the gloomy, cluttered workshop.

Rapid movement distracted him. Through the open door, he saw a stream of brown rats flood away from the fire, ringed tails lashing the air. The moment the Mercian turned, a crash sounded behind him. He was thrust roughly to one side as someone barged by. Stumbling to his knee, he glimpsed a dark figure scrambling through the door into the smoke.

Hereward threw himself in pursuit. Leather shoes clattered on the hard ground ahead. He glimpsed the figure in front and to the left, gone in an instant. Then to the right. The man was weaving across the road, trying to lose his pursuer or searching for a bolt-hole hidden by the smoke. His breath clouding, Hereward leapt log piles and heaps of rotting food, ducking down narrow walkways between houses. The ragged breathing of his prey drifted back to him.

When he burst on to a street filled with squealing pigs, a crescent of fire confronted him. The heat from the blazing ruins of the merchant's hall seared his skin. But he saw the conflagration had not been contained as Kraki had promised. Somehow the flames had leapt a narrow way and now two other houses burned close to a densely packed area of huts and workshops. On the other side of the hall, the blaze was also starting to spread.

Hereward cursed under his breath. That part of Eoferwic would soon be consumed. If he was caught there when the fire-rush began, he would be cooked as black as Thangbrand's face and then the huscarls would laugh that the gods had punished him in kind. Yet the dancing flames held him fast, the flickering colours, the heat, the swirling sparks, and he realized he felt no fear, only a dull thrill deep in his belly. He watched the straw of a roof glow red, and the timbers blacken and snap and crackle as if they were shouting in exultation. His head spun at the power he witnessed, one that made more sense to him than anything he had experienced in his short life.

Burn away, he thought. *Let it all burn away.*

He forced himself to break the spell. There was still time to carry out Kraki's order; Wulfhere had to be lurking in one of the buildings nearby. Hereward considered letting the rabble-rouser burn for his crimes – the one-eyed man's life would be forfeit anyway once he was dragged before Tostig. On the other hand, returning with such a prize could buy the earl's gratitude and make his own life easier.

The fire growled louder and bared its claws, stretching out on either side of him. Beyond the red and gold crescent Hereward could hear the shouts of Kraki's men as they searched the deserted houses for their prey. He would not let the huscarls snatch the trophy from his grasp.

With the heat burning his back, Hereward threw himself into the nearest house, then the next, and the one after. He felt a different atmosphere in the fourth, and smelled a hint of bitter fear-sweat in the air. Drawing his iron blade from its leather scabbard, he padded towards a wicker screen near the back of the gloomy space. As he neared, a figure burst out, arms flailing in a desperate attempt to reach the doorway. Hereward brought the hilt of his sword up in a flash, cracking the fugitive in the face. The man flipped back on to the hard mud floor, dazed. One eye, one hand. It was Wulfhere.

'There will be even less of you when Tostig has had his way,' Hereward muttered, looming over the prostrate form.

'Leave him be.'

The warrior whirled at the frightened voice from behind the screen. A second figure edged out. It was Alric, his pale face streaked with soot. 'If you wish to take this man, you must kill me first.'

Chapter Thirteen

Hereward stared at the monk's ashen face. 'Have your wits deserted you?' He jabbed the tip of his sword towards his former companion's heaving chest. 'I saved your life. And now you put it at risk again? Is this a game to you?'

Swallowing, Alric interposed himself between the warrior and the sprawling rabble-rouser. 'I know you do the earl's work. You must let this man go.'

Beyond the wattle walls, the guttural calls of the huscarls rang out, drawing closer. Hereward cuffed the monk around the head. 'Your brains have fallen out of your ears,' he said. 'If Tostig's men find you here, with him, you will face the same fate, man of God or not.'

Thrusting the monk aside, he stooped to grasp Wulfhere. Alric barged his way between them again. 'If you wish to take this man, you must kill me first,' he repeated. The young cleric held his chin up in defiance, but his eyes were filled with tears of fear. He blinked them away.

Hereward felt the familiar rage rising notch by notch. 'You know I will not flinch from taking any life,' he said in a voice almost lost beneath the snarl of the conflagration.

'I know.'

The warrior dug the tip of Brainbiter into the monk's black habit. The cleric squirmed under the pressure, making the sword waver. 'You think me a good man. You are a fool,' Hereward said. 'I am the wild animal I was branded from my earliest days. I care for nothing but myself.'

'You do not know yourself.' Alric jerked his head away as if he expected a blow. Shouts echoed outside. Kraki's men were searching the nearby houses. 'If you were the beast you say, you would have killed me already.'

Wulfhere tried to scramble to his feet. Hereward kicked the one-eyed man in the face, dazing him once more. 'You stake your life on that belief?' he snapped. 'Truly, you are a fool.'

'Kill me, then,' Alric shouted with a passion that surprised Hereward. 'God knows, I deserve it. But I will not allow you to take this man.' The monk held his arms wide and pressed his chest against the point of the sword.

More shouts, not far beyond the door.

Hereward felt unsettled. He could not find it in himself to drive the sword into the young monk's heart. With a flash of fury that he couldn't explain, he punched Alric in the face.

'Do not hurt him,' Wulfhere spat from between split lips. 'He is a good man.'

Out in the street, Kraki called to the huscarls to hurry.

Hereward yanked Alric back to his feet. 'This is not some sign that your stupid idea is right.' He shook the monk roughly. 'I do not want to hear you whining about me being a good man, do you hear?'

Alric nodded, wiping the blood and snot from his top lip with the back of his hand.

A shadow crossed the doorway, and Hereward spun, cursing. He had wavered too long. They had been discovered. Yet no one entered, and even as the warrior's brow knitted in sudden suspicion, what sounded like the rustling of autumn leaves raced over their heads. Crackling and spitting, the flames surged through the thatch and smoke swept into the hut.

'The house is afire,' Wulfhere cried, and began to scramble

95

for the door. Hereward grabbed him by the back of his tunic and dragged him towards the screen.

'You will see us burned alive?' the one-eyed man whimpered.

Alric was watching his former companion. 'Trust him,' he said. 'He knows death so well he can barter with his old friend.'

At the rear of the hut, Hereward aimed a kick at the wall. The daub had dried hard against the wattle beneath, but as the warrior repeated the action cracks appeared and large chunks fell away. When the hole was big enough, he propelled the monk through the gap, and then jabbed the one-eyed man with his sword to follow.

The three men stumbled out into thick smoke and air so hot it seared their throats. Hereward's mind raced with questions, but he urged the others past the stinking refuse tip by the well and into the back of a woodworker's shop. 'One wrong move and I will change my mind,' he growled. 'Lead the way to your hiding place. If we are caught by the huscarls, we will all enjoy the sleep of the sword.'

Wulfhere and Alric followed a mazy route along trails that were barely wide enough for a dog. The crackling of the fire faded away, and the deserted streets gave way to ones buzzing with crowds of anxious people looking towards the black cloud and wondering if all of Eoferwic was to be consumed. The three men slipped into the throng, keeping their heads down.

By the time they reached a house not far from the great stone church, the snow was falling in fat, heavy flakes, drawing a blanket of white across the thatched roofs and dirty streets. The throb of daily life became muffled. Glancing back, Hereward could see no orange glow and thickening smoke to suggest the blaze was spreading. For a moment he stood by the door, watching the low black cloud, and then he stooped to enter the warm, smoky interior.

A tearful woman was hugging Wulfhere; his wife, the warrior guessed. Two young girls clung to his legs, and a small dog ran in circles around the family, yapping. A silver-haired man squatted in one corner, eyeing the warrior with suspicion. Hereward suspected it was his house and he had risked all to offer a haven to Wulfhere and his family.

Alric was warming his hands over the hearth, beaming with relief. 'I knew you would listen to your heart,' he said.

'What did I tell you?' Hereward strode forward so purposefully that the monk cowered. The Mercian felt angry with himself for allowing the one-eyed man to go free, and still didn't understand why he had done it. 'Keep your whining to yourself or I will cut out your tongue.'

Alric squatted beside the fire. 'Why did you save us?'

Hereward grunted. 'My brain must be as addled as yours.' He glanced back at the door, and added, 'Your refuge could not have caught alight so quickly. It was too far from the seat of the fire.'

'What are you saying?'

'Someone knew we were there and tried to burn us.'

'Would Tostig's men truly attempt cold murder?' Alric stared into the glowing embers. 'Yes, they would. For the earl is an evil man.'

Hereward snorted. 'You speak with an ale-tongue. He is a Godwin. His kinsmen have stridden across England like giants since my father's father's time. His brother Harold is the king's most favoured adviser.'

'And you are blinded by gold rings.'

The warrior's hand twitched towards the hilt of his sword. 'Watch yourself, monk.'

Alric took a deep breath and stood to look his former companion in the eye. 'During your time in Eoferwic, you have been cosseted in the earl's hall, drinking his mead, eating his food, warming yourself by his hearth. I have watched from afar, my friend. You have been well cared for. But I have been sleeping on a cold floor provided by the archbishop and I do not feel so sanguine.'

Wulfhere's wife, a hard-faced woman with broken veins on her cheeks, interrupted them. With a grateful smile, she offered

Hereward a cup of ale and some bread. He accepted the gift with a curt nod.

When she left them, Alric glanced towards the one-eyed man. 'He is not what you think. Not what the earl says he is.'

The warrior swigged back his ale in a single gulp. 'So he burns no houses and does not incite the people to rebel.'

'Ask yourself why he does those things,' the monk pleaded. 'He is a woodworker, with mouths to feed.'

Hereward watched Wulfhere playing with his children, the rebel's hard face softened by a fond smile.

'These last days I have roamed across Eoferwic, looking for the reason God sent me here. You are one of those reasons, I know that now' – he ignored Hereward's snort as the warrior tore off a knob of bread and stuffed it into his mouth – 'and the other reason soon became as clear as the sun off the snow. Everywhere I turned, I saw misery, hunger, despair. The people are suffering. They are angry, and no one listens to them.'

'Not your God?' Hereward said with his mouth full. 'Not the archbishop? Is he not tending to his flock?'

Abashed, Alric peered into the fire. 'Ealdred is close to the earl; to all the Godwins.'

'Ha,' Hereward mocked.

'Tostig's unfair tax is crushing the spirit of the people of Northumbria. Since he became earl, he has increased the burden of the geld. His collectors are cruel and unjust. And any who voice opposition are crushed in the most brutal way. Homes are burned. Farms despoiled. There is talk of murder . . . murder! Of Englishmen, by the earl who governs them.'

The warrior shrugged. 'Is this a revelation to you, monk, that men who hold power over others abuse their position? Whatever Tostig does here, it is with the consent of the king. It could not be otherwise.' Returning to the door, he peered out to see if they had been followed. The snow was lying heavily on the street. 'Northumbria has always been a lawless place. It is the Viking blood, the Danish hearts. They make their own rules, and they are filled with rage when others try to tell them what to do. It takes a hard man to govern people like that.'

Alric beckoned Hereward back to the fire. 'What is happening in Eoferwic is beyond hard governance. It is unfair. There is true suffering. The people will only take this for so long before they rise up. For now, the thegns are loyal, but that can change if men like Wulfhere continue to give voice to the pain.'

The warrior studied the young monk. 'What compels you? From the moment I found you, like a frightened rabbit, you have been a riddle. I have spent time with many churchmen, but none like you.'

Alric would not meet the other man's eye. 'I seek to make amends . . .' He caught himself. 'I seek to live my life in a godly manner. Shepherding the weak, the hungry, the lost . . .'

'I save your life and you immediately throw yourself into more danger. I should have left you to your fate.'

The monk jumped to his feet, his eyes blazing. 'But you did save me. And now you have saved me twice. You reveal your true nature by your actions, a nature, perhaps, that you are not even aware of yourself. It seems to me that you fight yourself as much as everything that passes within a hair of your sword, and in that, you and I are not so different.'

'You are a fool. I am not. And I have wasted enough time here.' Hereward turned to the woman and thanked her for her hospitality, and then to Wulfhere. 'Take care. The next time you stand alone.' He strode to the door, but Alric jumped in front of him. 'Monk, you try my patience. I will not sully this good wife's floor with your blood, but I will bash the wits out of your head.'

'Join us in our battle.'

'You are mad.' The warrior shook his head in disbelief. 'How many times must I tell you? I care only for myself.'

'And what of Gedley? Would I be here now if you were driven by purely selfish motives?'

'I need the earl's aid to achieve my revenge,' Hereward said through gritted teeth. 'And he provides shelter from my enemies.

It would be foolish to stand against him. What gain is there for me in that?'

'Men achieve more together than they do alone.' Alric stuck his chin out.

'One man means survival. Two or more means the opportunity for betrayal.'

The monk softened his tone, holding his arms wide. 'Two men mean the opportunity for friendship and support and hope. Two men are the start of an army—'

His anger rising, Hereward shoved the cleric aside and stepped out into the stinging snow before he lost his fragile control. He felt as if the world were shifting under his feet. Before he met the monk, his life had been fraught but simple, his choices clear. Association with the churchman had brought only doubt and confusion. Looking over the thatched roofs of Eoferwic, under the pall of grey smoke from the homefires, he saw that the dull red glow on the town's southern edge had died down. He hoped his actions that day would not cost him dear.

CHAPTER FOURTEEN

Pressing his cheek against the icy stone wall in the shadows, Alric spied into the golden glow of the candlelit nave. The sweet scent of incense hung in the air around the copper censer. Two figures walked towards the main altar, heads bowed in reverence. A third waited near the font. Their whispers rustled around the vast, echoing interior, larger than any church the young monk had visited in his life. Thirty altars, he had been told when he accepted the Province's hospitality, though he had not seen even a third of them. Everywhere he looked chapels had been appended, seemingly in haphazard fashion. The place had grown out of all recognition in the four hundred years since King Edwin had ordered the small wooden church that had stood on the site to be rebuilt in stone. Shadows everywhere. Hiding places aplenty. He had hoped to find a sanctuary here, but the oppressive atmosphere that hung over all Eoferwic reached even into this sanctified interior.

Who plotted? Who weaved schemes in search of power and gold? Whom could he trust? Not the archbishop, he was increasingly sure, though it pained him deeply to doubt such a great man. Alric watched Ealdred drift along the nave, the candles casting a looming, hook-nosed shadow on the far wall.

His ceremonial mitre gave an odd, flat-topped appearance to the shadow's head, distorting the figure further. Alric shivered, his breath clouding, but the archbishop would be warm in his green and purple woollen chasuble.

Ealdred was a man who understood the world of power as well as the spiritual realm, the monk knew. He had the king's ear, and he was close to the Godwins, who wielded such great influence across England. Given a choice between the poor ceorls and the wealthy, where would he stand? Alric thought he knew.

Beside the archbishop, the earl's wife, Judith, listened intently to the advice she was being offered. Her expression was grave, the darkness in her features emphasized by her white headdress. She wrapped herself in her green woollen cloak, the red embroidery around the hem gleaming like blood.

'And what does the church think of these dark prophecies that consume the thoughts of the people?' she was saying in a quiet voice. 'They talk of voices whispering in the deep forests, and signs in the night sky. Their fears are fuelled by those who still pray to the pagan gods, I am sure. Is the world truly coming to an end?'

Ealdred clasped his hands behind his back, raising his face to the altar. 'The Revelation of St John tells us of the End-Times. It is . . . a difficult work and requires much reflection and study. But the words of our own Archbishop Wulfstan come down to us. His *Sermon of the Wolf to the English* is much discussed by my fellow churchmen and once was proclaimed from every parish pulpit.' The archbishop pressed two fingers on the bridge of his nose and closed his eyes, remembering. '*This world is in haste and is drawing ever closer to its end, and it always happens that the longer it lasts, the worse it becomes. And so it must ever be, for the coming of the Anti-Christ grows ever more evil because of the sins of the people, and then truly it will be grim and terrible widely in the world.*' Ealdred opened his eyes and gave a wolfish grin as if he was revelling in the apocalyptic message.

'And the Anti-Christ?' Judith asked. 'How shall we know him?'

'We will know him, fear not. Wulfstan thought the Vikings in their dragon-ships were harbingers of the End. But now . . .' Ealdred shrugged. 'The king is fading and with no issue, England faces a time of great upheaval. Perhaps this is the time when the Wolf hunts us all.'

Judith blanched and crossed herself.

'I am sorry. I did not mean to frighten you.' The archbishop pressed his palms together. 'We must put our faith in God who will save all good men and women. For now, a strong hand is needed to steady the course of our great ship in these turbulent waters.' He leaned in close and gave a conspiratorial nod. 'Now, I will leave you to your prayers. Should you require any more guidance, one of the acolytes will fetch me.'

When Ealdred's echoing footsteps had disappeared into the depths of the church, Judith knelt before the altar and bowed her head. Studying the slump of her shoulders, Alric thought how troubled she looked.

'Why do you spy upon my mistress?'

The monk jumped at the harsh voice. He whirled to see that the third figure had crept up on him. It was a woman with a face like the snow outside and hair the colour of raven's wings. 'I . . . I . . .' he stuttered.

'Answer me,' she hissed, leaning in close. Her eyes were like black pebbles.

Alric thought quickly. He couldn't say that he was spying on any visitor from Tostig's hall who might reveal the earl's plans to deal with the simmering conflict across Eoferwic. 'I would have news about a . . . a friend . . .' His words tailed away. The woman's stare was unsettling, and he decided he did not like her.

'What friend?'

'His name is Hereward. We travelled to Eoferwic together—'

'Hereward?' Her eyes flashed in recognition, but she hid the first glimmer of her feelings before he divined them. 'What do you know of him?'

'That he is a good man who hides his true nature behind a fierce face.'

Her laughter reminded him of stones falling on a frozen river. 'My name is Acha. I will take you to my mistress once she has finished her prayers and you can ask her all you wish to know.'

The monk told her his name and thanked her, though he would now have to spin his lie further. Acha did not soften, but they exchanged a courteous conversation about the festivities the earl planned for Christmas. His men had already selected the Yule log, which Ealdred himself would bless, and the holly and mistletoe would soon be collected. All-spice, nutmeg and cinnamon were ready for the baking of the festive cakes.

When Judith had finished her prayers, Acha led Alric over and introduced him. The younger woman stepped back, but listened with what the monk thought was keen interest. The countess's face softened when Alric told her of his mission to take the Word to the villages of Northumbria that did not yet have a church or a priest. The monk had heard that Judith was a pious woman who had made many gifts to the church of St Cuthbert in Dun Holme. Learned, too; she was said to own many books and illuminated manuscripts. She seemed surprisingly keen when the monk mentioned Hereward's name and spoke of the warrior with clear warmth.

'You knew him before he came to Eoferwic?' Acha asked.

The countess smiled at the younger woman's interest. 'Yes, I knew him. At court.'

'Hereward was at court?' Unable to hide the shock in his voice, Alric was filled with a crimson vision of the warrior rising from the pool of blood, eyes glinting with uncivilized fury.

Judith laughed. 'He is your friend, and you know nothing about him?'

'I know him better than he knows himself,' the monk asserted, 'but of the events of his life I know nothing at all.'

'Tell us,' Acha urged her mistress, unable to hide her curiosity.

'I remember a boy of barely twelve summers looking as if a great wind had blown him into the king's hall, golden hair filled with straw and dirt and bruises and dried blood smearing his face. He was a fighter even then, and a trouble to his father, Asketil, one of the king's thegns. Though he had a singing voice that could reduce men to tears and a face of beauty and innocence, there were some who said the Devil lived in his heart.' She looked from Acha to Alric, a shadow crossing her face. 'In his Mercian home, he and a band of friends were responsible for such unrest that Asketil feared for his son's safety. The boys were like wolves, untamed, they say. Stealing. Fighting. Burning barns. Attacking good men and women. Unable to control the boy, Asketil brought him to court where he hoped his son would learn to be an honourable man. Hereward promptly ran back to Mercia and hid for more than a year in the wilds.'

Acha covered her mouth to hide a laugh. 'And his mother? I have never seen a good wife who could not bring a child to heel with the side of her hand or the sharp of her tongue.'

Judith gave a sad smile. 'The boy's mother was taken by God when he was young. Asketil is as unbending as an oak and as cold as the ground outside this church. He played little part in the boy's upbringing, preferring to devote himself to the king's business and his own needs. Though he hides a hot temper. I found Hereward once so badly beaten he could not stand.'

'His father?' Alric asked.

Judith nodded. 'Asketil swung between uninterest and dealing out beatings that no just man would inflict on a beast. Yet Hereward wanted for nothing. The monks at Peterborough gave him schooling. He learned to play the harp. On his father's estates he was trained in fighting with spear, axe and sword, and he became a fine horseman. He learned the secrets of the watermen of the fens. He hunted boar and waterfowl and he was adept at hawking. And yet as the years passed, he caused such a tumult in Mercia that it was as if he cared for no man or woman.'

'I cannot believe that,' Alric put in.

'Nor I,' the countess said with a nod. 'He was a lost soul, but inside I saw a spark of goodness, if only someone could fan it into a flame.'

Alric felt his spirit rise. It was almost as if Judith were speaking directly to him.

'Perhaps it is too late,' Acha mused. 'Those who saw his treatment of Thangbrand said he was more beast than man. And I would agree.'

'Perhaps.' Judith rubbed her hands together to warm them. 'Asketil brought him back to court and kept him there for three summers, and though there were moments of fighting and drunkenness that shamed his father, he did seem to find some peace. When he returned to Mercia on the brink of manhood, I hoped he would escape the devils that haunted him.'

'And now he is in Eoferwic.' Acha stroked the tip of her index finger along her full lips. 'And no one knows why, for he refuses to tell a soul of his true reasons for being here.'

'His sword-arm is a valuable addition to the huscarls in these turbulent times,' Judith said. 'He is the best warrior here. At court, the men said he was unbeatable in battle because he has no fear.'

Because he cares for nothing, not even himself, the monk thought. He watched the raven-haired woman from the corner of his eye. Her expression was thoughtful, and he wondered what was passing through her head.

'Mercia's loss is Northumbria's gain. Hereward will serve us well here, I think. Now, this cold reaches deep into my bones and I would spend some time by my own hearth.' Judith was about to walk away along the nave when she added, 'Would you like me to remember you to your friend?'

'Thank you, Countess, but that is not necessary,' Alric replied with a polite smile. 'I will see him again soon enough.'

The tap-tap-tap of the two women's leather soles faded into the gloom. Just before the shadows folded around her, Acha glanced back and the monk thought he glimpsed something fierce in her face, a desire, perhaps, to seize an opportunity with both hands and never let it go.

Alone in the nave, Alric wondered what to do now. There was enough work in the church to keep him occupied until long after sunset, but then Wulfhere and some of the other men were meeting in secret to discuss their next move. The monk hoped to persuade the rebellious group to concentrate their efforts on urging the thegns to change the earl's mind, perhaps after Twelfth Night when Tostig would be replete and rested, without bloodshed or further burning.

Walking slowly towards the altar, he was distracted by the sound of approaching footsteps. Ealdred appeared, but Alric's smile of greeting froze on his face when he saw that the archbishop was not alone. Four men stood in the shadows behind the churchman, but the monk was rooted by the sight of the red-bearded Viking at Ealdred's side.

Harald Redteeth grinned, raising one muscular arm to point at Alric. 'That one,' he said. 'His hands are red with a woman's blood. He is a murderer who attempted to flee the punishment for his crime. Now he must pay the price for his sin.'

Chapter Fifteen

On the snow-covered bank of the grey river, in the teeth of a bitter wind, Hereward watched the sailors tie up a ship laden with lapis lazuli, amethyst pendants and silk brought from the lands beyond the whale road. It would be the last vessel to visit Eoferwic before the port closed for Christmas, for no one worked during the Twelve Days. The seamen, skin lashed red by the wind and the icy sea spray, struggled to work their frozen fingers despite the thick furs and leather they wore against the cold.

'News from the south?' the warrior asked a weary Saxon fumbling a knot on the rope looped round the wooden post by the jetty. Hereward had hoped the messenger Tostig had sent to warn the king would have returned by now to report that Edwin of Mercia had been imprisoned.

'It's cold,' the sailor grunted without raising his eyes.

'Is your blood as cold as the fish that swim in the river?' The voice at Hereward's back was laced with mockery. He turned to see Acha, her pale face peering from the depths of a hood, a wry smile playing on her lips. 'I cannot think of another reason why you would shun the fire on this icy day.'

'You follow me out into the winter gale to torment me now?'

'Torment? You are too sensitive. When I first saw you, I thought you a man who liked to play rough and tumble.'

At the clear tease in her voice, Hereward looked at her sharply, trying to guess what game she played. His instinct told him she was trying to keep him off-kilter. He felt sure she was used to making men run like dogs. 'Leave me be. I have no time for your diversions.'

He was surprised when she did not take offence, and instead slipped her arm through his. She leaned in close to breathe in his ear. 'Come. There is someone you should meet. And later, more comfort than you will ever find on these frozen banks.'

The promise hung in the icy air for a moment, then Hereward allowed himself to be led back into the filthy streets of Eoferwic. Under the pall of woodsmoke, the people were eagerly anticipating the coming feast and relief from daily toil, if only for a while. Faces were flushed and eyes gleamed. Freshly cut holly twisted round doorways, and sweating men dragged Yule logs across the frozen mud to their hearths. Under twirls of milky-berried mistletoe, men stole kisses from young women as they had done since the days of their most distant ancestors. Over the rooftops rang the squeals of the pigs and the honking of the geese facing slaughter.

'You are allowed greater freedom than many slaves,' Hereward said as Acha picked a narrow path into one of the oldest, dirtiest parts of the town.

'My reward for serving my mistress well.'

'I have watched you. You are filled with fire, and your tongue is as sharp as a knife, but you bite it whenever the earl or his wife is around.'

'We all do what we do to survive.' She skirted a spoil-heap where two hollow-stomached dogs fought over a cow bone, snapping and snarling.

'But you are not at ease with your lot.'

'You see that, do you?' Her eyes flashed.

Hereward saw more than she realized. Her flinty exterior hid a deep, unfocused yearning, much like the one he felt himself. He had never known peace, and Acha, too, was filled with unease, he was sure. The warrior knew that she thought escaping back to her homeland of mountains and forests would still the incessant drone in her head, but he guessed that the source of her troubles lay deeper than that. Perhaps it was the curse of all men and women that no one could see the road that would take them safely through the wilderness.

'Your king, Gruffyd ap Llywelyn, is raiding England once again. You know King Edward will not allow that to continue. Your people will face a bloody response.'

'Do not treat me like a girl,' she snapped. 'I know many things, and more than you. I know Edward is to discuss the English response at his Christmas court at Gloucester, the court Earl Tostig cannot attend because of the troubles here in Eoferwic. But he will be asked to invade Gwynedd and Powis to drive Gruffyd ap Llywelyn back, there is no doubt of that.'

'You keep your eyes and ears open in your mistress's presence, I see. Do you hope that your knowledge of your homeland might be of use to Earl Tostig should such an invasion arise? Perhaps that he might take you back to the Cymri? And then what? An escape? The information you have gathered on the earl would be of great value to your king.'

'Never. I am loyal to my mistress,' she replied, the lie apparent.

'You scheme and plot and twist men and women to your advantage more skilfully than anyone I know. I should watch you,' he said as they came to a halt outside a small, filthy hovel.

She gave him an enigmatic smile. 'Then if you are aware of my games, you are protected from them.'

Ducking down, she eased through the doorway. Hereward followed and found himself in a smoky space lit by the glow from the embers in the hearth. Unfamiliar plants smouldered in the fire, filling the air with an odd scent that was at first sickly-sweet but carried bitter undertones. The skulls of birds and small woodland animals hung from the roof in strings that rattled as the warrior pushed his way through them. He felt reminded of the house where the *wicce* had given them shelter after the escape from Gedley. By the fire sat a grey-haired woman with rheumy eyes, beating out a steady rhythm with a hollow wooden pipe. Her forearms were covered with faded blue-black etchings, and her cheeks too.

'Britheva, I have brought the one I told you about,' Acha whispered, crouching next to the elderly woman.

'He is welcome.' The woman's throaty voice held an accent that Hereward didn't recognize. He squatted on her other side.

'You are a wise woman,' he said. 'I thought the church had driven you out of all the towns.'

'The tide comes in, the tide goes out. The rocks remain.' Peering deep into her guest's face, Britheva held out a hand, snapping her fingers with irritation until Hereward offered his own. The woman grabbed his wrist and flipped it back and forth a few times, examining his skin. She nodded. 'Feeder of Ravens.'

The warrior flinched inwardly. The familiar vision of the black birds rising up from the lightning-split oak loomed large in his mind.

'What do you see?' Acha asked in a deferential whisper.

After a moment's silence in which there was only the wind whistling in the shadowy roof space and the crackle of the fire, Britheva closed her eyes and let her head fall back. 'These are the days we feared,' she croaked.

Acha bowed her head, her black hair falling across her face.

'From across the whale road they come, on wave-steeds, bringing doom to all,' the elderly woman continued. 'Amid the spear-din, the battle-sweat will stain the hillsides. A new breaker of rings will arise, but his rule will be brutal and bloody.'

'The End-Times,' Acha breathed, 'as the Bible foretold.'

'Starvation. Sickness. Many will die. This land will be blighted. And all the beauty we have made here, and the joy, and the songs, the wisdom of our ancestors, all the great things we have made and the great things we have done, will be washed away as if by the spring floods.' Britheva fixed an eye on Hereward through the swirl of blue smoke. 'Are you afraid, Feeder of Ravens?'

'There are prophecies and portents everywhere these days. If these dark times come, they come.'

'You are ready.' The elderly woman chuckled. 'You have been forged in fire. You know death as a friend, I see that, and not only on the battlefield.'

Hereward flinched inwardly once more; the wise woman struck too close. Unbidden, his mind flashed to his mother's dead face, her glassy eyes staring into his own, her features barely recognizable. And then to Tidhild, his love, lying in the pool of still-fresh blood, her pebble-eyes staring too, accusing. He had brought death to her hearth; he alone carried the responsibility for her ending. He had always feared he was cursed, and now it seemed this woman recognized it too.

He started to rise, but Britheva grabbed his wrist once more and held him back with surprising strength. 'Does the truth cause you pain?' she hissed. 'There is a reason for all things. The pattern unfolds around us, but we see only the smallest part of it.'

'And what do you see for him?' Acha asked.

Britheva peered into Hereward's face for a long moment. 'I see him surrounded by fire, a wall of flames.'

'No prophecy, that,' he replied with a shrug. 'It has already happened.'

'And it will happen again, and again, and again, for fire is your destiny, and blood too. The ravens will always follow you, their friend.'

'So be it. I have accepted who I am.'

The woman sniggered. 'You do not know who you are. Not yet. But you will learn. If you live.'

Hereward felt a spurt of anger at the woman's words. 'You cannot see inside me,' he snapped. Britheva only smiled.

'Is he the one you saw?' Acha pressed.

'It is possible. All things are possible. The gods play their games, but sometimes men resist.'

'And then they are punished?' the younger woman went on.

'And then they are punished.'

Acha stared at Hereward and in her face he saw something surprising: a desperate hope. 'Perhaps you will save us all,' she said quietly.

Chapter Sixteen

'Everyone is gripped by a fever,' Hereward said in irritation as he and Acha walked back to Earl Tostig's hall. 'If doom and destruction lie ahead, why fret? It will come soon enough.'

'Do you not fear Judgement Day?'

The warrior wrapped his cloak tighter around him against the stinging flakes. 'I fear nothing. My sword and my axe and my good right arm serve me well enough.'

The woman eyed him from the depths of her hood, but said nothing.

Twilight was giving way to black, and the snow swept down in sharp flurries. Outside the houses and workshops, men stamped their feet and blew on their hands as they prepared to end their last working day before Christmas. Conversation rang with good cheer, and the hails were loud and hopeful. Through the doorways, Hereward could see the comforting red glow of fires and smell the night's stew bubbling in the pot. Beyond Eoferwic, the night was deep and dark and still. No stars shone, and there was no moon.

As the great hall loomed ahead, Acha came to a halt and stepped in front of the warrior. 'You and I can find common purpose.'

'To betray Earl Tostig?'

'Though you refuse to acknowledge your destiny, it seems that great things lie ahead for you. I would join you on that journey. I am tired of this life here. I am weary of the struggle and the strife and the pawing hands of the men, and the sameness.' She leaned in closer so that it seemed she was about to kiss him. 'In Cymru, I dreamed of glory and wonder, not this sour existence. I want more.'

When the wind plucked her words away, a muffled silence lay across the hall's snow-swathed enclosure for just a moment before a deep-throated growl rolled out from the dark. The hairs on the back of Hereward's neck prickled erect.

'What beast was that?' Acha whispered, afraid. She pressed closer, looking round.

Hereward peered into the night. Nothing moved. 'All this talk of the End-Times has left you seeing the Devil in the shadows.' He flashed her a grin, making light of it.

Another growl rumbled out, and this time he could smell musk on the wind. Acha felt his muscles tense. 'What do you see?'

Hereward's hand dropped to his sword hilt. Wolves would not have ventured so far into Eoferwic, even if they were starving, he knew. Puzzled, he sniffed the air, and stilled his breathing so he could listen clearly.

A roar thundered out of the night. The ground vibrated from a heavy tread, gathering speed, and a moment later a shape as big as a cart burst into view. The unmistakable silhouette loomed against the snow.

Tostig's bear, the one shackled and penned in the corner of the enclosure. Free.

Acha shrieked. Hereward thrust the woman to one side, drawing his sword, but the beast was on him before he could pull the blade wholly from its scabbard. Another roar. His ears rang. A blast of meaty breath. A mouth torn wide, jaws strong enough to rip his head from his shoulders.

He flung himself back, too late. Talons tore through his cloak and into the flesh of his arm. The glancing side-swipe threw him from his feet in a shower of his own blood. Slamming into the frozen ground, he skidded on the thick snow. Through his daze he heard roars echoing all around him. Cries of alarm rose up, spreading out into Eoferwic.

Hereward scrambled to his feet and went for his sword, but the scabbard was empty. Flickering torches appeared in the dark of the nearby streets, accompanied by querulous voices growing louder as they approached. Feet pounded in the snow.

When the bear's bellows receded as it moved away in search of other prey, he shook his head to try to dispel the fog. But a moment later Acha's scream of terror rang out. Without a second thought, he lurched towards the sound. A rough hand caught his arm.

'Leave her. She is only a slave. That beast is more fierce even than you.' It was Kraki, his voice a low growl of warning. The other huscarls surged from the hall.

Hereward threw the Viking off and ran.

A crash of splintering wood. Terrified shouts. He sprinted towards a semicircle of dancing torches that swept back and forth as if a tide of fire washed against the enclosure. In their wavering light, he caught sight of Acha sprawled in the snow. The brown bear loomed over her, snarling jaws only a hand's breadth from the woman's petrified face.

Hereward hurled himself on to the bear's back, flinging his iron-muscled arms round its neck. The enraged beast thrashed from side to side in an attempt to throw off its burden, and then reared up. Enveloped in its musky reek, Hereward clung on to the greasy fur, knowing that one slight slip could see him torn asunder. Shocked faces flashed by as he was hurled around, his feet flying. Each mouth formed an accusation of madness.

'He has no weapon.'

'The fool tries to kill it with his bare hands. He has lost his wits.'

And he could not deny the charge.

Half slipping, his feet scrabbling for purchase, he glimpsed Acha stumbling away from the bear's claws. She cast one uncertain glance back at him before she plunged into the crowd. Relief sparked in him, a response that surprised him with its intensity, but he had no time to examine it. Inflamed, the beast threw itself across the rutted street like a ship caught in a storm at sea. Its flank shattered the shelter outside a metalworker's workshop, then punched through the wattle and daub of a house on the other side of the way.

Men and women in the growing crowd risked their lives for a sight of the spectacle and to marvel at this unarmed warrior who thought he could defeat a bear. In his excitement, a man stumbled too close. One swipe of a giant paw spilled his stomach into the snow. Before he had fallen, the creature's crushing jaws had splintered his skull.

By a pile of logs, the beast half staggered and Hereward was torn free. Lurching out of a drift, he sucked in a deep breath.

'Run, you fool!' someone called.

Sensing it had isolated its prey, the animal snapped round. The warrior took one step away, then came to a halt. How could he leave the cheering throng at the mercy of the fierce creature? An elderly man recognized the Mercian's dilemma and shrieked, 'Stand your ground!'

'Here!' The commanding voice crashed through the din.

Hereward glimpsed Kraki barging through the crowd just as the bear charged. Something glinted in the torchlight, turning quickly. The warrior caught the thrown axe, gripped it with both hands and braced himself.

Black eyes glittered. Blood and flesh spattered off bared teeth. The beast's bellow made Hereward's ears ring, and then the world around him fell into silence. He stood his ground until the bear's gaping mouth filled his entire vision.

Then, with all the strength he could muster, he drove the axe down. The impact jarred every bone in his body and the bear's skull split in two as if he were slicing meat off a roasting pig. A wave of blood crashed against his face, and a moment later the dead but still moving bulk slammed him off his feet. When he came round an instant later, he was fighting for breath, the full weight of the stinking carcass crushing the life from him.

After a moment, many men dragged the bear off him and he emerged to jubilation. Eager hands hauled him to his feet, and slapped his back and shoulders. Grinning faces flashed past with words of praise that he barely heard. Turning slowly, Hereward felt stunned by the adulation of the crowd. In his life of hatred, suspicion and contempt, he had never experienced anything like it.

'They will tell tales about this in Eoferwic in the time of their children's children's children.' Kraki reclaimed his dripping axe from the bear's skull. He looked the warrior's blood-drenched form up and down. 'Better get yourself washed. There will be women here eager to lie with the hero of the day, but not if he looks like a slaughterman.'

'Your name,' a man shouted. 'Who are you?'

'This is Hereward, the greatest warrior in all Northumbria, perhaps in all England,' the Viking announced. 'He has travelled to Eoferwic from the south to offer his sword in service to Earl Tostig. The earl has gracefully accepted.' Kraki gave a sly grin, satisfied that he had turned the act of heroism to the advantage of his master.

Unsettled by the attention he was receiving, Hereward retrieved his sword and broke away from the crowd, striding back to the hall with the huscarl. As his surging blood subsided, he felt suspicion rise. 'The bear could not have broken its bonds. It was set free. What madness would consume someone to release that monster?'

'The beast was half crazed from its imprisonment. No one would have ventured near it.'

'The hall was abuzz with preparations for tomorrow's festivities, and no one noticed a bear at loose?'

Kraki shrugged. 'Unless it had only just broken free.'

'The moment I entered the enclosure? During the fire, someone set light to the house I was searching.' Hereward came to a halt and confronted the Viking. 'Was it you?'

'Not I,' Kraki said, a flicker of indignation crossing his face at the suggestion. 'No honourable man would murder in such a way. I care little for you, but if I wanted to end your days I would do it face to face, with my blade against yours.' He snorted and walked on. 'Your trouble, you see enemies everywhere. But never friends.'

'I have no friends,' Hereward called after the huscarl, 'and I need none.'

Inside the hall, he found Acha waiting for him. She offered no thanks for saving her life, but they held each other's gaze for a long moment. Taking his arm, she led him away from the streams of servants decorating the hall for the feast. In the quiet of his home, she helped him to his bed and fetched a wooden bowl of fresh meltwater and a cloth to bathe the wounds on his arm where the bear's claws had torn his flesh. Hereward felt uncomfortable at her tenderness and pushed her away, taking the cloth himself. As he cleaned off the blood, he watched her face. Many would have considered her features cold, perhaps emotionless. But he knew better. The truth lay beneath, where the woman she'd dreamed of being still struggled to survive.

When he was done, her dark eyes met his once again. He saw the promise clearly. Holding his gaze, she leaned across him and brushed her lips against his. He felt the softness of her breasts and the warmth of her thighs pressing against him. Blood throbbed in his body, but it was not the consuming crimson passion of the battlefield; he had control over it, and he accepted it willingly. Unclasping her brooch, she let her dress fall away, and allowed him to explore her body with his hands. Pushing her on to her back, he eased into her, and they moved together, sweat slicking soft skin in the chill of the room.

When they had finished their lovemaking, they lay entwined in each other's limbs while their breathing subsided, listening to the throb of the hall and the soothing melody of the church bells marking the onset of the holiday.

Reflective, Acha twisted his blond hair around her finger. 'You have no woman of your own?' she asked.

Though her question was innocent, Hereward felt a tremor run through him.

'What is wrong?' she asked, concerned.

'I had a woman, once. Not long ago. She died.' He let his arm fall across his face, trying to drive the vision from his head.

'The sickness?'

'Murder.'

Tidhild, staring at him with glassy eyes, the pool of blood around her growing sticky. The guilt consumed him.

After a moment, she rested her head on his shoulder and whispered, 'Tell me.'

At first, Hereward thought he couldn't give voice to the stew of emotions that had bubbled inside him since he had fled London. But as she traced her fingers across his chest, he realized he wanted to unburden himself, and Acha was perhaps the only person he could tell.

He cast his mind back to the warm night when he had witnessed the murder in the shadow of the new abbey. He recounted the details free of emotion, but when he reached the point where he parted company with Redwald, his voice trembled and he had to pause to steady himself.

'Redwald told me to hide at Aedilred's house while he went to raise the alarm. I stayed there for a while, drinking ale, but a terrible melancholy came over me and I felt driven to visit Tidhild,' he continued, feeling the cold in the room for the first time. 'We had been together since the winter snows had melted, and . . . we had grown close.' He paused, recalling those days when it felt as though his life was finally turning towards peace. 'I had lain with women before, but Tidhild knew my heart.'

'Would you have married her?' Acha ventured.

'That question means nothing now.'

'I am sorry. I did not wish to stir up bitter memories.'

'I have hardened myself to it. I left Aedilred's and crept through the night like a thief. Tidhild's father was away and I knew she would be alone, but I felt something was wrong before I reached the door to her house. Some say we see the darkness ahead of us in our minds. That we all carry around with us the portents of the terrible things that will be.' He brought his arm round her back, finding comfort in the softness of her skin. 'I found Tidhild dead, her blood still warm. She had been stabbed with a knife many times.'

Acha leaned up on her elbow and searched his face. 'Did you slay her?'

'No!' Hereward exclaimed, his body snapping upright.

'I have seen the way you lose yourself to the bloodlust. You had been drinking ale—'

'I would never harm a woman.' The warrior lay back and closed his eyes. 'It was not the first time I had seen such a sight.'

Though he didn't want to revisit that time, another part of him demanded that he set free the memories. 'My mother. Murdered too.' He hesitated, a cold weight growing in his chest. 'By my father. He did not mean to do it, but his rage consumed him. He beat her with his fists until she was gone. When I looked at Tidhild, I saw my mother . . . I saw me, there, both times . . .'

'You were not responsible.'

'I was. It was clear the murderer went to Tidhild searching for me. Someone who wanted me silenced before I could reveal what I had learned that night. Tidhild was killed, perhaps as a warning to me, perhaps because she was there, and no reason beyond that. But her death lies upon me. I can never leave it behind.'

The sound of raven wings filled his head, and he thought he saw shadows flying across the wall of the room.

'I ran to my father. He is one of the king's thegns and had Edward's ear on Mercian matters for many years.'

'A thegn? After he murdered your mother?' Acha's furrowed brow revealed her incredulity.

'I was a child. Despite the horrors I witnessed, I kept my mother's murder a secret, out of duty to my kin. But there was little love between my father and me after that time. He despised me, because I reminded him of the crime he had committed. Because I reminded him of his weakness. And though I tried to earn his respect . . .' His words died in his throat. Shaking his head, he steadied himself. 'I went to my father and told him about Tidhild. I was afraid his life was at risk as well. But he was sure I had slain her, and was lying to save myself. He thought me like him.' Hereward hammered a fist on the bed. Acha folded her smaller hand over it. 'My father betrayed me. He ran to the king and raised the alarm. He accused me of murder.'

He fell silent for a moment and then said in a cold voice, 'And all who knew me at court thought me capable of Tidhild's murder, for they knew my rage, and my savagery. They knew my love of blood. No one would believe my account of the stranger's slaying. They would think it more lies to cover my tracks. And if I was arrested it would only be a matter of time before my life was taken by whoever ordered the killing of Edward Aetheling, the king's chosen heir. I had no choice but to run. And as I collected my sword, my axe and my shield, my brother, my loyal brother Redwald, told me that my own father had asked that I be declared outlaw.' He felt the cold in his heart spread throughout his body.

'Does Tostig know that you are outlaw?'

Hereward shook his head. 'Not yet. I hoped the earl would persuade the king of the plot before the truth came out. There is still hope. Word has been sent to London. If the throne can be made safe, then this hardship will have been worthwhile.'

'You are a puzzling man.' Acha leaned back and surveyed her lover. 'You fight without any sign of honour, yet you act only honourably in your sacrifices to protect the throne. You kill men as if they were nothing, yet risk your own life to save a woman. You show yourself to the world like the rocks along the coast, yet this night you have revealed only tenderness.'

Keen to lock the past behind him, Hereward rolled her on to her back and kissed her deeply. But shadows still moved across his mind. He thought of his mother, and Tidhild, and his father's blind fury, and he feared what the future held.

CHAPTER SEVENTEEN

'No one will hear your cries, monk. If death is what you want, it can be arranged quickly and silently.' With a black-toothed grin, Harald Redteeth shook his axe a finger's width from Alric's defiant face. The younger man slumped on the cold stone steps of the church tower where he had fallen.

'Archbishop Ealdred would never condone my murder within the minster,' he spat.

The Viking surveyed his prisoner's pale face and saw the fear behind the bravado. 'You think that old churchman cares one whit about you? His thoughts are on greater matters – power and glory, and who will soon be sitting on England's throne and whether that new king will have need of an even newer arch-bishop. Now walk, or die.'

Alric resisted for only a moment, and then dragged himself to his feet and continued up the tower steps. The monk still had some fire in him, Redteeth thought, but it would do him little good. He would have to endure the agony of one of the church's ordeals – water or iron – but the outcome was not in doubt. Death was the only sentence for his crime. Harald plucked at his freshly dyed red beard in brooding rumination. The Mercian was the one he really wanted. It was Hereward who had left the

Viking to a shameful death with a noose round his neck. And it would have come about if the men pursuing the English warrior had not followed the tracks through the woods from Gedley and chanced upon his hanging form. Unconsciously, his hand went to the pink welt where the rope had bitten into his neck. If it had been left to him, Hereward would already be dead, butchered and fed to the pigs. But his revenge would come soon enough, and all the more keen for being savoured.

As he hummed a lilting tune, the mercenary felt the last feathery fingers of the toadstools pluck at his thoughts. He glanced back at his second in command climbing the steps a few paces behind him. Ivar's skin was as grey as the stone of the tower walls, his blue beard bedraggled.

'Why do you haunt me still?' Harald asked.

'Valhalla is denied me, for I died trapped and screaming in fire, not in glorious battle,' the shade responded in a tone like cracking ice. 'I must walk the shores of the vast black sea for ever. No rest for me, Harald Redteeth, not until blood has been spilled.'

'And no rest for me until you have been set free,' the mercenary replied, understanding his responsibility. 'Not until blood has been spilled.'

Ahead, the monk flashed a puzzled glance back.

The two men emerged on to the flat roof of the tower in the bright of a Christmas sunrise. Eoferwic tumbled away from the minster into the white river plain, a black smudge misted with smoke from the homefires.

Alric shielded his eyes against the sun as he looked out over the landscape, his chest heaving in sadness at what he knew he would soon be losing for ever. 'Why have you brought me here?' he whispered.

'A kindness,' Harald Redteeth replied bluntly.

'A cruelty,' the monk snapped back. 'Dangling food before a starving man.'

The Viking shrugged. 'A cruelty. A kindness. Your choice.'

Alric held his head up defiantly. 'I will not betray Hereward.'

'He died long ago,' the mercenary replied, echoing the words he had first spoken beside the fires of Gedley. 'His spirit does not yet know that his life is over. He is a ghost who feasts and drinks and walks.' He glanced at Ivar, cold and grey against the tower's wall. 'The Mercian thinks himself safe behind the palisade of Tostig's enclosure. He is not.'

The monk flinched. 'The men who came into the church with you, they were not Northmen. They are the ones who have been hunting Hereward.'

Harald nodded slowly. The music in his head grew louder still. 'While I teetered on the block with a noose round my neck, we reached an agreement. The Mercian's enemies need him slain quietly, in a manner that will not draw attention to him or the secrets he holds. Though I am told he has escaped two such attempts on his life. Your friend is hard to kill, eh?'

'What agreement?' Alric flashed an unsettled glance.

Redteeth grinned. 'Those four men will capture the Mercian on the Feast of Fools when all order is turned on its head. And they will bring him to me.'

Harald felt a sly pleasure when he saw the monk blanch. On the shores of the great black sea, the Viking had been told that he would be feared, as Death himself, in these final days the Christians called the End-Times and his people knew as Ragnarok, the Doom of the Gods, when the world would be consumed in flames. And it would be good.

'You think this feast day belongs to your own God, Christian man,' Redteeth continued, prowling around the tower wall. 'But it is far older and darker than you know. This is a time for the dead, and for ghosts. It is a time of madness. It is the time of the Wild Hunt, when Odin rides eight-legged Sleipnir in pursuit of men.' The Viking pointed an accusing finger at Alric. 'Men who have turned their face against my people and the old ways.'

'It is a time for peace now,' the monk said. 'Your ways are gone.'

Harald Redteeth shook his head. 'My tradition is alive, in me. It has been passed down from father to son as long as man has walked this earth. In Yule, a sacrifice must be made. A blood sacrifice, which my people call *hlaut*.'

Gulls flying overhead called back to him, *Hlaut, hlaut!*

'Sometimes it is cattle, sometimes horses, and sometimes men. We smear ourselves with the blood and raise our mead-cups to great Odin, for victory and power to the king. Your friend, Hereward, shall be my sacrifice, and I will slake myself in his blood. In his final hours, he will know such agonies that he will plead with me to pluck out his heart. And then the final days will begin. Your friend does not know what he has unleashed.'

Chapter Eighteen

Christmas Day, 1062

The sword slashed down with one swift stroke. Hot blood gushed across the snow. Earl Tostig stepped back and grinned, resting the tip of his dripping blade on the frozen ground as the cheers rang out around him. In the centre of the circle of men and women, the goat squealed, jumping and slipping in the reddening slush. Hereward watched the beast's death throes from the ranks of the small crowd of guests invited to attend the annual ritual. The slaughter of the goat, they all hoped, would signal a prosperous new year to come, but Hereward struggled with darker thoughts. He looked from the dying animal to the wind-chapped faces gathered around, searching for any sign that would reveal his enemy: an unguarded look, a shared glance, a tremor on hard features like the first cracks on the ice covering the river's tributaries. He tried to find within him some of the warmth and hope he had felt when he first arrived in Eoferwic, but only a thin gruel remained. Deep in his bones, he could feel the threat mounting. Soon it would break, and then his sword would be drawn. It could not be sheathed again until it had tasted blood.

When the goat's eyes rolled back, its convulsions stilled, another cheer rose up. The jubilant sound wafted through the cold morning to mingle with the music of men and women travelling from house to house wassailing. Every full-throated song ended with the cheerful cry of *waes thu hael!*

Beyond the hall's enclosure, Eoferwic rested beneath a cloudless blue sky. Bright sunshine glared off the snow-swathed streets and houses. Not far away, the stark church tower soared from the jumbled rooftops, the bells now silent. The succulent aroma of roasting boar drifted from the hall, almost obscuring the pervasive scent of woodsmoke from the fires. Hereward's mouth watered. The feast would be good, and when his belly was full he would be ready for whatever was to come.

He caught Acha's eye. She was wrapped in a dark grey cloak so that with her gleaming hair and black eyes she looked like a raven in human form. The woman kept a sullen face – he had never seen her give an honest smile – but in her glance he saw a recognition of the night they had shared. Hereward felt warmed by the memory. The wound of his grief over Tidhild had not been erased, but to caress soft flesh, to feel the closeness of a kindred spirit, had soothed his turbulent thoughts. He yearned for that peace again.

The huscarls stamped their feet for warmth, and when Tostig and Judith led the way into the hall the fighting men followed, eager to fall upon the feast. Under festoons of holly and mistletoe, the guests raised cups of fruity Christmas ale and roared the oath to God and the earl. The serving women heaved in platter after platter laden with goose and beef, bread, salt-fish and smoked fish, blood pudding, cheese, honey and almond cakes and the centrepiece, a boar's head with an apple tucked into the mouth.

With the Yule log blazing in the hearth, the hall soon rang with song and jokes bellowed in increasingly drunken voices. When the food was consumed, the harp-playing began and then the Christmas masque was performed by talented players from the town. Amid the din, Hereward sat at the end of the table, drinking steadily while he observed the other men.

Fresh from doling out alms to the poor, Archbishop Ealdred entered, red-cheeked and misty-breathed, stamping the snow from his shoes. Tostig, who had seen the cleric only hours earlier at the morning service, greeted the man like a long-lost friend. The cleric joined the earl and his wife at the top table and was soon devouring a plate of boar meat washed down with ale.

Hereward watched the two men lean together, talking intimately and with great seriousness, and at one point they both glanced towards him. They looked away when they saw he had noticed their attention, but by then the warrior's suspicions had been raised.

The feast day drew on.

The drunken singing rolled out, more raucous with each passing hour, and men slumped across ale-puddled tables. When the guests were distracted by a Nativity performance by three men dressed as the Magi, Hereward caught Acha's eye once again and they slipped out unseen into the cold afternoon.

After a long kiss stolen round the corner of the hall, he asked her what she had overheard when she served ale to the top table.

'I heard no discussion about you,' she replied, her hands folded round his waist. 'Why would there be?'

'I saw how they looked at me.'

'You see plots everywhere.'

'The earl and Ealdred were discussing more than the Christmas ale. Their expressions were grave, their talk intense.'

Acha sighed. 'The archbishop told Tostig about a monk newly arrived in Eoferwic who worked at the church. He has been accused of murdering a woman.'

Hereward reeled. Surely it could only be Alric?

'What is wrong?' Acha asked, concerned by what she saw in his face.

'The monk killed the woman here?'

Acha flinched at the fire she saw in his eyes. 'No . . . before. Her family demanded blood and paid Viking mercenaries to hunt the monk down.'

In his mind's eye, the warrior saw Harald Redteeth and the bloody pile of his victims in the burning village. If this were true, every lost life rested on Alric's shoulders. Now he understood why the monk always looked so haunted, and whined about making amends at every turn.

It seemed he had been too trusting. He sensed his anger begin to rise at the monk's deception. Pretending to be a man of God, allowing the warrior to save his life, while in truth he really was no better than the bastards Hereward had slaughtered in Gedley.

Crying out, Acha wrenched away and he realized that in his anger he had been tightening his grip on her arm. Apologizing, he fought to control his simmering rage and asked, 'What now? He is to be brought before the hundred court? He will pay the weregild? Or will they throw him to those Viking dogs and be done with it?'

'The monk pleads his innocence. I overheard some talk of trial by ordeal. But for now, as he is a churchman, the archbishop aims to keep this matter secret while a decision is taken.'

'Innocence, you say?' Hereward brooded; perhaps the matter was not as clear-cut as it seemed. 'Where is he being kept?'

'They have him imprisoned at the minster, under the eye of the churchmen who pray for his soul.' Her brow furrowed. 'I met him at the minster. He is your friend?'

'I care less for him than the rats that run over the spoil heaps,' the warrior spat. 'Let him burn his hands to the bone with the glowing iron rod to try to prove his innocence. I will lose no sleep over him.'

Kraki lurched round the corner and paused when he saw them. Swaying, he tried to focus his eyes, then shrugged and pulled his member out of his tunic, spraying urine in a wide arc. 'You tamed her, then?' he grunted.

Hereward felt Acha grow tense in his arms. Her expression

became murderous. At that moment, the warrior thought she was capable of anything. Just as he was.

In the hall, the feasting and revelry continued long into the night. The archbishop left early with Tostig and his wife for the evening mass, accompanied by some of the guests, but not all, for though everyone there claimed to pray to the Christian God Hereward had heard some of the Vikings invoke their old deities. By the end of the festivities, the huscarls were slumped on the benches, the timber floor and the tables, soaked in ale and sweat. The servants nibbled on scraps of food, and only snoring and the crackling of the fire disturbed the quiet.

Hereward took Acha to her bed and they lay together, lost to their passion. But when he made his way to his own bed not long before dawn on the feast of St Stephen, he found his meagre possessions, his shield and his axe had been moved. The bed had been shifted to one side, as though it had been lifted to see if he hid beneath it. If he had been sleeping there, would he ever have woken, he wondered? Would he have been found in the morning in blood, like the man slain by the abbey in London?

His enemies were as close as he feared, and they had already made their first move against him.

CHAPTER NINETEEN

1 January 1063

The wolf howled to the rooftops. Red eyes shone in the sun-light as the man in the predator's mask prowled at the head of the crowd. Ducking down, he leapt up suddenly, howling once more, the delicately carved wood of the wolf head making the illusion complete. He whirled, sweeping one arm towards a boy of about twelve perched on the shoulders of a man in a boar mask. 'Here then is the Abbot of Unreason! Now let us turn this world on its head!' Someone tossed the boy a red cap and he slapped it proudly on his head. The crowd cheered loudly in response.

Shrieking with laughter, the throng surged through the streets of Eoferwic towards the church. More lovingly carved masks bobbed in the flow: horses, cows, ravens, salmon. Strips of colourfully dyed wool fluttered from wrists, waists and ankles. In the centre of the mass, swaying on the shoulders of his mount, the red-capped boy waved to his followers with the unspoken promise that chaos would rule.

Keeping his head down, Hereward allowed himself to be washed along by the rush of bodies. He ignored the horns of mead thrust in his direction by the drunken revellers. He wanted his wits clear.

The morning was crisp and bright, a perfect day for the Feast of Fools. The throng swept through the gate of the minster enclosure and milled among the halls, the barns and the school in front of the church's western door. For a moment, he watched the man in the wolf mask bound and frolic. 'Follow me now, good men and women,' the wolf called, 'into this stone house so that we may consecrate our boy pope. And when we are done, he will rule over an upside-down kingdom. The Lord of Misrule!'

Hereward pushed his way towards the edge of the crowd.

'Let the deacons, the priests, even the archbishop himself, keep well away from this festival,' the wolf-man continued loudly, 'or be prepared to pay the full price. A drenching in freezing meltwater. Let that wash their pious faces!' The crowd laughed. Hereward could sense the hope that one of the clerics would accidentally stumble out to get a soaking. The mockery served its purpose, he knew: release from the burdens of a straitened life, if only for a while. A moment when the lowest in the land could be the highest and dream the world their way before power was torn back from their fingers. The warrior saw true value in that disordered world. There were times when he felt every one of the highest in the land plotted only to their own ends. Where was concern for the weak, the innocent, the women? In this land of wolves, where was the strong protector? Perhaps the world *should* be turned on its head. And perhaps he should be its Lord of Misrule.

With raucous cries, the crowd thundered into the church. Few paid attention to the glory of the soaring stone tower as its builders had intended. When most were inside, the man in the boar's mask carried the boy in and approached the altar. Two men dressed in the white tunics of clerics followed, each wearing a mask with the nose and mouth shaped like human private parts, one male, one female. The mock-clerics intoned words in a made-up language that echoed the solemn Latin tones of the priests. The profane consecration of the Abbot of Unreason would have sickened the churchmen if they had not been in hiding, Hereward knew, but the throng laughed more loudly at each new mockery in the fake ritual.

Seizing his moment, he pulled up his hood and crunched through the deep snow from house to shack to hut in the jumble of ecclesiastical structures surrounding the stone church. Some were the dwellings of the churchmen, and he kept away from those, as he did Archbishop Ealdred's grand hall. But he searched the stores and the scriptorium and the school and all the other buildings where the churchmen organized their lives.

At the back of a room thick with a dusting of white flour where the daily bread was made, he found Alric slumped on dirty straw. Fettered, the monk looked miserable and exhausted, but his face lit up when he saw Hereward. His joy faded quickly.

'I should kill you where you lie,' the warrior spat. 'It would be a mercy, compared to what lies ahead for you.'

'You know, then.' The monk hung his head.

'That you live a lie? That you pretend to be a man of God, but are no more than a common killer of women? It is no surprise that you kept your filthy secret when I saved your life.'

Alric looked up with a fierce expression, his eyes bright with tears. 'Do not judge me. You do not know the truth. Nothing is ever as simple as it seems in the telling.'

Leaning against the wall, Hereward folded his arms, his face cold and accusatory. 'Enlighten me, then.'

Kneading his hands, Alric looked as if the strain of keeping his secret was finally about to tear him apart. 'I had taken the word of God to a village not far from where we met. They had no church, no priest, not even a stone cross where I could preach. It felt a godless place, and a lawless one too, with too many still worshipping the old ways, even now in this Christian land. It was a place where I could do good works. Or so I believed.' The young monk fell silent for a moment, and then wiped the snot from his nose with the back of his hand. 'I did my duty well. I was a good monk, hard-working, visiting every home, preaching whenever I could, teaching the children what I knew. The men and women accepted me, liked me even, I think. They kept me fed. There was one man, a merchant, who asked me to tutor his son and he would send payment to my monastery in return. And the merchant had a daughter.'

'You fell in love with her.'

'Yes. I am a fool. It should be me out there, made king of this feast.'

Hereward saw the remorse in the monk's face. 'And you murdered her because she gave you ungodly thoughts.'

'No!' Alric brushed the tears from his eyes. 'I . . . I followed the wishes of my father and mother. I had given myself to God. I was content with my path, dedicated. I wanted nothing else. But then the daughter and I talked about my mission, and God's plan, and she paid more heed to my teaching than her brother. And we laughed, and we walked together, and from nowhere feelings rose. Love, a pure love, of the kind I had never felt before for any human, only for my . . .' The word choked in his throat, and he almost spat it out. 'God.'

'What was her name?'

'Sunnild.' The monk swallowed. 'The force of that passion, it almost drove my wits from me. Something that powerful could only come from God.' He looked to the warrior for approval, and then hung his head again when he saw none. 'I fought against my feelings. Time and again I could have taken advantage of her. She made her own feelings for me clear. But I resisted, even though my heart was breaking. And then, one evening before the snows came, we walked in the woods and I became consumed by madness. I could hold my feelings in check no longer. And I kissed her.'

'That is all?'

'Yes, I swear. And, Hereward, though God strike me down, I felt as though I had been transported to heaven.'

'From one kiss?' the warrior asked with wry disbelief.

'But then her brother found us in the midst of our embrace.'

Alric's face darkened. 'He flew into a rage, accusing me of deceiving him and his father. He acted as though all I had done in that place had only been a ploy to steal Sunnild's honour. And he drew the knife he used for carving toys for the children, and attacked me to defend that honour.'

Hereward listened to the squeals of delight from the women and the drunken bellows echoing from the church. Time was short. Soon the ritual would be over and the people would rush back into Eoferwic to continue their celebrations.

'We fought,' the monk continued in a flat tone. The warrior guessed Alric had played the moment over so many times that all life and emotion had been sucked from it. 'There was no time to reason. I was struggling for my life. Sunnild was in tears, pleading with her brother to spare me. She claimed that she was to blame. Even then, when other women would have protected themselves, her love for me was clear. As the brother and I fell around the wood, she came between us to try to separate us. Somehow I had the knife in my hands. And I struck out, in panic, and the blade plunged into her heart.'

Alric held out his hands as if he could still see the blood upon them.

'She died instantly. In shock, I ran, with her brother's cries of vengeance ringing in my ears.'

'And her kin set those Viking pirates upon your trail. A blood-feud.'

'Believe me or not, Hereward, but in that moment I wanted to die too, so I could be with Sunnild, and for a while I considered taking my own life, to my shame.' The monk began to cry silently. After some moments, he steadied himself and added, 'But I would never reach heaven or Sunnild's side if I wasted what God had given me. I have to make amends in this world if I am ever to scrub the stain from my soul.'

'And you thought I was your path to salvation.' The warrior laughed bitterly.

'I must save a soul to balance the one I released from this world too soon.'

'You are a fool,' Hereward said, adding after a moment's thought, 'as are we all.' The warrior almost felt pity for the young monk, but a vision of the woman stabbed to death in the wood jarred too sharply with his own memory of Tidhild, and his mother. Three women dead, all stained in blood. And then he recalled with a flash of unease what the wise woman had told him in her smoky hut about hidden patterns.

The jubilant cries grew louder. The crowd was ebbing from the church.

His raw emotions receding, the monk started. 'Hereward, I *am* a fool. Forgive me. You are in great danger. I thought I would never have the chance to warn you and I had driven it from my mind—'

The warrior knelt and thrust his fist into the neck of the monk's habit, hauling him up. 'Then speak and stop your babbling. What danger?'

'I am rotting here because Harald Redteeth revealed my crime to the archbishop—'

'He lives?'

'The Viking was saved from your rope by four men who had been in pursuit of you. And so our destinies continue to be bound together.'

Hereward shook the monk roughly to quiet him, and then thought for a moment. 'And those four are here in Eoferwic?'

Alric nodded. 'Redteeth told me that for some reason, what I do not know, they would not confront you in public, only in stealth.'

'They fear drawing attention to me, or to themselves,' the warrior replied after a moment's reflection. 'You saw their faces?'

Alric described the four men. 'They are from the south. You will know them easily when they speak,' he added.

Hereward returned to the door and glanced back at the pitiful figure. 'Men are like wolves in the woods. Worse, for they have the capacity to deceive and betray as well as kill for base motives. But the life of a woman is a prized thing, and you have taken one. Whether accident or not, you must pay a price for that crime.'

The monk nodded, his face etched with grief. 'I know.'

And with that the warrior nodded in parting and slipped outside to join all the other fools.

Chapter Twenty

Merging with the throng, Hereward hid in the shadows of his hood until he was deep in the filthy streets of Eoferwic. He felt the blood already starting to beat in his head. His four pursuers were linked not only to the plot that had thrown his life off course, but also to Tidhild's murder. They hunted him. But now he would hunt them.

When he reached the earl's hall, he kept out of sight of the other huscarls until he could get Acha on her own. 'You may be in danger,' he warned her. 'Kraki saw us together, and now my enemies are close at hand they may attack you to reach me. I would not have another dead woman lying on my mind.'

'And do you expect me to hide like some frightened rabbit?' Acha bristled. 'I will cut off any hand laid upon me.'

The warrior felt a burst of affection for her. He would never forget Tidhild, but here was someone who could live in his heart. 'Then take care,' he said, 'for the peace of this Christmastime may soon be left broken upon the floor.'

As soon as he was certain no one was watching him, Hereward reclaimed his axe, his shield and his knife from his hut. Comforted by his weapons, he faded into the smoky streets, losing himself among the performers, the tumblers, the pie-sellers and the ale-addled crowds. When he was sure he was not being followed, he made his way to the house where Wulfhere and his family were in hiding.

The one-eyed, one-handed man emerged from behind a willow screen at the back. He greeted Hereward with respect, recalling how warmly the monk had spoken of the warrior. Hereward listened to the words without comment, and then asked the man for aid. For the outspoken protests that placed his life at risk, Wulfhere had found his own degree of respect among the over-taxed, hard-working people of Eoferwic, the warrior knew. He passed on Alric's descriptions of the four men who had pursued him and asked the one-handed man to spread word among everyone he knew. Whoever returns with knowledge of the men will be rewarded, he said, tapping one of his gold rings. When Wulfhere agreed, Hereward accepted the invitation to wait by the hearth, gnawing on a portion of the man's meagre supply of bread.

The day passed. Night fell, with the wind coming in cold and hard across the river flood-plain. Heavy clouds swept in from the north-east and soon the snow was falling fast once again. Large flakes covered the brown slush and a peaceful stillness descended on Eoferwic. Hereward stirred from his brooding at the sound of muttering outside the door. When Wulfhere returned to the glow of the fire, the warrior saw that the man's features were grave.

'You were right to be concerned.' Wulfhere squatted by the hearth, using the fingers of his good hand to balance himself. 'Your enemies have the protection of the earl. He has sheltered them in a house not far from his hall, where they have been hiding by day but emerge when dark falls. You fear some plot against your life?'

Hereward grunted. Rising to his feet, he took directions to the house and thanked Wulfhere for his help, stripping one of the golden rings from his arm to be given to his informant.

Beneath the howl of the icy gale, drunken singing rolled out from the doorways of the houses he passed. The Feast of Fools would continue until sleep came. Grim-faced in the depths of his hood, the warrior wondered why Tostig was sheltering his four enemies. There was no love lost between the Godwins and the Earl of Mercia and his kin. Perhaps Tostig was simply being cunning, he mused. Good hospitality after the long trek could lower the four men's guard. The earl could be hoping to draw out of them more information about the plot. Or he could be holding them as a bargaining tool once news of the conspiracy came into the open. Hereward felt unsure, but he could not risk his pursuers persuading the earl that he alone was the true enemy.

When he reached the earl's enclosure, the snow was swirling in a wall of white. He could barely see a sword-length ahead of him. Wild music and drunken singing boomed from the hall. The huscarls were in full throat, the ale flowing freely. Tostig knew how to buy his men's loyalty, Hereward thought. Head down, he forged into the gale through the calf-deep snow. The house Wulfhere had identified lay on the edge of the enclosure. It stood silent, a trail of grey smoke from the roof-hole whipped away in the wind.

He gripped his axe, enjoying the comforting weight in his hand. In response, his body flickered alight, every fibre burning, the blood thundering in his head. He was alive. He was the lightning and the oak. He was the feeder of ravens.

Hereward pushed into the house.

The howl of the snowstorm faded and for a moment there was only silence. The four men sat around the hearth staring at him, held fast by surprise. Hereward saw that his enemies were rough men, with faces like the cliffs of the Northumbrian coast and patchworks of scars that told long tales of lives lived in violence. Their hair was lank and greasy, their tunics stained with the road.

When they grasped who had burst into their midst, the four men lunged for their weapons. With a lupine grin, Hereward strode across the timber floor in four swift paces and swung his axe. The blade severed the top of the nearest opponent's head midway down his nose. As the skull-cap flew through the air, a gush of scarlet sizzled in the fire. A cloud of acrid smoke whooshed up. The second man half rose on one knee, his fingers closing round the hilt of his scabbarded sword. Hereward's axe came down again, lopping off his arm at the shoulder. The victim screamed and pitched forward, clutching at the stump.

The warrior felt as though he were floating across the face of the earth, untouchable, immaculate. He watched the blood drain from the faces of the two remaining men, noted the familiar shift of expressions like moonshadows on snow: shock, disbelief, dread. The world was silent, the air swathing him with the sumptuous muffling of goose-down. His grin broadened. Joy filled him. Euphoria. He floated across the timber boards and swung his axe a third time. To him, the weapon flowed like honey, but the third man moved even slower. The blade sliced through the chest and down towards the right hip, opening up his innards. And hard as the horrified man tried to hold them in, he could not.

And then there was only the fourth.

The ruddy-faced man threw away his sword and pressed his palms together in a prayer for mercy, as if that could turn back time. But in Hereward's mind, the man was already dead.

Yet the warrior dropped his axe, while still striding forward, and the relief in the fourth man's face was almost comical. A fist, driven hard, into bone and gristle. A resounding crack. And spatters of blood, a miserable amount.

Hereward caught one hand in his victim's tunic before the unconscious man hit the boards. Dragging him away from the spreading pool of gore and the dimly heard cries of the dying, the warrior stripped him and bound his wrists and ankles. Then he strung him up by the feet with a rope looped over a beam as he had done many a deer.

Hereward waited patiently, feeling the glow diminish and his wits return. The man came round soon enough, a reedy cry rising from his lips when he realized his predicament. The warrior pricked his knife beneath his victim's eye and whispered, 'Quiet.'

The man looked into his captor's face and fell silent.

'We will talk like men,' Hereward continued, 'and you will tell me all you know.'

'I cannot,' the man whimpered. 'I am sworn to silence, and God will damn me to hell if I break my vow.'

'You are a godly man. I admire that.' The warrior turned his knife so it glinted in the firelight. 'But we have different aims, you and I. We must see whose will is stronger.'

Hereward proceeded to cut the man's torso. The screams rang out, but the warrior knew they would be drowned by the storm and the revelry in the earl's hall. Their back and forth continued for a while, but Hereward whittled down his victim's resistance by degrees. Soon they were both so sticky with blood it was nigh-on impossible to tell them apart.

'Now.' Hereward leaned in close and whispered in the man's ear like a priest hearing the final confession. 'It is hell in this world or hell in the next. You may find peace, and a quick end, by answering me.'

The man muttered something unintelligible, his eyes rolling.

'What do you know of Edwin's plot against the king?' the warrior asked one final time.

'Edwin?' Blood bubbled over the dying man's lips. 'Not . . . not Edwin. I was sent by Harold Godwinson, who would have you dead and the memory of you defamed so that all who speak your name will curse you to hell.'

Hereward felt as if he had been speared through the stomach.

Harold Godwinson, the great protector, the brave warrior, admired by all Englishmen, who prayed he would take the throne once Edward was gone and lead them to an age of prosperity and peace.

Leader, protector . . . betrayer.

The warrior's blood burned. He had been betrayed once again, first by his father, now by the man who had the ear of Edward, the man who would be king. Betrayed and despised by all the powers above him. He was alone, as he always had been, and he would no longer bow down to any man. 'Then warn the Devil that I am on my way,' he growled, 'for you will be in hell afore me.'

CHAPTER TWENTY-ONE

Far from Eoferwic's streets, in the south-west, the night was just as cold, and just as bloody. The torches roared in the bitter wind. Song floated out from the king's hall where the Christmas court had gathered, yet beyond the palisade the dark over Gloucester was deeper and more threatening than it ever had been in London, Redwald thought.

Pressing his hand against his mouth in horror, he watched Harold Godwinson grab the Mercian's hair from behind and yank the head back. With one fluid move, the Earl of Wessex ripped the tip of his knife across the exposed neck. Drunken laughter from the hall drowned out the victim's bubbling cry. As the terrified man's hands went to stem the flood of blood, Harold rammed the head down to the ground and held the face against the frozen earth until the snow was stained crimson and the body had stopped convulsing.

'A lesson for you. This is how you survive, and grasp hold of power: by not being afraid to do the dirty tasks with your own hands,' the older man said with an unsettling calmness. In that one moment when Harold had held life in his hands, Redwald had seen his employer's face alter; the humour, the nobility, the wisdom, all of it fell away as if it were a mask. The young man felt chilled by what he saw rise up to replace it in the cold face and glittering black eyes. 'Do you see?' Harold's voice cracked with anger. '*Do you see?*'

Redwald nodded furiously.

'Good. Learn. Now help me.' Harold rolled the bloody body on to its back and wrapped it in its grey woollen cloak. For a moment, Redwald froze. The man's death might as well have been by his hand. At the Palace of Westminster, he had observed this Mercian, one of Edwin's men, following Harold as he rode out into London with his attendants. The young man had feared an attempt would be made upon his master's life and had informed the earl of his concerns. Nothing more of the matter had been mentioned on the long journey from London to the palace at Kingsholm. But earlier this night, while Edward was at prayer and the earls and thegns were in the middle of their feast, Harold had summoned Redwald out into the bitter night. Together the two of them had lured the Mercian away from the hall to this isolated place on the edge of the marsh beside the stream, and then Harold had struck.

When he saw his master glaring at him, the young man ducked down and grabbed the corpse's shoulders. Together they carried the remains to a small copse. Harold threw the Mercian down as if he were a sack of barley.

'What . . . what will you say when the body is found tomorrow?' Redwald ventured. 'Edwin will suspect—'

'Let Edwin suspect. He knows nothing and can make no accusations,' the earl snapped. 'But look . . .' He pointed to a mess of pawprints in the snow. 'In this cold weather, the wolves come out of the woods in search of food. They will smell the blood, and there will be no body here tomorrow, or none that is recognizable.'

When Redwald stared at the crumpled form in the snow, he flashed back to the sight of Tidhild sprawled amid the thickening pool of her blood. She had always been kind to him. He knew she felt sorry for him for losing his father and mother so young and she had stolen honey cakes for him when he had first arrived at the Palace of Westminster with Asketil and Hereward. So much misery, so much pain.

'That night,' Harold grunted, giving the body a kick, 'the night Hereward ran, you made a good choice. You could have gone to Asketil, or Edwin, or one of the thegns. But you came to me.'

Redwald's stomach churned. He saw the dead Mercian at his feet. He saw Tidhild.

'You recognized that only I had the strength to deal with the storm of weapons blowing up around England.' A whisper of a smile graced the earl's lips. 'And you knew only I could raise you up to the levels you dreamed of, out of the mud and into the world of gold.'

And even when I realized you were the true murderer of Edward Aetheling, I continued down this road, Redwald thought. *Because, God help me, I wanted what I saw within reach.*

Harold looked towards the hall, where the light from the torches around the enclosure formed a halo in the dark. 'Think no more of Hereward. You are a man now, not a boy, and men make hard decisions to grasp hold of the things in life that have value. Your brother could not be allowed to pass on what the dying man had told him. It would have left England in the hands of men who care little for the way we live our lives.'

'Hereward will be killed?' Redwald felt a constriction round his throat.

'In a manner that does not draw attention to the Godwins. We must be above all suspicion. I have received word from my brother in Northumbria, and these things are in motion.' The earl studied the young man's face for any sign of weakness or betrayal. 'You accept this is the way it must be?'

Redwald drove all thoughts of his childhood from his mind, of the kindness Hereward had shown him, the friendship and support. He felt the world whirl around him, cold and dark. And then he nodded.

'Good.' Harold rubbed his hands together for warmth. 'I have allowed you to see me take a life with my own hands. Few others have witnessed such a thing. We are bound by more than trust now, by something deep and unshakable. Should you betray this bond, know that I will kill you too. Your body will not be found. Your loved ones will never know your whereabouts. Do you understand?'

Once again, Redwald nodded, this time more quickly.

'I need a good man I can trust to do my bidding. My plans rush apace, and there is much business that must be conducted away from the harsh light if we are to win the prize. First, though, a blood-oath, to seal this thing.'

Leaning down, the earl dipped two fingers in the dead Mercian's blood and pointed them up to the stars and the moon. Redwald copied him, and when Harold spoke, the younger man repeated every word of the vow. 'My life is no longer my own. I swear to obey the word of my master, Harold Godwinson, Earl of Wessex, even though it go against my heart and mind. Even though it cost me my life.'

Once they had done, the earl gave a pleased nod. 'The throne will be mine. Stand with me and you will have everything you dreamed of.' Turning his back on the body without a second glance, he marched up the slope towards the lights of the hall.

After a moment, Redwald followed.

CHAPTER TWENTY-TWO

Clamping one hand over Acha's mouth, Hereward dragged her into the shadows inside her small house. She struggled with her unseen assailant, but the warrior's strong arms held her tight.

'Make no sound,' he whispered. 'No one must know I am here.'

Acha calmed when she realized who had hold of her. Whirling, she glared at him. 'You do not lay a hand upon me unbidden. Why are you here? Where have you been this evening? Your absence was noted. Even Tostig commented upon it.'

Hereward gave a bitter laugh. 'The earl noticed my absence? I am sure I am much on his mind these days.' He knelt to peer out of the door into the blizzard. The sounds of revelry drifting from Tostig's hall had subsided a little, but he saw no sign of movement in the snowbound enclosure. 'This night is far from done, and by the end of it I will no longer be able to call Eoferwic home.'

'You are leaving?'

Softening when he heard the hurt note in her voice, Hereward stood to face her. 'I must. And I would have you come with me.'

'I cannot . . . the earl . . .'

'I will face down any man Tostig sends to stand in my way. I care little about the consequences of my actions. If there is killing, so be it.'

'The earl will hunt you down—'

'I am already hunted, and friendless. There is no more he can do. I had hoped I might find an ally in Tostig, but now I know he is party to the plot I have uncovered and I have only survived until now because he cannot have me killed in a manner that will draw attention. So one of his men tries to burn me to death in the middle of a foray with his huscarls, and when that fails he sets a bear on me. An accident, and no further questions asked.'

Hereward watched the confusion in Acha's face strip away the brittle hardness that was usually etched in her features. Behind it, he saw the hidden woman he had identified on their first meeting, the one struggling to survive far from her home in a place where she was considered a worthless outsider. His heart was touched by this true Acha.

'You accuse the earl of trying to kill you? Why?' she stuttered.

'I learned this night that it is Tostig's brother, Harold Godwinson, who is plotting to seize the throne for himself once the king has died, if not before. Harold has always been an ambitious man, but until tonight I did not realize how much he valued power. He puts his own advancement, and that of his kin, ahead of all England.'

'Are you surprised that men of power seek power?'

'What makes men do the things they do? Truly? Some men seek power yet they have never gone to the depths that Harold plumbs.' Hereward looked past her to the dull glow of the fire, still trying to assimilate the revelations of the dying man. 'To order the killing of the king's heir, Edward Aetheling, the greatest obstacle in the way of his taking the throne, then to slaughter the man who committed that murder. To tear me from my own life, and the hopes I had, and make me scapegoat for his crimes, so that I am shamed and so are all my kin. To hunt me down like a beast. And . . .' he paused, trying to hold his incipient rage in check, 'to oversee the murder of Tidhild. A good woman who only thought the best of everyone she encountered. She was discarded as if she were a deer to be skinned. Betrayed.'

His final word resonated with such bitterness, Acha was silenced for a moment. 'You are sure he did all these things?' she eventually asked in a quiet voice.

'The man who told me was in no position to lie. Tostig is as tarnished as his brother. All the Godwins must be. Perhaps the foul corruption lies in the blood itself, and the entire family is born to deceive.'

'What will you do?' Acha asked. 'Surely you would not seek vengeance on the Godwins themselves.'

'I will no longer be run like a dog.' His voice burned with passion.

Acha gripped his arms. 'You are one man. Would you kill them all? Would you ride into London and fight your way into Edward's presence, when surely Harold will have all the king's swords raised in his defence?'

'If not I, then who?' He found his thoughts turning to Wulfhere and the other men and women of Eoferwic, suffering under the yoke of Tostig's taxes. The Godwins cared little for anyone but themselves, that was clear enough. The injustice of Harold's cold-hearted drive for power struck the warrior as acutely as his seething desire for vengeance. 'My plans must change,' he continued, trying to keep his voice steady. 'The Godwins and their allies – even Archbishop Ealdred who is so close to them – they are all my enemies now.' He paused, his mind flashing on a vision of Tostig impaled on Brainbiter. Could he get away with such an act?

'The Godwins are the most powerful family in the land. There will be no escape for you anywhere in England,' Acha ventured.

Hereward looked at her closely, trying to read the thoughts that chased each other like shadows across her face. He laid his hand upon his heart.

'We have known each other only a short time, but I feel we are of a kind,' he said. 'In here there is something that connects us. I have some business to attend to, but after I am done, before dawn, meet me at the wharf. I will protect you. And we will be together.'

'You will protect me?' she echoed, unable to meet his eyes.

'I know what you want.' He transferred his hand to her heart. 'I know your secret fears and hopes because they are my own.'

'And what is your business now?'

'I go to free the monk you told me of.'

'The murderer?'

He nodded. 'He deserves better justice than he will ever find in Eoferwic.'

A cry of alarm echoed through the storm. Hereward guessed the bloody evidence of his questioning had been uncovered. 'I must go before I am found here.' He stepped towards the door, then turned back. 'Meet me at the wharf before dawn,' he repeated, searching her face for a response.

Another cry, caught by a second throat, and a third. Hereward knew he couldn't afford to wait any longer. With one backward glance at Acha, he slipped out into the blizzard. Dark figures darted through the swirling snow, their calls disappearing into the howling wind. The warrior ran along the side of Acha's house to the enclosure fence, kicked his way through the gate and lurched across the knee-deep drifts. The flakes were falling so fast, he knew his tracks would soon be covered.

He put Acha out of his mind. Pulling his cloak around him, he forced his way through the bitter gale towards the church. Deep inside him, the drums beat out the word *betrayal* in a steady rhythm. His plans were shifting fast to match the new way he saw the world, a place of shadows where honour mattered little. He was beginning to think that the men who spoke of honour were the ones least likely to have it.

On the higher ground, the waves of white washed up high against the sturdy grey vessel of the church. The bell protested with faint musical notes against the wind's turbulent battering. Beneath the tower, the low houses of the clerics stood silent, their thatch now lost beneath folds of snow.

Hereward strode to the hut where Alric had been held, but he found the small, straw-covered room empty. Rats scurried away when he entered. He grew angry and that surprised him, a little. The monk meant nothing to him. But the order imposed by undeserving powers needed to be confronted, to be disrupted, and the monk, like all men, deserved a second chance. Prowling around the church enclosure, Hereward considered dragging the archbishop from his hall and prodding him with a sword until Alric's new location was revealed. Perhaps more than prodding him.

But as the warrior made his way to Ealdred's looming hall, he heard faint, discordant voices. Following the sound, he came to a sturdier house with a timber roof. He identified Alric's tones, and, he thought, the archbishop's. The two men appeared to be involved in an argument. Pressing his ear against the door, Hereward listened.

'Tell me what the Mercian knows.' It was the archbishop, his voice strained.

'If I knew anything, I would not tell you.' Alric's voice cracked.

'What others have heard his lies?'

'I do not believe he lies. He has always spoken with an honest tongue. Which is more than I can say for other men I have encountered in Eoferwic.'

'He is a murderer . . . a beast.'

'He is a man. Like all men.'

Ealdred snorted. 'The Mercian has shown himself to be corrupted by evil—'

'Like all men,' Alric interrupted in a loud voice, 'he has good and evil within him, and like all men he can be saved and brought to God. *Woe unto them that call Evil Good, and Good Evil*—'

'Do not quote scripture to me! You face punishment for your own crimes against God. First the court will hear your shame, and then you will endure your trial by ordeal. Your flesh will be seared. Your nose will be filled with the stink of your burning flesh, and your cries will rend your throat. Let us see then if you continue to protect this worthless sinner.'

'I care nothing for myself.' Alric's voice broke with emotion. 'You think to tempt me. You hint that I will face no trial, no ordeal, if I give up this man who needs me. I welcome the opportunity to proclaim my sins and beg forgiveness.'

'What vanity to think you alone can save a soul,' the archbishop sneered. 'Another sin against God.'

Hereward felt unaccountably moved by the monk's words. He had been as unyielding as the oak for as long as he could remember, but that night seemed to be one of transformation. Anger crystallizing from his stew of confusion, he tore open the door and stepped into the warm room.

The archbishop whirled, fear rising in his taut features as it had done in the faces of the four men who had died earlier that night. Lit by the golden light of the blazing fire in the hearth, Alric closed his eyes and gave a beatific smile. He was kneeling before Ealdred, his hands and feet bound. New bruises mottled his face. Two men stood guard over him, not churchmen. Hereward guessed they had been sent by the earl to extract the answers Tostig required.

'Stay back,' the archbishop hissed, 'or God will smite you down.'

'Your friend and ally, the earl, is already discovering God's will may not coincide with his. Now it is your time to learn this lesson.' He raised his axe.

'You dare attack a man of God? Truly, you are capable of any monstrous deed,' Ealdred gasped, backing to the far side of the house. He urged the guards forward with insistent hand movements.

With little enthusiasm, the two men grabbed the spears leaning against the mud-coloured wall and edged forward. The warrior faced his opponents, his eyes glinting.

'Spare them,' Alric said.

'They can spare themselves by throwing down their weapons.'

'Do not listen to him. Attack. The earl will reward you,' Ealdred cried.

The monk pleaded again.

'Quiet,' Hereward shouted back at the young cleric. 'Always you are like a fly buzzing in my ear.'

The guards attacked as one. The warrior spun between the spear thrusts and brought the axe down on one haft, shattering it. Continuing to spin, he swung his weapon towards the disarmed guard's head. At the last moment, he turned the blade so the flat struck the man's temple, knocking him cold.

'There,' Hereward snapped. 'I listened. Now, be silent.'

The other guard struggled to turn his spear to the warrior's new position. Hereward kicked the man's legs out from under him, and made to drive his axe into his chest as he sprawled.

'No,' Alric insisted. 'Let him live.'

Cursing loudly, Hereward wavered, and then kicked the guard in the head. 'I am already regretting my decision to come here this night.' He glared at the monk, then turned to the archbishop, still cowering against the far wall. Shaking his axe towards the cleric, he said, 'You play games with lives to see the advancement of the Godwins. I would be a fool to think you would ever reconsider your alliances, but know that judgement comes, sooner or later.' He grabbed the back of the monk's habit and dragged him towards the door. Slitting Alric's bonds, he hissed, 'My patience balances on a knife-edge, monk. It would be wise for you to keep your jaws clamped firmly shut from now on.'

Alric nodded, his smile unwavering.

Briefly emboldened, Ealdred called, 'Your days are numbered, Mercian. You will rue this night.'

Hereward flashed the archbishop a murderous look and then hauled the young monk out into the snow-blasted night.

CHAPTER TWENTY-THREE

Sickened, Tostig surveyed the blood seeping into the floor of the reeking house. His gaze roamed towards the bodies discarded and dismembered as if they were cordwood and then skittered away. Though he was battle-hardened, the earl had never witnessed a scene of such dispassionate slaughter. He glanced at the corpse still hanging by its feet from the beam and muttered, 'What kind of man is capable of such things?'

Kraki levered one of the bodies with the toe of his shoe and shrugged. 'A good man if he is at your shoulder. Less so if you stand axe to axe.'

Tostig kneaded his brow in thought. 'Find him. Do not let him leave Eoferwic.'

The Viking nodded. 'The slave might know his whereabouts. The Mercian has been trapped by her thighs and she is one who can steal a man's wits in the process.' Still drunk from the festivities, he lurched out into the night.

The earl hesitated a moment, eyeing the marks of torture on the hanging body and wondering how much Hereward had learned from the dying man. He had promised his brother he would hold the north in the name of the Godwins, and every day he felt he was failing a little more. And now his chance to prove to Harold that he was worthy of respect was on the cusp of being destroyed by a Mercian who was more beast than man. He could hear his brother's condemnation ringing in his head, as he had heard it ever since he was a child. Tostig the Worthless. Tostig who would amount to nothing.

Frustration turning to anger, the earl followed Kraki out into the bitter night. He found the Viking in the woman's house. Acha sprawled on the floor, teeth bared like a cornered wildcat, her cheek pink from the blow that had been struck.

Tostig stood over her. 'Where is your man?'

Feigning deference, Acha stood and bowed her head, but her eyes flashed with defiance. The Viking grasped for her, but the earl held him back with one hand. He stroked his chin for a moment as he studied her and then said, 'I understand you, woman. You are cunning and clever. I know you had standing among the Cymri and here you are as nothing. You secretly despise all around you and would seek to overturn the established order, if you could.'

Acha returned his gaze boldly, but said nothing.

'You saw in this man . . . strength? Protection? Hope that he could help you achieve your aims? But you must now know that he cannot protect you, or serve any purpose that you hold dear. With him, your only future is an outlaw life, hunted and despised, and eventual death. A woman like you . . .' Tostig shook his head, choosing his words, 'would find no value in anything a man like that could offer.'

The space following the earl's words was filled with the crackle of the fire and the howl of the wind outside. Acha let her gaze drift down to the floor and said in a bitter voice, 'He has gone to the church to free the monk who is held prisoner there.'

Tostig nodded. Turning to Kraki, he ordered, 'Bring the huscarls together. Find Hereward. Slaughter him as he slaughtered our guests. Leave no trace.'

The earl followed the Viking out, leaving Acha still seething, filled with murderous intent. Returning to the hall, he found

Judith waiting for him, her troubled expression at odds with her festive emerald dress.

'You will not harm him?' she asked.

'He is our enemy and he has committed terrible crimes.'

'Hereward is a lost soul. Better to pray for him.'

'It is too late for that.' He would have turned away, but Judith caught his face between her hands and pulled his gaze back to her eyes.

'You are a good man, husband. You will destroy yourself following your brother's path.'

'I am worth as much as Harold.'

'You are. More.'

He kissed her hand, enjoying the fleeting moment of tenderness. His face fell when he heard Kraki's barked orders outside the door. 'I must go,' he said, averting his eyes to hide his shame.

The Viking had lined up his men in the space beyond the hall's doors. Each huscarl held a torch that guttered and snapped in the gale, the light casting monstrous shadows across their fierce faces. In their other hands, the warriors gripped their axes or spears, hungry for blood.

Kraki glanced at Tostig, who nodded his assent. With a battle cry in the old tongue, the Viking turned and loped into the blizzard. The earl watched the flickering torches move away into the dark and hoped the dawn would come soon.

CHAPTER TWENTY-FOUR

'What is that?' Shielding his eyes against the biting flakes, Alric pointed across the thatched roofs of the town. In the distance, dancing flames gleamed off the deepening snow.

'Torches,' Hereward replied. 'They come for us. I had hoped we would have more time before my work was discovered. Still, this is our lot and we must deal with it.'

'You have horses ready? We could ride away from Eoferwic before they find us.' Shivering in his tunic, the monk wrapped his arms around himself. Despite the cold, he felt infused with a glow of mounting hope. All he had prayed for was coming to pass.

'And freeze to death before sun-up,' the warrior replied. 'Besides, we must wait for another.'

Alric's brow knitted. 'Another?' He studied Hereward for a moment, and when the warrior didn't meet his gaze, he nodded. 'A woman.'

Hereward silenced the monk with a glare. 'I told you. No more talk.' He watched the ebb and flow of the torches moving in their direction. 'They head for the church,' he muttered in a puzzled tone. 'How do they know I am here?'

Grabbing Alric by the tunic, he propelled the monk into

the narrow space between two houses. They waded through the knee-high snow, stumbled across the stinking spoil heap and over a low fence into a workshop yard. Skirting the well, they fought their way through a deep drift along the side of the workshop and emerged on to the next street.

Glancing down the white way, the warrior glimpsed the glow of two torches and cursed under his misting breath. 'Kraki, the bastard.'

'What is it?' the monk gasped.

'The Viking who leads the huscarls knows his work too well. He sends his men along every street leading to the church to stop us slipping by.'

'We could hide until they pass.'

'They will find our tracks soon enough in the torchlight, and they will lead them straight to us.' Hereward looked round until he saw a cowshed. 'In there,' he urged. 'Hide among the beasts until I come for you.'

Alric began to protest, but the warrior barked the order once more, with such a fierce gaze that the shivering monk ran to the shed and hid in the dung-scented dark. The cows stamped and shifted at the strange presence, their snorts so loud the young man was fearful the noise would draw unwanted attention. Creeping to the door, he peered out into the black and white night, and watched Hereward ease into a deep drift and pull the snow over him like a blanket. Alric wondered how the warrior could appear immune to the bitter cold; sometimes it seemed that nothing touched the man at all.

The two huscarls lurched up the street, heads down into the buffeting wind, torches guttering ahead of them. Their hoods remained low so that their faces were hidden, but their cloaks billowed behind them like bat-wings.

As the two men passed Hereward's hiding place, the warrior burst from the snow like a churchyard revenant. The howl of the gale drowned the cries of shock. Gripped by the speed and fury of the attack, the monk crossed himself. The warrior's sword flashed. Blood spurted across the drift from the first man's throat. When he stumbled to his knees trying to stem the flow, Hereward leapt past him at the second man, who was struggling to whip his axe out from his flapping cloak. The warrior lopped off his head with one bone-juddering strike.

Alric felt horrified by the brutality, and entranced. He saw a poetry to the killing, the gleam of the dark blood against the white flakes, the glimmer of the blade in the torchlight, the speed and elegance of the warrior's exquisitely balanced turns and thrusts. Hereward was moving away before his second victim had fallen, a fleeting shadow across the snow.

The monk knew he couldn't hide any longer. He told himself he was concerned for his companion's safety, but a part of him wanted to see more. Here were revelations of God's work that were usually denied him, and he wanted to make sense of them. Stumbling across the street, he skirted the still-twitching bodies and entered a narrow path between two houses in the footsteps of the warrior. When he left the street, he heard a cry behind him. A man had stepped out of his house to investigate the disturbance and was now turning back with an anxious expression.

Although Alric moved as quickly as he could through the blizzard, he found he had lost sight of the Mercian. He grew uneasy, aware that he had abandoned a safe haven for a labyrinth where an attack could come from any direction. His heart pounding, he crept to the edge of the next street and peered round the corner of a small house. Another huscarl stalked up the incline towards the church.

A figure leapt from the edge of a low roof. Alric had not even noticed the dark shape hunched there in the swirling snow. Silently, Hereward fell, driving his sword down like a spike. The monk glimpsed the warrior's face contorted in a bestial snarl, and then he ghosted away once again, leaving a body leaking steaming life.

Alric hurried in pursuit of his companion. The lethal dance bewitched him. Death occurred in the corner of his eye, a flash of a blade here, a lunge from the shadows there. Hereward was everywhere and nowhere, appearing from the blizzard and gone in a swirl of flakes. Bodies littered the streets. Yet the only sound was that of the wind roaring across Eoferwic from the flood-plain beyond the clustered houses.

Dazed by the brutality of one eviscerating kill, the monk staggered out into a street only to realize his mistake a moment later. A huscarl was emerging from the side of a pigsty nearby. Before Alric could retreat, the man bellowed a warning and raced to investigate. Waving his torch in the monk's face, he barked a query. Alric was tongue-tied. The bearded man glanced down at the monk's habit and his eyes gleamed with suspicion. He raised his spear towards the younger man's chest.

Movement flashed on the edge of Alric's vision. Hereward bounded from his hiding place, sword raised for a killing stroke. But the huscarl glimpsed the movement too, and he whirled, swinging his spear. The weapon clattered against the side of the warrior's head, pitching him into the snow. In an instant, the spear-tip pressed against Hereward's neck. The monk glimpsed a bead of blood rise up.

'I . . . I am sorry,' Alric called, realizing how pathetic he sounded.

The huscarl grinned at Hereward. 'No devil. No ghost. Just a man.' Tossing his torch to one side, he gripped the spear-haft with both hands and prepared to ram it down. With a cry, Alric darted forward, but the huscarl lashed out with the back of his hand, catching the monk full in the face. The younger man tumbled backwards, seeing stars. When his vision cleared, the huscarl was hunched over the spear once more, ready to make the killing blow.

Four men swept out of the blizzard and wrestled the Viking to the ground. Before he could cry out, the attackers rained blows down upon him. Two of the men were armed with cudgels. By the time Hereward scrambled to his feet to help, the huscarl had already been beaten senseless.

As Alric staggered upright, another man slipped from the lee of a house. He glanced round and the monk saw that it was Wulfhere. The rebel beckoned with his good hand. Within moments, the four men, Hereward and the monk slipped into a deserted textile workshop. In the dark, they crouched beside the loom amid the bitter smell of dyes.

'Thank you for your aid,' the warrior whispered, looking round at Wulfhere and his men. In Hereward's face, Alric saw an expression of bafflement, as if the warrior couldn't understand why anyone would have risked their own life to save him.

'You have opposed Tostig's cruel rule,' the one-eyed man replied, 'and the people of Eoferwic have taken strength from that. We could not stand by and see you killed.'

'We hope you will join us in an uprising against the earl,' one of the other men said.

Hereward shook his head. 'This is not my fight.' When he saw the disappointment around him, he added, 'And this is not the time for an uprising. You will be crushed.'

'The taxes bleed the life from us. Tostig steals our freedom and tries to bend us to his will. He is a man of the south. He does not understand how we do things in Northumbria.' Wulfhere waved his good hand with passion. 'We fight or we are broken anyway.'

'I understand. But this is war, no less for lacking axes and spears. Fight it as you would any battle, choosing the time and the territory. And ensuring your forces are strong and well ordered.' As Hereward spoke, a hint of a cold smile lit his face. Alric could see his companion was relishing giving the strategic advice that could damage his enemies.

'What do you suggest?' Wulfhere asked.

'You must get the thegns on your side. If they support the earl he will never be moved from his hall. They are the true source of his power across Northumbria. Speak to them. Tell them your concerns. If it takes a year . . . two . . . win them over. Then your victory will be assured. Tostig cannot oppose all of Northumbria with only his huscarls at his back.'

My thoughts exactly, the monk said to himself, pleased. *And that will weaken Harold Godwinson.* The warrior was clever; he didn't need a sword to wound.

Wulfhere and his men agreed that Hereward's suggestion was a good one. 'What now for you?' the one-eyed man asked. 'There are places where you can lie low, but—'

'Tostig will not rest until I am found,' the warrior interrupted. 'He will burn your houses and make trouble for your neighbours until you are forced to give us up. I would not wish that upon you. We must leave Eoferwic this night. Where we go . . .' he glanced at Alric, 'we have yet to decide.'

He thanked Wulfhere again and slipped out into the night. When the monk followed him to the door, Wulfhere handed him a cloak. 'Keep warm,' the one-armed man said. 'It is a bitter night, and you will freeze out there. Go well, Alric, and with all our thanks.' Touched, the monk clapped the man on the shoulder and hurried after the warrior.

By the time he caught up with Hereward, Alric realized the wind had dropped a little, and the snow was falling more slowly, in larger flakes. He felt a tranquillity that brought back sharp memories of childhood Christmases, but the recollection was fleeting. Barked orders filled the air. Feet pounded through the snow. In the direction of the church, a red glow lit the sky accompanied by a distant crackle and spit. Twists of golden sparks rose up to meet the snowflakes. Other ruddy glows appeared on every side, and Alric's nose wrinkled at the sting of smoke.

'Do they burn Eoferwic to the ground to find us?' he asked, filled with mounting trepidation.

'They have lit the bonfires the Northmen were preparing for their fire festival three days hence,' Hereward said, his mood darkening. 'With this snow all around, reflecting everything, they will light up the night, leaving fewer shadows for us to hide in.'

'They must hate you greatly to go to such lengths.'

'They fear me.'

The monk heard no boasting in his companion's words, only

a calm acceptance of the facts. Hereward crept along the narrow path between the houses until they heard raised voices and puzzling peals of laughter. Peering over the warrior's shoulder, Alric saw a knot of men further along the street towards the church. Tostig was there, with Kraki and two other huscarls. The earl's expression was severe as he conversed with an equally grave Ealdred. The archbishop was wrapped in a thick woollen robe, as grey as his face now appeared to be. But the laughter came from Harald Redteeth, who prowled around the group of men, occasionally throwing his head back and roaring his humour to the heavens. He looked, Alric thought, quite mad.

A man ran up to pass on some urgent information and disappeared just as quickly, and then another. The monk saw they were not huscarls. Tostig had bought more aid with his gold.

Hereward was watching the patterns the men made as they darted among the houses. 'They scour the streets in an ordered way,' he said. 'They will have covered the gates and the walls. There is little chance of escape.'

'What can we do?'

'Burn Eoferwic down. In the confusion, we may be able to find a way out.'

'We cannot kill good men and women,' Alric said, horrified. 'Our lives are not that important.'

Hereward bunched his fists in frustration and for a moment looked as if he might knock Alric to the ground. 'Very well,' he replied, calming. 'You have probably ensured our own deaths, but so be it.' Glancing back at the group of men, he murmured almost to himself, 'There are now too many to fight, and they are too well organized.'

'I have a plan,' Alric said.

A few minutes later, the two men were creeping down a street where several families kept their pigs in a single large sty. Alric went in and herded the animals out while Hereward waited to slap their flanks as they passed. The squealing pigs bolted into the street in a frenzy, and within moments their owners ran out of the surrounding houses, bellowing their anger. Nearly twenty men, women and children chased after the pigs to round them up, calling incessantly, while more people emerged from their houses to see what was going on.

But that was only the start, Alric thought.

While Tostig's men hurried towards the outcry, Hereward and Alric slipped among the houses towards the church. As they hoped, the enclosure was deserted.

'And so we risk everything,' Hereward muttered. 'I must have lost my wits to take battle advice from a monk.'

Alric ran into the church, his footsteps echoing along the nave until he reached the door to the tower. 'Help me,' he called back to the warrior. Together, they leapt on the bell-rope and pulled with all their strength. High overhead, the bell tolled.

Within moments, the sound of running feet drew near. Hereward slipped behind the door, drawing his sword. A young deacon burst into the tower.

'Quickly. You must help,' the monk cried. 'Eoferwic is under attack by raiders from the sea, just as in the times your father's father spoke of. Raise the alarm. Let all know of the peril we face.'

Ancient fears burned in the man's face. Without a word, he grabbed the bell-rope and began to pull. Racing back down the nave with Hereward beside him, Alric knew their time was short. The archbishop would send men to investigate, perhaps even some huscarls if he suspected Hereward was behind the alarm.

Outside, though, he saw that their plan was already taking effect. Men, women and children streamed from every house, some drunken, others bleary-eyed from sleep. The meaning of the alarm bells was encoded in the deepest parts of them. They swarmed into every street, every public place, yelling questions, searching for arms, demanding to know the direction of the attack. The blazing beacons only added to their fears.

Confusion filled every public space of Eoferwic. In the din and the madness, Hereward and Alric pulled up their hoods and merged into the swirl of bodies.

CHAPTER TWENTY-FIVE

The harsh wind blew along the wharfside. Ice edged the black ribbon of river reaching out into the rolling white plain as the two hooded men darted out of the shadows. Their feet only slowed when they could hear the lap of the water against the banks. Beyond the natural noises of the river, all was silent. The daily bustle of the port had stilled for the Twelve Days. The workshops of the shipwrights stood dark and quiet, the smell of new wood still hanging in the cold air. The smaller boats lay like beached fishes on the snowy banks. The larger vessels strained against their creaking ropes along the quay and jetty.

Hereward picked a path to a large mound of ballast rocks and found a hiding place behind it. Once they had settled out of the wind, the two men rubbed their hands, trying to bring some life back to their numb fingers.

'My plan worked well, then,' Alric said.

'No one likes a braggart, monk,' the warrior said. 'And there is still time for both our heads to end up on sticks.'

'The rule of law—'

'Forget the rule of law. That is for ceorls. Men like Tostig, and Harold Godwinson, make their own rules.'

'Still, we should offer up prayers of thanks for our survival.

Without God's mercy, we would never have made it this far.' Alric closed his eyes, recalling his darkest hours after Harald Redteeth had delivered him up to the archbishop. He had hoped and prayed for a chance to be redeemed, but he had never truly believed it would come. Silently, he cursed his own lack of faith, and made another promise to God.

The clanging bells died away, and the hubbub of voices began to ebb.

'Who is she?' the monk asked when he realized why Hereward kept peering round the ballast heap.

At first he thought the warrior was not going to answer, but then he replied with studied detachment, 'Her name is Acha. Taken from the Cymri and brought here to fetch water and keep the fires burning. She said she met you at the minster.'

Alric nodded. 'And you are in love?'

Hereward clipped the monk round the ear and went to sit on his own for a while.

Time passed. The snow stopped falling, and the black clouds began to drift away. In their absence, icy stars glittered in a majestic sweep across the heavens, and a full moon cast shimmers across the water.

In the town, the bonfires still burned and the questioning call and response of Tostig's search parties continued to echo. When footsteps trudged nearby, Hereward drew his sword and crept on to the heap of rocks. Alric crawled beside him. They saw the newcomer was only a sailor making his way to one of the larger ships. Another joined him, and then a stream of them meandered up. The seamen stumbled, sleepy-eyed and still half drunk from the tavern, chattering in tired voices. But as they prepared their vessel for sailing, they began to sing. Torches sparked into life to light their work, and to warm their hands.

'An early start to cross the whale road to their homeland,' Alric muttered.

'We have nothing to offer them to buy passage.'

'It is our only way out of Eoferwic.'

'What do you suggest? That I kill them all and steal their ship, and the two of us man it on the whale's way, with your prayers for help? A great plan.' Hereward slithered down the slope and sat brooding.

Alric continued to watch the sailors, turning over ideas but finding no solution. After a while, he noticed a dark figure, cloaked and hooded, gliding along the quayside. From the elegant steps, he could see it was a woman.

'Hereward,' he whispered.

The warrior scrambled back up the slope, his face lighting when he saw her. Climbing over the ballast heap, he crunched through the snow towards her. The woman stopped, hesitated for one moment, and then pulled back her hood.

Hereward came to a sharp halt, arms outstretched.

It was Judith.

The warrior backed away a step, as if Tostig's wife was the first sign of an attack. But then she smiled, a little sadly, Alric thought, and beckoned the warrior to step closer.

'She does not come, Hereward,' the woman said, her face lit by the sailors' torches.

The warrior's expression revealed nothing. 'Why?'

After a pause, Judith forced a smile. 'It is not the time for her. Perhaps in future days . . .'

Hereward's laughter couldn't hide his disappointment. 'Why are you here?' He looked past her along the dark quayside.

'My husband does not know I have come,' she said, answering his unspoken question. 'I am here alone.' Alric saw a hint of affection in her gleaming eyes that surprised him. She pulled her cloak tighter. She was shivering. 'What happens between man and wife is kept in their hearts only, but sometimes a woman can see things a man cannot. Whatever you might think, my husband is a good man, but he has his troubles and sometimes he strives for things that will harm him, or listens to men who give poor advice. I would never speak out against him, but I pray for him at the church every day.'

Alric watched Hereward hanging on her every word. The

monk saw an odd look to the warrior's face, almost childlike, or perhaps it was the shadows flickering in the torchlight.

'I have seen you grow into a man over the last few summers,' Judith continued. 'You were as wild as they say when you first came to court, but you have learned the ways of your elders. Do you hear my words?'

'I am not a good man,' the warrior replied, as if the woman had asked a different question.

'You are a wounded man. And like all who have been wounded in battle, sometimes your pain consumes you, and it turns to rage, and you lose the part of you that searches for peace. Yet still, I think, you are a good man, Hereward, and you would be a better one, if only hands of kindness reached out to you.'

Alric felt his heart swell. It was as if the woman had looked into his own mind, he thought.

'This is my kindness to you, in the hope that it will help you find that peace you need.' Judith glanced back at the sailors busying themselves on the ship. 'Those are my countrymen. They sail home tonight to be with their families after the storms kept them trapped here over Christmas. The whale road is still dangerous, but they risk all for love.' She let the word hang in the air and then continued, 'I spoke to Acha, and she told me where I could find you. She has not told my husband. She will not. She has her own wounds, you know that.' Hereward nodded. 'I have arranged free passage for you on the ship. What you do when you reach Flanders is your choice, but you deserve a second chance. If you heed me, you will give your life to God, and in that way you will find all that you search for.'

Hereward remained mute for long moments. Alric searched the man's face and saw him struggling to accept that anyone had done him such a kindness. In that moment, the monk was gripped with curiosity about what made this man so different, so confusing. There were many caverns inside him, all of them dark, he thought.

'Should I depart,' the Mercian said, 'in days to come I will sail back and kill Harold Godwinson for his crimes against me.'

'If you take that course, you will cede England to William the Bastard. Harold is the only man who can stand against him.'

The warrior remained silent.

'You think life harsh when the Godwins play?' Judith continued. 'See what it will be like if the duke seizes the prize he covets. Normandy has run red with blood for years. Rivals poisoned at court. Villages laid waste. Rebellious voices stilled with axe and sword.'

'It is the Viking blood that courses through the Normans,' Hereward said.

The countess nodded. 'And yet William has thrived. What kind of man does it take to rule such a violent place? A brutal man. A cold man. A man for whom no price is too high to pay for power. Now see him on the throne of England and imagine what our home will be like.' The monk watched a shadow cross his friend's face as Judith shook her clasped hands in pleading. 'Harold Godwinson can be as hard as the duke, and that is what England needs at this time. Not a sapling, but a broad oak that will not bend in any storm. Would you deprive your people of that stout resistance?'

The warrior bowed his head. 'No.'

'You are a strong man with a brave heart, Hereward. For once, the strongest thing you can do is walk away and never come back.'

He assented with a curt nod. Thanking his benefactor, he asked, 'Will you arrange passage for my friend, too?'

Alric felt surprised once again.

Judith smiled. 'It is already done,' she said. Then she leaned in to whisper something into the warrior's ear, and for the briefest of moments Hereward looked unaccountably sad. Then the woman pulled her hood back up and hurried away into the night.

'What did she say?' Alric asked when he had scrambled to his companion's side.

'She said all monks should be beaten whenever they speak.' He glanced towards the eastern sky where a thin sliver of silver was just appearing. 'The course of my life has changed this night,' he said in a reflective tone. 'Before, it meandered its way to the sea. Now it plunges into a deep, dark chasm, and where it will finally emerge I do not yet know.'

'All waters run to the sea eventually.'

Bowing his head, Hereward drew a deep breath. 'My old life ends here. Harold has won. I cannot help the king. I have been betrayed on every side, even by my own father, and now I am driven from my homeland, shamed, hunted, despised. What does the future hold?'

Alric rested a hand on the warrior's shoulder. 'Now we wait for God to reveal your purpose to you. The terrible things you have endured may be the Lord's way of shaping you for the road ahead. There is a pattern to all things, though we cannot see it.'

Together, the two men strode towards the singing sailors. The torchlight lit a path to the ship, but beyond it lay only dark waters.

CHAPTER TWENTY-SIX

4 January 1063

For two days, the ship battled heaving seas and freezing northern winds that left the sailors' beards and eyebrows white with frost. In the harsh conditions, Hereward found little time to brood on what he had left behind. Alric spent the hours huddled by the brazier that swung from a chain at the stern, or heaving over the side as the deck bucked beneath his feet. And then, on the second night, a storm swept in like a hungry wolf.

Iron waves whipped up into towering cliffs. Under pitch-black skies a lightning flash froze faces in expressions of terror as the ship's dragon-headed prow soared almost vertically on the convulsing ocean. 'O Lord, save my soul!' Alric cried in fear above the booming thunder. His sodden tunic clung to him as he gripped the mast with rigid fingers. A wave crashed down, wrenching at his arms, but he held on for dear life.

'Here!' Hereward bellowed, throwing a length of rope for the monk to wrap around his wrist. 'Hold tight.' The warrior felt numb to the bone from the freezing brine. If they were pitched into the water they would not last long, he knew. All around him the sea-hardened sailors prayed for dawn as they battled with the oars.

The ship careered along black valleys like a leaf caught in the wind. The sail had long since been torn free. The cloth flapped wildly, threatening to wrench the mast from its moorings or turn the vessel over and drag them all down to the depths. The untethered rigging lashed the air. Hereward ducked as a greased hemp rope flashed towards his head, but the seaman next to him reacted too slowly. The tip of the rope tore across his face, ripping out his left eye. Stunned, the sailor crashed to the flooded deck. Before Hereward could grab him, a wave plucked the man up and threw him overboard.

Catching the rigging on its next pass, Hereward wrapped the rope around his wrist for support and braced himself, legs apart. Bitterness welled up in him. To be caught up in such a calamitous storm so close to their destination seemed unjust.

Along the deck, the sailors shivered in their rancid-smelling greased furs and clung to whatever support they could find. In their drawn faces, Hereward could see their fear of the fate that awaited them. Soon they would succumb to the warm-sleep from which no man ever awoke, he knew.

Another freezing wave smashed into him with the force of fifty hammers, ripping his feet off the deck. His mouth and nose flooded with salt water and his head spun, but the rope around his wrist held tight.

The straining ship soared high on the swell, hung for a moment and then plummeted prow-down into the next trough. Hereward's stomach shot up into his throat. The monk retched. The vessel slammed into the water as if it had hit rocks. Men flew into the air and crashed back down on to the boards, fumbling for hand-holds. The warrior felt sure he could hear the hull screaming in protest. Beneath the deck, the ribs had been lashed into place with pitch-soaked cords to allow the hull to flex in strong water, but even that would barely cope with this ocean's brutal punishment. The treenails were holding for now, but Hereward knew the wooden rivets couldn't last long.

At the stern, one of the seamen struggled futilely with the steering oar. A crack sounded louder than the booming of the sea, and the oaken rudder snapped. The remnants drove up into the sailor's face, pitching him back and into the towering stern-post. Another, quieter crack echoed as his back broke.

'This wave-steed is dying beneath us,' Hereward shouted. The ravens flew so close now he could almost feel their wings on the back of his neck, yet he felt no fear. A part of him welcomed what lay ahead, although he would have preferred an honourable death, with his sword in his hand. He glanced at the monk, trying to find some final words of kindness that would ease the man's soul at the last. But the monk's face now gleamed brightly, his eyes wide with hope.

'A beacon,' Alric gasped. 'I saw a beacon. Our prayers have been answered.' He would have pointed if he could have torn his frozen hands from the mast.

Hereward peered ahead as the ship plunged into another trough, but saw only the impenetrable dark. 'It was a star,' he said. 'There is only water.'

'I saw it,' Alric protested. 'We are close to land. Thank the Lord.'

Hereward decided to let his companion find some comfort in his wishful thinking.

Bracing himself again, he clung on to the greasy rope as another cold wave crashed against him. The vessel moved like lead, spinning round and rolling low in the water. The warrior knew the waves had almost filled the below-deck.

It will not be long now.

The thought had barely flashed into his head when he realized he was staring into a wall of black water. The wave came down.

He was drifting. His mother was there, as beautiful as he remembered from his earliest days, her pale face unmarred by blue bruises, her lips and nose not split, not bloody. And Tidhild was there too, taking his hand and trying to whisper something to him. But the more insistent she became, the more he resisted.

'The oak is split in two,' his mother called. 'But it is not the end.'

Birds were shrieking. *Ravens*, he thought, his head awhirl with the reedy cries. *The ravens have come.*

Not ravens, he realized after a moment. Gulls. All around him, in his head and out, their cries rising and falling.

Cold pebbles, hard under his face.

The boom of the waves, the sucking sound of water retreating over stone.

His eyes opened to a thin silver light. Every fibre of his body burned and his head felt as if it were filled with iron. Heaving, he wrenched himself up on his arms and retched seawater. Scarcely able to believe he was alive, he glanced around at a pebbly beach littered with the remnants of the ship. Strakes washed on the surf and a pile of rigging lay nearby. Several bodies lay face down along the shore, suspicious gulls padding around them.

Though sodden, he did not feel cold. The sound of crackling and spitting and a heat at his back drew his gaze to a bonfire being fed by a tall, thin man with a pockmarked face. He cast a bored eye over Hereward and stooped to pick up more driftwood. Eight survivors of the wreck sprawled around the fire, which was keeping them from dying from the warm-sleep. Some were still unconscious, he could tell. Others sat staring into the flames in shock. Lurching to his feet, Hereward was relieved to see Alric on the other side of the fire. The monk was still lying face down, but twitching like a dreaming dog.

'You saved us?' Hereward asked the pockmarked man.

'He speaks no English,' one of the seamen muttered. 'He is Flemish.' The sailor waved a hand in the direction of three other men wading into the surf to search for anything worth salvaging from the wreck.

Peering down the beach, the warrior could make out a broad river estuary gleaming in the early morning light. The landscape at his back was flat and scrubby, skeletal black trees bowing away from the harsh sea wind.

'It seems a long way from England.'

Alric now loomed at the warrior's shoulder, looking over the Flemish countryside. Hereward saw that his companion was shaking, more from the aftermath of their experience than from the cold.

'England waits for us. We will return one day,' the warrior muttered.

The monk slumped back on to the pebbles, squeezing the seawater from his hair. 'I am starting to believe that you bear a charmed life. However often you lead me into brushes with death, you always pluck me back from the brink.'

'If memory serves me, you did a good enough job yourself of welcoming death into your life.' Standing, Hereward shielded his eyes to watch three men on horseback riding across the pebbles towards them. His hand slipped to Brainbiter, still in its scabbard despite the sea plunge.

Alric pressed his fingers against his companion's wrist. 'We have been reborn into a new life. This is your opportunity to leave behind the man you were and become the man you would be.'

'We are who we are,' Hereward said, but he let his hand fall to his side none the less.

Reining in their horses, the three men eyed the shipwreck survivors, trying to discern who was the spokesman for the group. In an insistent, querying tone, they made their demands in the rolling Flemish tongue, which reminded Hereward of the waves breaking upon the beach. The seaman who had first spoken to the warrior translated the men's orders, in accordance with which the survivors lumbered wearily to their feet and traipsed behind the horsemen into the cold morning.

They trudged along rutted tracks, thankful to be free of the snow that gripped England. After an hour, church spires appeared on the silver-grey horizon and soon the ramparts of the town of Guines loomed up. They passed an abbey, the quiet broken only by the rhythmic rattle of a waterwheel, and skirted a leper-house, the morning's bread left outside the door still uncollected. Within the walls, three church towers rose above the thatched and timber roofs, but Hereward found Guines sleepy after the bustle of Eoferwic. Dogs yapped in the street, and men emerged from their workshops to eye the cause of the disturbance, returning to their tasks a moment later with a sniff and a shrug.

Though Alric had promised a new dawn, the warrior found he could not forget England or his hatred of Harold Godwinson. Without vengeance, how could he ever free himself from his shame, his grief and his loneliness?

The riders dismounted and led the seamen into the hall of the local ruler, where they warmed themselves by the hearth, waiting to be seen. Not long after, a snowy-haired man, bent by his years, shuffled in with his retinue. His face was hollow-cheeked and crumpled by wrinkles. With a groan, he lowered himself into a carved oaken seat on a low dais at the far end of the hall while his attendants gathered on either side. His barely audible words creaked like leather, but the seaman translated for his companions.

'He is Count Manasses, who rules this county and has rights over all shipwrecks on this coast. He would know our names and our purpose here.'

One by one the seamen stepped forward to announce their identity, but when Hereward advanced the count leaned forward and eyed the warrior curiously. The older man noted the blue-black markings of the warrior inscribed on Hereward's arms, and the gold rings, and his stature and his sword.

'My name is Hereward Asketilson. I am exiled from my homeland, a fighter, trained in spear, sword and axe, a huntsman, a rider. I seek to earn my way in Flanders.' His voice echoed clearly across the hall.

Manasses studied Hereward for a moment, and then spoke. 'The English have been coming to Flanders since the days of his youth,' the sailor translated. 'High-born men and women as well as merchants. But there is always a need for warriors with strong right arms. The counts of this country fight over any slight, real or imagined, and all dispute their territorial boundaries. You will earn your way here as a sword for hire, he says, but only if you are good enough. If you are not, you will be dead within the week.' Manasses' laugh rustled across the hall.

'There is no man in this country I fear,' Hereward replied.

The count gave a slow nod and beckoned with one finger to a figure standing at the back of his attendants. A man strode forward who appeared as big as the bear Hereward had killed in Eoferwic. The Mercian took in the wild red hair and the untamed beard that fell almost to the man's navel, both streaked with grey, and the heavily scarred arms that looked as if they had been carved from oak. A leather patch covered the giant's left eye. Despite his fearsome appearance, however, his mouth was split in a warm grin and his chest shook with silent laughter.

'Little man,' he boomed, 'my name is Vadir. I am a man of Mercia and I welcome a brother from my home to these unfamiliar fields. Count Manasses would see your claim put to trial. Let us test your bravery and strength before all in this hall, and if your reputation survives there will be no shortage of gold to hire your sword.'

'You may be tall and broad, but even oaks will fall with enough cuts of the axe.' Hereward knew he was weakened by the shipwreck and the long march, but he put on a cold face and started to draw his sword.

'No weapons, little man. There is no need to spill blood here, for we are all friends. It is play, no more, for the benefit of our hosts.' The bear-like man clapped a hand on the warrior's shoulder.

'Play, you say? Though the loser will be humbled before the eyes of all here? This is serious business.'

Vadir laughed. 'You are a true warrior. Come, let us see if we can complete this trial without too much harm to you.'

When the red-haired man led Hereward towards the hearth an excited whisper rustled through the attendants, but two young men jeered and pointed, laughing together.

The warrior glanced at them, then directed a questioning look at Vadir.

'They say the English are weak,' the big man translated. 'Weaker than the Vikings. Weaker than the Normans.'

Hereward simmered. 'Then they have not seen a true Englishman in battle.'

'Let us teach them, as we would children.' Vadir stripped off his tunic and motioned for his opponent to do the same. Naked to the waist, his torso was a patchwork of pink scars.

'You are old,' Hereward said. 'I will restrain myself.'

The other man boomed with laughter. 'Ah yes, poor me. My body fails me.'

One of the attendants tossed him a length of greased rope. Vadir tied one end tightly round his right wrist and offered the other end to Hereward, who did the same. When the two warriors faced each other across the hearth, the big man waved their bond in the flames with a shake of his arm. 'A simple game. Your aim is to survive until the rope burns through. Should your strength falter, you will be dragged through the embers and face a burning.'

Two attendants stoked the fire until the flames roared up higher than a man.

Hereward tested the rope. 'One of us will be roasted like a hog, but it will not be me,' he said with a nod to signal he was ready.

Vadir's broad grin gleamed through the twirling grey smoke.

Both men took the strain on the rope. For a moment they sized each other up, and when the circle of attendants began to shout encouragement to their favoured competitor, the contest started. Vadir yanked on the rope, almost propelling Hereward into the flames. The warrior braced himself, reassessing his opponent's strength. In a fair fight, he could see he would be no match for his fellow Mercian. He had to make it a contest more of guile and skill than of muscle.

Playing to the crowd, Vadir roared with laughter. He flexed his right arm again and drew Hereward towards the fire. Beads of sweat trickled down the warrior's brow. The jeers of the crowd rang in his buzzing ears; they sensed a quick defeat. His leather shoes slid on the boards, and his arm shook from the strain of resisting.

Vadir laughed louder, punching the air with his free hand.

Then, with one sharp yank from his opponent, Hereward's exhausted legs gave way. His face plunged towards the embers, and he flashed back to Thangbrand sizzling in the hearth in Eoferwic. God was surely punishing him for his sins. Ramming his hands against the rocks circling the fire, he stopped his momentum, but the heat seared his skin.

Vadir chuckled, allowing his younger opponent to scramble back to his feet. This time Hereward changed tactics. He leapt to his right and wrenched on the rope. Vadir stumbled towards the fire, off balance. Shock flashed across his face. Reasserting himself, he narrowed his eyes and nodded, but his grin remained.

For long moments, the two men feinted and fought, Hereward dancing with a light foot that the heavier man would never be able to match. Vadir, in turn, planted his feet firmly and strained his back and arms to haul the warrior over the embers whenever he appeared wrong-footed.

The greased rope sizzled and blackened.

Unimpressed by both combatants, the two young attendants jeered more loudly. Though he couldn't understand their words, Hereward felt stung by the obvious mockery. He saw Vadir had the same feelings. His grin fading for the first time, the big man flicked his eyes towards the two Flemings, who laughed again at their private joke and slapped each other's backs.

When Hereward felt the strain on the rope loosen, he realized Vadir had reached the limit of his tolerance. Glowering at the two men, the giant cursed in Flemish and then raised his eyebrows at the warrior. Hereward responded to the silent communication with a nod.

Vadir roared. Leaning back, he bunched his arm muscles and hauled with all his strength. Hereward leapt through the fire.

At the last moment, he swung his legs round and thundered into the two attendants. The Flemings spun away across the hall, their wits smashed out of them.

Laughing, Vadir grasped Hereward's hand and hauled him up from the floor. Though the contest had not ended as planned, from his chair Manasses clapped and croaked his approval.

'It seems we achieve more fighting side by side,' Vadir laughed, laying a heavy hand on Hereward's shoulder. 'You need gold. I need gold. And I know just the way to get it.'

Chapter Twenty-Seven

27 September 1064

Beyond the ramparts, the stark church towers of Bruges pierced the blue sky. A steady stream of the curious made their way out from behind the walls. It was the biggest fair of the year, Vadir had told Hereward, and their last chance to find employment during the wolf-season. On a trestle, a man from one of the drinking houses sold cups of ale to men who lay back drunk in the sun. Two boys turned a sizzling hog on a spit over a fire. Poets recited their latest compositions to small groups waiting for the real entertainment to begin, wandering harpists sang of past glories and jugglers spun balls of wood high into the air. To one side, a churchman in his white tunic preached against the ungodly ways of the tournament, but few listened. There would be time enough for that in church the following morning.

Sweat slicked Hereward's brow and trickled down his back beneath the chain mail as he surveyed the growing crowd. Summer still lingered, although the apples had ripened in the orchards and the berries had all been picked. It had been a good year and a half in Flanders. The voices in his head had faded, and the rage that had simmered in his heart often seemed a distant memory. He had Vadir and Alric to thank for that. As they travelled the flat, green countryside selling their services to anyone who would have them, his two companions had attempted to teach him the honourable code of the knight. With his unquenchable good humour, Vadir had begun by instructing him in the etiquette of combat. Most of it had made little sense to Hereward, and the red-haired Mercian had often been forced to lay his charge on his back with a punch or a turn of his spear. But gradually Hereward had listened and learned, as he would have done at the feet of his father, if Asketil had ever paid any attention to him during his early years. Over time, the terrifying force that lurked inside him was shackled and imprisoned so deeply that Hereward hoped it would never possess him again. And after the day's tuition was over, Alric had eagerly offered his own instruction, in the biblical lessons and the teachings of St Augustine and the ways of living a life in service to God. Most days the words washed over him, but Hereward was surprised to find their friendship deepening.

Under Vadir's guidance, he had kept his fiercest instincts in check during their employ by various counts involved in minor territorial disputes. No wild slaughter, no murder, all kills made honourably in the manner of a knight. And so his reputation had grown, to the point where at their last stay in Picquigny he had been employed to train the younger fighters. Once again, he had felt some of the respect that had touched him in Eoferwic, a puzzling sensation. He still felt haunted by the shadows gathering in England. He still found himself concerned for Alric, who battled his own demons. But for the first time in his short life he thought there might be a chance for inner peace.

As he waited for the battle-fair to begin, a knight strode up with his retainers close behind him. Hereward could tell from the noble's red and blue banner that he was a Fleming, slender, with piercing eyes and an aquiline nose, a head shorter than Hereward but five years or more older. The warrior sensed trouble. Competition in the battle-fair was fierce, with women, work and gold all at stake. Vadir had warned him that some of his rivals would attempt to unsettle him.

The knight jabbed his sword directly at Hereward's heart. 'You are just a common fighting man,' he sneered. 'Not a knight at all. You do not deserve my respect.'

'I do not need to be a knight to kick your arse across this field of combat,' Hereward replied, rattling his sword in its scabbard. 'Here, this makes us equal.'

The Fleming laughed in a studiedly contemptuous manner. With a swing of his arm, he clattered his blade against the side of Hereward's head.

The warrior lunged, grabbing the startled knight round the neck with one hand. 'I was mistaken,' he mocked. 'We are not equals after all.' The Fleming's eyes bulged as Hereward increased his grip.

Four of the knight's retainers succeeded in dragging their choking master free. Vadir stifled laughter behind his hand.

Spluttering, the knight hid his dismay. 'English dog,' he snapped, darting forward to slap Hereward across the face with the back of his hand. He leapt back behind his retainers before the warrior could respond. 'We shall see who has the upper hand at the end of this day.'

When he had gone, Alric sighed with relief. 'In the days when we met you would have snapped his neck or skinned him alive. We should be thankful you only assaulted his pride.'

Hereward grinned. 'I am a new man, monk. Though losing an ear would have taught him to curb his tongue.'

Vadir shook his head in weary disbelief. 'He says you are a common fighting man so you attempt to strangle him like a drunken ceorl,' he sighed. 'Honour!' The red-haired man whacked Hereward on the chest with the back of his hand to emphasize his point. 'Honour. Learn that and we will make a man of you, perhaps even a knight.'

'I wake in the night with the word buzzing in my ears. How could I not learn it?' He watched the disappearing knight. 'And who is that weak-armed son of a whore?'

'That is no way to talk about Hoibrict, the grandson of our old friend Manasses,' Vadir chuckled. 'He's been asking around about you. You made an impression in the count's hall that cold morning.'

'If he is the worst I encounter on this field, we already have enough work to see us through until the snows melt and the flowers bloom.'

'Watch your pride,' Alric cautioned. 'With your ability to conjure enemies out of thin air, you may find surprises ahead.'

Shrugging, Hereward let his attention drift to the gathering crowd. Plenty of wealthy merchants wandered around the edge of the field, talking business or showing off their new amulets or gold rings to the many bright-eyed young women who always gathered for the contests. Hereward noted at least three counts too, with their retinues trailing behind.

Remembering Acha's sullen features with a surprising pang, Hereward looked around the flushed faces of the watching women. They clasped their hands together, whispering in clutches. Sparkling eyes flashed towards the most favoured combatants, and many women, unmarried and married, offered blue or yellow ribbons to the young fighters to tie around their wrists. The victors would win a greater prize later that night.

One young woman was looking his way. Beneath her white headdress he glimpsed the tease of brown hair curled at the ends with tongs, and her feline face wore a wry, interested expression. A gold brooch gleamed at her breast.

'Who is that?' he asked, his eyes locked on the woman.

Vadir followed the warrior's gaze. 'Someone you should know. Name's Turfrida. She brings fire to the loins, does she not? But that is the least interesting thing about her. Her father is the castellan of Saint-Omer, Wulfric Rabe, and a man with gold to hire swords like ours.'

While Hereward was still considering asking Turfrida for her favour, Hoibrict sauntered up to her and after a moment's conversation walked away with her yellow ribbon. He saw the Mercian looking and added a triumphant swagger to his step.

'You have to be quicker than that with women,' Vadir grumbled. 'They're fickle, easily flattered and always looking for the best offer.' He shrugged. 'Behind their hands, the locals whisper that she's a witch, but I'd wager that's more to do with how she bewitches men's hearts.'

Hereward continued to stare at Turfrida, wondering what it was about her that attracted him so, but now that she had offered her favour to another she studiously avoided his gaze.

Alric stepped into Hereward's line of vision to inspect the chain-mail coif protecting the warrior's cheeks and neck. 'This time remember what we told you,' the monk said. 'Whisper a prayer to God. Chew upon your tongue. Do anything but give sway to that demon inside you. *Are* you prepared?' The monk fixed a warning eye on Hereward.

'I know this is only a game, if that is what you mean.'

'It would not do for you to start slaughtering the contestants, even with a blunted weapon. Your potential employers look for men of honour, not wild beasts as likely to turn on their own as on their enemies. The fullness of our bellies depends upon you.'

'Words, words, words. I am already too weary to fight.'

'Leave him be, monk,' Vadir sighed. 'God knows, his temper is like a forest fire, even without you fanning the flames.' The big man slapped Hereward on the back. 'Besides, has he let us down yet? No. He keeps us fed. And these women who so influence their husbands and fathers would rather see a strutting young cock than a greying old wolf like me. Now, make sure your arse stays on the horse and your head stays on your shoulders. We want to open those gold-stuffed purses of our good and noble onlookers.' Shaking his mane of hair to disperse the horseflies, Vadir held up the heavy iron helmet so that it gleamed in the autumn sunlight. Hereward studied the decorative band of metalwork that ran from the base of the skull over the top and down the front to protect the nose, the plates sweeping under the eye sockets. A few dents marred the shining surface, but the helmet had served him well during the long months since he had left Guines with Alric and the red-headed brawler.

Lowering the heavy helmet on to his head, Vadir said, 'There's gold aplenty out there. And many men who want to deprive us of our fortunes.' Glancing towards Hoibrict, he added, 'The monk is right . . . you have a habit of making enemies wherever you go. Let us hope that one of them doesn't leap back and bite you on the arse.'

Alric led up the warrior's chestnut horse, a fine beast, strong and brave, and held it steady for Hereward to mount. The warrior eyed the other men riding into position. The lots had been drawn, near a hundred warriors on each side. Many of the riders wore layers of thick wool under their mail to protect against the blows from the blunted weapons or the falls from horseback that killed many at each battle-fair, but Hereward had refused that protection. It was a hot day, and he wanted nothing that would drain his fire or slow him.

On the edge of the field, the count, a slim man with a drooping moustache, raised one hand. Silence fell across the crowd. His voice droned out in the lazy afternoon, but the words meant nothing to Hereward. When the count waved his hand and ordered the battle-fair to begin, Hoibrict turned to the English warrior and levelled his sword in an unmistakable threat.

'For Mercia,' Hereward cried with pride. 'For England.' He dug his heels in the horse's flanks and propelled himself towards the melee.

CHAPTER TWENTY-EIGHT

The thunder of hooves drowned the crowd's cheers. His view restricted by his eye-holes, Hereward saw only a heaving sea of men on horseback. Helmets and mail glinted in the sun. Full-throated war cries and bellowed insults closed around him as he crashed into the midst of the fighting. Blunted swords flashed in front of his eyes. Horses smashed against him like the waves on the black rocks at the coast. Elbows and fists rammed into head, shoulders, ribs. Blades crashed against his nose and face, and bruised his arms and chest beneath the mail, but he fought on. The red and yellow strips of linen tied around the combatants' thighs to signify membership of their side disappeared in the confusion. Survival became the priority.

Hereward lashed his sword back and forth to carve a space for himself. The blade rang off helmets and clattered against mail coifs, smashing the chain into cheeks and necks. Unseated, one rider tumbled beneath the surging bodies and pounding hooves. Hereward couldn't tell if the man was an ally or an enemy.

The crush rolled around the field. Some warriors broke from the tight knot to pursue each other through the wood edging the grassland, searching for a superior position. Bodies littered the torn-up turf. Many lay still, others cried for help, all twisted and broken. Horses galloped riderless. Some men dragged themselves towards the sides, trying to hide their shame.

Hereward fought the urge to lose himself in the fighting. Drawing the attention of the wealthy men looking to hire swords was all that mattered, he knew. He guided his mount near to the crowds, then yelled and waved his blade to catch the eye of four other horsemen. He could feel the gaze of the onlookers turning towards him. Sitting high, he raised both arms to demonstrate his fearlessness, then leaned across his horse's neck and dug in his spurs. The ground whirled under him in a green blur. He felt the familiar rush of blood and grinned. Now they would see who was the bravest, he thought. The four riders bore down on him, but he held his line towards the centre of the rank. He watched heads begin to come up in anxious anticipation when his opponents realized his resolve was not going to weaken.

At the last moment the four warriors scattered before him. Two horses crashed into each other, unseating their riders. When he passed the third, Hereward flicked up his sword with outstretched arm, smashing his opponent under the chin. His wits scattered, the rider flew over the rear of his horse and down.

Hereward brought his steed round to face the last of the four horsemen, his breath rasping beneath his mail coif. Sweat stung his eyes, and when he blinked the droplets away he glimpsed a familiar helmet, with slanted eye-holes and a nose-shield tapering and hooked at the end so that the wearer resembled a bird of prey. It was Hoibrict. Hereward's eyes fell to the yellow ribbon round his opponent's wrist and he grinned.

Hesitating as he brought his steed round, Hoibrict recognized Hereward in turn, the Mercian knew. The nobleman reined in his horse, weighing his course of action. The warrior imagined his opponent's eyes narrowing, his temper rising at the recognition of a true rival. More lay at stake here than gold. He sought out Turfrida at the front of the crowd.

He spurred on his mount. With a shout, Hoibrict raced his own steed forward. The sounds of battle drained away. Hereward lost himself in the rapid drumbeat of hooves, the wind tearing into his helmet as he hurtled towards the other rider. His grin broadened. Sods flew up all around him. The falcon helmet filled his entire vision. Gritting his teeth, he readied himself for the bone-breaking impact. Just before it came, the Fleming drove his horse to one side, swinging his sword at Hereward's head. Hereward ducked beneath the blade, jabbing his own weapon into his rival's side. He allowed himself a triumphant smile when Hoibrict's pained curse rang out.

Hereward brought his horse round and charged once more. He could see his rival begin to panic as the nobleman struggled to bring his mount under control. Balancing on the saddle, Hereward drew alongside his opponent and launched himself into the air. Both men slammed into the turf. Hereward was prepared for the impact, rolling back to his feet in an instant. Limping and dazed, Hoibrict gamely raised his sword, but he fell back step by step under the assault until he stumbled. Whisking up his blade, Hereward saw the fear in the downed noble's eyes.

'I am a better man than you,' the warrior whispered. 'Yield.'

The Flemish warrior grunted assent. Stepping back, Hereward plucked the yellow ribbon from Hoibrict's wrist.

'You will pay for this shame you have heaped upon me,' the nobleman hissed.

'You brought it upon yourself. Pride . . .' he smiled, remembering Alric's words, 'goes before a fall.'

As Hereward left his rival lying in the churned mud and turf and walked towards the cheering crowd, he felt Hoibrict's gaze heavy upon his back. He knew he had made a bitter enemy that day, but he didn't care.

At the side of the field, a grinning Vadir crushed the warrior in a bear-hug and boomed, 'Women will be your downfall. But your performance did all that was needed. We have our winter shelter and food and pay. Bishop Liebert of Cambrai requires our services to protect the building of a new monastery.'

Alric congratulated Hereward on his self-control. 'How far

you have come from cold Northumbria. Why, not a single man was flayed alive. How disappointed you must feel.'

'There is still time, monk.'

'You have my token.'

Hereward turned to see Turfrida. Her dark eyes held him. He thought she looked even prettier at close hand, with clear skin and high cheekbones. She peered into the shadows of his mask's eye-holes. Behind him, he heard Vadir and Alric shuffle away, accompanied by the big man's rumbling chuckle. 'My name is Turfrida,' she added.

Hereward removed his helmet and held it in the crook of his arm. 'I know your name.'

Taking this as a compliment, the woman smiled her approval. 'You defeated my champion.'

'You deserved a better man to defend your favour.' He held out her yellow ribbon.

'A pity I did not offer it to you,' she said, 'or you would have won a prize beyond value.' Her eyes teased him.

'You speak English well.'

'My father saw me well schooled. And there are so many of your countrymen in Flanders these days, I will find good use for the tongue. Your king has always encouraged close ties with us. They say he plays a cunning game with those who seek the throne of England.'

'He plays a dangerous game. William the Bastard will not sit quietly in Normandy while Edward's suitors dance around him.'

'Ah, you fear William of Normandy,' she replied with a knowing nod.

'I fear no one. But William would have England kneeling before him for no reason but to swell his head. Englishmen do not kneel to invaders,' he added with a note of defiance. 'The throne will stay in English hands.' He flinched, seeing Harold Godwinson's face.

A shadow crossed Turfrida's features. 'Walk with me a while.' She led the way from the tournament fields back through the walls into Bruges. The timber-framed houses and wattle-and-daub huts were crammed hard on each other, the narrow tracks between them twisting and turning with little plan. Among the houses, Hereward saw more stone buildings than he had ever seen in one place in England. He remembered an abbot telling him that one day there would be stone houses everywhere, as there had been in the days before the Vikings. Men and women trailed back from the tournament, pausing to chat beside chickens scratching in the dust. The lowing of cattle and grunting of pigs echoed over the thatched and timber roofs.

'You have many riches here,' Hereward said, eyeing a necklace of amber beads that must have been shipped from the east.

'But it is not England,' Turfrida replied. 'Knowledge of your great art has spread far and wide. The women here fight for English jewellery. Your illuminations are praised in our monasteries, your tapestries exceed those of the Normans. The laws of your land, and the way in which all men and women cleave to them, are admired everywhere. If only we had them here. Two days ago a merchant brought my father an English silver brooch so beautifully engraved it took the breath away, the manner of depiction so real, so powerful, it can have had no equal. All struggle to keep up with England, but you race ever further ahead. What heights can you reach in the years to come?'

He listened to the woman's breathless praise and felt a pang of regret for the fields of his youth. 'I know little of art,' he replied, 'except the art of battle.'

Turfrida hesitated at his comment. 'And have you heard of wars to come? There are portents—'

'There are always portents,' he interrupted. 'Ever since I left London, I have heard nothing else. From churchmen and wise women and those who still pray to the old gods. The End-Times are coming.'

'And would all of them, all so different, say these things without good reason?'

Hereward shrugged. 'Would you know? I am told there are some who consider you a witch.'

The woman's cheeks flushed. 'I am skilled in the mechanical arts.'

'Magic, then?' He saw in Turfrida's face a quick intellect and imagined that some might think that a threat; not he. She intrigued him.

'And the study of the stars and the future they hold. All the mysteries of the world around us, the patterns of animals and the stories the trees whisper when they are alone.' Her eyes flashed. He could see she found excitement in her knowledge.

'The Church will damn you.'

'Let them try. I am a God-fearing woman. On some matters, even the priests are wrong,' she said defiantly. 'There is no sin in learning. Though some churchmen believe there is sin in *women* learning.'

Impressed by her passion, Hereward smiled to himself. Turfrida was strong, and in some ways he was reminded of Acha. But this woman was better schooled, and, he felt, more honest. 'Do not fear. I have no desire to fetch the priest to you.'

Her face darkened again. 'When you fought upon the field today, I thought I saw ravens flying overhead, a cloud of them, turning the sky black.'

He felt a chill despite the heat of the day. 'More portents?'

'I would know who you are, English man,' she said as if she had not heard his question. He saw her put on a bright face as she swept her hand in the direction of a hall. 'Come claim your reward. We shall feast with my father at the count's hall and I will hear the tales of your past. And let us speak only of good things.'

But as they moved away, he saw her glance behind him, and her smile fade, as if she saw something walking there in his shadow.

CHAPTER TWENTY-NINE

The boy lay on his bed of rushes, mumbling incoherent words in the throes of his fever. Sweat slicked his flushed face in the glow from the hearth. At the door of the hut deep in the woods, Hereward watched Turfrida bend over the lad as she eased a creamy paste between his lips. The mother and father stood to one side, their faces crumpled by worry. When the boy had taken in the mush, Turfrida bowed her head and muttered a few words in a language the warrior didn't recognize.

Rising, she turned to the parents and gave an exhausted smile. 'Pray over your son until dawn, and, if God is willing, he will recover.'

Hereward had looked around the ceorls' shack and noted their meagre possessions, yet still the relieved couple tried to press offerings of food upon Turfrida. She took only a fragment of bread so as not to offend them, and bid them farewell.

'The boy will live, then?' he asked, once they were on the narrow winding path leading back through the trees.

'I would not lie to his mother and father.'

'Is this how you repay the Church for all the attention they give your kind – by being honest and aiding sick children?' He hid his smile. 'Where is the shape-changing and the night flights and the curses?'

'Perhaps I have secretly bewitched you.'

'I am protected from your charms.' He feigned aloofness.

'Ah. Your kisses were to ward me away. Now I understand.'

'Or perhaps I bewitched *you*.'

She laughed at that, but not unkindly. 'Now, speak no more of witches. Words travel far. It is a mark of my trust in you that I have made plain what I do.'

'Made plain? All I see are crushed herbs and balms. All I hear are whispered words that mean nothing to me.'

After a moment's thought, she said, 'I was taught the secret ways by my mother, who learned from her mother before her. They were people of the woods, but I am the daughter of a castellan, yet still I carry on the ways of those who have gone before me. I can do no other. We are all in thrall to our pasts.'

'Then you do not consort with the Devil?'

'Only one.' She laughed. 'The mechanical arts are no more terrifying than the teachings you received from the monks as a child. Is finding your way by the position of the stars the work of the Devil? Is knowing which plants heal? Listening to the whispers of the trees and the animals, finding wisdom in the patterns of all we see around us?'

'But you do not worship the Christian God?'

Her smile tightened, but she gave no reply.

They talked of other matters as they walked home, of his friendship with Alric, and with Vadir, and of the dangers of his mercenary work. He made light of the threats to his life, but Turfrida showed only concern, and as she gave voice to her fears for his safety tears sprang to her eyes. Under the shade of a twisted elm, his reassurances turned to kisses, and in the warmth of her lips all thoughts of Acha and Tidhild ebbed away. In that moment he wanted only Turfrida for the rest of his days.

Before he could find the words to express his feelings, a scream tore through the woods. Turfrida pulled away, looking back along the path.

'The boy took a turn for the worse?'

'Impossible.'

When a tumult of shouts and cries rang out, Turfrida picked up her dress and ran towards the hut that they had just left. Hereward caught up with her, grabbing her arm to stop her from racing into danger. He steered her off the path and into the cover of the trees where they had a view of the clearing around the shack. The mother was on her knees, sobbing, her hands clasped together in a desperate plea. Beside her, her husband sprawled on the ground, clutching a bloody forehead. Five men surrounded them with graven faces. The one who loomed over the woman wore a priest's white tunic. Under a thick black moustache, he snarled questions in Flemish, his eyes cold and cruel.

'What does he ask?' Hereward whispered.

When no reply came, he glanced at Turfrida and saw that the blood had drained from her face. 'He demands to know the whereabouts of the witch.'

Uneasiness filled him. Time and again, he had heard church-men promise to 'punish pitilessly the witches, the healers, the ones who deal in auguries and omens and work magics'. The words had become an oath, repeated at stone crosses through-out England. Death by burning or drowning or exile would be her fate.

When his hand went for his sword, Turfrida grabbed his wrist. 'No,' she whispered, her gaze fierce. 'You cannot risk your life. I will not allow it. If you harm the priest or his men, the Church will not rest until you are hunted down and executed.'

Hereward hesitated – for Turfrida he would risk even the wrath of the Church – but he saw the worry in her eyes and relented.

In the clearing, the sobbing woman tore at her hair and screamed. The priest was directing one of his men towards the house. A spear prodded the father's chest. Hereward watched the aide venture inside and return with the sick boy in his arms. The warrior could only guess at the threat the cleric had made to the distraught mother. Turfrida's nails dug into his wrist. Tears shone in the corners of her eyes, her own fear now forgotten.

As he weighed his response, Turfrida jumped to her feet and called out to distract the men. The priest and his aides spun towards her. Their shock gave way to fierce expressions as the cleric stabbed a finger and snarled a command.

'Are you mad?' the warrior shouted, but Turfrida was already racing back through the trees. He caught up with her as she scrambled down a grassy bank towards a tinkling stream.

'We will not outrun them,' he said, glancing back in the direction of the noisy pursuit.

'Then we shall hide.'

Hereward saw no safe refuge in the wood. Nor would the churchmen slow, filled as they were with holy fire. He had seen time and again the torments and tortures they inflicted on those they believed to be in opposition to God's will. As he splashed through the cool water, his thoughts turned to making a stand with sword in hand, sacrificing himself, if necessary, to allow Turfrida to flee.

Before he could draw his blade, he noticed her cocking her head as if she were listening to some voice in her ear. 'Follow me,' she gasped.

'What is this? Witchery?'

She ignored him, weaving away from the stream through a sea of bracken, her eyes fixed ahead as if she were following some unseen figure leading the way. They slid down a steep incline to where a section of land had slipped in the heavy rains. Among the tangle of exposed roots, she crawled on her belly, working her way into a dark space behind. Hereward followed, afraid there was no room for his broader shoulders, but within a moment they were pressed tightly together in a dank hole. Turfrida was shaking beside him, as aware of her fate if caught as he was. He held her tight for comfort.

The sound of feet skidding down the incline echoed through the earth. Through the narrow tunnel, Hereward watched the men jabbing their spears into the undergrowth as they searched. The priest had the cold face of a warrior, he thought, a hard man accustomed to inflicting pain, a seasoned campaigner who would go to any lengths to achieve his aims.

He had no idea how long the grim-faced churchmen prowled around the woods, but when they finally disappeared from view down the slope, Turfrida began to relax in his arms. Her deep, juddering breath echoed in the small space.

'Your blasphemy will cost you your life,' he said with no little tenderness.

'I am what I am,' she replied. 'I can be no other.'

Once silence descended on the wood, they wriggled out and made their way back up the slope. Hereward saw in Turfrida's dirt-streaked face that she was still afraid. 'By his looks, the priest is one who goes by the name of Emeric, a Norman,' she said, biting her lip. 'He was directed by the Pope himself to travel the land hunting witches, and it is said he loves his work as much as he loves God. He uses a hot rod to burn the flesh or weighs women down with rocks and throws them into deep water.' She began to shake again.

'Let us see his God-given courage when he faces my sword.'

'You cannot protect me if accusations are made. No one can. The Church is more powerful than even you.' She forced a smile, but it looked uncharacteristically sad.

'I cannot stand by—'

'A good warrior knows the time to fight and the time to wait, so you once told me.' She took his hand and added, 'I am moved by your concern for me, but know that I have faced these trials all my life and I have survived. As the castellan's daughter, I am offered some protection, and I have many friends who will guide this priest in another direction. For now, though, I will stay with my mother's sister until he moves on to torment some other poor woman.'

Frustration welled in Hereward's chest. 'How long will that be?'

'Fear not. We will be together again.'

He searched her face. 'Is this one of your auguries? Is it written?'

She smiled. 'In my heart.'

When they parted company in the shadow of the palisade, he realized how much Turfrida had settled into his thoughts. He found it a strange feeling, at once unsettling and promising the peace of which he had always dreamed. For once, he looked to the future with hope.

But as he moved into the oddly quiet streets, he felt a shadow descend on him. He saw unease in the faces of everyone he passed, and eyes darting in suspicion and mistrust. When he reached the pond beside the tavern, he understood the source of their fear. From a distance, it appeared a bundle of linen floated in the dirty water. It was an elderly woman, dead, the back of her dress torn open to reveal numerous pricks from a blade. Emeric the Priest had already been here.

Hereward struggled to comprehend the feelings rising through him. In all his life he had never tasted fear. But at that moment he felt afraid, for Turfrida, and dwarfed by a threat that could not be cut down by even the sharpest blade.

CHAPTER THIRTY

3 October 1065

It seemed as though all Northumbria was burning, perhaps all England. Church bells tolled the alarm as a wall of fire roared out across the wealthy merchants' homes and the southern palisade of Eoferwic. Yet in the choking pall of black smoke, warriors waved bloodstained axes and swords in the air and people danced and cheered with voices made hoarse by passion. Bands of men moved through the streets, flushing out their hiding prey. Whenever a fugitive broke cover, they would be hacked down, their head lopped off and hauled up on a pole as a warning to others.

Acha cowered beside the line of burning houses, her pale face seared by the heat. Ashes flaked across her raven hair and streaked her coarse slave's dress. Her eyes darted around in fear that she would be caught by the blood-crazed rebels. Most of the day she had spent running and hiding, afraid for her life, listening to the screams of the dying as the circle of iron drew tighter around her. Even the slaughter of her own people in the thickly forested hills of Gwynedd had not been so terrifying.

Through the thunder of the fire and the crash of falling

timbers, she heard men chanting, 'Hereward! Hereward!' Over the seasons since he had disappeared, the bear-killer had become a symbol of resistance to the people opposed to Tostig's rule. Why, she was not quite sure, but she had heard the Mercian's name whispered with awe in the marketplace. *Oh, what a tempest you have unleashed, Hereward*, she thought bitterly. It will blow us all away. She had needed a protector and he had failed her, and now he would see her dead.

A hand grasped her wrist and she screamed in shock. It was Kraki, dried blood caked across his beard from a new wound on the bridge of his nose. 'Our time here is done,' the huscarl growled, glancing around.

'We cannot escape—' she began breathlessly.

'There is a way. Come. I will look after you.'

Keeping his head down, the Viking led Acha along a puddled path beside a workshop, the route as clear as day in the golden glow from the fire. At the far end, they emerged on to a street among the burning houses. Acha could barely stand from the heat scorching her throat. She felt sure then that she would never see her homeland again.

A cry rang out through the din of the burning. Whirling, she saw the one-eyed, one-handed rabble-rouser, Wulfhere, leading a band of rebels through the smoke. A triumphant grin split his face as he pointed at the two fugitives.

'Run like the deer, slave girl. Run faster than you ever have in your life,' Kraki shouted.

She followed the huscarl towards the inferno consuming Tostig's hall as the hungry roar of their pursuers echoed at their backs. Yet she slowed to a halt when she realized his intended path lay between the hall and a burning barn. A sheet of flame and swirling amber sparks blocked the way.

'No,' she cried. 'We will die.'

'Die by fire or die by axe,' he snarled. 'Trust me.' The Viking tore off his cloak and threw it over her head. As she protested, he grabbed her and hauled her along. The roaring of the fire drowned out her panicked squeals, and then, even through the thick wool, Acha felt the heat envelop her. For a moment, she was convinced she had died and gone to hell, and then Kraki's thunderous battle cry echoed around her as the air grew cooler.

When the cloak was torn away, she saw they stood on the ramparts on the southern edge of the town with the conflagration behind them. Hacking out coughs, Kraki rested for a moment with his hands on his knees. Sparks flickered in his beard and his face was black.

'Thank you,' Acha said, overwhelmed with gratitude. 'You risked your life for me. I . . . I would not have thought it.'

'You're a sullen cow with a savage tongue, but you deserve better than that,' he muttered.

They stumbled through the ditches and across the plain in the October chill, heading for the high ground where they knew the remnants of those loyal to Tostig waited. Not far beyond the ramparts, two bodies hung on poles, the flesh green and bird-torn. Acha recognized Amund and Ravenswart, two of the huscarls, who had been butchered on the first day of the insurrection when the Northumbrian thegns had attacked with two hundred men. The earl had been over-confident, she realized, believing he could contain the long-simmering uprising with even more brutality and desperate pleas to his brother for support. Within hours the treasury had been sacked, the armoury looted and Tostig and his forces driven beyond the walls. A fool, she thought, like all English men, seduced by their own bragging.

They fell silent as they trudged across the grasslands, their lungs protesting from the smoke they had inhaled. Briefly, they halted before a vast field of armoured corpses reeking of decay. A sad red banner fluttered on a pole. Though the blood had long since soaked into the black soil, Acha knew the slaughter of so many of Tostig's men would linger in the earl's mind for as long as he lived. Never had he suffered such a defeat.

Her legs were shaking with exhaustion when they reached the high ground and heard the snort of horses and the low murmur of strained voices. She felt shocked to see barely fifty men gathered on the edge of the wood, their heads low in dismay. With his wife Judith beside him, Tostig looked towards the fires of Eoferwic painting the night sky a dull red in the distance. His face was drained of blood, and he looked at that moment many years older than the last time she had seen him, Acha thought.

'Did you know they have declared me outlaw? That they have sent for Morcar of Mercia to rule here in my stead?' the earl said to Kraki, his voice drenched in bitterness. 'For all I did to bring law and prosperity to Northumbria, the ungrateful bastards have brought me down to nothing.'

'While there is life in your breast, the end is untold,' the huscarl muttered.

'True. Though Eoferwic is lost, this is a time for plotting. There are other roads ahead.'

'You will meet your brother?' Kraki enquired. 'If Harold Godwinson still backs your claim—'

Tostig shook his head forcefully. 'My brother has betrayed me. He sees his own power under threat if this uprising spreads south and so he has thrown me to the wolves. He supports Morcar as earl. Morcar, the Mercian bastard, as bad as his brother Edwin, our bitterest rivals. And so the poor souls who cleave to me are put to the sword and wild lawlessness spreads across the land.' He glanced at Judith and said, 'I wish I had listened to you, wife. I thought the blood I shared with my brother meant something, but Harold thinks only of himself.'

'You will still meet him, though?' she asked. Acha thought her mistress's face looked unbearably sad.

'I will speak to him, and the king, though I fear I know the outcome already.'

'What, then?' Judith enquired, her voice tremulous.

'We will flee to Flanders and entrust ourselves to *your* blood. Count Baldwin will welcome us, I am sure, and then we shall see what price shall be paid for this shame.' His voice grew as hard as iron.

'I heard the rebels chanting the name of that Mercian,

Hereward,' Kraki muttered. 'I thought him dead. Has he played some part in this uprising?'

'Hereward left England behind for Flanders long ago,' Judith replied.

Acha saw Tostig snap round to his wife, as surprised by this information as everyone else there. Anger burned in his eyes at his wife's secrecy, but gradually he softened, and then shook his head. 'No matter. Hereward was as much a victim of my brother's plotting as everyone here. I hold no grudge against him.'

Judith reached out and took her husband's hand, though both kept their eyes on the distant flames. After a moment, the earl said, 'Kraki, you have been a loyal servant, but I now free you from your oath to me, and from your contract.'

The huscarl bowed his head and thanked him. Acha felt surprised by Tostig's reward to his most faithful follower in this darkest hour. Perhaps there was some honour in the earl's heart after all. As the Viking wandered away towards the other men in the trees, she hurried after him. 'Wait,' she called, and when he half turned she added, 'I would come with you. If you will have me.'

Kraki laughed. 'How sly you are. You see an opportunity where many see only defeat.'

Acha felt her ears burn, though she set her jaw defiantly, expecting a refusal.

'Very well, then,' the huscarl said finally. 'I could do with some comfort on the road ahead. You will get your protection. But if you believe you can bewitch me into returning you to Gwynedd, think again. I travel south where there will be work aplenty for my axe, I wager.'

Relieved, Acha skipped beside her new companion. But as they walked into the woods, a movement caught her eye. In the trees stood a dark figure, close enough to have overheard every word Tostig had uttered. When the shape moved, she realized it was Harald Redteeth, the wild Viking who had left such a trail of blood in his wake when he had joined the earl's huscarls all those seasons ago. With a shudder, she realized she was happy to leave that red-bearded madman far behind her.

When she glanced back a moment later, Redteeth was gone. And in the distance, the flames of Eoferwic burned higher.

CHAPTER THIRTY-ONE

Two men hunched in silence over black and white counters on a tabula board which had been carved around the edge with scenes of warriors at arms. Only the spit and crackle of the logs in the hearth broke the silence. Harold Godwinson studied the arrangement of the ivory counters, one finger resting on his chin. But Redwald watched the older man's face, as he scrutinized all that the earl did. The young man had learned that his master approached everything in life with the same degree of preparation and strategy as he did battle. Nothing was left to chance.

Redwald watched, and learned.

Good advice at the right time, remaining silent at all others, loyalty in the face of harsh treatment, all these things had secured his place within the earl's trust, the young man knew. As the seasons passed, Redwald had kept himself close to the older man's shoulder, for power bred loneliness, and the great always needed a friend and honest adviser. Promoted by degree, he had fetched mead when his master's cup was empty, and passed on whispered secrets he had become privy to in the gossip of the court. Redwald had become Harold's eyes and ears, and sometimes his strong right arm, and the rewards had flowed to him accordingly, slowly at first, but now there was no man in all England who could benefit more from Harold's coming ascension.

Harold rolled the dice. In making his move, he left two of his men exposed. When it was Redwald's turn, the young man broke up his defensive position to attempt to gain an advantage. By the next round, Harold had carved through Redwald's counters and was on his way to victory.

Redwald slapped his right palm on the table in annoyance.

'A lesson,' Harold said, with a grin. 'Sometimes it is necessary to sacrifice the things we most cherish to win.'

Redwald feigned irritation. He had long since seen the older man's ploy and had let the earl win. 'And that is what you did in Northumbria?'

Harold scooped up the dice and dropped them on the board. 'Tostig had failed,' he said with a crack of anger. 'He moved too fast, demanded too much. He did not display the cunning of a king. The uprising by the lawless Northumbrians could easily have spread, and they might have damned all men of Wessex for Tostig's failings. How could I then ask them to follow me into battle once I am on the throne?'

'But you have strengthened the Mercians by advising Edward to make Morcar Earl of Northumbria?'

'For now.' Harold grinned. He stood up to stretch his legs. Redwald followed him to the hearth. 'Neither Edwin nor Morcar has any experience of leading. And now Morcar will be too distracted by bringing order to the unruly lot in the north to plot and connive with his brother. No, the Mercians are not a problem for now.'

'A wise move,' the younger man said, adding in a wry tone, 'If only those Mercians realized you led them by the nose.'

'Know, then, that you and I are the same,' Harold said, laying a hand on his attendant's shoulder. 'We have both been forced to abandon brothers we love for the greater glory. But our sons and our sons' sons would never forgive us if we showed weakness and failed to grasp our true destiny. Men cannot afford to give in to their hearts. That is for women and boys.' The earl lowered his voice, and the younger man thought he heard warmth there, as if Harold were speaking to one of his two sons. 'But you understand that well, I know.'

'You have prodded and poked me enough to ensure that my skin is well calloused,' Redwald replied with a confident smile.

The earl poured himself some mead and let the cup linger on his lips for a moment, his gaze searching far beyond the walls. 'My own father taught me these lessons when I was young. He tried to teach Tostig too, but my brother would never learn. He always cried and ran to my mother, hiding in her skirts until my father flew into a rage and threatened to beat him with the stick he kept by the door.' Harold swallowed a deep draught of the mead. 'Once, when I was very young, he took me out to the hills at night. The moon was full and turned the grass to silver. I could hear the wolves howling in the woods in the valley, and I began to tremble. My father knelt before me and took my shoulders in his big hands. He was not a harsh man. He did not strike me, even though I could see in his face that he was disappointed that I was scared. "Here, take my knife," he said, and he gave me the blade I had seen him use to skin a deer and once to kill a man who had offended him. It was a fine knife, well balanced, with a handle made of antler, and it had belonged to his father. I have it still, though the blade is tarnished and weak.

'And he said to me, "Harold, this is the night when you become a man. I will leave you here now and you must let me go, without tears. You must sit and tell yourself the story of the loaves and fishes, as the priest told it to you, and when you are done, you must try to find your way home. It will be hard and there are many dangers along the way." "The wolves—" I began, but he only placed a finger on my lips to silence me. "If you return to our hall, what you learn about yourself on the way will change you for ever. You will become the man you need to be, you want to be, in your heart." He watched me for a moment, and although I wanted to cry, I held the tears inside. And then he was gone.'

'*If* you return,' Redwald repeated, imagining how terrifying it must have been. 'How old were you?'

'I had entered my ninth year,' Harold replied, still lost to his memories. 'And my father was right. I remember little of that night, apart from the terror and my certainty that I would die. I do not know how I found my way back to the hall in the dark – I could not have done it in the light. But the next day, when I woke, and my father greeted me as if it was any other day and the previous night had not happened, I was changed.' He flashed a curious, unreadable smile at Redwald. 'But later my father told me there was but one more thing I needed to learn: the only question in life that matters.'

'What is that?' Redwald asked, his curiosity piqued.

'How far will you travel along the road to damnation to achieve your heart's desire?'

'A good question.' Redwald refilled his master's cup.

Reflecting, Harold sipped his mead, and then said, 'Perhaps I will give you that knife one day.'

Redwald flashed a polite smile, but he didn't want the knife. He already had one. From outside, the throb of voices intensified. 'By the sound of it, they are almost ready.'

Harold grunted and finished his mead. 'We cannot leave this moment all to Edward. Let us reward the waiting throng.'

Sweeping on his best cloak, the red one edged with a design of looping yellow circles that made him stand out in a crowd, Harold stepped out into the crisp morning. He made his way across the palace enclosure towards the edge of Thorney Island where the grey stone tower rose up against the blue sky. Shielding his eyes against the sun, Redwald could see the stonemasons making the final preparations at the summit. Most of the timber platforms and the greased fibre ropes had been removed to give a clear view of the magnificent abbey. It must indeed match any of the great churches across Europe as Edward proclaimed, the young man thought.

The crowd had gathered around the sunlit western wall of the abbey, the women in their white headdresses, the men garbed in their finest embroidered woollen clothes for the occasion. Gold glinted everywhere, in brooches, amulets, sword hilts, rings and bracelets. All heads craned upwards in awe.

When they saw Harold nearing, the men, women and children turned and cheered. Redwald's chest swelled. He saw in the flushed faces the respect they held for Harold, yes, and the love too. To be loved by so many people must be a wonderful thing indeed, he reflected.

The king approached unnoticed from the direction of his hall. His jewelled crown gleamed on his snowy hair, but his face was as grey as his cloak and he leaned heavily on Edith's arm. The queen deposited him by the west door and, beaming, hurried over to her brother. She kissed Harold on the cheek.

'I won our wager,' she whispered, breathless with excitement. 'The abbey will be stocked with three times the relics that Edward found. It is my name that springs first to the lips of the abbot.'

'Well done, sister. And Edward?'

'Survives.'

Resplendent in his tunic and cap, Archbishop Ealdred caught Harold's eye and sidled over. Redwald knew the cleric's journey from Eoferwic for the ceremony served another purpose: to inform his close ally of the current state of affairs in Northumbria. Redwald left the group to discuss their business and slipped inside the new abbey. He smelled the freshness of the wood and clean-cut stone, and marvelled at the stained glass in the windows. His attention was drawn to the wooden box on a table in an alcove. Inside lay the shankbone of St John the Baptist, the relic he had recovered from the village near Winchester. Hurrying over, he rested one hand upon the casket and bowed his head. His heart beat faster at the thought of what was within: a secret so profound that it seared the deepest part of him. For a moment, he stayed there with his thoughts, and then he returned to the throng, wishing he could leave that box well alone.

A slender hand caught his arm as he pushed through the crowd and he turned to see Hild smiling coyly. She was the daughter of Blacwin, one of the king's thegns, and as beautiful as any woman at court. Her eyes were as lush as a summer forest, her well-defined cheekbones setting off plump lips. Redwald had admired her from the moment he arrived at the Palace of Westminster, but Hild had spurned all his initial advances. Now she was more than happy to hold his hand and let him steal a kiss, and her father was happy too.

'I saw you walking beside Harold Godwinson,' she breathed. 'You have grown well into the role he has granted to you.' Glancing around, she whispered, 'Let me stand with you during the ceremony. So all can see.'

'I would be honoured.'

Her cheeks flushed with excitement. Redwald imagined the soft warmth of her thighs, but that would be a joy for another day. For now, there was serious business at hand, and it would only grow more testing in the days to come. He could not afford a distraction like Hild. 'I must speak to someone first, but catch my eye when I return and I will take you to stand with Harold.'

'And has your master any more gifts? Some amber, perhaps, or ivory?' She jangled the bracelet he had given her after Harold had advised him how to make the most of the attention Hild had been showing him.

With a smile, Redwald tapped his nose and slipped away. He would find a different route back through the crowd to avoid seeing her, but give her a gift at sunset to mitigate her disappointment. He knew exactly how to play her.

Returning from a merchant, who had little useful information, the young man found Asketil waiting for him. Hereward's father looked as though he had aged ten years in the last three, but he beamed when he saw the man he had adopted as his son.

'You have put some strong meat on you since last we met,' he laughed, gripping Redwald by the arms.

'I work hard. It is good to see you looking well. How are things in Barholme?'

'Quiet, which is good. But your name is spoken often in the taverns and fields. A local boy, now advising Harold Godwinson. It is a source of great joy to all who remember the young lad who fished and hunted and made mischief among them.' Redwald could hear the pride in Asketil's voice. The young man glanced down at Beric, who stood silent and sullen beside his father. Hereward's brother was now on the cusp of manhood, but Redwald could see he was still broken.

'He has still not spoken since that night,' Asketil hissed when he saw Redwald looking, 'and now I fear he never will.'

'And no news of Hereward?' the young man ventured.

The thegn's features darkened. 'His name is never mentioned in Mercia. He must be dead.'

Redwald wondered whether Asketil was right. If Hereward was still alive, he hoped his brother had finally found some peace.

A cheer rippled through the crowd. The ceremony was about to begin. The young man bid goodbye to Asketil and Beric and hurried back to Harold's side. Edith had rejoined her husband beside the abbey wall, but she looked impatient.

'In the dusty heat of eighteen summers and the bitter wind of eighteen hard winters, we have laboured here to build our monument to God's glory. And now we are almost done,' the king began, his dry croak almost lost beneath the murmur of the crowd. 'This great abbey is more than a testament to our devotion. It is a beacon to all Englishmen, reminding us that even in our darkest times God watches over us and listens to our prayers.'

Redwald felt surprised to hear the smack of his master's cunning in the king's words. England faces dark times. God watches over us. And Edward's good work here is the bond that joins the two. The old monarch was establishing his great legacy, a man of God, a protector of the people. As the king's words rustled out, the young man thought it sounded as though

Edward knew his days were ending, and that what was to come would be terrible indeed. So terrible, in fact, that people would look back on his rule with fondness. Redwald glanced aside and saw Harold's brow was knit, his expression angry. Was Edward damning the Earl of Wessex's rule before it had begun? Perhaps, as Harold had often suspected, the king hid his cunning behind a mask of weakness.

When Edward had finished his speech, all heads turned up towards the tower's summit. The master mason held the final stone aloft for all to see, and then set it in place with a flourish. A great cheer rang out. The abbey was done, and ready for the consecration that had been planned for three days after the Christmas feast.

When the crowd began to disperse, Harold grabbed Redwald's arm and steered him away from the flow of bodies. 'I have had my fill of Edward weaving his web. King or not, he is an old man and a fool. First he leads William the Bastard on. Then he makes plain to me that it is all to keep William's sword in its sheath and I am the one who will take the throne. Enough!' In a cold fury, Harold punched his right fist into his left palm. 'The time has passed for these things. Edward must name me as his chosen heir. And he will do so, by his own volition or with the edge of my axe against his neck.'

CHAPTER THIRTY-TWO

9 November 1065

In the lee of Cambrai's fortifications, Hereward strode along the ranks of the apprehensive young men he now commanded. 'The enemy will come at you with their shields held high, like this.' He raised his own shield in demonstration. 'Each one will be pressed hard against another so there will be a wall in front of you. Do not attack a wall. It does not bleed.' He grinned, hoping some humour could raise the spirits of his ramshackle group. Wan smiles appeared on a few faces.

'Do we run?' one youth asked, leaning on his spear.

'No. Never turn your back upon them. The wall will open and their axes will cut the bones from your shoulders to your arse. You stand your ground with your own shields. Watch out – they will reach underneath and try to hack your knees or your ankles. Do the same back and they will think twice.'

'Then how do we drive them back?'

'With your strength. Force hard enough, do not yield a step and in time their wall will break. Wait for that moment, then ram your spears into the gaps.'

Hereward turned to look out into the thick mist shrouding

the damp Flemish countryside. The post-dawn birdsong was muted, the only sound the steady drip of moisture from the branches of the black trees clustering at the foot of the slope leading down from the town's fortifications.

'You have nothing to fear,' he said. 'Our enemies are no better men than you.'

The young men appeared to relax a little at their leader's words. In the awkward way they gripped their spears, Hereward could see their lack of experience. He knew many had been called from toil on the land to join Bishop Liebert's force in his struggle with the castellans, John of Arras and Hugh of Havet, and he hoped they were up to the battle ahead. Many of the hardened swords for hire were still recovering from their battles against incursions from neighbouring counts during the long, hard winter, the sodden spring and the baking summer. He was learning to hate Flanders, with its constantly shifting allegiances and petty rivalries. It made England seem like a land of peace and calm.

Since their parting, he had not seen Turfrida, but she had stayed in his mind when the snows fell and when the thaw came. Vadir had taunted him long and hard, calling him a love-sick girl, but Alric had welcomed the romance as a sign that Hereward was moving away from his blood-soaked past into a blessed and peaceful future. 'Every step you have taken away from England has taught you to be a better man,' the monk had said in his gentle way. 'My work will soon be done and I will be able to find my own peace.' To avoid seeing Turfrida's face, Hereward had lost himself in his new work commanding and teaching the younger men. At first it had seemed odd – he felt too raw himself to be in such a position of authority – but as the days passed he realized how much he had learned at Vadir's side.

He shook off his introspection and turned to see Vadir himself watching from the top of the ramparts. A broad grin split the red-haired warrior's face. Hereward paced up the slope to his friend. 'What do you mock now, you great bear?'

'Mock? Nothing. My heart is warmed to see how you have grown, little man. From the wild one that all feared to a commander of men, respected by the young, in such a short time.'

The warrior waved away the other man's taunting. 'You taught me well.'

'And you listened. Few have ever paid heed to me.' Peering past Hereward, Vadir leaned in and whispered so the younger soldiers couldn't hear. 'Now listen once more. The men I sent out before dawn have returned with news. Only one small force of around twenty men makes their way through the fog, seeking to take us by surprise and rout us. But they are battle-hardened. Leather-skinned, scarred old warriors like me.' His gaze fell to the small knot of young men below them and his expression grew grave. 'Tell them to take care.'

Hereward passed on the warning. Then, with a whistle and a flick of his fingers, he summoned the men he had chosen to fight to fall in behind him. With reluctance, they plucked up their shields and their spears and trudged down the incline into the misty woods. The fog muffled the steady tramp of feet over the leaf-mould, but the warrior knew it would also mask the approach of their enemies. Underfoot, brown leaves crackled and the dying bracken crunched. Falling droplets pinged off helmets and shields, but the men remained silent, their wide eyes trying to pierce the folds of grey. In their faces Hereward saw the flush of childhood play and memories of hands gripping mothers' skirts. They were only a little younger than he was, but by their age he had seen things most people would never encounter in their worst nightmares. He had robbed. He had beaten stronger men until they cried for mercy, their faces unrecognizable. He had killed, many times. He had lain with a woman. And he had seen his own mother beaten to death. He had never been a child. Hereward hoped he had trained them well.

Under cover of the trees, he brought the men to a halt. For long moments, he cocked his head and listened, past the drips and the rustling of rabbits and mice in the undergrowth, past the ragged breathing of his frightened men. All was still.

Satisfied, he turned to the broad-nosed farmer he had chosen to lead the attack. 'If I could go with you into the battle, I would, but the bishop has ordered me to prepare the defences along the ramparts. But you are all strong and brave. You have nothing to fear from the enemy.'

The youth nodded, his anxious gaze darting around over Hereward's shoulder.

Once the small force had disappeared into the woods, Hereward waited for a while, listening and praying, and then made his way back to the fortifications. As he directed the rest of the men to collect their spears and take position along the ramparts, he found his thoughts turning back to Tidhild and his mother, the betrayals of his father and Harold Godwinson, and to Redwald. He hadn't thought of them with such force in many months. Had Redwald taken revenge on his behalf? Had his shame been expunged? In response to the questions, he felt his devil stir deep inside him; it had been asleep for so long, he had thought it gone.

Still there, he thought bitterly. *Why has it chosen this moment to remind me of its presence?*

Unable to answer his own question, he kept himself busy for the rest of the morning. But as the daily bread was handed out to the men, a shout rang out through the mists, and then another, and another. Racing to the ramparts, he saw the remnants of his fighting force fleeing back up the slope from the trees. They were bloodied and scared. Many had lost their spears. But his anger died in his chest when he saw how few remained. Catching hold of the nearest man, he demanded to know what had happened.

'They came out of the mists.' The man's eyes looked dazed and faraway like those of someone drunk on ale. 'We stood our ground, like you taught us. Behind the shield wall. Striking out low and high. We drew first blood with our spears, and more too. It was going well. Then . . . then . . .' He pressed the back of his hand to his mouth. 'Those bastards found a gap in our wall. Drove a spear into Blavier's eye. That was the start of it.'

'The shield wall did not hold?'

'When Blavier fell, two broke ranks and fled. One fell beneath an axe before he had taken three steps. A spear drove into the back of the other. Then fear struck us all. The wall crumbled. The enemy fell upon us like wolves.'

Hereward turned away, unable to contain his disappointment. He saw Vadir standing on the fortifications watching the bedraggled remnants of his force scramble up the slope. Every man shook, their eyes filled with tears. Vadir exchanged a look of condolence with Hereward, wise enough to know words would not help. He led the survivors back to their camp, and left Hereward alone to deal with his emotions in his own way.

In the distance, the jubilant cries of the castellans' men rose up for a while, then died away, letting silence creep back to the foggy wood. Hereward watched and brooded. The grey day inched on, and when twilight fell he lit a campfire, still hoping for another attack so he could release his simmering feelings. In the growing chill of the night, the dancing flames illuminated a lone figure trudging from the direction of Cambrai.

'If you have come to talk to me about God, you will receive a response from my fists,' Hereward said when Alric appeared on the edge of the circle of light.

'Do you think I only preach the Lord's word?' The monk squatted next to the fire. 'I have come to sit with my friend.'

Hereward grunted. 'I thought I was only a soul to be saved.'

Alric prodded the fire, watching the sparks fly up in the smoke while he chose his words. 'No man can save all the innocents that cross his path.'

'You wanted to say "Only God", didn't you?'

The monk smiled sadly. 'Only God, and we do not know his plan.'

'I commanded the men who died this day. I taught them. I failed them.'

'You did what you could. But in the end their choices are their own.'

Hereward peered up at the stars sprinkled across the vault of the heavens. 'My heart aches when I recall their faces. Yet in days past I would not have mourned them. Death is the price of battle.'

Alric cast a sympathetic glance at his friend. 'Raw feelings are the price we pay for striving to be good men.'

'You think I have now moved to the side of the angels?' Hereward gave an empty laugh. 'That I have been saved because I mourn a few poor souls?'

'I think you struggle with the burdens of your early days. But you no longer allow them to turn you away from God.'

'And if I was still the devil you said I was that first cold night in Northumbria, would I have saved those men from slaughter?' Hereward glared at the monk through the flames. Disturbed by whatever he saw in his friend's face, the monk flinched.

'I do not profess to know God's will, but I know you. I started along this road to save myself by saving you. Now I see the peace that lies within your grasp and that is reward enough.'

Staring into the fire, Hereward muttered, 'The ravens never leave me.'

'You have Vadir to keep you on the straight path now. He knows of battle and blood. He knows your mind, and he is wise. He is like a father—'

'Do not mention my father.'

Alric recoiled at the vehemence in his friend's voice. And in that moment, Hereward saw that the monk recognized the truth: that his devil could only be chained, not killed, and that it was always straining to break free.

The burning wood popped and crackled, shattering the uncomfortable silence, and then the tramp of leather shoes echoed over the dark fortifications.

Vadir cast a searching glance at Hereward, but appeared satisfied by what he saw. 'All of Cambrai is afire with news from Saint-Omer,' he boomed.

'What news that excites the Flemish would be of interest to us?' Hereward said with a shrug.

'This news will interest you more than most.' The big man squatted beside the fire, looking from one face to the other. 'Tostig Godwinson now stands on Flemish soil. No longer an earl, he has fled England an outlaw, with his wife Judith and a handful of loyal men by his side. He seeks refuge at the court of Count Baldwin. There is talk that he even seeks an alliance with William the Bastard.'

Hereward laughed without humour. 'Tostig, an outlaw. We are brought to the same level.'

Uneasy, the monk eyed his friend. 'What lies on your mind?'

The firelight glimmered in the warrior's eyes. With a lupine grin, he replied, 'Revenge.'

Chapter Thirty-Three

Hoofbeats thundered through the moonless night. In pools of dancing torchlight, the sentries opened the gates of Bruges to admit the riders. Seven there were, cloaked in black and distinguished by their close-cropped hair in the Norman style. Grim-faced, they cast only cursory glances at the deferential guards as they rode hard towards the hall occupied by two visiting Normans.

From the shadows outside the tavern, Harald Redteeth watched the riders rein in their steeds and dismount in a flurry of cloaks. He had known they were coming. The *vaettir* had told him as he had wandered the shores of the vast black sea, and they whispered still that here was purpose and meaning that would ripple out into days yet to come. While servants took the horses to water, two well-attired men, heavy with gold rings, marched out to greet the new arrivals with cheery hails. The Viking knew the wealthy men were William of Warenne and his brother-in-law Frederic. William had the ear of his namesake, William the Bastard, and had arrived in Bruges to encourage wealthy Flemings to support the Norman duke's plans to seize the throne of England. An offer of gold or ships would result in a grant of land once William took the crown, Redteeth had learned.

He studied the black-cloaked Normans' hard faces and warriors' gait as they followed William and Frederic into the hall, and felt he knew their minds. They shared blood, he and they. Normans were the spawn of the *vikingr* in days long gone. Did they still listen to the *vaettir*? Did they have fire and iron in their hearts? If only the English knew what terrors they encouraged with their kingly games.

Once the hall's door had closed, Harald Redteeth returned to the smoky confines of the tavern. In a corner, a group gathered around two men arguing over the black and white bone pieces on a merels board. On stools next to the hearth, four other men sat drinking ale from wooden cups, laughing as they swapped bawdy tales. The Viking didn't understand the words, but he recognized the rhythms of the speech and the gleam in the Flemings' eyes.

Taking his seat in the shadows, he supped his mead and waited.

When two further cups burned in his veins, the door swung open and three men sauntered in. Their bearing spoke of power and wealth, a swagger at the hips, superior gazes cast across the drinking men grown timid, sword hilts inlaid with gold. He identified the leader of the group from his aquiline nose and piercing eyes. A weak man, spoiled by good living, Harald noted. Yes, this was the one he awaited.

As the men collected their ale and settled into a corner to laugh loudly, the Viking mercenary rose, stretched, and wandered over. Ivar, his second in command, watched with dead eyes from the other side of the tavern. Redteeth grinned at his old friend. 'Soon, now,' he whispered to himself, to Ivar.

The three men looked up when he arrived at their side, still grinning. They snarled at him in Flemish, no doubt warning him to leave them alone. Harald fixed an eye on the hawk-nosed leader. 'You are Hoibrict, grandson of Count Manasses?' he asked.

The knight looked startled, but quickly regained his

composure. 'If you value unbroken bones, leave now,' he sneered in faltering English.

'But we have much to discuss,' the mercenary said, holding his arms wide.

One of the men started to stand, his fingers falling to his sword hilt as he snarled some epithet. His hand a blur, Harald snatched the man's wooden cup and drove it into his face. Teeth smashed, lips pulped. The Fleming crashed on to his back unconscious. Before the other man could rise, the Viking whipped his axe Grim against the bare throat.

'Now,' Harald said, still grinning, 'we shall talk of matters of great import, of blood-oaths, and vengeance, and death.' He ignored the tumult rising up from the other men in the tavern and fixed his gaze on Hoibrict's apprehensive face. 'My journey to this point has been long and hard. I have followed a trail of words and memories that at times seemed to take me in circles. Until I heard of a nobleman who had been shamed in a contest by a raw English warrior. The whispers I hear . . .' he fluttered the fingers of his left hand against his ear, 'tell me this proud Flemish man may lead me to the one who has wronged both of us. And then, perhaps, we can have a reckoning that will lighten both our hearts. The warrior's name is Hereward.'

He saw the light of recognition in the knight's eyes and knew all would be well.

CHAPTER THIRTY-FOUR

'Confront Tostig and he will have you killed,' Alric protested, throwing his arms around Hereward to hold him back.

'Listen to the monk,' Vadir boomed. A wall of muscle and bone, he stepped in front of the younger man. 'Normally he speaks with an ale-tongue, but this time he's right.'

Hereward's anger burned. He threw Alric to one side with a ferocious sweep of his arm and drew his sword, pressing the tip against Vadir's chest. 'Out of my way, old man. I have waited too long for this moment.'

With his good eye, the big Mercian peered down his nose at his younger companion and then stepped aside. Hereward pushed by him towards the hall.

'What are you doing?' the monk shouted at Vadir. 'Stop him.'

'He is his own man. He lives or dies by his choices alone.'

Behind them, the horses stamped the wet turf and snorted hot, clouding breath into the cold air. The bishop had offered them double their wage to stay on in Cambrai, but Hereward rebuffed all his pleas. Only one thing now mattered. The ride from the monastery had been hard and fast, with Hereward just managing to stay ahead of his two pursuing companions. Saint-Omer had been abuzz with talk of Tostig and his wife's arrival, and it had been easy to locate the hall Count Baldwin had already presented to his English son. Partly constructed long ago from stone and now extended with a timber frame and roof to emphasize its status, the building stood in its own estate with views across the town and the green, and the gold and brown Flemish countryside beyond.

Hereward seethed that Tostig should be so rewarded even in his time of failure. Bursting through the door, he found the former earl and his wife in conversation with three loyal Northumbrian followers. Recognizing Hereward, the men stepped back, hands falling to their sword hilts, but the Mercian could see they were afraid.

When he marched across the hall, Judith gathered her dress and stepped to meet him. The warrior kept his gaze firmly on Tostig. 'You would hide behind your wife now?'

'Hereward, there is no need for threats,' Judith urged, concerned. 'You risk only your own life. Things are not as they were—'

'Who here is going to stop me gaining my revenge for the plot that took the life of my love?' His eyes glittered.

'They are,' Tostig replied with a faint sneer. He waved a lazy hand towards the door.

Glancing back, Hereward saw Alric and Vadir forced in at spear-point, followed by a stream of soldiers in mail and helmets. The force flowed around the edge of the hall. Men caught his arms and knocked his sword from his hand. These were not inexperienced men torn from the land to support Tostig, but well-trained, professional troops, part of Saint-Omer's standing defence.

'Count Baldwin has saved your neck,' Hereward said, 'for now.'

'More than that. The count has made me a trusted ally,' Tostig replied.

A man with long black hair streaked with silver and a drooping moustache and pointed beard pushed his way past the soldiers. Hereward saw from his gold amulet and rings and his fine ochre tunic that the new arrival was a man of standing.

'This is Wulfric Rabe, castellan of Saint-Omer,' Tostig said.

Turfrida's father. Hereward recalled the gentle time he had spent with Turfrida and wished it could have been longer.

'Count Baldwin has made me the deputy commander here,' the former earl continued, 'and working alongside my new friend I will ensure peace and stability in Flanders.'

'As you did in Northumbria?'

Judith cautioned Hereward with her eyes.

Tostig looked as though he was about to fly into a rage. But then his shoulders sagged and exhaustion crumpled his face. 'Set him free,' he muttered, waving the back of his hand towards the soldiers. 'You were unfairly treated in Eoferwic, I see that now. We were both victims of my brother's plotting.' His right fist bunched. 'Though we are blood, Harold and I, we are brothers no more.'

'He betrayed you.'

'Harold betrays everyone sooner or later,' Tostig snapped. 'He has made one of your own Earl of Northumbria. A Mercian.' He shook his head in disbelief. 'Kin of his greatest, most hated rivals, but now they serve a purpose – to unite England and thereby keep William the Bastard in Normandy. And I . . . I am sent into exile like some murdering criminal.'

'Like me,' Hereward said.

'Work with me against our common enemy. I need good fighting men. I have lost my huscarls, and though I have these Flemings under my command—'

'You cannot take them to England and risk starting a war.'

Tostig nodded.

Hereward spat. 'And you believe I could raise my sword in your defence?'

'Listen to my husband,' Judith said. He turned to look at her and saw deep lines etched in her face, the mark of the toll taken upon her by the flight from England. 'You are more alike than you might think,' she continued. 'Listen to your heart. Listen to God. Find forgiveness.'

'We do not need to fight any longer,' Tostig said. He beckoned to a slave for a cup of mead and downed it in one go. 'I was misled by my brother. And now, see, we are two Englishmen in a strange land, far from the fields we know, both exiles, both cut adrift. We can find common purpose.'

'Listen to him,' Vadir urged. When Hereward glanced back, the elder Mercian gave a knowing wink.

Three years earlier, Hereward knew he would have ignored all entreaties, ignored even his own safety, and carved a path to kill the man with his bare hands if necessary. Yet now he could see his one-time enemy was right. Tostig was just as much a victim of his brother's plotting as was Hereward.

Steadying himself, he said, 'My sword, and the employ of my friends, comes at a high price.'

'Done.' Tostig broke into a triumphant grin, as if he had already struck a blow at his brother. 'Count Baldwin has not only put his forces at my disposal, but also granted me the taxes collected in Saint-Omer. I will pay you well. And with the fleet he has promised me, we shall see who eventually sits upon the throne of England.' He hurled the mead-cup across the hall in an explosion of defiance.

Out in the thin sunshine, Hereward pressed the heel of his hand against his forehead. 'For nigh on two years I have dreamed of closing my hands around Tostig's throat and in the blink of an eye he is my ally. I feel as if I am moving through yesterday's fog.'

'This is the business of leaders, little man,' Vadir laughed, slapping his friend on the back. 'It's all fog and smoke, as murky as hell. You cannot trust any of the bastards, but if you keep your eye on an advantage you'll come out of it with gold at the least.'

'All I want is Harold dead and Tidhild avenged.'

Vadir smiled. 'Do not turn your nose up at gold.'

Hereward still felt unsure he had done the right thing. He allowed himself to be led into the crowded streets of Saint-Omer to find a tavern. When they had eaten their fill of bread and blood pudding, and Vadir was preparing to settle in for a day's drinking to celebrate the confirmation of their winter employment, Hereward took his leave. He felt as adrift as he had during the days of his youth when he had drunk and fought and robbed and tormented the good people around Barholme. Would killing Tostig have satisfied him? Would killing Harold?

He found Wulfric Rabe's house easily, a newly built timber hall with two floors set in a sprawling estate, grand enough for a military leader and the defender of the people. Turfrida stood in the doorway, smiling.

'When did you return?' Hereward asked, shocked.

'Three days ago. I knew I would meet you here.'

He laughed. '*I* did not know I would be here until last night.'

Turfrida's eyes sparkled. 'Come. Let me show you the streets of my home. Which is your home now.'

She took his hand and led him back among the houses and workshops, amid the scent of woodsmoke and the apples stored in the barns, and she whispered the stories of her childhood that made the town and the past come alive for him.

By the time the frosts whitened the fields and bejewelled the cobwebs hanging from the thatch, they had become closer still. On windswept hilltops, she pointed to the sky and told him the meaning in the patterns the crows made, and the secret words in their calls, and she led him to the magic pool and sacred wells where wishes would be answered. When Christmas neared, they kissed beneath the mistletoe, and were caught mid-embrace by Vadir who mocked in a good-natured way before punching Hereward firmly on the arm in a gesture of respect. And as the church bells pealed in joyous celebration on Christmas morn, the warrior found himself at peace.

But there was little peace in Saint-Omer. Mercenaries flooded into the town from all over Flanders, many of them Englishmen. Hereward came to understand that Tostig was amassing his own army, paid for by Count Baldwin: to attack Harold Godwinson, perhaps, or to invade England, to take the throne for himself.

Rarely seen, Tostig hid away in his house, plotting and brooding, but Hereward often saw Judith trudging alone through the snow or the icy rain to the church to kneel on the frozen flagstones and pray. Turfrida's father was a serious man, too, but he laughed loud and long when drunk, and under his daughter's subtle spell he grew to like Hereward. He put the Mercian in charge of training the Saint-Omer force, pulling him to one side one cold morning to urge him to pay particular attention to the young, inexperienced men.

His memories of Cambrai still burning hot, Hereward trained the young recruits better than he ever had before. They learned to hate him, for he forced them to practise with their spears until long after the sun had set, and a circle of torches illuminated the field. They repeated strategies and tactics until they were sick and weary, and he cursed them and berated them, and lifted them up when their spirits fell.

One morning when the snow was thick, Vadir arrived at the door swaddled in furs and a thick woollen cloak, blowing on his hands and stamping his leather-shod feet. 'Stop hiding by your hearth like a sewing woman,' he boomed, 'there is work to do.'

Baffled, Hereward wrapped himself in his own cloak and followed the elder Mercian out into the bitter morning.

Clapping a hand on his friend's shoulder, Vadir said, 'I watch you, little man, with this one good eye. And I have seen your dedication to teaching the apple-cheeked, bright-eyed, wooden-headed boys. But you must not neglect your own skills.'

'My skills are already honed.'

'And that is where you show your inexperience. If you want to keep your head fixed on your shoulders, you can never stop learning. Someone, somewhere, will always find a new way to kill you, and you must be ready and at your best.' The big man led Hereward to the field outside the ramparts where a bad-tempered soldier waited, his hood pulled up against the bitter wind. He held a bow and a pouch filled with newly fletched arrows.

'What is this?' Hereward asked, suspicious.

'It is called a bow, little man,' Vadir replied with sardonic humour. 'Your education truly is limited.'

'What need do I have for that?' Hereward recalled using the bow for hunting when he roamed the Mercian countryside, and had even seen a few men use arrows in battle.

'Across Flanders, Normandy . . . everywhere on this side of the whale road, men are skilled in archery to kill other men.'

Hereward snorted. 'When you kill, you need to see a man's eyes, feel his blood pumping over you. A sword, an axe, a spear . . . these are the honourable ways to slay. That . . .' he pointed at the bow, 'is for cowards, who would hide behind a tree, fire an arrow into a man's back and then run away before they are seen.'

Vadir roared with laughter. 'Will you protest as much when you are lying on the ground looking like a spiny-backed igil, or will you fight fire with fire? Learn. You may need this skill one day.'

Irritated, Hereward took the bow from the soldier and listened to the instructions on where to place the arrow and how to draw the greased hemp string. He sniffed with contempt, set the arrow in place and flexed the bow. When he released the string, the arrow flipped into the air.

Resting his hands on his knees, Vadir laughed until he wept. Hereward snatched up the shaft and tried again. The string slipped out of the notch and the arrow flopped impotently to the snow.

'Not as easy as it looks, is it?' the big man chuckled, wiping his eyes.

Determined to excel, Hereward persisted. When his fingers were numb and he was chilled to the bone, he could finally send the arrow across the field, but with little accuracy. 'Enough,' he snapped. 'You waste my time. I will never have a need for this weapon.' He thrust the bow into the hands of the soldier and marched back into Saint-Omer, with Vadir's mockery ringing in his ears.

*   *   *

Few would risk travel when the coldest weather bit, but men trailed into town every few days and made their way to Tostig's hall with snippets of news from England. Rumours swirled like the last season's leaves caught in the wind. King Edward was ailing; his days were numbered; he had fallen into a fever-sleep, never waking, but ranting and raving about angels and devils hovering over his bed. William the Bastard had sent men to hide in London and report back to him on the plans of Harold Godwinson. Those who failed to provide useful information were put to the sword. And in his Normandy redoubt, the duke drew up plans for war. Gold was donated to the Church by the sackful, and William played the part of a devout man to gain the Pope's support for invasion, so Hereward heard in the tavern.

Tostig emerged from his gloom on the eighth day after the Christmas feast, proclaiming to all that the coming year would be better than any in living memory. A messenger from Count Baldwin had told him that his ships would be ready when the worst of the cold weather passed, so Alric heard from a slave in the house.

On Twelfth Night, when the festivities were long concluded and Hereward drifted in drunken sleep, Turfrida called his name. Lurching to the door, he found her with a tear-streaked face peering from the depths of her hood. She pushed her way inside and threw her arms around him beside the red embers in the hearth.

'What is amiss?' he asked. 'Your father—'

'My father is well and wrapped in ale-sleep.' With a shudder, she threw off her hood. 'I dreamed of ravens, a cloud of them blackening the sky.'

'What does that mean?' he asked, trying to throw off his stupor.

Turfrida took his hand. 'You must not sail with Tostig. You must stay here with me.'

'How can I? I have taken his pay.'

'We must marry. My father will be happy that his new son is a military man of great reputation and he will want you to stay here to defend Saint-Omer.'

Hereward gaped. 'Marry?'

'If you sail with Tostig, you will never return. This is a truth that has already been written.'

'But if I am needed—'

'You are needed here more, by me. And you will be needed by many others in times to come. A great destiny is being written for you, Hereward, but it will all turn to ashes if you do not heed me this night.'

Struggling to understand, Hereward prowled his house for the rest of the night, torn between Turfrida's warning and the fear that he would bring shame upon himself if he walked away from the call of battle.

The time of peace had passed.

CHAPTER THIRTY-FIVE

5 January 1066

Shadows flickered at the edge of the room. In them, Death waited. The king lay on his bed, clinging to the last of his life. His skin was the colour of ashes, his face little more than a skull draped in parchment. His breath rasped out slowly and then stopped for what seemed like an age until the two watching men felt convinced it was the monarch's last. Time and again. Beside the hearth, Redwald struggled to warm himself against the roaring fire. His bones felt as cold as the thick, grey ice that lined the banks of the Thames. A log cracked and spat and the young man jumped, then felt foolish. He realized he was holding his own breath tight in his chest.

Harold Godwinson ranged around the bed, casting hate-filled glares at the dying man. Sweat stained the armpits of his brown tunic and left a black streak down his back. The gold rings at his wrist jangled with every grim step. In the firelight, the earl's shadow appeared to move of its own accord. Every time it loomed over the bedridden form, Redwald winced and stared at his master's flexing fingers and the pale curve of Edward's throat.

Had they been in that sour-ale-reeking room since the autumn leaves had fallen? Since the summer fields of golden barley, or the spring flowers? Time had no meaning here, Redwald thought. His head spun with echoing moans and cries and shouts and threats, and a mounting desolation. He had stood by and watched, and done nothing, when perhaps he could have ended the king's suffering with a word of guidance, or warning. But the torrent of abuse had crept up on him. At first, only sly urging had echoed around the room, then insistent demands, then menaces. By the time Harold had hurled himself on to the bed to shake the supine form, Redwald had realized it was too late. Trapped in his complicity, his silent observation had been an encouragement to his master. He might as well have joined in the persecution. He felt only numb.

How had he sunk to such depths? Redwald recalled the Christmas feast and Harold pressing the king to name him as heir to the throne. Edward had smiled politely and whispered, 'In good time.' The next day had seen the rehearsal for the consecration of the abbey, the chanting of the monks ringing off the stone walls and the sweet smell of the smouldering spices filling the air. From the back of the nave, Redwald had watched Harold berate the monarch under the arch of the great west door. In the candlelight, the earl's face had appeared like a snarling beast, his teeth bared, his hands shaking with passion. And, trembling from the cold, the weakening monarch had nodded thoughtfully, and smiled, and then shuffled away to join his wife for the Mass.

That was the moment Harold had decided to leave any vestige of morality behind, Redwald now realized. He remembered the earl's face framed in the candlelight, and how he had puzzled over the fixed stare and strange calm that had come over his master. Harold had made his peace with what he needed to do. Redwald remembered hurrying to the casket that contained the relic of John the Baptist and pressing his forehead against the cold wood. What lay within was not comforting. It taunted him with visions of mortality and sacrifice.

How far will you travel along the road to damnation to achieve your heart's desire? Harold had said. How far? To the end, if the prize is great enough.

Edith appeared at the door, kneading her hands together in worry. 'What news . . . ?'

The earl silenced her with a cold stare. 'Leave. You should not see this.'

'The bishops would pray at the bedside,' Edith whispered.

'No. Are you a fool?' Redwald thought his master was about to strike his sister. 'Tell them the king has woken and insists that no one troubles him.'

When Redwald saw the ivory cross clutched in the queen's slender fingers, he almost laughed. What prayers had passed her lips, he wondered? How could she ever make her peace with this, watching the man she had wed destroyed by degrees by her own brother, urging it on, in fact, with the aid she had given by keeping the earls and the thegns, the servants and the healer away. It was the queen who had lied to the court that her husband was sick with the fever, and who had reported back to the concerned men of the Witan that Edward had slipped into the unwaking sleep.

'The healer has prepared another salve of the healing herb,' she ventured.

'Leave it outside the door.'

'The healer wishes—'

'Leave!'

Bowing her head, Edith scurried out, the hem of her sapphire dress sweeping across the worn boards. The emotion drained from Harold's features. He turned to watch the juddering rise and fall of the king's chest for a moment.

'This man . . . this weak old man,' the earl said bitterly. 'What drives him to deny me such a simple thing? One word. That is all it would have taken to prevent so much suffering. One word and he could have been left alone to slide easily into the arms of God. His days are numbered. You can almost see the life slipping from his weary limbs, yet still he resists. Why?'

The room reeked of impending death, a bitter odour that Redwald had come to know well. He tried to answer his master, but his mouth was dry.

Harold leaned over the bed. 'Name me heir,' he roared at the king, grabbing Edward's shoulders and shaking the old man so that he flopped like a child's woollen doll.

Stepping forward, Redwald put on a grin and a honeyed voice. 'Hold fast, my master,' he urged, 'or what remains of his wits will fall out of his ears.'

The words died in his throat when the monarch's eyes snapped open. Redwald leapt back, afraid of the accusation he might see in the milky orbs.

Calming, Harold let the old man fall back on to the bed. 'Now,' the Earl of Wessex said, 'make your peace with God and leave everything right here. Name me as your heir.'

Harold snapped round at a disturbance outside the door. Fast feet echoed on timber, accompanied by muffled voices. Edith burst in with Stigand, Archbishop of Canterbury, striding at her heels. He flashed a warning glance at the earl before pausing at the foot of the deathbed to study the king. His gaze wavered over the bruises and the cuts, but he said nothing. The cleric was a dour man, as old as Edward, but filled with a vitality that belied his years. Redwald didn't like him. Stigand had a sharp tongue and a sour manner and was cruel to those he felt were unimportant to him. Yet he tolerated Harold, recognizing the power the earl would one day wield. Over his long life, five popes had excommunicated him for holding two sees at once, Winchester and Canterbury. But he had clung on, amassing both power and wealth until he was now perhaps the richest cleric in England. And it showed in his fine garments, Redwald thought: a brown linen robe, delicately embroidered with yellow crosses underneath a sumptuous black woollen cloak edged with fur and held at the neck by a golden clasp.

'The archbishop insisted he pray over the king,' Edith stuttered.

'You have no right to keep me from Edward's side.' Stigand levelled his cold gaze at Harold. 'He needs my ministrations.'

'Pray for him, then,' Harold snapped. He dismissed Edith with a brusque wave of his hand. The queen shuffled away, casting worried backward glances.

Pressing his palms together, the archbishop knelt at the end of the bed and began to intone in Latin. The earl paced around in mounting frustration. The rolling rhythm of Stigand's voice washed over Redwald, but the young man didn't feel the knot in his stomach ease as it would have done in church. He feared he was beyond God's help now.

The archbishop finished his prayers and stood. He eyed Harold for a moment and then said, 'I understand your heavy heart. If Edward does not name you as heir, it leaves many questions still to be asked, and a degree of uncertainty over your worthiness.'

The earl ground his teeth, then forced a smile. 'If Edward had been well, we both know I would have been his only choice. William the Bastard would destroy everything we have built here. The king understood that.'

Stigand nodded.

'There would be no place for true Englishmen like you or me,' Harold continued, warming to his theme as he searched the archbishop's unwavering gaze. 'And Edward's ties to Normandy were not as strong in private as he liked to make us think. Though he sent me to the duke to discuss these matters of succession, it was simply a ploy to keep William sweet.'

Stigand nodded again. Redwald knew this was a lie, but neither man appeared ready to recognize it.

'When I sit upon the throne, I will need a good adviser with your long experience. Indeed, I would say I could not rule well without it.'

Stigand smiled, and suddenly Redwald understood the reason for the archbishop's abrupt intrusion. Here was a man as skilled in the games of kings as Harold.

A low moan shattered the two men's silent communication,

and they turned to survey the dying monarch. Edward's lips worked soundlessly, his eyelids flickering.

'He tries to speak,' Redwald called, one hand clasped to his head, the other pointing.

'About time,' the earl grunted, and pressed his ear close to the dying man's mouth. Stigand hurried to the other side of the bed and leaned in too.

When the king's lids fluttered open, his eyes rolled, pausing now and then to focus on the shadows in the corners as if he saw things standing there.

'He is dreaming,' Redwald hissed. 'He does not know we are here.'

'I know.' The king spat the two words like an epithet. 'Listen, then,' he croaked. 'Listen closely, Harold Godwinson, for this is the moment you have worked so hard to reach, and sold your soul to gain.'

Harold smiled.

Edward's whispery voice barely reached beyond the end of the bed. Eager to have an end to the long period of suffering, Redwald strained to hear what was being said, but he knew it would be beyond his station to draw closer.

'No.' Stigand's hoarse exclamation sounded like a pebble dropped on wood. Redwald saw that all the blood had drained from the archbishop's face. His features had grown taut, his wide-eyed gaze fastened upon each movement of the king's mouth. Harold's triumphant grin was slowly fading.

The cleric jumped to his feet, staggering back, one hand to his mouth. 'A prophecy,' he gasped. 'The dead have spoken to him.' Spinning on his heel, he almost ran from the bedside. Harold rose too, running one trembling hand through his hair.

'What did the king say?' Redwald uttered, not wanting to hear the answer.

'Lies.' Harold stood for a moment, lost to his thoughts. Then he replied in a distracted voice, 'He said he was visited by two monks he knew from his youth. And they told him that all those who held the highest offices in his kingdom were not what they seem. They were servants of the Devil. And within the year they will be washed away in a tide of blood, and England will be delivered into the hands of the enemy. By fire. And sword. And the havoc of war.'

Redwald felt gripped by terror. The dead had spoken through Edward. God had cursed them all for their sins.

In a rage, Harold flung himself on to the bed, striking and shaking the king. Redwald could only watch, though he thought the monarch would be torn apart. In his heart, he knew he should stop the assault. But as God was his witness, he wanted an end to it, as if only death could expunge the terrible prophecy.

And so he watched as Harold's rage burned as fierce as the fire in the hearth. Tears glinting in his eyes, his master pressed a hand against the king's mouth and nose and held tight. And after long moments Edward lay still, and would never move again.

Calming himself, Harold wiped his mouth with the back of his trembling hand. He looked deep into the king's dead eyes, but what passed through his head Redwald would never know. Turning to the young man, the earl glowered beneath heavy brows. 'Nothing of this must ever pass your lips.'

'I am your trusted servant. It will never be spoken of.'

Harold accepted the vow with a curt nod, and his mood lightened. With a smile, he said, 'Now hurry from this place and spread the word that with his dying breath Edward named me as his chosen successor. I will speak to Edith and she will support us in this account, as will Stigand, so the Witan can be convened. Then find a scribe who can record an account of this ending that meets our needs. Let us be jubilant, and proud, for a new day dawns, and a new age for England. Make haste. I would be crowned king before tomorrow is done.'

Chapter Thirty-Six

6 January 1066

The gold crown gleamed in the flickering candlelight.
Though shadows danced across the stone walls of Westminster Abbey, the emeralds and rubies incorporated from the
circlet of the great King Alfred shone with an inner fire. An
apprehensive hush fell across the shivering men and women
pressed into the dark confines for the second time that day. Misty
trails of breath drifted in the icy air. His forehead shimmering
with holy oil, Harold Godwinson relaxed in the coronation
chair and allowed himself a slight smile of satisfaction. Edward
lay interred in the cold ground beneath the abbey's flagstones,
and though the funeral feast still cooled on the table in the
king's hall, the Earl of Wessex already had everything he ever
wanted. Nestling the jewelled sceptre in the crook of his right
arm, he grasped the blackwood rod in his left hand, stared at
the gold cross on the high altar and waited.

Redwald felt a swell of pride. Turning his attention from
his master, he examined the faces of the congregation, the
earls, thegns, bishops, wives, and Westminster's community
of monks huddled at the back. In them he saw an odd

mixture of relief and worry. He knew they were all relieved that the long period of troubling uncertainty was over and the succession had been decided. Yet they also dreaded what was to come. Thanks to the archbishop's loose lips, news of Edward's dying prophecy had swept through the court, out into London, and in all likelihood was making its way across England despite the winter snows. They were poor subjects, he thought, these frightened sheep. In taking the crown, Harold had saved all gathered in that church from the terrible deprivations they would surely suffer under a man with as bloody a reputation as William the Bastard. England remained free to enjoy its wealth and its art and its law. And the highest in the land were free to enjoy the comforts their status had brought them.

The coronation had gone well under the stern but self-satisfied eye of Stigand. In his madder-dyed red robe, Harold had been a splash of blood amid the golden candlelight. Redwald thought he had seen his master's hands shaking when he processed into the abbey church, but now he looked calm. His white pallium luminous, the Archbishop of Canterbury had intoned the liturgy drawn up by St Dunstan. When his clear voice had soared to the shadow-cloaked roof, a clearly humbled Harold had taken communion. Yet his words rang out as he delivered the oath to govern faithfully, with justice and mercy. The solemn choir of monks had been in fine voice, their stirring rendition of 'Zadok the Priest' from the Book of Kings washing into every corner of that vast space. And then Harold Godwinson had removed his robe and sat rigid in the coronation chair while the archbishop consecrated him sovereign with the anointment of the holy oil. He would be a fine king, and Redwald's own future would be assured. Here was the culmination of the young man's choices, and they had all been good ones. He felt his eyes drawn once more to the casket holding the shankbone of John the Baptist, and shook his head clear of the thoughts that threatened to tarnish the day.

What would Hereward have said if he had been here to

witness this momentous event, he wondered? Would his brother have forgiven him?

With an acute awareness of spectacle, the Archbishop of Canterbury raised the crown high over his head. Redwald's chest tightened. When the crown came down on Harold, tumultuous shouts of 'The king! The king!' boomed out across the congregation.

It was done. And whatever would be, would be.

When the new king processed out of the abbey into the bitter night, the archbishop followed, and then Ealdred of Eoferwic, the earls and the thegns. Redwald waited until the church was almost empty, enjoying the growing quiet.

In the king's hall, the fire roared high. Cloaks were thrown off and cups of ale downed and filled once more from the iron cauldrons hanging in the corner. Servants heaved wooden plates and bowls laden with goose, pork and beef on to the feasting table, a grand spread that made the funeral meal look like a beggar's scraps. But Redwald thought too many faces remained taut, and the urgency of the drinking was more to quell fear than in celebration.

Flushed from the ale, Harold swept over when the jugglers and tumblers danced around the tables, raising laughter and cheers. He pulled Redwald to one side and whispered, 'The coronation went well?'

Redwald, who had remained sober as he always did when in attendance on Harold, heard a querying note at the end of the sentence and knew his master was seeking approval. He thought it a sign of weakness, perhaps fuelled by guilt at how he had achieved the crown, but he smiled and replied, 'The majesty of the occasion brought tears to the eyes of all present.'

'Really?'

Redwald nodded. 'England now has a king who will be loved at home and feared by enemies wherever they might be.'

Harold nodded. 'Do not think that I am not aware of your loyalty, and the talents you have employed in my rise to power. You will be well rewarded.'

I expect to be, the young man thought, and for the briefest moment his head swam with visions of two brothers laughing as they hunted waterfowl in those long-gone Mercian days.

'Your wise advice must be close at hand at all times from now on,' the new king continued. 'I will ensure you have a station that meets both our needs.'

When Harold returned to the feasting, Redwald slipped away. The celebrations bored him. He saw little gain in them now that everyone was drunk. He needed to attend to the maggot squirming deep in his head.

Was Hereward still alive somewhere? Had he been wrong to put his brother from his thoughts once the warrior had vanished from Eoferwic?

Brooding, he tramped through the crisp snow to the abbey once more. It lay silent and still now. Pausing at the door, he peered through the dark in the direction of the small house he had shared with Asketil, Beric and Hereward when they were at court. Memories still haunted him of the night that Hereward had fled. Absently, he rested his hand on his gold and whale-bone sword hilt and thought of a black river of days stretching behind him and ahead. That terrible night had set his life on a new course.

Inside the abbey church, he went straight to the reliquary, unable to resist the lure of the casket any longer. Flicking open the lid, he let his fingers encircle the old bone. He found no peace there.

'Redwald?'

The young man jumped so sharply at the voice, he almost threw the casket away. It was Hild, wrapped in a blue cloak, her pretty face flushed from the cold. 'What is that? I have seen you visit it many times,' she said, peering at the box.

'A memory.'

She nodded and smiled sadly. 'A memory of Hereward. I understand.' Her voice became comforting. 'You were close, but he is not blood. You must put him out of your mind.'

Redwald laughed inwardly at the unconscious irony of her

statement. How could he ever forget his brother, the man who had befriended him when he felt lost and alone? Who had given him a place in the world, and offered only loyalty? He closed the casket and stepped away from it.

'I saw you leave the feast.' Hild's eyes fluttered, saying more than her words. Then, as if she realized she had been too brazen, she added, 'I would not have come here at this hour, unannounced, but—'

Redwald waved his hand to dismiss her excuse. Hild was younger than him by a year, but she had a drive that would have done Harold proud. Since Harold's patronage had become clear, she had set her sights upon him, the young man knew, and she had been relentless in her pursuit. 'It is good to see you,' he said.

She smiled, pleased at the attention. Redwald saw in her eye a hint of triumph; she considered her manipulation was working. His black mood still enveloped him, and he felt colder than he had done even in the snowy night. He needed more. She seemed to sense his thoughts for her eyes widened, but when he leaned in to kiss her plump lips she placed a cold finger against his chin. 'No,' she said with mock indignation.

Removing her finger, he slipped his hand round her waist. She resisted only a little. Pulling her close, Redwald enjoyed the weight of her breasts on his chest and her hips against his.

'What drives you?' she breathed.

'I have given my life to one aim and I cannot rest until I have achieved it. But sometimes the road is a lonely one.' He let the words hang, knowing that she would respond.

'I . . . I would accompany you on your journey.' On tiptoes now, her hands on his shoulder, her face filled his vision. He felt surprised to see the desire there.

For one moment, he pressed his lips against hers, and allowed himself to float in the peaceful dark of the embrace. The rush of emotions shocked him. He became afraid he might cry like a child. Distracting himself, he allowed his hand to move to the curve of her breast.

'I . . . I cannot,' she stuttered, although he knew she felt the opposite. 'I would not be used by you and discarded.'

'You and I are much alike,' he said, staring into her dark eyes. As he spoke, he made up his mind. 'And would you resist if I said I would marry you?'

Hild started as if she had been burned. Her lips worked, but no sound came out.

'I will marry you and protect you and be the husband you long for. But tonight I need comfort from you, for I cannot face the long hours till sunrise alone.'

After the briefest hesitation, she nodded. 'But . . . but you must not tell my father. Or anyone at court. I would—'

'I will never tell a soul.'

Redwald pulled her out of the abbey and across the snow to the large house Harold had secured for him not far from the king's hall. Pushing her towards the bed, he tore off her headdress and grasped her lush brown hair in his fists, pulling her face towards him. He kissed her long and hard this time, and when he broke the embrace her breath caught in her throat. Fire burned within him, and a desperate need for release. He pulled off her dress and her white linen shift and thrust her on to the bed, running his hands over her breasts and down between her legs. She was ready for him and there was no longer any pretence of resistance. Holding her wrists with his left hand, he bit her neck and breasts and pinched her, and when she cried out he was surprised how much it excited him. The more she gave in to his advances, the rougher he played. Here was his release, he thought; here was his escape from the pain in his heart.

The next morning they locked eyes across the snow-swept palace enclosure, and shared a secret smile, and in the days to come they began to make plans to wed. Redwald informed Harold, who slapped the young man on the back and roared with laughter. Amid a stream of crude humour, he thrust a cup of mead into Redwald's hands and said it was the best thing that could have happened. A man needed a wife, and a soon-to-be-great man needed a wife like Hild. Her father, a balding Wessex thegn called Blacwin, was just as enthusiastic.

Barely two weeks after Harold's coronation, the joyous mood faded. A strange ship sailed up the grey Thames and moored on the frosted bank beside the palace. In shining helmets with broad nose-shields and long mail shirts, the crew looked dressed for war, but one ship was not a threat. Yet from their armour all could see these grim-faced men were Normans. A dark mood fell across the palace as word spread, colder even than that bitter winter.

Five men disembarked, the only ones not wearing armour, but in their black hooded cloaks and with their fierce dark eyes they appeared just as menacing. At the gates they waited, seemingly oblivious of the cold, while Harold's advisers debated the appropriate course of action. When they were admitted to the palace, the five Normans strode directly to the king's hall. Harold waited on his throne. On either side of the monarch, the ranks of earls and thegns stood like sentinels; a show of strength. Barely visible, Redwald waited in the shadows just behind the throne, studying the new arrivals.

The Norman leader was a tall, slender man with a sharp nose and a heavy brow. The translator introduced him as Odo of Bayeux, the representative of William, Duke of Normandy. Redwald had spent much of his time since the coronation diligently learning all he could about the Normans from Harold. He knew Odo was much more than that pallid description. As the half-brother of William the Bastard, the Norman was one of the duke's most senior advisers, both a cleric and a warrior, renowned for crushing all opposition to William's word. Angel and Devil.

Harold knit his brow. 'I welcome you to my hall,' he said with little enthusiasm. 'What is the reason for this visit?'

Echoing his master, the translator said in halting English, 'I bring a message from William of Normandy. He would know why you have usurped the throne that was promised to him.'

Harold sniffed. 'There was no promise, as your master

knows full well. He seeks any excuse to claim what he has always wanted, a prize far greater than he deserves. I am King Edward's chosen heir and that is the end of it.'

Odo seemed unmoved by Harold's dismissal, almost, Redwald thought, as if he expected the response and a decision had already been taken on how to proceed. The Norman nodded slowly, then spoke quietly to his translator, who said simply, 'Then only one course can lie ahead: war.'

CHAPTER THIRTY-SEVEN

3 June 1066

'Kiss her! Kiss her! Then take her home for a good plunging!' Vadir bellowed from the back of the hall. The assembled friends and family of Hereward and Turfrida laughed. Still drunk from the previous night's feast, the red-haired man's good eye struggled to focus. Alric dug his elbow in his companion's ribs in a futile attempt to shut him up.

Cheeks flushing, Wulfric Rabe glared at the towering bear of a man. Intoning 'I give you care of my daughter', the castellan nodded to Hereward. Cupping the back of his bride's head, the new husband pulled his wife close and kissed her firmly on the lips. The throng trilled their support for the union, and patted their chests above their hearts. When the warrior pulled back from the embrace, the monk saw Turfrida's eyes flash with affection and knew the decision had been a good one.

Taking his new bride by the hand, Hereward led her through the hall. Alric allowed himself a sly smile. He knew the fierce warrior had been like a frightened child, tossing and turning all night at the prospect of the morning's ceremony. The long negotiations with Wulfric over his daughter's future had gone smoothly, and the scribe had been summoned to draw up the contract that would stand Turfrida in good stead in the eyes of the law. The monk muttered a quiet prayer. This was God's work indeed, he thought, a soul saved. He marvelled at the calm he now saw in the man he had first encountered rising from a pool of blood. Perhaps there was hope for him too, Alric thought. The wound of his own crime still felt raw, and barely a week passed when he did not shed a tear for the life he had cruelly stolen. But the blackness that had enveloped him in those early days had lifted, a little. He could see the light.

When the men gathered around Hereward and clapped his back and whispered crude hints in his ear, the women took Turfrida to one side and danced in a circle while the harpist played a jaunty tune. Alric cast one eye towards his friend's new father, who was engaged in intense conversation with two wealthy men. Gilbert of Ghent and William of Warenne both had close ties with the Norman court, Alric knew. He had overheard that Wulfric sought to uncover what they knew of William the Bastard's plans and what it would mean for Flanders. In one corner, Judith stood alone, watching the conversation. Although she had given her blessing and smiled through the ceremony, Alric thought how sad Tostig's wife looked, almost as though she were in mourning. She feared for her husband, he guessed.

Hauled to the back of the hall where the wedding feast of goose, pork, beef, bread, cheese and sweet cakes was laid out on a creaking table, Hereward found a cup of ale thrust into his hand with a rousing encouragement to down it in one. When his oath had been sealed and the other men had fallen upon the food and drink, Alric and Vadir pulled their friend to one side.

'You do not regret staying here while our former master sails to wreak his revenge on his brother Harold?' Vadir asked, gulping back his ale. 'Tostig spent long enough persuading you to go with him.'

'You too,' Hereward pointed out.

'You are such a little man. How could I leave you to drink all this ale alone?'

'I am sure he is filled with regrets,' Alric said in an acid tone. 'Why, he could be grunting in the company of sweat-stained men like you instead of falling into the soft embrace of his new wife.'

'I would wager he still dreams of sticking his sword into flesh,' Vadir replied with a broad grin.

'The sooner we get a new king on the throne, the sooner I will live without the yoke of exile around my neck.' Hereward swilled down a cup of ale.

Vadir levelled a cautionary eye. 'Tostig's fight is not your fight.'

When the fire had died down to glowing embers, Hereward took Turfrida's hand and together they leapt the hearth to seal their handfasting. But the cheers ebbed away as a messenger burst in, searching for Wulfric. The two men exchanged insistent whispers in one corner before the castellan hurried to speak with Gilbert and William, and then finally edged to Judith. Her features grew pale as if she knew what was to come. After Wulfric had spoken to her for a moment, she bowed her head, her eyes filling with tears, and hurried from the hall.

'Looks grim,' Vadir muttered, swaying from the ale. 'That cannot be good for Tostig.'

Seeing the two Mercians eyeing him, Wulfric came over. 'Tostig will not be returning,' the castellan said in his thick Flemish accent. 'He sailed his fleet to the Isle of Wight, where he took on provisions, and then proceeded to raid the English coast.'

'I wager Harold Godwinson took that well,' Vadir growled.

'The new king called out all his ships and his army and drove his brother back. Tostig would not have taken such a defeat well. He has been consumed by rage for his betrayal for too long.'

'Then why does he not return to Flanders?' Hereward asked.

'He took his fleet to raid England's east coast, and there your own – the earls Edwin and Morcar – soundly thrashed him,' Wulfric replied, his tone grave. 'With his tail between his legs, he has sailed to Scotland. He plans to stay with his old ally King Malcolm for the summer. But . . .' He paused, lost to reflection for a moment. 'My messenger tells me Tostig has sent word to Harald of Norway, requesting council.'

'What does Tostig want with that cold-hearted knife-tongue?' Vadir asked.

The castellan glanced back at the feasting wedding party to make sure he would not be overheard. 'Tostig plans to persuade Harald to reassert his claim to the throne of England, and to raise a levy so the two men can invade by the end of summer.'

'He would hand the throne to that Viking pirate?' Hereward exclaimed. Alric felt troubled by the fire he saw in his friend's eyes. It burned too quickly, too brightly, still.

Vadir dropped a heavy hand on the younger warrior's shoulder. 'Stay calm, little man. This is not our fight, unless someone seeks to give us gold and lots of it to get involved. It will all be over soon enough and then we will see how things stand.'

'It may not be over as soon as you think,' Wulfric said, his voice low and grave. 'I also have news from Normandy and from Rome. The Pope has assented to Duke William's invasion plans. Seven hundred warships and transports are being readied at Dives-sur-Mer, to sail before summer's end. An attack from the north and the south. King Harold's forces will be divided. It seems William the Bastard's prophecy that England will be swamped in a tide of blood will come true, one way or another.'

Chapter Thirty-Eight

25 September 1066

Under a merciless sun, a dark cloud was charging across the verdant Northumbrian plain. Billowing grey dust swept in its wake, licking over the trees and water meadows. The baked ground throbbed with the pounding of hooves and leather soles. The still air rang with the jangle of mail shirts. In that stifling autumn heat, a storm of spears and axes was descending on a river crossing sixteen miles beyond the ravaged defences of Eoferwic.

When barbs of brassy light glinted off the snaking River Derwent, the commanders brought the swollen English army to a rumbling halt. A lull gradually settled on the horde, broken only by snorting horses and creaking leather. No man uttered a word.

Ahead of the mounted warriors, two men rode out to get a clear view of the terrain. Harold Godwinson wore the tarnished armour that had served him well during his long, uncompromising ascent to the throne. His helmet was of the old style, with broad plates covering the ears and cheeks, and it was dented and scratched from the spear-points and axes it had deflected. His mail was brown, rust and dried blood from years of campaigns merging into one. In contrast, Redwald gleamed in the morning sun. His armour was all new, a helmet with a mail coif to cover his neck and a mail shirt he had taken receipt of only days earlier.

'Our enemies will have seen the dust-cloud and heard the hooves,' the young man said, shielding his eyes against the harsh light.

'Good,' Harold replied with a tight smile. 'Let them know their death approaches and let them fear.'

Glancing back over the sea of fighting men, Redwald felt a stirring deep in his heart. Never had such a force been amassed on English soil. Harold's own huscarls were the elite core of the army, their heavy armour combat-worn, their axes nicked and stained. Alongside them stood a coterie of mercenaries, the most fearsome warriors the king's gold could buy. Flanking them rode a group of mounted javelin-throwers of a kind never before seen in England. Harold had witnessed the lethal effectiveness of such a force on his travels in Europe, the younger man knew. The javelins would rain down on their enemies as they advanced, pinning men in place to die screaming. Redwald cast his eye over the field-workers who stretched beyond the hardened soldiers, almost as far as he could see. They had been collected along with the West Mercian and East Anglian *fyrd* as the army drove north, marching almost day and night for four full days. Once the call to arms went out, each man had raced to his home to collect his spear and shield from under his bed. Many carried the bows and arrows they used for hunting, but others were armed only with stones fastened to pieces of wood. They wore no armour, these levy men. Most of them still had straw in their hair and dung on their tunics, but though their eyes were fear-filled, Redwald saw determination in their ruddy faces.

Harold stretched out a steady arm to point to the river crossing two miles away where men swarmed like ants on both banks. 'See? They are not ready for us. Too confident, like all the Northmen. The Vikings thought we would be as weak and slow as the men who faced them in the time of our fathers' fathers' fathers. They thought we would creep like whipped dogs, not strike like wolves.'

'They did not reckon with Harold Godwinson.'

The king smiled.

Redwald cast his mind back to the beacon blazing in the night on the hills to the north of London. It was the last bonfire in a long line stretching from the north along the east coast. At first, the young man's heart had filled with ice, but Harold was hot with passion. He had been ready for this moment and his blood was up for battle. If he had waited for mounted messengers to deliver the news of the Northmen's attack, his war preparations would have been delayed too long. But Harold had been proved right in overriding the Witan, and his system of bonfires meant the news had arrived before the ravens had even taken wing. On the hard ride north, they had encountered white-faced messengers with stories of three hundred dragon-ships blotting out the whale road with their red and white sails. Thousands of fierce Viking warriors under the command of Harald the Ruthless. And Harold's own brother, Tostig, was among them. The Northmen had sailed up the Humber and sacked Skaresborg before tearing through the forces of Edwin of Mercia and his brother Morcar at Fulford. Eoferwic had fallen with barely a whimper. When the English army had arrived in Tatecastre after the great march, Harold had prepared for an attack. Redwald recalled his master's fire, the clarity of his planning during the long tactical discussion with the huscarls; for the first time the strength of the Wessex man's leadership seemed to match his grand ambition, Redwald thought. But the attack never came. The Vikings were indeed over-confident. They waited to resupply thinking they had all the time in the world.

And that morning, the storm of English spears and axes had made their lightning advance to Stamford Bridge.

Harold swept an arm towards the enemy, who raced back

and forth to prepare their defences. 'And now we are here, how would you attack?'

Redwald knew the king was testing him. As in all things, this was part of his education, the knowledge that would help him become great. He thought for a moment and then made two slashes in the air from the north and the south.

The monarch nodded, but his sly smile suggested the answer had not been correct. 'Look at the men we have arrayed behind us. Why halve the enemy's attention when we can break it into seven.'

'Seven?'

'Seven warbands.' Harold marked the lines of attack in the air. 'We strike quickly and tear the Northmen apart. That is only a small part of their full force. The rest of Harald's men will be with his fleet at Riccall, and he will have sent messengers to call them here. Our victory is assured if we crush the Vikings before the rest of the army arrives.'

'They will try to hold the bridge to stop us crossing the river to the east.'

'Of course they will. Only a handful would be needed to make a stand. But we will come like the hammers of a thousand smiths and smash them upon the anvil.'

Redwald stared at the churning Vikings, feeling his heart pound faster as the battle neared. He feared the attack would not go as cleanly as his master suggested. Around the campfire the previous night he had listened to the murmurs of the huscarls as they discussed the coming attack, and he soon understood why the king of the Northmen was called 'the Ruthless'. Harald had left the ravens feeding on the remains of his foes across all the world, from Byzantium to the frozen rivers of Kievan Rus where the Slavs gnawed on the bones of those they had killed in battle.

Harold's eyes narrowed as he peered towards the river crossing, the current weak and the waters low after the long weeks without rain. 'My heart is heavy for my brother. He still feels the pain of his treatment. Let the word go out to take him as our prisoner, if it is within our power. I would have him at my side again, and his good advice in my ear.'

Redwald flinched and quickly turned away before his master could see his concern. If Harold brought Tostig and the rest of his brothers into his closest circle there would be no room for other advisers.

'You will lead one of the warbands,' the king said, as if to reassure him. 'Give the order.'

The king urged his mount back towards the waiting huscarls, and after a moment Redwald followed. Leading a warband into battle was a great honour, yet still he felt uneasy. The warriors, even the men of the *fyrd*, all carried tokens next to their skin, a strip of linen from the garment of a loved one, a bone cross, secret amulets bearing the marks of one of the old gods. He had nothing except what was in his heart.

'Let the spears of the English pierce the hearts of the Northmen!' Harold bellowed as he rode along the front of the huscarls. 'Let the river run red with their blood! Into battle, English, with God on our side!' He wrenched his horse around and dug in his heels, leaning across its neck as he roared his fury. Thousands of throats responded, the cry resounding like the waves crashing on the shore. Redwald thought how terrifying it must be for the enemy to hear that sound.

Within moments he was lost to the pounding of hooves and the wind tearing at his face. The army moved behind him like a great beast coming to life, lumbering at first but gathering strength and speed as it thundered towards its prey. Oak and elm flashed by. Lost to the drumming of blood in his head, Redwald could only sense the men riding at his side, their gaze fixed, their lips drawn back from their teeth, spears or axes clutched in their right hands as they gripped the reins with their left.

As the turf blurred by beneath the horses' hooves, Redwald glimpsed the Northmen jostling against each other as they waited along the river bank and realized yet another error they had made. Many were naked to the waist, their only armour their helmets. In the burning heat of the day, they must have left their mail shirts at their ships. Wooden shields would offer scant protection to the smiting that would be dealt them.

On the extremes of his vision, Redwald saw the mounted javelin-throwers leading the charge from either flank. Each man carried seven javelins in deep leather pouches strapped to their harness. Redwald found himself riveted by the sight of the riders pulling out each narrow, weighted spear and hurling it in one fluid motion before selecting the next weapon. The iron tips caught the sun like fire as they rained down. One Northman threw up his arms as if praising God when a javelin rammed through his right eye socket, down through his body and out of his side. A red mist sprayed upwards. Across the ranks, Vikings convulsed, pinned to the ground by the falling spears like rabbits caught in traps. Fascination gripped Redwald. Truly Harold was a great war leader to bring such a devastating tactic to England.

Shields stretched along the river bank in a bulging semicircle centred on the river crossing, reds, blues and yellows, marked with black and white crosses or stripes, all newly painted for the invasion. Redwald saw gleaming helmets poking out from behind the wall and wondered what thoughts were going through the Northmen's minds. Did they fear their death was near? Did they trust that even with the vast army ranged against them they could still win? He had been told that the *vikingr*'s belief in their own prowess was unshakable.

Spreading oaks and beeches dotted the approach, but the huscarls surged among the trees without checking their pace, before leaping from their horses and attacking on foot. Redwald joined them. With a roar, the English wave broke on the shield wall. Northmen staggered back under the pounding, ripe for the hack of an axe. Spears bristled from behind the shields.

Within a moment, Redwald found himself enveloped in the din of battle cries and the crashing of iron upon wood. Huscarls pressed tightly on either side, the constant motion of chopping axes and thrusting spears like the flapping of birds on the edge of his vision. Redwald threw his blue shield in front of him without a moment to spare. A spear burst from behind the wall towards his face, the tip splintering the wood as it raked across his defence. Before the Northman could withdraw his weapon, Redwald rammed his own spear into the warrior's face. Blood gouted from where the tip ripped through the cheek and out of the back of the head. The man's dying convulsions wrenched the spear from the Englishman's grasp.

Cursing, Redwald withdrew to snatch up his axe. As he spun round, he glimpsed the seam of corpses littering the reddening turf in front of the shield wall. Even outnumbered, the Northmen were taking their toll on their English foe. On either side, the plucky ceorls swarmed forward. Many fell within moments, but the sheer weight of bodies began to drive the Vikings back. Redwald felt a rush of blood, but no fear.

Whipping up his axe, he lurched forward with a snarl. Gaps were appearing in the shield wall. Through one, he glimpsed a man who could only be Harald, taller than most of the Northmen who surrounded him, his blond beard glowing in the harsh sun. The red and white banner fluttered above his head.

Raising his fist in the air, Redwald ordered his huscarls towards the enemy king. As the warriors thundered nearer, the Northmen along the front of the shield wall raised their spears. All Viking eyes focused on the attack. Redwald beckoned to one of the archers loosing his shafts from the cover of a broad oak and pointed at Harald. The archer nodded and notched his arrow. Drawing the greased fibre string of his hunting bow, he took aim and fired. The arrow whistled through the gap in the shield wall. Distracted by the huscarls, the king of the Northmen did not raise his red and white shield, and the shaft plunged deep into his throat.

Redwald thought his own heart would burst. The Viking leader went down in a spray of blood, clutching at his wound. Instantly, Redwald could see the dread burn through the ranks of all the Northmen standing near him. Encouraged by the sight, the English crashed once more against the crumbling shield wall, splintering the wood with their axes and driving the enemy back step by step.

Wiping the sweat from his eyes, Redwald felt his jubilation ebb away when he saw another man take the enemy king's place. But this was no Northman. Shorter than Harald, but with an English helmet and mail, Redwald guessed it could only be Tostig Godwinson. The outlaw barked orders in English, and whether the Vikings understood or not they marshalled their forces to the frantic waving of his hand. The gaps in the shield wall closed as the men began a steady retreat to the bridge.

Redwald realized that Tostig intended to regroup on the other bank. For an instant, the two leaders locked eyes before the outlaw took up his axe and waded to the wall. Gritting his teeth, he hacked with a fury that dwarfed even that of the seasoned Viking warriors. Bodies piled high in front of him. Of all there, only Redwald truly understood him. The young man alone saw the potent resentment, the pain of betrayal, the bitter grief that came only between kin.

Redwald felt a cold calm descend on him. 'Let my hand be true,' he whispered to himself.

Stalking forward, he drew his sword and threw himself into the seething mass of English warriors. Voices roared all around him. Buffeted side to side as if by a winter sea, he elbowed his way through the men until he came within sight of Tostig. The outlaw dripped with blood and brain-matter, his teeth clenched in a constant, bestial snarl. His axe fell, again and again. Helmets split and mail shredded. Waiting for his moment, Redwald kept his head down and hoped he would not be recognized.

One English warrior fell, his jaw torn free by Tostig's axe. Into the gap, a ceorl stumbled with his spear. He was younger than Redwald, plain-featured and simple, with hair like straw. His face looked drained of blood, and his weapon wavered in his untutored hand. Probably never used a spear in battle before, Redwald thought.

When Tostig raised his axe, the ceorl retreated a step to avoid the blow. Redwald lunged into the man's back, propelling him forward. The axe crunched into the spearman's skull, killing him instantly, but, wrong-footed by his victim's forward motion, the king's brother struggled to withdraw his weapon. Redwald saw his opening. Avoiding the mail that could deflect or break his blade, he drove his sword upwards with both hands, under Tostig's chin and into his brain. He slid his weapon out of the wound just as quickly and instantly pressed back through the ranks of men before anyone recognized him. Bursting out of the English warriors, he ran to reclaim his mount.

Back on his horse, he saw that Tostig's death had broken the enemy's resistance. On the far river bank, the leaderless Vikings massed for a final stand. The reinforcements left at the fleet were finally making their way to the rear, bolstering the ranks. Red-faced and sweating, they had clearly raced all the way from Riccall in the heat. Several collapsed with exhaustion; others threw off their mail.

When all the Northmen had fled to the eastern bank, a lone Viking took a stand on the bridge to prevent the English from swarming across. Clean-shaven, with long brown hair tumbling from under his helmet, he stood as tall as Redwald with a boy upon his shoulders. English warrior after English warrior tried to take him down, but the Northman swung his axe with blows that could have felled a tree. The bodies fell into the now-red river or heaped at his feet so that it was even harder for the English to reach him.

Removing his helmet, Redwald mopped the sweat from his brow. He heard a blast from a horn on the other side of the river and within moments the king's huscarls tore into the waiting army from the south. The king, as cunning as a snake, must have redirected some of the English army to cross the Derwent at an older bridge a mile further south. For all its ferocity, the battle on the western bank had only been the mildest precursor to what was to come.

A galloping horse distracted Redwald from the furious clash on the far bank. It was Harold, slaked in blood. Where his men massed at the bridge, he leapt from his horse and barged through the ranks, yelling, 'Stand aside for the king.' The warriors parted in an instant. At the front, Harold watched the big Viking hack down two more men, his frustration rising. Snatching a javelin from the chest of a dead Northman, he snarled a curse and hurled the weapon with a force that seemed impossible in one who had spent all morning in combat. The javelin flew true. It rammed into the surprised Viking's chest, ripping through his mail and bursting out of his back in a shower of blood. The man teetered for a moment, clutching at the wooden haft protruding from his front, and then he toppled over the bridge to splash into the river. Harold spat and returned to his horse. Cheering, his men flooded across the bridge to join the bloody battle on the other bank.

By late afternoon, Redwald was sitting in the suffocating heat at the foot of an elm. He looked across a field of bodies seething with black-winged carrion crows to the sunlit high ground rising up in the east. Too weary to stand and sleeked in sweat, he was aware that his arms were burning from the thousands of blows he must have struck that day. His helmet and mail lay beside him, tarnished and dented now.

Blood trickled in thick streams down the bank into the slow-moving Derwent, which had long since turned the colour of rusted mail. The feeding birds cawed hungrily, and behind the din he could hear the cries of the wounded and the dying. The English army had suffered terrible losses. Even leaderless, the Northmen had fought like devils, the reinforcements instilling renewed purpose in their weary fellow warriors. But in the end, the English numbers had proved decisive. When the rout was assured, Harold had ordered the West Saxon mounted troops to hunt out all the enemy survivors. Redwald had watched the Vikings cut down as they fled, or drowned in the river. Some had been trapped in barns and bothies and burned alive. He had just heard from a messenger returning from Riccall: of the three hundred dragon-ships that mounted the invasion, only twenty had escaped. It was the greatest defeat inflicted on the Northmen in their long, brutal history.

'You fought well.'

His eyelids drooping, Redwald started at the familiar deep voice. The king strode over with the energy of a man half his age. Gathering all his strength, the young man pulled himself up the tree's rough trunk and rested his back against the bark. 'I wished to serve in a manner that would make you proud,' he replied with an overstated flourish of his right arm. He put on a cocky grin.

'And you did.' The king removed his helmet and held it in the crook of his arm. 'This was a great victory. All Englishmen should be proud.' A shadow crossed his face as he glanced back to the western bank. 'Tostig is dead.'

'I saw your brother brought down in battle,' Redwald said, the lie springing easily to his lips. 'Who slew him I do not know, but I failed to prevent the killing blow.'

The king shook his head. 'It was always a vain hope that Tostig would survive. He was a Godwin. He would fight until his last breath.'

'Still, though we never met, I grieve for him, for he is your kin.'

Harold turned away to look across the field of the dead. 'Our victory was hard-won. We have lost many men this day.'

'But the throne is safe.'

'For now, though I fear . . .' He killed the words in his throat and pointed towards the Archbishop of Eoferwic picking his way through the corpses, his white tunic aglow. Five black-garbed monks accompanied him. 'Ealdred looks for his pickings. The Northmen left behind a block of gold among their treasures as big as this.' He put his hands a sword's length apart. 'Harald looted it from Greece on one of his raids. It was his talisman, but it failed him this day. That should buy my way to heaven.' He grinned, his teeth smeared with blood. 'I need no great churches to earn my final reward.'

'And now?'

'Now we begin the negotiations for surrender with Harald's son Olaf. We will bury our dead, like good Englishmen, but we will leave the Vikings unburied. Their bones will be a warning to all who dare covet English soil.'

'And then rest,' Redwald croaked, overcome by weariness.

'And feasting and drinking,' Harold roared, grinning, 'for we have earned it.'

The negotiations ended two days later and Redwald recovered his strength in Eoferwic with the king and the remnants of the army. Five days after that a mounted messenger thundered through the gates. Scared witless, the man struggled for long moments before he could babble his message to the monarch: the omens and portents had all come true. Two days gone, William the Bastard and his army had landed at Pevensey on the south coast. Villages were burning. Men and women lay slaughtered in their homes. The end was near.

CHAPTER THIRTY-NINE

14 October 1066

England was dying. Silhouetted against the blood-red setting sun, the tattered remnants of Harold Godwinson's army clustered on the hilltop around the fierce Golden Dragon of Wessex. Beside the king's once majestic gilded leather standard, a banner depicting the Trojan hero Ajax fluttered limply in a chill north breeze. Silence hung over all for the first time that day. A lull, not peace. Falling away below the warriors, butchered bodies obscured the hillside turf. Red streams bubbled down towards the foot where the vast Norman army washed all around like an iron sea. Beyond the invaders, shadows marched across the wooded slopes and lush valleys of southern England.

The eyes of the gore-spattered huscarls turned towards the king. Cuts slashed his cheeks and blood dripped from his right brow. He stood proudly, looking into the growing gloom, but his hand shook where it gripped his spear for support. In the exhausted warriors' drawn faces, Redwald saw a pitiful acceptance. One by one, they raised their axes for their final stand.

And then the quiet of the late afternoon was shattered. The

clatter of iron upon iron, a susurration of voices, low at first but growing louder. Norman nobles, troops from Normandy, Flanders, Brittany and France. Mercenaries from as far away as Rome. All of them joining together. Swords clashed against mail-covered chests, beating out the rhythm of their war chant.

'What are they singing?' Redwald asked, not really caring.

'They are singing open the gates of hell.' Harold's voice cracked with weariness, his bravado disappearing into the wind.

Redwald felt bitter and fearful. How had it come to this, when only days before victory had seemed assured and all his careful planning was about to bring him his just rewards? Racing from Eoferwic after the messenger had delivered his disturbing news of William the Bastard's incursion, the elite force of huscarls and mercenaries had attempted to raise a new *fyrd* along the way. But so many men had been lost at Stamford Bridge. Some villages in the east were near deserted, an entire generation lost. In London, Harold had attempted to rebuild his army, but old King Edward's prophecy clung to every lip. As the coming battle neared, a steady stream of deserters fled the already depleted ranks. No support came from the Mercians or the Northumbrians. The Godwins had long since burned their bridges. And as the small army rode south to where William the Bastard's men were stockaded, Redwald had sensed a draining of power from the once great king, a man now seemingly crippled and making one last desperate attempt to cling to the throne. But still Redwald hoped, for where else could he turn?

The king had arranged a Sussex levy to bolster his ranks, but the meeting place was the hoar-apple tree at the crossing of the old tracks where the London road emerged from the dense forest of the Weald north of Hastings. It was too close to the Norman encampment, and the noisy gathering of straw-hatted, terrified men had alerted William the Bastard's scouts. The king's plan to repeat his strategy from Stamford Bridge, of a last-minute race to a dawn raid, had to be abandoned. Redwald had cursed under his breath. Harold would never have made such an error before. But the long struggle to the throne and the months of battle to hold on to it had taken their toll. Now Redwald glanced down the steep slope at the chilling array of power and his heart fell: cavalry, the best in Europe, armed with lance and sword; missile-troops, swaths of archers and others armed with something he had heard tell of but never seen, the fearsome crossbow; troops carrying shield, spear, axe and sword, all of them heavily armoured in long ring-mail shirts and thick helms. Eyes like a winter heath, and hearts too.

Redwald gripped his spear more tightly and tried to drive that unsettling chanting from his head. The English had been too slow-witted, too lead-footed, and in their weakness they had sold England like a goose at the market, ready for the slaughter.

But still he hoped. Harold had never let him down before.

And yet why had the king not responded faster when he saw William's scouts thundering back towards the palisade? Had he really expected the devious Normans to wait until the full English army had arrived and all their troops were in battle order? The Bastard's rapid attack with his eight-thousand-strong army had devastated the ragged English ranks when they had barely reached half that number. Most of the levied English men had still been straggling along the London road. Harold had responded with the only tactic open to him, ordering his bloodied troops up to the high ridge and leaving the Normans to occupy the swampy lowlands. When the shield wall had locked into place, the king knew he had bought himself some time. Redwald cast his mind back to the Norman archers racing up to the English line and loosing flight after flight of arrows. The shafts had rattled into the huscarls' shields, and been met with a hail of rocks, javelins and maces that stunned the enemy. And when the two sides had clashed together, the Normans had soon found their mail was no match for the huscarls' axes. Yet this advantage had only been short-lived.

Less disciplined than the elite force, the *fyrdmen* and the levied troops broke ranks to pursue the Normans, and William the Bastard saw his opening. When he ordered in his cavalry, the men had been slaughtered, the ranks fragmented, and

Harold's own brothers Gyrth and Leofwine left lying among the dismembered corpses.

Redwald thought back to the shattered look that had flashed across the king's face. Did Harold realize then that the age of the Godwins was truly over? No longer able to hold the ridge, he had withdrawn the standards to the top of the hill.

The harsh beat of iron and the full-throated singing ebbed away. Only the moan of the wind with its whispers of the coming winter drifted through the stillness.

Harold peered down to the long Norman line without expression. 'We are English,' he called in an unsettlingly calm voice. 'When death looks in our face, we kick it in the balls. Come then, Norman bastards. Run up this hill in your heavy armour and meet our axes.' The king looked round at his huscarls. 'For every whoreson you slaughter this day, you will be rewarded with gold. We have the high ground. The Normans must come to us . . . to die. Kill well, my men, and by the end of the night we will be raising our mead-cups to victory.'

Redwald felt his heart stir. Was there yet a chance? When he glanced around the English, he saw there was no shield wall left. No defence. Harold was right; killing was all they had.

The red sun edged towards the horizon, the shadows pooling around the huscarls. The Norman horn sounded, low and mournful.

Harold turned to Redwald, clapped a hand on the young man's neck and pulled him in close to whisper in his ear. 'You have been more son to me than adviser,' he said, 'and you have made me proud. This day make me prouder still, and if die you must, do it with honour.' He looked Redwald deep in the eye with an unflinching gaze, and for the first time the younger man thought he saw a hint of tears there. But then the king snapped back to the Normans and the final battle began.

The cavalry charged. Behind them, the archers raced in waves. The sky blackened with arrows.

'Shields up,' Harold bellowed.

Driven to his knees by the thunder of shafts, Redwald saw a

score of tips bursting through the splintered wood. Fear gushed through him. With so many Norman archers, the high ground meant nothing. The realization had only a moment to sink in, and then the storm broke upon them. Redwald glimpsed mere flashes in the whirl of his panic. The huscarls stood their ground, swinging their axes in furious rhythm. But the arrows flooded down upon their heads as the Norman archers fired over the top of their own cavalry.

Madness, madness, Redwald thought.

Shafts burst through faces, rammed into chests and shoulders. Heads leapt from necks. Arms fell still twitching. Grey chunks of brain sprayed from split skulls. A mist of blood descended on them all.

Redwald realized he was rooted with dread and tried to jab with his spear, but his hand shook too much. Never had he expected such horror. Through the whirl of axes and streams of arrows, he glimpsed the faces of the Normans, and thought they all looked like death's heads, hollow-eyed, pearly teeth grinning with insane delight. No men these! Things from the night, or devils from hell.

Tears flooded down his cheeks.

Beside him, Harold threw his head back and cried out, clutching his face. Sickened, Redwald saw a wooden shaft protruding from the king's right eye. Yet still the monarch fought on as if he could feel no pain, the arrow flashing back and forth with every movement of Harold's head.

The sky was darkening. Redwald glimpsed the ghost of the moon, and a thought skittered through his head that he had black wings, like a raven, and could fly away.

Madness.

Gripped by the horrific sight of that arrow in Harold's eye, Redwald only sensed the Normans were attacking from two flanks until it was too late to shout a warning. Torn apart as if by a winter gale, the huscarls could offer little resistance. Six knights on horseback rammed through the crumbling defensive line and thundered towards the king.

Redwald saw his duty flash before his eyes: with spear in hand, he should defend the king to the last, even though his master's death was inevitable. He hesitated. What good would it do to give up his own life? Harold looked from the attacking knights to Redwald, and in the moment their eyes locked the young man saw the king's shocked dismay at the final betrayal. Redwald cared little. He threw himself backwards, away from the line of pounding hooves. Rolling down the hill, he caught flashes of swords slashing down on the man who had raised him up to such great heights. A blade stabbed through his master's chest. The king's head flew from his shoulders and bounced across the sticky grass. A knight swung his axe down, rending open Harold's mail shirt and the flesh beneath. Guts tumbled out to glisten in the fading light. And still the Normans hacked and slashed.

Dazed, Redwald came to a halt. *Run*, he told himself. *Do not look back*. But a grim fascination dragged his gaze back to the hilltop. The Normans were cheering around his fallen master. One knight stooped down with his knife and sawed at the king's corpse. Jumping to his feet, the man waved his trophy over his head and the others roared with laughter. Sickened, Redwald realized the knight had cut off Harold's cock.

Hot tears came for the failure of all his dreams. Turning, he careered down the hillside into the growing night.

CHAPTER FORTY

Still and silent under sable skies, London held its breath. Moonbeams limned the glistening roofs of the cramped houses, casting long shadows across the rutted streets. A dog barked; a cow lowed. The insistent clatter of hoofbeats broke the quiet as Redwald rode hard from the direction of the river crossing towards the Palace of Westminster. Snorts of hot breath clouded in the chill air. Digging his heels into the flanks of his foaming horse, the young man urged the last vestige of strength from its weary limbs. Sweat dripped from his brow. Hot despite the cold, he had taken no chances, swaddling himself in a stolen cloak with the hood pulled low to hide his identity.

He could almost sense the apprehension leaking from the dark houses on either side. He pictured the men sitting by the hearths, unable to sleep, the women anxiously tossing and turning in their beds. If they only knew the horror that would soon be marching towards their doors. Stifling his own desperation, he guided his mount towards the barred gates in the high enclosure fence. Above the palisade, cold lamps of faces glowed in the moonlight, each one filled with trepidation. The guards called for news of the battle. They looked pitifully hopeful when he said he had an urgent message from the king and could not be delayed.

Leaping from his horse, he glanced once over his shoulder to ensure he was not being watched, and then raced for the abbey church. A full day and more had passed since he had seen Harold butchered, the most dismal day he could recall. A dark night of running and hiding from Norman troops scouring the countryside for escaping English soldiers to slaughter gave way to a red dawn, a near-bungled attempt to steal a horse, and the long flight home. Ahead stretched grey days of worry. All his plans had turned to ashes, all the long years of scheming wasted. He had less now than when Asketil had taken him in after his parents' death. And if William the Bastard's men recognized him, his life would be lost too, his head planted on a pole beside the Thames, food for the crows.

Consumed by despair, the young man crashed through the heavy oak door into the echoing vault of the church. Candles guttered along the far wall, left by the monks for sinners desperate to pray for their souls in the long dark of the night. The dancing flames sent jewels of light shimmering across the stained-glass windows. Above the altar, the Christ glared down at the young man. Redwald saw angels too, but no devils. They already walked the earth.

His leather shoes echoed on the stone flags. Redwald snatched one of the candles and hurried to the reliquary containing the shankbone of St John the Baptist. He thought back to that frozen night when he had retrieved the relic for the old queen, Edith, Harold Godwinson's sister. How long ago it seemed. With that simple act, he had earned the first step of his advancement. Power had felt within his grasp.

Fighting back tears of frustration, he placed his hands upon the casket, almost afraid that it would burn him, and then flipped open the iron-banded lid. With the candle held in a trembling hand, he pushed aside the brown bone to find what he had hidden beneath.

'It *is* you.'

Redwald almost cried out in shock. Clutching a hand to his mouth, he whirled in fear of his life only to see Hild standing in the doorway. Hild, his wife of four months, already with child, whom he had kissed goodbye barely a week ago. He hadn't even remembered she was at the palace.

'Leave me,' he snapped, the thump of his heart returning to normal. 'I have business.'

'Here? Do you pray for divine help?' She crossed the nave, the embroidered hem of her yellow dress swishing across the flagstones. Her hands fluttered in front of her, her voice rising. 'Why have you returned alone? What of the battle? Where is the king?'

'The king is dead.' Turning his back on his wife, Redwald delved into the reliquary once more.

Only silence followed. He glanced back to see Hild's face frozen, tears springing to the corners of her eyes.

Forcing himself to soften his tone, he continued, 'England is done. You would do well to flee before the Normans come. Their soldiers will not treat women kindly.' He stifled a bitter laugh at his understatement. The Normans' reputation for rape, cruelty and brutality was unparalleled.

'You wish me to travel alone? But you are my husband . . . you should protect me,' his wife said, aghast.

Wearied by the exchange, Redwald shook his head and returned his attention to the casket. 'Go.'

'How can your heart be so cold? Do you not love me?'

'I never loved you. You were . . . necessary.'

Hild gulped like a codfish.

'You look foolish like that. Leave now.' Redwald's voice hardened.

'No.' Her cheeks flushed with indignation. 'You will protect me, as you promised my father. The Witan will find a new king. We will stay here, safe within the palace. And if the Norman is to be king, so be it. We will throw ourselves upon his mercy. You served one monarch, you can serve another.'

Angry, Hild grabbed her husband's arm to drag his attention

from the reliquary. Redwald snapped round, eyes blazing. 'There is nothing for me here. Nothing.' He felt a spiralling rage at so many wasted years. Every moment in that place only added to the miserable total. Lowering his voice, he threatened, 'You will not hold me back.'

'And you will not abandon me.' Hild's eyes flashed. Redwald could see she would not be deterred. 'You are a coward,' she spat. 'A weak child of a man. Come with me now, or I will tell all how you fled from the battle, abandoning the defence of England.'

'Lies!'

Hild smirked. 'Is it? You think yourself so clever, moving everyone like chess pieces to win your game. But in the night when you lie with me I see the true you.' Redwald coloured at her mocking laughter. His fingers fumbled in the bottom of the reliquary. Lost to the rush of things she had kept unspoken for so long, Hild thrust her face into his and hissed, 'And I used you.'

Redwald stiffened. His ears burned, his hand shook.

With a cruel look of triumph in her face, Hild twirled away. 'Now follow me back to the house and all this will be forgotten.'

'No.' The word whispered away like candle-smoke in the vast belly of the great stone church.

Hild spun back, her small teeth clenched. 'Then I will hail the king's men and make my claim.'

Redwald felt all the fury born of failure rush through him like a spring flood. His fingers folded round the knife hidden for so long under the old bone, and without a second thought for the life growing inside her he plunged it into her belly. He thought the shocked expression on her face almost amusing. Blood bubbled from her lips. A calm descended on him as the heat of his emotions ebbed away and he realized he felt nothing. Before she could call out, Redwald stabbed again.

When Hild lay dead in a growing red pool, he stepped back to steady himself against the wall. In his open palm lay the knife, a handle of whalebone carved into the shape of an angel; Hereward's old knife. Pressing the back of his left hand against his mouth, he stared into the wide, frozen eyes of his wife, but felt no grief for her or his unborn child. Instead, his thoughts flashed back to the last time he had wielded that knife. He recalled Tidhild, Hereward's love, lying on the floor of her home, the same staring eyes, the same spreading, dark pool.

Tidhild, stabbed three times by his own hand, with the knife he had stolen from his brother.

Those dead eyes staring.

Redwald sucked on his teeth. The vision had haunted him ever since, day and night, but not in a troubling way, he understood now. He had been fascinated by what it represented, the power he held over all things. And still he felt no regrets. For a long time he had worked to inveigle his way into the confidence of Harold Godwinson, and thereby earn his own advancement. Small tasks here and there, difficult work, earning trust. He knew how the earl's mind worked, for they were alike in many ways. So it had not surprised him when he had overheard Harold meeting with his two accomplices to plot the murder of a man who demanded gold in exchange for keeping his lips sealed. That was simply the game men played in pursuit of power. But then Hereward had come to the house that night, threatening to tell the king of the plot he had uncovered. Harold would have been exposed. What choice did he have, Redwald thought? He had to stop Hereward speaking to anyone. His brother's rage was well known; everyone would believe the warrior had it within him to kill his own love in a drunken argument. And then Redwald could encourage Hereward to flee, and Harold would reward his loyalty and his cunning and all would proceed as planned.

With bitterness, he stared at the bloodstained knife in his hands. The weapon had drawn him back time and again to relive that night of power. And now he would be running, as he had made his brother run, an outlaw in all but name, powerless, friendless, without land, or woman, or gold. Redwald laughed hollowly at the joke God had played upon him. Balancing the knife in his palm, he closed his eyes, still feeling some of the power it held. His path had been deflected, but not blocked. He would find another way to prevail. Stooping down, he wiped the blade on Hild's dress, and then he ran from the abbey into the night and an uncertain future.

CHAPTER FORTY-ONE

29 August 1067

The warship ploughed through the choppy waves towards the brooding island. Warriors heaved on the oars as they sang their song of blood and death to the beat of wood on water. With the sharp smell of new paint swirling in the wind from the freshly decorated shields hanging on the outside of the vessel, Vadir leaned against the bowpost. 'How many men wait there, unseen, silent among the trees with their swords and axes and spears?' he said, his mood grim. 'I tell you, Hereward, this expedition reeks of disaster. There will be blood on the water before we are done, and it will not all belong to our enemies.'

Shielding his eyes against the afternoon's late-summer sun, Hereward scrutinized the dappled islands dotted among the strong currents of the wide Scheldt estuary, each one black with dense tree cover. 'When the count needs his taxes, he is not likely to listen to fighting men.'

Vadir snorted. 'He has everything to gain here and nothing to lose. It's not his neck at stake.'

That morning Hereward had dutifully reported his assessment of the dangers to Count Baldwin's son Robert, their new commander. But Robert was a man intent on making his name as quickly as possible. His attentions were focused upon extending his influence deep into Zeeland, a power struggle that ebbed and flowed like so many of the rivalries around Flanders. The expedition to recover unpaid taxes from the rebellious residents of the scattered islands was merely to keep his father quiet. Robert expected it to pass without incident. Gold would be heaped upon the beaches once the islanders were terrified into submission by the sight of the warrior-laden warships sweeping up the Scheldt. Any man who had held a spear in battle could see what was lacking in that dream, Hereward thought. Fear rarely made men run – initially it made them fight harder.

'Still, the gold and mead that Robert has paid us since we joined his ranks has been most welcome,' Vadir said. 'It seems our reputation is growing, and that can only be good.'

All true, Hereward thought. It seemed that wherever they went they were now well known. Even Robert had sought them out, at Saint-Omer, when it became clear that Tostig was not coming back to Flanders. The count's son needed good commanders, if only to keep his men in line. And the warriors knew Hereward and Vadir understood their complaints, where Robert never would.

The two men watched the other eight warships cutting through the white foam with Robert's blue banner flying from a pole on each one. The fleet drew towards Wacheren, the largest island, with the stone steeple of the church of St Willibond just visible above the treetops. The Abbot Thiofrid, of the monastery of Echternach, had been encouraging the residents to refuse to pay their taxes. Hereward had suggested burning the monastery to the ground, but Robert had been less than keen to consider this course of action. 'In my experience, men like Abbot Thiofrid are only pious when they pray,' Hereward had told Robert. 'The rest of the time they play the games of kings and counts and do a better job of it by hiding behind their God-given masks.' But Robert would not be moved.

The foreman barked the order to the starboard rowers to

slow their strokes. The warship turned through the narrow gap between the sandbanks. Wacheren loomed up ahead of them.

'Your monk must count himself lucky not to be here. He seems at ease sitting at home with the women and trying to interest your wife in Bible stories,' Vadir muttered, scanning the treeline near the rock-strewn beach for any sign of resistance.

'Alric believes there is a natural goodness in all men. He is sickened by the sight of blood because it shows him, more often than not, that his view is misplaced.'

'Ha,' Vadir laughed, 'you are as sour as early apples when it comes to people.'

'I know what I see with my own eyes and feel with my heart.'

During the five seasons since his marriage, Hereward had found himself at peace in Saint-Omer. More than a good wife, Turfrida had been a good companion, advising him on the best course suggested by her understanding of those mechanical arts which the Church would prefer were never practised. When England fell to the bloody William the Bastard, Hereward had been keen to sail to offer his resistance, but both Turfrida and Vadir had counselled against it. 'All the omens show you will never return to the life we have here,' she had told him, her cheeks flushed with concern. 'The bloodshed in Hastings was only the beginning. William now has to bend your unruly land to his will, and he has never shirked from a task like that. If you must return, wait until the moment is right.'

And so he had waited, and waited, and had grown close to his father-in-law, Wulfric Rabe, and he and Vadir and Alric had wanted for nothing. His time with Turfrida had been enjoyable, and his campaigns had brought them wealth. They had not yet been blessed with a child, but it would come. Alric had seemed happier still, and had spent his days working at the church and teaching the children. Hereward felt pleased that the monk had found his peace.

But still England would not leave his thoughts, hovering like a black cloud on the horizon on a summer's day.

'What is on your mind?' Vadir asked as he eyed his friend

askance. 'You have that look on your face. The one that makes my heart sink.'

'I was thinking of my brothers, young Beric, and Redwald.' He paused, his throat tightening. 'And my father. I wonder how they fare, now William has been crowned king. I wonder if they still live.'

The red-headed man made a non-committal noise deep in his throat, but Hereward could tell his friend did not like the course the conversation was taking.

'I was thinking, perhaps, of a journey to Mercia, to see my old home. It would be good to drink mead with Redwald again.'

'A journey home means no pay,' Vadir grumbled. 'And with a monarch as bloody as William the Bastard upon the throne, I would expect England to be much changed.'

Hereward studied Wacheren. It looked like an upturned bowl floating on the grey waters, steep, tree-covered slopes rising from the boulder-strewn shores to the village on the summit. 'If only the islanders defend their home without help from warriors we should be done before there's sweat on our backs,' he mused. Vadir dismissed the thought with one raised eyebrow.

Three of the warships broke away to patrol the channels among the islands. No sly attack would come from silent ships disgorging fighters at their backs. The other vessels sailed around Wacheren, each dropping anchor at a different point.

As the Mercians' ship neared the shore, the sun dipped behind the island and the chill of the shadow fell across the oarsmen. The black water lapped against a small stony beach where a cracked, grey-wood jetty on rope-lashed pillars protruded out into the sea. The two English warriors searched the dense bank of trees rising up to the skyline. All was still.

When the anchor splashed into the shallows and the creaking boat strained to a juddering halt on the greased rope, the dripping oars were raised from the water and drawn into the vessel. Hereward held up one hand. Helmets gleaming on bowed heads, the men sat in silence, unmoving. The two Mercians turned their heads and listened.

'No birdsong,' Vadir hissed. 'Our enemies wait under leaf-cover.'

Twirling his hand, Hereward thrust it in the direction of a path disappearing into the shadows among the trees. 'Take the sleep of the sword to all who stand in our way,' he yelled, leaping over the side into the shallows. The cold water splashed on to his mail, but beneath his helmet his head burned. Drawing Brainbiter, he shouted, 'For Mercia! For Robert!' With an answering roar, the warriors grabbed their shields from the side and their axes and spears from under their seats and leapt into the water behind him.

But as they splashed towards the small rocky beach, the air filled with whistling. Arrows whizzed from the trees. A shaft flashed a hand's width from Hereward's head. Throwing up his shield, he ordered his men to do the same, but his voice was nearly drowned by cries behind him. Turning, he saw arrows ram into eyes, into chests, into necks. Many shafts lashed harmlessly into the black water, where blood now pooled. Vadir's prophecy had been correct. Thrashing, the wounded men slumped beneath the surface until the nearest warriors dragged the still living towards the shore.

Another flight of arrows sped through the air. This time they thudded into raised shields. The men clustered into a knot, heads now protected by a roof of wood. 'Stay together,' Hereward shouted as his force stumbled out of the sea and rattled up the stones to the treeline.

'When this business is done, I will find three of the best Frankish whores in all Saint-Omer and you will not see me for an entire week,' Vadir growled.

'Only three? You are getting old.'

Under the cool green canopy, the men broke formation. The path was only wide enough to travel single file. It had been cut into steps and edged with wood to keep it in use when the rains came. The two Mercians bounded up the track, their men close behind. Among the trees, ferns and rocks, they glimpsed shadowy figures scrambling up the steep slope towards the village. Arrows flashed past the trunks intermittently, but the warriors kept their shields high and their bodies low.

'Cowards' weapon. I told you,' Hereward hissed, darting from cover to cover.

'You cannot deny that the bow does its work well, though,' Vadir puffed. Wrenching an arrow from his splintered shield, he tossed the shaft away.

Glancing through the swaying blades of emerald grass up the hillside, the younger warrior came to a sudden halt. For an instant, he had a view through the trees to one solitary sun-drenched clearing amid the dark. A figure had stood there briefly, almost as if it had wanted to be seen. Something about that fleeting outline tugged at the depths of his memory. Unease rippled through him.

'What is wrong?' Vadir was watching him suspiciously.

'Nothing. Keep your wits on staying alive, not on me.'

The path turned sharply, following the contours of the hill. A tangle of exposed roots and dense vegetation blocked any other easy access to the summit. Ahead, Hereward noticed yellowing turf and branches spread across the beaten mud. When Vadir moved to cross, the younger Mercian blocked him with an outstretched arm. Crawling on his knees, he stabbed his sword on the dead vegetation and some fell away into a gulf beneath.

Peering into the hole, Hereward reported, 'Sharpened wood . . . spears rammed in the bottom.'

'A Viking trick,' the big man replied with a curse. 'If more of these bear-traps lie around, let us hope the other commanders are as sharp-eyed and sharp-witted as you.'

As the warriors edged round the pit, arrows tore into two more men who failed to keep their shields up. Both soldiers plummeted into the hole, the sticky impact followed by their dying moans.

When the force neared the top of the winding path, Hereward raised his hand once more to slow his men. From around the island echoed the sounds of battle, punctuated by the agonized cries of the dying.

'Let us hope that is the enemy howling their way down to hell,' Vadir said, unconvinced.

Hereward looked out across the flat, broad summit of the hill. Past the fields, a system of ditches and low ramparts protected the cluster of timber-framed houses with the stone church at the centre. No smoke drifted from any of the houses. Nothing moved. The only sound he could hear was a dog's barks floating across the grassland.

'The islanders are gone,' he hissed to his waiting warriors. 'The only men you will encounter here are our enemies. Cut them down without a second thought.'

When the order had been translated, the Flemish warriors beat their shields with their weapons. A moment later they burst from the trees, helmets aglow in the sunlight. Their battle cry resounded across the summit of the hill. Arrows whistled around their ears, but the men moved too fast to be easy targets. From the trees, two clutches of enemy warriors erupted, the variety of shield designs marking them as spears for hire. A third group emerged from the village on to the ramparts, and a moment later a fourth appeared. Within moments the other bands of Flemish warriors began to straggle on to the summit.

Iron clashed upon iron amid a tempestuous din of throat-rending screams and frenzied shouts. Gritting his teeth, Hereward led the way into the melee. Roaring men thundered towards him, their eyes glazed by battle passion. An axe strike glanced off his helmet, a spear skimmed his chain coif. In the crush of battling bodies, he washed back and forth as if he were being tossed by a churning ocean. Snarling faces filled his vision. The choking stink of sweat, blood, piss and shit burned his nose.

Then, through the swirl of bodies, Hereward glimpsed a familiar hawk-like face. Piercing eyes fixed upon him with a burning intensity as if he were the only important one on the field of battle. Memories skittered through his head between thrusts and parries. And then the name sprang to his lips: Hoibrict, the grandson of Count Manasses whom he had shamed on the tournament field in Bruges so long ago.

The swamp of mud and blood sucked at his leather shoes. Round and round he spun, with barely a moment to think, but the sight of the Flemish noble nagged at the back of his head. He glimpsed Vadir, roaring with laughter and drunk on battle, burying his axe in a collarbone.

Again Hoibrict fell into view. His eyes burned with hatred as they locked on to Hereward's gaze. The Fleming yelled some threat or other, the words lost to the din of battle. As the nobleman disappeared in the swell once more, a warning jangled through Hereward's head. Something here was not right.

He searched the sea of helmets as he fought until he found Hoibrict, and this time the Fleming was cutting a path through friend and foe alike. Towards Vadir.

A cruel revenge, Hereward thought, and what he expected of a weak man like Hoibrict. 'Vadir,' he barked. 'Your back!' But the din of battle drowned his voice. He set out to close the gap, cutting his way through the mass.

The hawk-faced man loomed closer to his prey.

Hereward bellowed again, and this time Vadir heard. As he spun round he swung his axe to deflect Hoibrict's thrust with ease. Faced by the towering warrior, the nobleman recoiled in shock. For a moment, the Fleming hovered, unsure. His eyes flickered between Vadir and his approaching rival.

'Seek your revenge face to face like a man,' Hereward yelled.

Hoibrict turned and ran. A moment later another man joined him, the two of them bounding like rabbits towards the village.

'That bastard.' Hereward glanced around at the dying battle. 'Something stinks here even worse than you.'

'Then let us ask what it is . . . with the help of your sword and my axe.' Vadir laughed loudly, whisking his weapon in the direction of the fleeing men.

Leaving the clash behind, Hereward and Vadir raced across the ramparts. As they skidded down the final slope to the edge of the houses, the two warriors could hear running feet ahead.

'The coward tries to hide.' The big man stooped to peer between the buildings. 'You take that side, and I'll go this way. Between us, we'll surprise him.'

Hereward nodded, pressing one finger to his lips. He kept low as he edged past a barn and a plot where herbs grew. He felt a simmering anger at Hoibrict's cowardice. The Fleming betrayed his knightly status and shamed his own bloodline. Better to die under a hundred axes than to flee honest combat. On the other side of the village, the dog began barking again. The nobleman had revealed his position and it would cost him dearly, Hereward thought with contempt. He sprinted silently past one house and to the lee of the next one, keeping one eye open for the man who had accompanied Hoibrict.

When he passed the third house, a shout rang out, and another – Vadir, he was sure. The clang of iron upon iron resounded across the rooftops.

Hereward ran. His friend must not have all the fun.

Following the hound's barking, he charged on to a green next to the church. Hoibrict waited there with the second man, who had drawn an arrow from a pouch on his back. This time the Flemish nobleman was grinning as he unsheathed his sword. A poor trap, Hereward thought, already searching for cover from the arrows. It was then that he saw Vadir. Beyond the church, on the edge of the village, his friend lay on the turf, blood seeping from gaping wounds on his arms and neck. Hereward felt his thoughts burn slow as he struggled to comprehend the scene and the identity of the man standing over his fallen friend. *Harald Redteeth.*

As the Viking raised his axe over his head for the killing blow, he began to sing a jaunty song. He paused when his weapon reached its highest point and grinned at Hereward. The Mercian could almost read his enemy's thoughts. *I have travelled across land and sea with only the heat of my yearning to drive my legs on. I have hunted through wild woods and empty grassland, past rushing rivers and in the reeking depths of towns to find your trail. And now that I have found you I will take my revenge – by stealing the life of your friend as you took the lives of my men. By driving guilt into your heart as you brought shame to mine.*

Guilt, Hereward thought, because he had let down Vadir: he couldn't reach his friend in time to prevent the fall of the axe.

If only he had realized the lengths Harald Redteeth would go to achieve his vengeance. If only he had watched the path behind him instead of the road ahead. If only he had killed his enemy outright when he had the chance.

Hereward refused to submit to this destiny. He hurled himself at the archer with a roar. The man loosed his arrow, but his arm trembled in shock at the ferocity of the attack and the shaft sped by. Hereward drove his sword through the archer's gut so hard the tip ripped out of his back. Snatching up the bow and arrow, the English warrior cast one lowering glare at the advancing Hoibrict. Whatever the Flemish man saw in that look, his features drained of blood and he turned and ran.

Harald Redteeth grasped the badly wounded Vadir's hair and yanked it up, exposing the man's neck. Holding his axe high, the Viking cast one final taunting look towards his hated rival.

Hold steady, Hereward thought, trying to calm the blood rushing through his head. *Be strong.* He notched an arrow, took aim and fired. Harald Redteeth stared back at his enemy, unruffled.

The shaft sped past its target by a hand's width.

Cursing, Hereward flashed back to the wasted moment on the snowy field outside Saint-Omer when Vadir urged him to learn to use the bow.

You may need this skill one day.

Sickened, he drew another arrow.

Harald Redteeth swung his axe down.

Silence closed around the Mercian, and filled his head. It rang with regrets. With trembling hands, he let the bow fall.

The Viking was laughing and dancing, a comical, soundless performance. And from his raised left hand, Vadir's head swung by the hair, dripping blood. Once, twice, the wild man swung the thing around his own head, and on the third circuit he let go. Vadir's head landed on the thatch of the nearest house, bounced and rolled down to fall in the dirt.

Hereward felt overwhelmed by a rush of grief so powerful he thought his legs would fail him. Vadir had been more than friend, more than guide; he had felt almost kin. In an instant, fury supplanted the grief, a long-suppressed rage that drove all civilized thoughts from his head. Hurling the bow and arrow aside, he ran towards the Viking. Harald Redteeth braced himself, whistling that unsettling tune as he gripped his weapon.

As the Mercian neared his prey, he glimpsed movement on either side. Ahead, he saw the Viking's expression darken. Victorious in battle, the remnants of Robert's men were sweeping into the village. Redteeth sensed any advantage he might have had was gone, and he turned on his heel and ran from the village. Consumed by passion, Hereward pursued him, over the ramparts and across the fields to the trees lining the hillside.

Nothing could have stopped him, not mountains, nor sea. His vision closed in on the fleeing Viking, and only death would free him from the bloodlust that now gripped him.

On the edge of the shadowy woodland Vadir's killer slowed and glanced back. His satisfied grin sprang back to his lips when he saw that only one pursued him, the man who had haunted his thoughts for nigh on five years.

Tearing off his helmet and throwing it aside as he ran, Hereward drew his sword without slowing his step.

His pupils so wide and black they appeared to be tunnels into his head, Harald Redteeth swung his axe with a grunt. With a yell, Hereward clashed his sword against the Viking's weapon, for a moment fearing his blade would shatter. The impact threw both men off their feet. The Mercian scrambled up first and launched himself at his enemy. His head rammed into the Viking's stomach and both warriors pitched down the slope. Initially they rolled in unison, bouncing off outcropping rocks and careering off trees. Gathering speed, they flew apart.

Hereward cracked his head, saw stars, but somehow kept hold of his sword. Skidding through fern, he glimpsed blue sky ahead.

Bursting from beneath the verdant canopy, his legs swung over the edge of a cliff. The grey sea churned far below. One hand caught hold of an exposed tree root, almost wrenching his arm from its socket. For a moment, he dangled above the dizzying drop, and then his leather shoe found purchase and he eased his way back up to solid ground.

Dazed, he drew himself upright. A flash of reflected light dazzled him. Harald Redteeth burst from the shadows beneath the trees, his axe already in flight.

Instincts afire, Hereward threw himself back, but not far enough. The axe ripped through his mail into the flesh of his chest. The force of the blow propelled him back over the cliff.

Wind tearing at his hair, he felt guilt that at the last he had failed Vadir, and he had failed himself. The final thing Hereward saw was the Viking's grinning face before the cold sea claimed him.

CHAPTER FORTY-TWO

The keening cry echoed through the small house next to the great church of Saint-Omer. Startled from his duties, Alric hushed the frightened children and instructed them to continue repeating the Latin he had taught them. Racing into the sun-dappled street, the monk found Turfrida clutching her arms around her, her face streaked with tears.

'You are hurt?' he asked, concerned.

Racked with silent sobs, the woman couldn't speak for a moment, and then she gasped only, 'Hereward . . .'

Alric felt a pang in his heart. He had learned to trust in God whenever his friend marched off to fight, but he always knew that sooner or later Hereward's battle prowess would fail him. 'You have had word back from the Scheldt?'

Turfrida shook her head. Wiping the snot from her nose with the back of her hand, she stuttered, 'A vision came to me as I stood on the hill where my husband and I always walk . . . a raven, falling from the sky. And when I looked at my feet, the bird lay there, crawling with white maggots.'

'You think God speaks through this vision?'

'The raven is Hereward, I know it. He has met death.'

Alric forced a comforting smile and said softly, 'Your husband has met death many times. Indeed, the two are close friends, and he has introduced death to others.'

'Perhaps that is it,' the woman replied, her chest heaving. She took long, deep breaths until she calmed and then she allowed the monk to lead her back to her house, where she sat by the hearth with her uncompleted sewing. But a dark cloud hung over her that no comforting words could dispel. Her sadness would only ease when she held her husband in her arms once more. Alric hoped that time would come, and soon.

He returned to the children, but he was in no mood for any more teaching and sent them all home. For the rest of the day, he prayed in front of the church's plain wooden altar, seeking solace among his troubled thoughts. He followed the contours of his mismatched friendship with the Mercian, from the suspicion and dislike of that first frozen night in Northumbria to the ease with which they spent time together in Saint-Omer. The monk realized he'd grown to like the surly warrior, for all his many flaws. Perhaps he even admired some of the qualities he found lacking in so many others: courage, loyalty, love, even honour, something the monk had thought to be entirely absent during their early days together. Their destinies had seemed entwined, both seeking salvation from a bloody past, both unable to achieve it without the help of the other. Now he wondered if he had been mistaken.

For some reason that Alric couldn't understand, he woke at dawn the next day and felt the urge to go to the road out of Saint-Omer and look to the horizon. He stayed there until mid-morning, and returned again near sunset.

The next day he did the same.

And on the third day, not long after sunrise, he glimpsed a lone figure riding towards Saint-Omer at a funereal pace. The monk waited, his heart pattering.

When the figure neared, Alric saw that it was Hereward. Yet his friend looked quite different, as if worn down by a terrible weight upon his shoulders. Even when the warrior saw the monk waiting, he didn't increase the pace of his mount.

Finally, he reined the horse to a halt. A bloody strip of linen had been tied across his bare chest, and there was dirt under his fingernails from, although the monk didn't know it then, the grave he had dug with his bare hands. He was filthy and he smelled of the road, but Alric was shocked when he saw the fire burning in his friend's glowering eyes.

'Say your goodbyes among the children and the churchmen, monk,' Hereward said in a cold, flat voice. 'Our time here is done. We sail for England.'

Chapter Forty-Three

5 October 1067

The gulls shrieked in an iron sky. Spray salted the wind, and the morning throbbed with the roar of the grey ocean, the creak of timber and the splash of dipping oars. At the prow of the Flemish warship Turfrida's father had arranged to transport them home, Hereward and Alric felt the first lick of autumn in the air.

Unable to hide his anxiety, the monk gripped the bowpost until his knuckles grew white. Memories of icy water closing over his head still haunted him. 'Let me soon feel dry land under my feet,' he muttered.

'Were yesterday's constant prayers not enough?' Hereward enquired, distracted. He had not taken his eyes off the swell since daybreak. Such a grim mood afflicted the warrior that it seemed he would never know joy again.

Suddenly a shaft of sunlight punched through the dense cloud cover, illuminating a hazy band of green across the horizon. Pointing at the sunbeam, Alric forced his first smile of the day. 'God looks down upon England.'

'And what does he see awaiting us in William the Bastard's

newly forged realm?' Hereward's eyes narrowed. He let his lamb-fat-lined furs fall open, already thinking of setting foot upon the quay.

'You always fear the worst,' Alric said. He thought of making light of it until he saw Hereward's darkening expression. Following the warrior's gaze, he glimpsed columns of smoke rising here and there across the coast. 'Burning off the crop stubble,' the monk said without conviction.

No more words passed between them for the remainder of the sea journey.

As his relief rose with the proximity to land, Alric thought back over the last few days. When Hereward returned from the expedition to the islands in the Scheldt estuary, he had seemed a broken man. For two days he slept, and for two days after that he barely spoke, apart from demanding food and ale and sending Alric away to make arrangements for the coming crossing. Turfrida had been so overjoyed to see her husband alive, she made no attempt to question him. 'He will speak in his own time,' she had whispered on the third morn. But she had disappeared to the woods where the *alfar* walked, and she had listened to the tongues of the birds and the foxes, and communed with the trees, and when she had returned her mood had darkened once more. 'The shadow is rising within him again,' she said. 'We must work together or we could lose him.'

Alric chewed a nail. He had tried to maintain a calm disposition, but it was not within his nature. He feared for his friend. One night beside the hearth, the words had tumbled out of him as he pleaded to know what was wrong. Hereward had glared at him in such a way that at first he thought his friend might strike him dead. But then he said simply, 'Vadir is dead,' and returned his attention to the fire. The monk recalled waking with a start the next morning and finding the warrior looming over him. Hereward's face was like the statues the Normans carved on their churches, but his eyes swam with grief. In flat, halting words, the warrior had described the older man's death, and Harald Redteeth's triumph, and how Hereward believed it to have been a plot long in the making; revenge for what transpired on that frozen night all those winters ago when they had first met.

Once again the monk felt the guilt that had consumed him that morning. If not for him, Hereward would never have encountered the mad Viking, or attracted his wild attention, and Vadir would still be alive. Hereward had pressed a cup of ale in Alric's hand, and ordered him to drink up – it felt like an oath, though no words had been spoken – and then told the monk not to blame himself. Turfrida had spoken to him of the *wyrd*; who was to know the schemes of God, he had said. But as he walked back to the fire, he had added something like, 'That does not mean I cannot make amends,' but what he meant by that he would not say. Turfrida had pleaded with her husband to stay. He had earned himself a new life of peace and love. Why would he risk all that for the uncertainty of a journey to England? But he would speak no more on the matter.

The ship ploughed a white-rimmed furrow through the waves. Alric knew they had skirted the south because of William's strength around London, and the vessel had been making its way up the whale road to the east coast. Hereward had set his sights on the place he knew best: Mercia.

When the ship put in to Yernemuth, Hereward leapt to the quay before the ruddy-faced sailors had even tied up. Urging Alric to follow, the warrior threw off his sea-furs and flapped his grey hooded cloak around him. Alric found his black woollen habit disguise enough. No one gave monks a second glance at the best of times. Along the quay, merchants haggled over boxes and barrels and sailors argued with shipwrights. Men with arms as hard as iron hauled bales from the seagoing ships to the smaller vessels that would carry the goods along the rivers inland. All appeared as it should at the port; bustling, focused upon the day-to-day activity of trade. But Alric thought he could already see signs of the Norman occupation. Faces everywhere looked beaten, eyes downcast or suspicious. Children ran from trader to trader begging for food or coin.

Pushing through the crowd at the waterside, the two companions forged into the narrow streets amid the sound of hammers and the whirr and rattle of looms. Hens scratched in the mud. Donkeys trudged under piles of wood for the workshop fires. Women carried baskets of fresh-baked bread covered with a sheet of white linen. Alric let his attention drift over the scene, searching for whatever was causing the knot deep in his belly. Then he had it.

'Look at them,' he whispered to Hereward. 'Everyone carries an amulet, a token, to ward off misfortune.' A woman grasped a roughly made wooden cross. Rabbit's feet hung from leather wristbands and bracelets. Others wore small, flat stones hanging round their necks, each one bearing a symbol. The monk noted the runes that the Northmen still used, and the horned circle that he knew represented the old heathen god Woden. Fingers fumbled for the amulets every moment or two, fluttering, unconscious actions once inspired by prayer, Alric guessed, but which had become second nature by constant use. 'They are scared,' he said. 'All of them.'

Hereward said nothing. The monk realized his companion had long since noticed the signs.

Asking around, the two men took directions to a merchant who had horses to sell, and some bread, blankets and a bow for hunting. Soon they were riding west along the narrow paths through the flat, green land.

'When do you plan to tell me where we are going?' the monk asked.

'I did not ask you to come with me.'

'You did not ask me to stay behind with your wife,' Alric snapped.

His words must have touched something in his companion, for after a moment Hereward pointed to one of the columns of smoke and said, 'First, we go there.'

When they neared their destination, Alric could smell that it was not crop stubble burning. The smoke caught the back of his throat with a bitter edge, and underneath the odour lay something sourer still.

Emerging from the wood into a clearing, the two men fought to control their skittish horses. In a vast circle of blackened grass and burnt mud, grey-white clouds drifted up from blackened stumps of timber punching up from the ground like the carcass of a long-dead beast.

'An entire village, burned to the ground,' Alric gasped. 'What wretched fate.'

'Not fate,' Hereward replied, his voice free of all emotion. 'This is the work of men.'

Raising one arm, the warrior gestured through the folds of smoke. Alric squinted, trying to see what had caught his companion's eye, but all he could make out was the dark line of trees on the far side of the clearing. When Hereward urged his mount to skirt the blackened area to get a clearer look, the monk felt his chest tighten with apprehension. On the other side of the destroyed village, he understood what he had sensed, and recognized the source of the sour smell caught on the wind.

A makeshift gibbet stretched between two elms. From the line hung not foxes and crows, but human remains. Six men and a woman swung in the gentle breeze, their skin grey-green, their bellies bloated, their eyes already food for the birds; poor souls left as a warning.

Hereward stared at the faces of the corpses for a long moment, and then said under his breath, 'The Norman bastards.'

CHAPTER FORTY-FOUR

'Say nothing. Do not even breathe.' Hereward unclamped his hand from Alric's mouth and peered into the monk's brown eyes to ensure the message was understood. Satisfied, the warrior pulled his companion back behind the spreading willow where Alric had been waiting for his friend to return with food for his empty belly. A cloth of red and gold leaves had been unfurled across the floor of the wood. Grey mist drifted among the trees, and the air was heavy with the brackish odour of the meandering watercourses. Rooks cawed in their tangled roosts high overhead.

The monk questioned with his eyes, then saw with bafflement that his friend was soaking wet.

Hereward mimed cupping a hand to his ears. Muffled, the insistent thud of hooves on soft ground emerged from the autumnal stillness, drawing nearer. When Alric continued to make questioning faces, the warrior slapped the man on the chest to stop him and then crawled away through the rustling leaves. The dry ground rose up a slight incline to a ridge marked by a long exposed net of roots.

Peering over the top, Hereward studied the group of three riders, easily identified as Norman knights from their dress: a conical helmet with a long nose-shield, a woollen cloak over a tunic and a linen shirt, baggy breeches, and bindings round the lower legs. Each man carried the long shields which tapered to a point at the bottom and offered more protection to the legs and flanks than the English shields. With envy, the warrior noted the double-edged, sharp-pointed swords that were so much more effective at ending a life than anything his own people wielded.

The knights reined in their mounts and conferred in quiet voices, all the time scanning among the trees. Hereward silently cursed himself for being overconfident. A winding journey from the coast through the wildest parts of East Anglia kept the two companions well away from villages and farms during daylight. But at each nightly camp, he had crept away to spy on the small communities. Steeling through the dark streets, he had listened at doors or to the men muttering as they lurched out of the taverns. It seemed that everything he had heard from the merchants arriving in Flanders had been correct: in all of England, only East Anglia had not yet wholly fallen to William the Bastard. Disturbing stories of terror had started to leak out of the north, but in the windswept, watery east the Normans had only started to exert their control over the larger trading centres. The hinterland remained as harsh and unwelcoming to invaders as it had for generations.

Hereward dug his fingers into the leaf mould and sensed the deep power of this inhospitable land. Alric had called it 'the Devil's land of mist and bogs', and it was. Fed by a network of rivers and streams, water flooded along hidden courses to create an inland sea dotted with islands that could only be reached by the shell-shaped craft that the local people used, or by narrow causeways that became lethal traps after night had fallen. Even what appeared to be dry land was deceptively perilous. Swamps lurked everywhere beneath seemingly solid meadows, threatening the unwary traveller. One wrong step could see them sucked down to their deaths. With the bleak hills of West Mercia on one side, the swamps and sea to the north, and wild forests to the south and south-east, the fenland remained isolated behind its own natural defences.

Knowing the land as he did, he had allowed his guard to fall while he had been hunting waterfowl in the reed beds for that day's meal. Crouching on the bank with his small bow and arrow, he had been listening to the voices made by the east wind moaning through the reeds and had not heard the knights ride up the track behind him. With a contemptuous demeanour, they had questioned him in faltering English and then attempted to take his bow and his sword. It might have been easier to give them what they wanted, he knew, but his instincts had taken control and he had resisted. The knights had drawn their swords, and he knew from the familiar look in their eyes that they had decided to kill him, dump his body in the icy water and take their loot anyway.

And so he had dived into the reed beds, sending the water-fowl flapping and screeching. Swimming through the shallows, he had stayed out of reach of the men on the bank and then had picked up the secret paths through the marshes that only some-one raised in the fens would recognize. He thought he had lost them. But here the Normans were, as relentless as the stories about them always said.

Hereward weighed the option of stalking the knights and trying to kill them one by one, but his plan had been predicated on remaining invisible. If these three went missing, more would come searching for them, and more after that. That was the nature of the Normans.

From nearby, the baying of hounds pierced the folding mists. The three knights laughed.

The warrior cursed quietly once more. Another error of judgement. He had presumed the Normans were scouts ex-ploring the deepest reaches of their last unclaimed land, but it seemed they were not alone. Were they outriders for a corps of reinforcements? Part of a hunting band of nobles? How many rode out there in the fog?

As the dogs drew nearer, he crawled back down the slope and

ran to the monk. Grabbing him by his robes, the warrior hauled his companion in the direction of the camp they had made the previous night.

'What have you done now?' Alric wanted to know.

'If you value your life, be quiet. Follow my lead.'

Alric glanced back, unsettled. He almost stumbled as Hereward propelled him through the draping sheets of willow.

'The Normans came across me while I hunted. You see how they are. Not a people who will allow even the most harmless opposition to their word. Now they have decided I am better prey than birds or deer.'

'Why do I let you go off on your own? I always know what the result will be.'

Hereward set his jaw. 'Do you wish to have your own gibbet here?'

'We could talk to them,' Alric grumbled. 'Tell them we are poor travellers who have lost our way—'

'Monk, sometimes you are blind to what lies before your eyes, or else you wilfully ignore it. Either way, you will be the death of us both.' On the edge of the camp, the warrior turned and grasped his friend's shoulders. 'If they catch us, they will kill us. Do you understand? You are in the land of the Normans now. Words mean nothing here.'

Uneasy, Alric looked back in the direction of the hounds. 'The dogs will scent our trail.'

Hereward ran to the tethered horses, untied the leather straps and slapped their flanks to send them cantering off into the woods. He hoped they would be able to avoid the bogs on their own.

'What are you doing?' the monk protested. 'They cost us good coin. And how will we travel—'

His eyes blazing, the warrior grabbed his friend with both hands in the neck of his robe. 'Do what I say. This is my world now, not yours, and if you listen to me you may live through it.' The excited barks echoed just beyond the low ridge of exposed roots. 'Run!'

Turning, he ducked low beneath the trailing willow branches and sprinted without checking whether the monk was behind him. Soon the pounding of leather soles and ragged breathing sounded at his back. Before they had settled on the campsite, Hereward had scouted the lie of the land. He knew the location of the overgrown watercourses, the old tracks, the marshes. The barking of the dogs grew closer. The warrior imagined the curs snapping at their heels and the smirking knights encouraging their fellows to the hunt. He set his teeth, holding back the blood-rush.

'We will not outrun them,' Alric gasped, the fear in his voice palpable.

Bursting from the trees, Hereward skidded to a halt where the ground fell away before a sheet of bright green rippling under the grey mist. He snaked out an arm to grab his friend before he careered into the deadly marsh. Panic flared in Alric's face.

Momentarily, Hereward held his companion with his eyes, reassuring him while the hounds' baying raced nearer. When the monk gave a hesitant, trusting nod, the warrior grabbed the man's robes and jumped with him into the swamp. Hereward felt arms of liquid mud encircle him and drag him inexorably down. Alric flailed in panic as his head dipped beneath the slimy surface. Snaking one hand up, the warrior caught hold of an exposed tree root beneath the overhanging lip of bank where the woodland floor had fallen away into the marsh. With his other hand he snatched his friend's robes. The monk gulped and spluttered, his face smeared with filth. Hereward pressed one finger to his mouth. With an effort, Alric silenced himself, and the two men eased under the lip of hanging grass and crumbling brown soil just in time.

The curs' barking resounded over the two mens' heads as the dogs ran along the edge of the bog, snuffling in the undergrowth. A moment later, the thump of hooves reverberated through the soil. His eyes wide, the monk held the back of a hand against his mouth to stifle a moan of dread.

The sound of leather shoes hitting the turf; one of the knights had dismounted. Then another. Footsteps approached the edge and came to a halt directly over Hereward's head. A curt command from further back. The hounds' snuffling and yelping receded. Silence fell.

A bubble rose on the slimy surface of the swamp, then burst with a *pop* that sounded jarringly loud in the misty stillness. Alric grew fixed and still. Hereward felt the blood rumble in his head.

A hint of a shadow fell across the rippling green marsh-water. The knight was peering over the edge, looking where the bubble burst, listening.

Alric screwed his eyes shut tight.

Do not whimper. Do not cry out, Hereward thought.

A grunt from the knight, still hovering on the edge. A comment with a querying note. Laughter among the knight's two companions. Had the dogs identified the fugitives' location? Was the knight toying with them?

Hereward felt his muscles grow tense.

The rapid beat of more riders arriving. Voices raised, conversation flashing back and forth.

The warrior tried to estimate how many knights now stood a whisper away. For long moments the conversation ranged across the group, and then the knight barked something in his gruff tongue and returned to his horse. Someone else shouted an order and the dogs padded away. The thunder of hoofbeats disappearing into the quiet wood echoed across the marsh. The knights would be following the tracks of the horses he freed, Hereward hoped. It would buy time.

Alric sagged. Shaking with the release, he whispered, 'Is this how it is to be now? Fear everywhere? English hunted like animals?'

Hereward felt a wave of respect for his friend. By no means a fighting man, the monk had endured much at the warrior's side yet still continued to be a true companion. Silently, the warrior vowed to keep Alric safe, even at the cost of his own life. 'Let us wait before we pass judgement,' he replied, trying to raise the monk's spirits but fearing the worst. 'Now, hold tight. I will have you out before you drink too much of this stew.' When Alric fumbled for the root, Hereward reached out to grab a handful of turf and hauled himself slowly out of the sucking mud.

Once they were on the bank, the shivering monk gasped, 'If the roots had not been there to support us, we would have been sucked down to our deaths.'

'I knew the roots were there.'

'You knew?'

'Yes.'

'You searched the area for an escape from all possible encounters,' Alric persisted, incredulous.

'That is how I survive, monk.'

CHAPTER FORTY-FIVE

On weary feet, the two men pressed westwards for the rest of the morning. The mist lifted, treating Alric to the beauty of a world turned silver as the pale light glinted off sheets of water that reached almost to the horizon. Islands of green grass with dense orange, gold and brown copses splashed colour across the fens. A suffocating stillness lay hard on the land.

Hereward picked a path across a narrow causeway snaking only a hand's width above a treacherous bog. Amid the stink of decaying vegetative matter, the warrior felt the exuberance of their escape dissipate and a familiar brooding descend upon him. 'Monk,' he called to the man trailing along the uneven path behind, 'I would know God's plan for us.'

For a moment, Alric held his tongue. 'God's plan is that we do God's work.'

Hereward heard the dissatisfying uncertainty in his friend's tone. 'I was a man when you first met me, but I was not a man,' he said. 'I saw the world as a child would. You, and Vadir, have taught me things that my father never did. But the more I have learned, the less I feel I know. Is this right, monk? Why do I feel this emptiness . . . this disquiet? You told me I was more than a devil in human form, as I have been called time and again since I was a child. More than a feeder of ravens, leaving only sobbing widows and fatherless children in his wake. If what you say is true, then what is my purpose in life?'

'The questions you ask . . . there are no easy answers,' Alric began, choosing his words carefully. 'I wish God had given me the skill to divine the purpose you need, but I am just a man, Hereward, with all the failings of men. I can reflect. I can offer guidance. But in the end, every man must look into his own heart to find the answers he seeks.'

'In my own heart?' the warrior murmured.

'Yes.'

Hereward's head dropped as he turned his thoughts in on himself. For a long while, he lost himself to the dark reaches inside him, and when he next looked round the causeway was far behind. Familiar landmarks rose up on every side: the field where he learned to hunt with his father's falcon, the copse where he first lay with a woman, the fair Cengifu, the farm of his childhood friend Ailwin, who died when the sickness took him and his two brothers and sisters. Memories of happiness, pain and grief locked into the dark soil, the stark trees, the shimmering pools. For a moment, he stood and drank in his past.

'Enjoy the view,' Alric sniffed, 'but I am cold and wet and filthy and I would know what you plan to do with us here.'

'Once I know, I will tell you.' Hereward sifted the strange feelings rising within him.

The old straight track knifed from the ancient stone marker post to the church tower dark against the pale sky. Growing silent, the two men followed it along the side of a watercourse edged with brown reeds rustling in the breeze. The day drew on. When they passed a row of skeletal willows, cheery voices rose up from the near bank.

Alric came to a halt, gaping. A stocky, ruddy-faced man floated through the air, his head and torso just visible above the treetops. 'What is this place you have brought me to?' the monk hissed.

Hereward roared with laughter at his friend's expression, bending from the waist to steady himself with his hands on his thighs. When Alric backed away, still gripped by the frightening sight, the warrior grabbed his companion and dragged him along the track past the willows. The monk stopped, marvelling. The 'floating' man towered above them on a pair of stilts, which he was using to move across the watercourse and the treacherous pools that lay beyond.

Enjoying the respite from his brooding, Hereward watched the stilt-man's familiar looping gait as he spun across the water with such skill that he appeared to be flying. 'We are a people of the wetlands,' the warrior explained to his entranced friend. 'Our entire lives are lived on and around the water, learning ways to enjoy the bounties it offers and to navigate its hidden dangers.'

'This is a wonder indeed,' Alric muttered.

'The Normans may have their fine swords and their maces and their archers, but they will struggle to thrive here. Only people who know the safe, secret routes through the fens can escape death by drowning. The water here is a living thing. It breathes and waits and hunts for prey, and claims the lives of many strangers. Land can be dry one day and a marsh or a lake the next.'

Half distracted by the stilt-man, Hereward felt the first stirrings of an idea, as yet unrealized. Before he could examine it further, a snowy-haired man burst from the long grass on the bank and stabbed a spear towards the two wanderers.

'What do you want?' the man barked. He wore a coat of rabbit pelts smeared with lamb-fat to keep the elements at bay.

'Holbert?' Hereward could see the man was scared.

'Who are you?' The man leaned forward, squinting. The warrior grasped what a sight he and Alric looked, filthy with dried black mud from feet to neck and more of it splattered across their faces. Stepping closer but not lowering his spear, the white-haired man peered for a moment and then ventured, 'Hereward Asketilson?'

The warrior nodded, remembering the time he stole a line of fish that Holbert had spent two days smoking. He felt a pang of guilt.

'Are you here to steal from me again? Because I have little and I will fight till I die to keep it.' Sensing danger, the stilt-man strode towards them, glowering.

'I am not the man who tormented you, Holbert.'

'You tormented everyone, you and your wild friends,' the elderly man grumbled, the feelings still raw after so many years. 'We heard you were outlaw.'

'We heard you were dead.' The ruddy-faced man leaned forward on his stilts and just at the point when he seemed on the brink of falling he dropped like a cat to his feet.

'Then I am a ghost.' Hereward smiled.

'And what a time you picked to haunt your home grounds.' Holbert lowered his spear. 'There are worse things abroad in the fens these days. There must be, if I look on a bastard like Hereward Asketilson with something like fondness.' He shrugged and turned to the stilt-man. 'Sawin, get some ale. Let us welcome home this son of the fens with a moment of joy before he realizes what hell he has returned to.'

Sawin pushed through the waist-high, yellowing grass and skidded down the bank. Holbert, Hereward and Alric followed. Hidden among the undergrowth beside the willows and above the spring flood-line was a small shack with wattle walls and a roof of branches covered with turf. Scattered along the water's edge lay the detritus of Holbert's business. Wooden tubs of reeking fat. Hides drying over willow frames. Creamy curls of wood shavings. Mallets, bow-saws, adzes, wedges, planes and awls. Hereward remembered lying in the long grass, watching Holbert's meticulous labour as he built the shell-like boats that the fenlanders used to traverse the watercourses, shaping the willow frames, stretching the hides and waterproofing them with the fat, cutting the short-handled paddles.

Cup in hand, Holbert looked Alric up and down as if he had only just noticed him. 'Who are you? Monk? Your kind are as bad as the bastard Normans.'

Alric recoiled. 'My kind?'

'The clergy. They were the ones pushing for William the Bastard to be made king.' The white-haired man threw back his ale and wiped his mouth with the back of his hand. 'They watch us. They pass on what they see to our new masters.' He spat. 'And they get their rewards. They're living fat while we pay our taxes. But you'll see. William will bring his own kind in sooner or later. And when there's Norman bishops giving out the orders, then there won't be so much chest-puffing and strutting.'

Hereward sat on the bank and warmed himself against a smouldering fire made from the off-cut timber. 'And the Normans, here?'

Holbert shook his head, frowning. 'The bastards won't be happy until there's nothing of England left. They don't care for us, for our families or our wives or our children. They raise our taxes, and put us to work building their castles and garrisons. Speak out, you'll find your house burned. Two speak out, the village gets burned. Look at one of their knights the wrong way, you'll be hanging from a tree the next morning with the rooks feasting on your eyes. William the Bastard won't be happy till he's crushed the life from us. Till we're nothing but cattle in the field, keeping the Norman bellies full.' He looked into his empty cup, his mood dismal. 'You should have stayed away. There's nothing for you here.'

Hereward set his jaw. 'Fight back.'

'Me? On my own? Or me and him?' Holbert nodded towards Sawin, laughing without humour.

'We are English. We fought against the Vikings in our fathers' fathers' fathers' time. We fought against each other until we were all raw head and bloody bones, God knows. And now we lie down and do nothing?'

'You haven't seen what it's like,' Holbert muttered. He didn't meet Hereward's eyes and shuffled away in search of more ale. The warrior thought how broken-backed the boatwright looked. Was all England like this?

'There is no place anywhere like the fens,' the warrior pressed, waving his cup at Sawin. 'It is a fortress, protected on all sides, and riddled with traps and dangers that the Normans would never be able to navigate. Why, a few good men here could start a rebellion that would bring all William's plans crashing to the ground.'

'There have been rebellions aplenty,' the ruddy-faced man murmured, 'and they all ended the same way.' He saw the look in Hereward's face and snapped, 'Do not call us cowards! You have been away from the worst of it. If you had been here you would be like the rest of us.'

His nose turning pink from the ale, Holbert returned with another full cup. 'Entire villages are starving because the Normans have taken the food for their own garrisons. The sickness has returned, some say. People are dying in their own blood, puke and shit all over England. These are the End-Times, just like all the prophecies said, and there's not a thing you can do about it.'

Anger flashed across Hereward's face, but he controlled himself. 'I am not here to wage war with the Normans. I am outlaw. You, Holbert, all the men and women here, none of you wanted any part of me. England wanted no part of me. I was driven away from my home, and saw my woman murdered by others who sought to use me for their own ends.'

'Then why have you come back?'

'To see my father one final time, and find some peace between us for what has gone before. To talk to my young brother Beric and make amends for the blight I must have placed upon his life. And to speak to Redwald, if I can, about a matter that may interest him.'

Hereward could feel Alric's sympathetic gaze upon him, but it was Holbert who caught his attention. The elderly man blanched almost as white as his beard.

'What troubles you?' the warrior asked, his eyes narrowing.

'It is not for me to say. You will find out soon enough.' The boatwright glanced towards the western sky. 'It gets dark early this time of year. If you leave now, you should be home by dusk.' He caught himself. 'But your father is not at his hall.'

Hereward flinched. 'The Normans have taken it?'

Nodding, Holbert flashed a glance at Sawin that the warrior couldn't read. 'He is staying in the house that used to belong to Berwyn the leatherworker. Before Berwyn saw fit to anger the bastards.'

Hereward could see a dark mood had fallen on the two men, but neither would discuss what haunted them. He finished his ale and thanked Holbert for his hospitality before making his way back to the old straight track.

'Why did you not tell me you wanted to visit your kin?' Alric asked.

'I should tell you everything?'

Alric looked hurt. 'If I am to help you—'

'Some things are beyond help.'

For a moment the monk hesitated, and then he said, 'I find myself afraid, and I do not know why. But the look on Holbert's face—'

'It is too late to go back.' Hereward ended the conversation and closed his own mind to conjecture. Instead, he fixed his attention on the grey light moving towards the horizon and set off along the track.

He felt his mood darken with the fading of the day. No comfort came to him from the old trees that had been friends in his youth, places for hiding or trysting. No old memories stirred him. Barholme was silent. A chill wind blew across the scattered farms, some unidentifiable sour odour caught up in it. Suddenly he realized he was not yet ready to face his father. Troubled thoughts had been stirred up in him, and he would wait until they stilled. He needed to find the right words, and not be driven by rage or loathing or grief.

'I would see my father's hall first,' he said.

Alric looked pleased that the uneasy silence had been broken. 'This is your home?' he said, looking round.

'Asketil Tokesune is a wealthy man. He holds land in many places, freely with sake and soke, but Barholme was always close to his heart.'

'And you have fond memories of it?'

'I have . . . memories.'

Hereward strode on, determined to avoid more questions. He followed the track through the leafless trees until he saw his father's hall loom up in the half-light. It was an old, timber-framed building, the thatch wearing thin in many places. From within echoed the raucous sound of drunken singing.

The warrior stiffened. Alric caught his friend's sword-arm and whispered, 'You have learned some wisdom in your years on the road. Do not throw it away now you are back on your own soil.'

Hereward nodded. 'The wisdom is all yours.' The loud voices told him there were many Normans inside the hall, too many to confront. Still, the building called to him. He thought of his mother lying on the boards, her glassy eyes devoid of the warmth he had known. Her ghost still walked here, the ghost of the woman she had been, the reminder of the only days of peace he had known in his life. His chest tightened as the visions rose up.

Each step along the track to the arched gateway in the enclosure brought another memory of her, teaching him the harp with giggles and teasing, singing, smiling, calling to him to come home. *Come home, Hereward. Come home.*

And then he looked up the tall elm poles that formed the arch and his heart stopped.

Alric must have noticed that his friend had grown rigid for he hissed, 'What is wrong?' Standing beside the warrior, the monk followed his line of vision to the top of the arch, squinting in the growing dusk, not believing what he was seeing. And then all he could say was, 'Oh.'

Hanging on the arch was a head, turning green, eyes gone, mouth sagging. The decay had not been merciful, for Hereward recognized it in an instant. His young brother, Beric.

CHAPTER FORTY-SIX

Blood flooded Hereward's head. In the thrum of arterial flow, he heard his young brother's dying screams and the laughter of the Normans hacking through muscle and gristle. Rage, burning hot. And then whispers, the seductive voice of his devil, throwing off the shackles that had been forged so carefully over three years, and rising up in him, filling him, destroying him.

Someone tried to grab him, urging him to restrain himself, to grieve but not to hate, but the words came to him as if through deep water. The warrior threw the arms off him and rounded on the one trying to restrain him. It was the monk. Whatever Alric saw in his friend's face, he recoiled in horror.

'There must be blood for this,' Hereward hissed. Flames closed in around his vision.

'If you give in to your urges, you will lose everything you have gained,' the monk pleaded.

'It is too late for that. Too late for everything.'

'Please, I will pray for you . . .' Alric clutched at his companion's tunic.

'I do not need your prayers,' Hereward snapped. 'Only revenge. He . . . he was barely a man.' Caught by a rush of grief, he glanced back at the rotting head above the archway. The stink of decomposition drifted down to him.

'Then at least do not confront the Normans now. You will be killed.' The monk let go of the tunic and stepped back, clutching his hands together in desperation.

Hereward's head swam. His devil urged him to enter the hall and slaughter all he found there, telling him that then, and only then, would the pain be eased and he would find peace. The monk sensed his inner battle and grabbed him once again. As if dashing in a skull with a rock, the warrior threw his friend to the floor. Unsheathing his sword, he almost drove it into the man's chest there and then to end the sanctimonious pleadings.

Alric threw his arms wide. 'Kill me then. If it will end your rage and save your soul, I give you my life.'

Blood closed over Hereward's vision and he thrust down with the blade. The monk cried out. His vision clearing, Hereward glared down at a torn robe and a bloody shoulder. Some hidden part of him had twisted the sword at the last moment, but he had been poised to kill the man who had tried to save him.

Sickened, the warrior sheathed his sword and lurched away through the growing gloom. The blood still pounded in his ears, filled with screams and whispers. Stark trees lashed in a howling wind that had blown up from nowhere, and in that gale he thought he could hear the voices too, or was it just the *alfar* stalking him, ready to steal his life and his soul? The moon was out, and the stars, glittering like ice.

Down winding tracks he ran into the haunted night, and gradually his rage seeped away and his blood subsided and the devil returned to its cave. When his thoughts calmed, he recognized the small, timber-roofed house that had belonged to Berwyn the leatherworker looming out of the dark. Now, though, it was the home of his father.

Standing on the threshold, Hereward felt unsure if he could enter. His stomach had knotted, and though he told himself it was his mounting grief at Beric's death, he knew he was simply afraid. How had he come to this? So many hearts had been stilled by his sword, and he was frightened of an old man. His father could do him no harm. And he had travelled so many miles across the whale road, just to be here. Why could he not bring himself to go inside?

Cursing his weakness, he called, 'Asketil Tokesune.' When there was no reply, he repeated, louder this time, 'Asketil Tokesune. It is your son. Hereward.'

A low growl emanated from the quiet interior; it could almost have been that of a beast.

Hereward entered the dark, chill house. Only a few dying embers remained in the hearth. The floor was beaten mud covered with dry rushes, not the fine timber boards of a thegn's hall, and in the gloom he could see little sign of comfort, no tapestries, no ivory or gold, no cauldron of ale. A grey figure hovered in the shadows near the far wall. When it stepped forward, the warrior felt shocked by how greatly his father had aged. Asketil's face was the colour of ashes, hollow-cheeked and sagging around the eyes so that the shape of the skull could be identified. The thegn's silvery hair was thinning on top and hung lank around his shoulders. But the warrior felt most struck by his father's loss of potency. The man of iron who had ranged through the days of Hereward's youth with fists like hammers and a heart like an anvil had been replaced by a bent-backed, hollow-chested wisp of straw.

Visions flashed through the warrior's head. Broken bones and bloody noses. Split lips and black eyes. A night of terror buried beneath the boards of the hall while the rats scurried all around. Cruel words delivered from a cold face, accusations of weakness and failure. And then the memories he wanted to keep locked away for ever, surfacing in a rush that took his breath away: those fists raining down on his mother, even while she pleaded and cried until her lips were so pulped she could not form words, and the sounds like the cracking of dry summer wood, and the wet, sticky splatterings on the boards, and the low moans slowly fading away until there was only silence.

For a moment, Hereward reeled as if he had been struck again. And when the visions finally cleared, his father still stood there with eyes like coals.

'I should have known that in this lowest tide of my life, the harbinger of all that has gone wrong would sail back in.' Asketil spat each stony word.

Hereward fought to restrain himself. He had played this meeting over in his head so many times, promising himself he would not give in to rage or accusations. All he wanted was the final spade of earth upon a grave.

'Beric,' the warrior croaked. 'The Normans killed him.'

'You killed him.'

Though he recognized the absurdity of the statement, Hereward still felt the blow to his heart.

'When you took the life of your woman—'

'I did not kill her,' the warrior interjected. 'I do not know whose hand held the blade, but Tidhild died at the order of Harold Godwinson.'

'When you took the life of your woman,' Asketil continued as if he had not heard Hereward's denial, 'and fled like a coward rather than accept judgement of your bloody actions, Beric's heart was broken. His wits fled. In that boy's eyes, you were hero, not outlaw.'

Because he saw me as his saviour from your hand, the warrior thought.

'He never spoke again after the day you abandoned him. One week gone something stirred within him, some madness, and he ran to my hall and taunted the knights and threw stones. And they meted out their punishment in the harsh manner that is the Norman way.' The older man flashed a sneering look at Hereward as he went to the hearth. 'You failed the boy as you have failed all of us.'

For a moment, the warrior let the words hang in the air. 'I have come here—'

'. . . to beg my forgiveness?' Asketil's humourless laughter rolled out. 'You will never get that.'

'To give *you* the opportunity to ask for forgiveness.' Hereward's voice hardened. 'So that you can atone for your crimes and all the matters that lie between us can be laid to rest.'

Asketil whirled. 'My crimes?' he snapped. 'All the misery that has been inflicted on this house has come from your actions. The shame you have heaped upon me over the years . . . your crimes as a child . . . the robbing and the beatings of good neighbours . . . the mockery you brought to me at court with your misbehaviour. And then' – he smacked his lips with distaste – 'you took an innocent life in drunkenness or rage, and you forced me to plead with Harold Godwinson, a Wessex man, to intercede with the king on my behalf so our kin would not suffer the greatest shame of all. If your crime had been debated by the Witan all of England would have learned of my humiliation.'

Hereward hung his head. 'I know my failings. You are right to chastise me. I was a weak child, and I gave in to my devils too easily.'

'Blame it on the Devil, but it is you.' Asketil strode forward, bunching his bony hands into fists that still wanted to inflict pain. 'You are black to the core, and you will never be anything else.'

Hereward knew he could have knocked the man to the ground with a single blow, taken his life with one strike, but still he stepped back. 'You killed Mother and you blamed her death on an accident.' The words came out blunter than the warrior intended, but Asketil appeared to be untouched by them. 'That night has left a wound in me that I fear will never heal.'

The thegn snorted. 'And if not for you, she too would still live.'

The warrior's chest tightened. Some deep part of him believed every accusation his father made. 'How so?'

Unafraid, Asketil pushed his cold face into Hereward's. 'She tried to protect you. You went too far, as you always have, as you still do. You defied my word—'

'I was barely a child,' Hereward protested.

319

'Black to the core, from the very beginning,' the older man roared. 'I saw it in you when you were born. It is your nature.'

The warrior wiped a shaking hand across his mouth. He felt a child once more, waiting for the inevitable. 'We should not have these years of loathing lying between us any longer. There is no gain. We must start afresh.'

'And that is why you have come here?' Asketil sneered.

'We are joined by blood—'

The thegn slowly shook his head. 'You are not my son. I scarce believe you have any of my blood within you.' He made no attempt to mask his contempt. 'Your mother was a whore. Who knows who truly sired you. Some wild beast?'

Hereward felt a rush of anger. His hand fell to the hilt of his sword.

Asketil advanced, unbowed. 'I will do all I can to aid the Normans in ridding this world of you.'

'Even after Beric's death?'

'Because of his death! In the memory of my good son, betrayed by you. If I still had my sword, I would drive it through your heart and make this world a better place. God would forgive me.' Asketil struck the warrior across the cheek with all his strength. Hereward let his hand fall from his sword and turned his face towards his father again. The thegn struck once more.

Hereward swallowed, searching his father's hate-filled gaze. He could see now that whatever he had hoped for from their meeting would never be. The past could not be laid to rest. The pain could never go away. They both were what they were, and they would always be that way. For a moment, he bowed his head and then he walked to the door.

'Run,' Asketil called after him, 'as you always have. You show your cowardly nature in everything you do. Run, for I go to the Normans now and I will stand beside them as they hunt you down.'

When the warrior stepped out into the cold night, he saw a shadow waiting along the track. It was the monk. 'What did you hear?' he snarled.

'N . . . nothing,' Alric stuttered.

Hereward felt sure his companion was lying. But a turmoil whirled inside him and he thrust the monk to one side and ran, away from his father, away from his past, knowing he could escape neither.

CHAPTER FORTY-SEVEN

The raised sword burned like a brand in the red rays of the rising sun. Beneath the potent symbol, the mounted Norman knight grinned at the ten English men standing in a semicircle in front of him. Their faces were sullen and sleepy-eyed, but they watched him with unmistakable loathing. He cared little. Power resided with the conqueror. Nothing else mattered, Aldous Wyvill thought.

Cawing rooks broke the misty stillness of the morning. At the gateway to the ramshackle enclosure surrounding the thegn's former hall, seven other Norman knights stood like sentinels. Their polished helmets were aglow, the finely woven woollen cloaks as black as night. The contrast between the imposing smartness of the military apparel and the worn, mud-flecked tunics of the rag-tag peasants could not have been greater, Aldous noted.

'Work hard,' he ordered in a clear voice, his English only slightly inflected with his Norman tongue, 'and you will be allowed to return to your farms in good time. You will be given bread and ale once the job is done. Dissent, or laziness, will be dealt with harshly.' He glanced up at the rotting head of the thegn's son to illustrate his point. 'Begin.' The sword slashed down to his side.

Grudgingly, the peasants plucked up their spades and set to work digging the deep ramparts and replacing the palisade with fresh wood, taller and cut to a point at the top. Soon they would be building a castle here, but for now the hall needed to be fortified, Aldous knew. There had been little resistance in this part of the fens, but it would come.

His legs bound with linen strips in the criss-cross style that signified his high status, the knight urged his horse back under the gateway into the enclosure. He breathed deeply of the aroma of damp leaves and the woodsmoke from the morning's hearth-fire. Though a long way from his home in Hauteville, there was some peace here now the fighting was over, he decided. But the English were an odd breed, and he wondered if he would ever understand them. Their government and their art, their trade and their financial system, were jealously eyed by all Europe, but the people themselves were an unruly, intemperate lot, given to drunkenness, fighting, coarse humour and moods that swung between raucous high spirits and maudlin introspection. They would not take orders, even if refusal brought them harm. They would do everything in their power to cause delays, distraction and minor irritations, and they seemed to find pleasure in the slightest disruption they engendered. But they would learn, in time. The Normans were the mighty ocean waves pounding any rock-like resistance into meaningless granules of sand.

'Sire.'

Aldous glanced back to see a young knight striding from the gate.

'Sire. You have a visitor. The old thegn, Asketil.'

With a sigh, the Norman commander looked to the gateway where a grey wisp of a man rested against a gnarled staff. Aldous removed his helmet and rubbed a hand through his close-cropped hair. His nose was long and sharp, ending at a moustache that curved down to his chin. 'Is he begging for food again?'

'He wishes to tell you about a coming rebellion.'

'Oh?' Aldous raised his eyebrows. 'Bring him into the hall. He may find the surroundings familiar and comfortable.'

The two men laughed.

The Norman commander dismounted and marched into the warm hall. Ornately embroidered tapestries hung on the walls and gold plate and bowls glinted in the firelight. He had made no changes to the opulent surroundings since he had become the lord. Indeed, he barely recognized them. Their only value was to mark his power, he thought. With three quick strides, he bounded on to the low dais and took the old wooden chair where Asketil had once sat, and his father before him. Aldous felt only contempt for the old thegn. A weak man, pathetic in his whinings, who still came to bow and scrape before the men who killed his son. Aldous would have attacked the murderers single-handedly with his sword and died with honour in failing.

The grey-haired Englishman shuffled in and stood uneasily in the doorway, looking around his former home.

'Draw closer, Asketil. Welcome to my home,' the Norman commander boomed, making no attempt to hide his smirk.

'I am here to warn you,' the thegn began, his croaking voice almost lost in the hall's vault, 'of a sword raised against you.'

'And who would dare to challenge me, old man?'

'His name is Hereward, and he is my son.'

Aldous's eyes narrowed. He had heard the name before. A great warrior whose fearsome exploits had gained the attention of Baldwin of Flanders. *Bear-Killer*, the mercenaries had called him when they had joined the invading Norman force, to a man fearing they would face this Hereward on the field of battle in England. Was this the same warrior? If it were, he would need to send word to the court in London. More supplies, more mercenaries. The fens would need special attention.

'Why would you warn me about your own son?' the Norman commander asked.

'Because he is a black-hearted outlaw who has brought shame to his kin.'

It had been the right decision after all to keep the old thegn alive, the commander thought. With the information he supplied, they could set a fine trap to catch the English rebel before even a weapon was raised. Aldous smiled. 'Tell me more.'

Chapter Forty-Eight

Icy black water swilled around Alric's neck. Panic surged through him. He thrashed his arms to find the narrow causeway, but it was lost in the impenetrable night and the activity only dragged him down further. Kicking his leather shoes in the muddy depths, he fought to stay afloat. The swamp-water sluiced into his mouth, stinking of rotting leaves. He gulped, choked, threw his head back and cried out although he knew there was no one within miles to hear. The weight of his habit dragged him down. Alric passed from the black of the moonless night to a deeper black as the water closed over his head. Silent prayers gave way to sheer terror. Pressure filled his mouth, his nose, his lungs burned, and down he went, and down.

I am a fool, he thought, his last thought.

And then, through the mad whirl in his head, he felt his descent arrested. Water tore at his face and hair as he was dragged rapidly up and out into the chill night. Vomiting swamp-juice, he sucked in a huge gulp of breath. The dark enveloped him. He couldn't see what was happening, or where he was, but then he became aware of hands grabbing the shoulders of his tunic. Roughly thrown to one side, he crashed on to a hard surface. The flint shards of the causeway ground into his cheek. He lay there for a moment, recovering, and then rolled on to his back. A dark figure loomed over him.

'You are a fool, monk.' It was Hereward's voice, as if he had read Alric's mind. 'Why would you try to make your way through the bog with no torch to light your way and no fenlander to guide you?'

'Because you abandoned me,' Alric spluttered, realizing how pathetic his response sounded. He let his head fall back and closed his eyes, drinking in the joy of living. He had let his desperation get the better of him, he understood that now. But when Hereward had raced off into the night after leaving his father's house, the worst had seemed a distinct possibility. Alric had overheard the bitter conversation between the two men and now understood his friend's inner darkness in a way he could never have grasped before. The pain was still raw. But was it a pain so acute that Hereward would take his own life?

Though he had raced in pursuit, Hereward had outpaced him, and soon he had been left alone on the old straight track. He was filthy, exhausted, and there were no friends to offer him a bed. A cold night passed in fitful sleep under a willow, waking repeatedly, afraid of wolves. By dawn, his bones ached and his stomach growled. He had retraced his steps to the boatwright, but the snowy-haired man only treated him with suspicion, and if he knew where Hereward might have gone he wasn't saying. And so the monk had spent the day searching and calling. At some point he had wandered off the track and found himself lost in the unforgiving waterlands, surrounded by endless pools and bogs and copses and scattered islands with no landmarks or clear path to find his way back to the village. And then night had fallen, and he had started to believe that Hereward had killed himself. His despair had turned to panic and he had foolishly started to jog, then to run as fast as his weary legs could carry him. Halfway along the narrow causeway, he had wrong-footed himself and pitched into the water.

'Here is a rule for you,' Hereward said. Alric could see the silhouette of his friend squatting further along the causeway.

'No man born outside the fens can find his way across these treacherous bogs and keep his life. This time God watched over you, or I did. Next time you may not be so fortunate. Do not attempt such a risky journey again. Do you understand?'

'Oh, yes. I plan to dance across this stinking hell every night,' the monk snapped. 'How long have you been watching me? Could you have spared me this misery? If you tell me you could have, I will not be responsible for my actions.'

Hereward laughed softly. Alric found it a strange sound, devoid of humour. Something had changed in his friend.

'I thought you had returned to Flanders. Or worse, lost your life,' the monk explained.

'There is work to do here first.'

It was an unsettling reply, mainly because Alric didn't know to which part of his statement Hereward was responding.

The warrior hauled the sodden monk to his feet. 'Come. There is a warm campfire waiting. Once you are dry and full, your spirits will rise.'

He led the way back along the causeway, on a winding path beside a bog, and across a second causeway to a thickly wooded island. Pushing through the dense vegetation, Alric realized they were following a path that only Hereward could see. The monk could smell smoke on the breeze, but could see no light ahead.

When he had struggled up the steep incline until the breath burned his chest, his friend suddenly disappeared from view. Baffled, Alric caught an ash branch to pull himself up and found himself standing on the lip of a broad hollow lit by a flickering campfire. The meaty aroma of cooked fowl hung in the air. White willow and ash continued across the dip, but some saplings had been newly cleared, by Hereward, Alric guessed, and the hill continued up to the tree-shrouded summit on the far side.

Skidding down the bank, Alric followed Hereward towards the campfire, only to come up sharp when he saw another man hunched on a fallen branch, gnawing on a bone. Big as an ox, with shaggy brown hair and beard, the man let his flickering gaze drift over the new arrival and then returned to his meal. 'We feast on fowl, but now you bring me a drowned rat,' he muttered. By his size and his wry tone, Alric was reminded of a younger Vadir.

'Guthrinc,' Hereward said by way of introduction. 'This is the monk I told you about.'

'Monk,' Guthrinc said with a nod.

'Who are you?' Alric asked, his eyes flickering towards the carcass resting on a flat stone in the ashes. Hereward tore off a leg and tossed it to him.

The large man shrugged. 'This and that.' He eyed Alric up and down. 'God has not looked kindly on you. What have you done to offend him?'

'Leave him be,' Hereward said. 'He has had a fright in Dedman's bog.'

Tossing his bone to one side, Guthrinc wiped his hands on his tunic and said, 'I'll keep watch.' He hauled himself to his feet and disappeared into the dark towards the lip of the hollow.

Shaking from the cold and the shock of his brush with death, Alric almost leapt on to the branch next to the fire. 'You trust him?' he said, warming his hands.

'We ran together when we were youths. He likes his ale and his meat and his women, but in any fight he is like a wolf at your side.'

Alric chewed on his bone for a moment, then said, 'You plan to fight?'

'The Normans are a blight on all England. They must be driven out, like rats from the grain store.' The warrior's voice hardened, his face becoming thunderous. 'Their blood must turn the rivers red and their bodies pile up like stones on the beach as they flee to their ships.'

The monk considered the new-found vehemence in his friend's tone, trying to make sense of this sudden rebellion. 'And this great victory will be accomplished by two of you?'

Hereward's eyes narrowed. 'Three, I would hope.'

'Three, then. But what can three men do against an army?

The Normans have crushed any resistance. Destroyed whole villages.'

'Three is only the start. As word spreads of the resistance we mount here in the fens, Englishmen will rush to take up arms alongside us.' The warrior stared into the middle distance, imagining the picture his words conjured up. 'They will come in their tens, their hundreds, their thousands, and we shall rise up, with one voice, one weapon, and smite our enemy. We will crush the ones who make our lives a misery, who steal our freedom, our dreams, our hope. And then, when we are one family once more, peace will reign in England and our future will be assured.'

The passion he heard in the warrior's voice frightened Alric. Yet in the fire flickering in Hereward's eyes, the monk saw hints of a deeper truth. Though terrifying in number and strength, the Normans were an enemy the warrior felt he could defeat, whereas a grey-haired, beaten man remained invincible. 'Take care,' he whispered, 'that you do not win the battle but lose your soul in the process.'

Hereward laughed. 'Always you worry. We have all the time we need to raise our forces and to plan. William the Bastard's men still slumber, unaware that we are here. The battle in the fens will be over before the Normans know what hit them. And then we will take it to all England.'

CHAPTER FORTY-NINE

25 October 1067

Fat white candles flickered around the High Altar. Shadows swooped across the stained-glass window and the dressed stone wall above it to the vaulted roof, as deep and dark as the black robes of the abbot kneeling in prayer. Only the soft muttering of the Latin devotion disturbed the peace.

Abbot Brand breathed in wisps of sweetly aromatic incense and opened his eyes. He was a gaunt man, as hard as a cold flagstone, with piercing black eyes and thin lips that appeared to be sneering at comfort. Rising to his feet, he crossed himself, and only then did he hear the soft click of a closing door and the echo of feet padding along the nave.

Alric watched the man turn, gauging the abbot's nature from the intensity of his stare and every line in his face. Suspicious at first, the man absorbed the monkish robes of the new arrival and said in an iron voice, 'What is the meaning of this interruption?'

'Father, I waited until you had finished your prayers, but there is an important matter which needs your attention.'

'Who are you to make demands of me?'

'I am merely a humble servant of God,' Alric replied. 'Like yourself.'

The abbot took a moment to consider if there was any insult implied in the comment. The monk continued, 'My companion and I have travelled long and hard here to Burgh Abbey, and we are weary from the road. Would you deny us a brief moment?'

'It must wait until morning,' the abbot snapped. 'The business of the abbey calls to me.' He moved to walk past Alric along the nave to the door, but the monk stepped into his path. Anger flashed across the abbot's face at the disrespect.

'In truth, Father, I approached you in advance of my companion to be sure the abbey was not swarming with Normans at prayer. I am only just returned from a long stay in Flanders, but I have been told the clergy enjoy a fruitful and warm relationship with our new masters.'

Suspicion once again burned in the abbot's eyes. 'And why would you, a monk, have any reason to question the king?'

'I answer only to one master, Father.'

The abbot's patience had almost worn through. As he prepared to call out, Alric said quickly, 'I see you are alone here at this late hour, and this abbey remains a place of tranquillity, so I would usher in my companion. He is of your blood, Father.'

Abbot Brand started. 'My blood?'

'All of this business is about blood, in one way or another.' Hereward's voice floated from the deep shadows at the rear of the church. He had entered unnoticed while Alric had been speaking. At the sound of the familiar voice the monk saw a flash of unease cross the abbot's face, perhaps even fear, but it was gone before he could be sure.

From the shadows, Hereward slowly emerged. The candlelight illuminated the blue warrior marks on his bare arms, his fair hair, his strong jaw. The flames danced in his pale eyes. Alric caught his breath. For the first time, he thought that here was a man who could defeat an entire army of invaders if he put his mind to it. When had this warrior emerged from the wild youth who had sprayed blood across frozen Northumbria? In the misery he had witnessed in Eoferwic? During the long march through the bloody battlefields of Flanders? With Turfrida's kiss, and her love? On the day's march from the camp to Burgh, the monk had realized how truly changed his companion was. The warrior, it seemed, had developed a strategy shaped by wisdom and patience instead of the raw passions and rage that had once filled him. But, as always, Hereward kept his plans close to his heart, and Alric had been surprised when he saw the church tower rising up against the grey sky from the top of a hill. It was a grand abbey. Behind the enclosure, halls, houses and stores sprawled across an extensive estate. What, he wondered, could his friend possibly want here?

'Hereward?' the abbot began. 'I thought you—'

'Dead. Outlaw. Yes, Uncle, you are not the first to tell me these things.' Hereward came to a halt in front of the older man and looked him deep in the eye. 'I expect my father has had much to say about me.'

Brand's face remained impassive. 'I have prayed for you.'

'Many have died by my hand, Uncle, but not the woman I was accused of murdering. That was a lie, designed to keep small men in great power. But God has dealt out his punishment for their sins.'

Abbot Brand folded his hands behind his back. 'It has been many years since you were here as a boy. Though your learning improved, we failed to tame you. I always saw that as my failing, and I told your father so.'

'Then you can make amends now.'

Alric studied the two men. He saw suspicion lying between them, a hint of unease in the abbot, but Hereward's true thoughts were unreadable.

'What would you have? Food? Clothing?' The older man paused, his eyes narrowing. 'Sanctuary?'

Hereward laughed. 'I need no protection. No, Uncle, I need you to make me a knight.'

Taken aback, the abbot's studied aloofness fell away.

'You seem shocked. Am I not suitable? My father is a thegn.

I hold land – or did before the bastard William came. I have my sword and mail, and I am well versed in all the knightly ways. And was I not a good protector of this very church for many years?' From a leather pouch at his side, Hereward removed a smaller pouch tied at the neck. The coin in it jangled. The warrior held out the payment for Brand to take.

After a moment's hesitation, the abbot took the pouch with a sigh. 'What gain is there in this for you? It will not clear the stain upon your name.'

'England needs a defender, Uncle. It needs an honourable man who will inspire hope in the hearts of our neighbours and fear in the hearts of our enemies. When I am knight, men will flock to my banner more readily. All will look to what I am now, not what I was before.' Hereward's eyes twinkled. Alric thought he saw mischief there.

'You would rebel against the Normans?' Brand said with horror.

'Why would I not? The invaders crush the life from us.'

The monk felt impressed by his friend's cunning. In the eyes of others, the title would transform the warrior from savage killer and outlaw to a man who fought for the highest principle, a warrior blessed by God.

'Consider the consequences. If you stand against the Normans, you will bring all of William's wrath down upon the fens,' the cleric pressed. 'We have kept our peace here as best we could. It has not been perfect but we have survived. William will brutally crush you, and all who stand with you, and he will not care what innocents get in the way. Do you wish that fate upon your neighbours?'

'I would not wish upon my neighbours the life they now have.'

The abbot wrung his hands together, pleading. 'There is only a small force here now. Just fourteen knights of high rank commanding barely five times that number.'

Hereward nodded. 'And those fourteen slaughtered my brother? A good number. They will be the first.'

Brand looked sickened. 'William will burn the whole fenland

if he has to. He will go to any extremes if he feels his word is challenged.'

'I will do the same. We will see who has the stomach for this battle.'

Seeing his nephew would not be deterred, the abbot relented. 'Give me your sword and kneel. I cannot deny this request from my own blood, but my concerns are great.'

Hereward smiled. He knelt on the cold flags in front of his uncle, and bowed his head.

'Then repeat the knight-oath.' The abbot laid the tip of the sword upon Hereward's right shoulder. 'In the eyes of God, swear now to be just and honourable at all times.'

'I so swear.' Hereward's clear voice echoed along the nave.

'Swear now that you will defend the weak and uphold the virtues of compassion, loyalty, generosity and truth.'

'I so swear.'

'Swear now, by all that you hold sacred, that you will honour and defend the Crown and Church.'

'I so swear . . . that I will defend the Crown, but not the invader who now wears it.'

Brand hesitated, still struggling with his reluctance, and then said, 'Rise. In the eyes of God, you are now a knight.' He balanced the sword on the palms of his hands and offered it to Hereward.

Alric saw a change in his friend, as if a mask had suddenly slipped away. His eyes afire, Hereward took the sword and slipped it into its sheath. 'So be it.'

The abbot frowned. 'When this reaches the ears of the Normans—'

'Why would it?' Hereward interrupted, his smile sardonic. 'There are only we three present.' He laughed. 'I expect this to reach the ears of the Normans, Uncle. That is why I came here. I want them to dwell on the nature of the enemy they face. I want this night to ripple out across the fens, across all England, to wash up to the very feet of William the Bastard as he sits upon his stolen throne.'

Abbot Brand looked white in the pale candlelight. 'What will you do?'

Without answering, Hereward showed the cleric his back and strode to the edge of the shadow at the end of the nave. As if as an afterthought, he turned back and said in a cold voice, 'I will bring terror. I will bring blood. And England will be made free once more.'

In the instant before the dark folded around his friend, Alric glimpsed something in his friend's face that turned him cold. It was as if another peered out through the eyes of the man he knew, something inhuman that had been hiding away but was now set free. Frightened, the monk hesitated for a long moment before following his companion.

When he slipped through the door and called after his friend, a cowled figure that had been spying upon the meeting separated from the shadows and followed him.

CHAPTER FIFTY

The torches guttered and spat in the breeze. Smoke stinking of pitch swirled in the thin light breaking through the branches where a few gold and copper leaves still clung. Holding aloft the burning brands, the Norman knights waited on the edge of the green. They were dressed for war, in helmets and hauberks, double-edged swords hanging at their sides. In front of them, the village men knelt on the turf, their heads bowed. They still wore the thin tunics they had been dressed in when they rose from their beds at first light, before the Normans had hauled them from their homes. Whimpering, the women huddled against the wall of one house, casting fearful glances at their menfolk as they wrapped their arms around their sobbing children.

Aldous Wyvill felt only contempt for the cowardly English. They had brought this upon themselves. 'One final time,' he said, his eyes moving over the sullen peasants. 'What do you know of the outlaw Hereward?'

Only the wind answered him.

Grim-faced, the Norman commander nodded to his knights. He would brook no resistance. In response to his silent order, each knight raised a sizzling torch towards the thatch roofing the eight dwellings ringing the green. The village men looked up, their faces drained of blood, but still they remained defiant. The commander sighed inwardly.

'Wait.' A young, thin-faced man with straggly blond hair and unsettlingly pale eyes lurched to his feet. The men about him cursed him, insisting he hold his tongue. A woman, the man's wife, Aldous guessed, begged him to stay strong.

Aldous held up his hand to stay the burning. He looked the man in the face with as respectful a stare as he could muster. 'You know something of this Hereward?'

The man nodded.

'Then speak, and know that you do an honourable thing in trying to save your village.'

'We have all heard talk of him, in the market and the inn. He has returned to defend us in our time of need.'

The commander snorted. 'He will be the death of you all. What do you know of him?'

'That he is more than man. That he is filled with the spirit of a bear, which he killed with his bare hands in the north, or so the stories say.'

'He is a man, be sure of that, and a weak one too.'

'You say. But that is not what the English hear. Already the stories are reaching out beyond the fens, and a steady stream of men and women draws towards this place.'

'To join the rebellion?'

'Some. Others to seek protection from the grip of your king.' Burning insolence flared in the man's eyes.

Aldous struck him across the face with the back of his hand, splitting his lip and raising blood. 'He is *your* king,' he hissed. 'Show respect or you will lose your head, here, in front of your woman, and your neighbours.'

The man flashed an affectionate look towards his tearful wife.

'One more thing I would know,' the commander continued. 'Where does this Hereward make camp?'

With one voice, the village men roared their opposition, shouting threats of violence to their young neighbour.

'For your village,' Aldous whispered. 'For your women and children.'

Looking down, the man swallowed. In a quiet voice almost drowned out by the clamour, he described the location of the outlaw's camp.

Once he was done, Aldous allowed himself a triumphant grin. He would begin making his plans immediately to attack the rebel. This Hereward would not know he was doomed until it was too late. Striding back to his men, he nodded curtly. 'Burn it down. Then kill the men.'

CHAPTER FIFTY-ONE

'Keep your eyes ahead,' Hereward whispered.

Alric barely heard the warrior above the music of the fens. Wind whistled through the high branches of the willows. Dry wood cracked under the monk's shoes. Leaves rustled. Rooks cawed. Since they had left Burgh Abbey, Alric had concentrated on the burning in his thighs as they waded through black mud, skirted silent lakes shimmering with a brassy glow as morning broke, stumbled along flinty causeways and splashed across white-foamed rushing streams. He felt tired and hungry and he feared what was happening to his friend. All the good work of years appeared to be draining away by the moment.

'What is there to see apart from water and wood?' he grumbled.

The warrior slowed his step so that he dropped back alongside his travelling companion. 'We have been followed ever since we left the abbey,' he muttered, his gaze fixed on the way ahead.

'How do you know? I have seen nothing. And heard nothing above this din.'

'He is skilful and cunning. In the dark, he shrouded himself in black cloak and cowl. Since sunrise, he has put just enough distance between us to prevent us from hearing his footsteps, but not enough to lose sight of us.'

'A Norman scout?' Alric's chest tightened.

'Mayhap,' the warrior growled, 'which is why I drew him on. Knights could have been hiding at Burgh Abbey, and if the alarm had been raised there we would have had little chance of escape. But here . . . this is my land.'

Before the monk could ask another question, Hereward melted away. Alric felt the warrior by his side one moment, but when he glanced across he saw only swaying branches and heard only the ghost of footsteps disappearing across the muddy ground. He tried to steady himself, but they had spent most of the journey talking about Norman tactics, the swift strikes from their cavalry, their use of bowmen to bring death from a distance, but most of all their cruelty, which he had witnessed at first hand in the head of Hereward's brother hoisted above the hall gateway. Of all potential enemies, the Normans were the worst with their coldness and efficiency.

His heart hammering, he continued to struggle through the undergrowth, unsure what the warrior wanted him to do. Suddenly Hereward's battle cry shattered the peace of the woodland. Rooks took flight as one with a thunder of black wings from the treetops, their raucous cries alerting everyone within miles.

Turning on his heel, Alric weaved back through the swaying willow branches which obscured his view. He was afraid of what he would find: his friend dead in a bog, a horde of well-armed Normans closing in from all sides? The final sweep of branches fell aside and he stumbled across Hereward wrestling on the sodden ground with the black-cloaked stalker. Clearly no stranger to battle, the other man fought as furiously as Hereward. Alric was shocked to see that his friend had already been disarmed, his sword lying half buried in a bank of rust-coloured fern. Yet Hereward refused to allow his opponent a moment to catch his breath, raining down punches and butts with his head.

'Wait,' the other man croaked. 'Hereward . . . wait.'

At the sound of his name, the warrior came to a halt. One fist raised, he tore the cowl away with his other hand. Alric saw curly brown hair and full lips that made the features seem oddly innocent, like a child's. The warrior's bafflement gave way to a broad grin.

'Redwald?' For a moment, he stared at the battered figure, and then jumped to his feet. Hauling the other man into his arms, he hugged tightly, slapping his brother on the back. 'Redwald! I thought you dead!'

'And I you.'

Hereward held the cloaked man at arm's length to study him. Alric watched a shadow cross his friend's face. Redwald looked gaunt and pale, his gaze skittering like that of a whipped dog. Forcing a grin, the warrior said, 'You look well. How did you find me?'

'I took revenge for you, Hereward,' the other man said with an almost childlike desperation to please. 'Harold Godwinson died with prayers for forgiveness upon his lips . . . prayers in your name.'

The warrior nodded. 'Then Tidhild can rest easily. Her death has been avenged.' He shrugged, throwing a puzzled glance at Alric. 'For so long, seeing Harold Godwinson suffer for his crimes was all that filled my heart and mind. Yet now I feel grief for Tidhild's passing, but no joy at Harold's death. Other matters loom larger.'

The monk smiled. 'As we march along life's road, we see the trees and hills we pass in a different light. What was is not always what is.'

Hereward sighed, waving an arm towards his friend. 'This is Alric, a monk, who sees it as his life's work to save my soul. We must pity him for that thankless task. But beware, Redwald, he talks. And talks. And ties your wits in knots. When you want to feast, or drink, or lie with a woman, he talks. *What was is not always what is.*'

'It is good to have friends,' Redwald said with a hint of regret.

'Since the Normans invaded, I have spent all my days running and hiding. They are a fierce enemy, Hereward. They never slow, they never stop. Once William arrived in London, he collected the names of all who were close to King Harold and resolved that he would not rest until each one was accounted for.'

'And thereby tried to cut out the heart of any future resistance.'

'Many ended their days with their heads upon poles outside the palace or tied to a stake at low tide on the river, where the waters slowly washed away their screams.'

'But you were always a cunning one, Redwald. You survived.'

The cloaked man nodded with little enthusiasm. 'This spring, at my lowest ebb, I threw myself upon the mercy of your uncle at Burgh Abbey. He owed it to your father to take me in, and give me a new life as a monk, and a new name. So when the Normans came, as they regularly did to see the abbot, they never gave me a passing glance.' He paused. 'Your kin have always shown me kindness, Hereward. Taking me in when I had nothing, not once now, but twice—'

'Enough,' the warrior interrupted. He rested a comforting hand on Redwald's shoulder. 'Though we share no blood, we *are* kin. We offer each other a hand in hard times. And you have proved your loyalty time and again, not least in your devotion to avenging Tidhild and the crime against me.'

Redwald smiled and nodded. 'And I would join you now. So we can fight shoulder to shoulder, as we did in the days of our youth.'

'Would you not be safer in hiding at the abbey?' Alric asked.

'Is anywhere safe in these times? The monks all mutter of the End of Days. They speak of the sickness sweeping through villages and towns in the west. Of starvation brought on by William the Bastard, who steals the food and razes the fields of those who fail to bow to him.' Redwald wrung his hands as long-buried worries rushed to the surface. 'And then the stories reached us of a new rebel, who killed bears with his bare hands and had brought all of Flanders to its knees. And they said his

343

name was Hereward, and I would not believe . . .' He bowed his head, his voice growing quiet. 'But last night I saw.'

'Why did you not speak out at the abbey?' the monk pressed.

Redwald shook his head. 'I thought you would not have me,' he whispered.

Hereward laughed in disbelief. 'Have you lost your wits?'

Trying to lighten the atmosphere, Redwald clapped his hands together and forced a broad grin. 'Yet here I am. I will join you. I will be a loyal servant, and I ask only for your protection.'

'Servant?' The warrior shook his head in mock bafflement. 'We are equals, brother.'

'As I followed you, plucking up courage to speak, I have been thinking . . .' Redwald's tongue moistened his dry lips. 'If any man could stand against William, it would be you, Hereward. But the Normans are great in power and they have their hands round England's neck. If we could get Earl Edwin on our side . . . perhaps his brother Earl Morcar too . . . We men of Mercia could start a grand rebellion that would shake the invaders to the core. Even the throne could be within our reach.'

Alric saw a puzzling fire flicker in the man's eyes. Hereward, though, appeared overjoyed that his adopted brother had walked back into his life. 'That is the spirit I remember.' The warrior shook a fist. 'See, monk? You feared we would be a poor force against the Norman might, but with men like this by our side we can achieve anything.'

'We have time to plot and plan and build our strength. The Normans will not be able to find us in the fens,' Redwald said. 'Yes, brother, we can achieve anything.'

Alric watched the two men set off through the willows, arms round each other's shoulders as they exchanged raucous stories of the time they were apart. Yet when Hereward roared with laughter at some joke or other, the monk glimpsed something that puzzled him. Redwald glanced sideways at the warrior, and in that unguarded moment his features showed no brotherly love. Alric thought he saw something sourer there, resentment, perhaps, or contempt, but the look flashed so quickly he could not be sure. He followed at a distance, deep in thought, but his suspicions would not subside.

CHAPTER FIFTY-TWO

The sunrise set fire to the fenland waters. Mist hung over the marshes and drifted among the stark black trees as the Norman knights mounted their steeds in the quiet enclosure. Aldous Wyvill felt pride as he studied the gleaming helmets his men had spent all night polishing ready for the coming battle. In their hauberks and with their axes sharpened on the whetstone, they would descend upon the rag-tag band of rebels like a storm of iron. The English would not know what hit them before their heads were separated from their shoulders.

The horses snorted and stamped their hooves as if they too were anticipating the inevitable rout, the commander thought. He inhaled a deep draught of the chill, damp air, his nose wrinkling at the stink of rotting leaves and marsh gas. He yearned for the green pastures of his homeland, but there was no virtue in sentimentality. It was a weakness.

'Ride out,' he barked, 'and let our swords drink deeply before this day is done.'

The newly constructed gates rattled open and the column of knights moved out into the wild, fog-shrouded fens. Yet they had barely travelled beyond the edge of the village when the sound of many hoofbeats echoed further along the muddy track. Aldous brought his men to a halt and ordered them to draw their weapons. Who could be approaching at that hour?

When the riders galloped out of the mist, the commander's tension eased at the sight of familiar armour and a familiar face. Here were the reinforcements he had requested from London when he had learned of the rebellion. Some were knights, many were clearly mercenaries. But at their core, Aldous recognized a man with a long rodent's face and small eyes that appeared set in a permanent scowl. He wore only the finest clothes, a warm woollen tunic dyed purple and embroidered with yellow diamonds, and a furred cap that made him appear feminine among the scarred faces and harsh armour. He was Frederic of Warenne, who had been given land in the vicinity in return for funding a ship for the invasion. Aldous knew this wealthy man had married well, taking the sister of William of Warenne, who had the ear of King William.

Holding his chin at a haughty angle, Frederic urged his horse out from the protection of his guards and approached Aldous. 'I was troubled by your message,' he said in a reedy voice. 'I would not have my lands put at risk by rebellious English.'

'My words were sent too early.' The commander removed his helmet as an act of respect, though he felt little regard for the man. 'This rebellion barely merits the name and will be crushed before the day is out.'

As a contemptuous laugh tinkled out, Frederic raised a hand to summon someone from the column of reinforcements. 'You speak too soon once again, Aldous Wyvill. The leader of the rebels is known as Hereward, yes?'

'He is.'

'Then you presume too much. My brother William was a guest at this man's wedding in Flanders, and he returned with tales of the warrior's exploits. When Hereward arrived in exile from England he was raw and wild, but during his stay in Flanders he learned to hone his natural talents for slaughter. He carved a bloody swath across battlefield after battlefield and earned the praise of none other than Count Baldwin, who took the warrior into his employ. The most fearsome man in all of Flanders, the count said. Hereward is far more dangerous than you could ever imagine.'

'He is just a man.' Aldous restrained an urge to wipe the sneering smile off the aristocrat's face.

A jangle of mail echoed from the reinforcements as a rider dismounted and walked towards them. He was a Viking, his beard and hair dyed the colour of blood, the skulls of birds and rodents rattling against his rusted mail where they had been tied by strips of leather.

'This man has more experience than you or I. His axe has already tasted the blood of this Hereward.' Frederic waved his hand flamboyantly towards Harald Redteeth. 'He was employed in the army maintaining order across the south when news of your rebellion spread throughout the ranks. His knowledge will prove invaluable.' Frederic smiled. 'As will his passion to see your enemy dead.'

Aldous felt unsettled by the Viking's eyes. The pupils were so dilated the irises had all but disappeared.

'Hereward has killed me once,' Harald intoned, his black, unblinking stare fixed on the Norman commander. 'And I have killed him once. We are equal. Now I would see whose fire burns the brightest.'

CHAPTER FIFTY-THREE

The camp was abuzz with voices. Men and women milled around the fires among the clustering trees. Old friends and neighbours greeted each other with cheery hails. Strangers clasped hands, finding common cause, but struggled to make sense of accents from the north and south and west. Hereward counted more than twenty heads as he strode through the throng with Alric at his side. The paltry collection of spears and shields were a poor match for the Normans' might, but he anticipated some strong fighters among the new arrivals.

'Word spreads fast,' the monk remarked.

'To hear tell, the suffering inflicted by the Normans reaches across every part of England. Anger is everywhere.'

'But they are drawn here by your name. It seems your exploits in Eoferwic have caught alight.' Alric restrained a grin. 'The English needed a hero and there you were.'

'I am no hero,' Hereward snapped, rising to the bait. The words died in his throat as he saw two familiar faces across the camp. Unsure of his feelings, he left the monk and pushed through the crowd. Kraki and Acha sat on a log beside the campfire, eating some of the fowl that Guthrinc had roasted. The Viking had earned a new scar over his left eye since the last time Hereward had seen him, and a few more strands of silver gleamed in his hair and beard. His creaking leather and stained mail were splattered with the mud of the road.

Acha's eyes met Hereward's before her companion looked up from his meal, and the warrior was struck afresh by her fierce beauty. Though she wore a worn woollen dress, her raven hair gleamed. She flashed the warrior a smile that appeared to hold a hint of contrition.

When he saw Hereward, Kraki wiped the grease from his mouth with the back of his hand and tossed his bone into the fire. Rising to his feet, he held the warrior with an unwavering gaze. 'You and I, we had our troubles. But your courage and fighting skills were never in doubt. Let us put the past behind us and start afresh, for together we can spill enough Norman blood to turn this wet land red.'

Hereward searched the Viking's face. They would never like each other, but Kraki had proved himself loyal when he had taken Tostig's oath. The warrior accepted the man with a firm nod. 'Your axe will be put to good use soon enough.' He turned to single out Alric. 'The monk will tell you our plans.'

With a grunt, Kraki pushed his way through the crowd. The moment he was out of sight, Acha jumped to her feet. 'There is little I can say about Eoferwic,' she began. 'I was weak.'

'It is behind us now. You have not returned to the Cymri?'

Her eyes flashed. 'He would not let me,' she snapped, nodding in the direction of the Viking.

'You are with Kraki now?'

Acha looked down, trying to hide the shame she felt. 'He was—'

'You do not have to answer,' Hereward interrupted, his tone gentle. 'I know your mind, remember.'

Hope flared in the woman's eyes. She stepped forward, almost pressing her hands against his chest. 'I would rather be with you.'

'I have a wife now.'

'Then take another.' Acha looked round. 'Where is she?'

'Where she is safe.'

'You would never have to keep me safe. I would stand at your shoulder at all times.' Her dark eyes widened as she looked up at him. 'We know each other's hearts. We are the same inside. You told me that. You know it.'

Hereward hesitated, knowing that what she said was true. Before he could respond, a cry echoed across the camp. Bodies fell aside as someone pushed their way through the crowd. Redwald burst from the gathering, flushed and breathless. Rushing up to the campfire, he grabbed Hereward's arm and gasped, 'The Normans are coming!'

CHAPTER FIFTY-FOUR

Golden eyes shone like torches through the grey mist drifting among the skeletal trees. Beneath the wind hissing across the silver water, Harald Redteeth could hear the whispers of the *alfar* as they watched the world of men. They were warning of the raven-harvests to come. A crow cautioned him as it swooped across the still landscape. When he peered into the mirror-surfaces of the lakes, he saw the yawning skulls of the dead looking back at him from the other world. Oblivious, the Normans rode on, along the edge of the stinking marshland where stagnant pools reflected the lowering sky. But Harald listened, and he heeded.

Scouts galloped back from one of the islands rising out of a sea of reeds in a brown bog, their tunics smeared with mud where they had crawled on their bellies. Aldous Wyvill listened to their insistent reports and nodded. The rebels milled about, not yet realizing their end was upon them, Harald overheard, and Hereward was there, with the monk. The Viking's fingers folded around the haft of his notched axe. What would it take to send the English warrior to the Grey Lands? In Flanders, Redteeth had been convinced he had struck a killing blow, but still the life-bane had survived. Now his quest had become more

than a matter of vengeance. The *alfar* had told him there had
to be a balance in life and only one of them could continue on
the road in the days to come. Hereward or Harald. Harald or
Hereward.

Urging his horse alongside the Norman commander, the red-
bearded mercenary said, 'Hereward is more than a man. He
is ridden like a mare by some night-walker, and he has all the
powers of the dark world on his side. You must take special care
with him.'

Aldous eyed Harald with contempt, then glanced back to
see if the superstitious comment had affected his knights. The
Viking was used to the look, and cared little. Fools lay everywhere.

'No risks will be taken,' the commander replied, turning
his attention away from Redteeth to study the approach to the
island. 'We will strike quickly and hard before the rebels have a
chance to mount a defence.' Looking across the boggy ground,
he turned up his nose. 'If we could use our cavalry, this would
be over in the blink of an eye. As it is, we are still better armed.'
He smiled at the chink of the heavy mail hauberks and the
swords rattling against thighs.

Harald settled back into the rhythm of his mount and continued to listen to the whispers from the trees.

On the edge of the bog, the knights dismounted and left their
horses with two of the young hands who had accompanied them
from the hall. A narrow, low ridge of grassland ran towards the
foot of the island. The Viking scrutinized the dense bank of
black trees covering most of the island and the marshland and
floodlands surrounding it. The rebels had chosen their camp
well, he thought. But if the English were not prepared for the
attack, their new home would be the perfect trap, with little
opportunity to flee across the causeway that stretched across
the water on the western side.

Aldous raised one hand to draw his men in line on top of
the grass ridge. Harald settled into position midway along the
column. The knights kept low, moving slowly so they would

not be heard. The Viking sniffed the air. Woodsmoke. Two campfires, perhaps three.

At the foot of the island, the grey mist swirled among the willows and ashes. Harald smacked his lips, tasting the blood that was to come. As the knights steadily climbed the slope, muffled voices floated back through the fog. The rebels sounded busy. Preparing to flee, Harald wondered? Finding a position to make a stand?

When the calls and chatter were clearly close at hand, Aldous raised his hand again to bring his men to a halt. Whisking his arm left and right, he ordered them to move out in a line. The scouts had told him the island summit was flat and sloped gently down to the bog on the far side. A jaunty tune meandering through his head, Harald resisted the urge to whistle as he gripped his axe. He fixed his eyes on the Norman commander. The whispers of the *alfar* faded away. Silence fell.

Holding his hand high, the Norman commander waited, listening to the ebb and flow of voices. All eyes were upon him. He whisked the arm down. 'Dex aie!' he called in his own tongue. *God aid us.*

Echoing the cry, the knights rushed up the final few steps of the slope and over the rim. Through the mist, Harald saw the English scatter like rabbits. There were fewer than he had anticipated.

Careering down the incline, the footfalls of the heavily armoured Normans sounded like thunder. A wolf in human form, Harald outpaced them all. His eyes darted this way and that, searching for Hereward. A rebel in a brown tunic bounded through the ferns to his left. Two men disappeared into the mist to his right. The ghosts of others flitted ahead.

Plunging down the slope, Harald realized the fog was growing thicker still. He saw that all but one of the knights on either side had disappeared from view as they followed the muffled yells echoing from across the island.

His breath rasping in the chill air, the Viking skidded to a halt on the edge of a bog. He had reached the far side of the small island. The knight clanked to a stop beside him, then began to range along the edge of the marsh, looking around.

His senses tingling, Harald dropped to his knees to examine the muddy ground. It had not been churned up by fleeing feet.

'No one came this way,' he grunted.

The Norman ignored him, prowling past hanging willows.

The red-bearded mercenary stood up and tried to pierce the dense fog. Deep in the cave of his head, the voices of his ancestors rang out in warning. 'Wait,' he cautioned. 'Something is wrong here.' The knight stopped, lifting a sweep of branches with his sword.

Silence fell across the island. No fearful shouts or cries of fleeing rebels. Harald raised his axe, turning slowly.

From somewhere nearby, a throat-tearing scream shattered the quiet. Then another. And another.

Death cries, the Viking warrior knew.

The Normans had been too confident, he saw now. He felt sure the rebels had been aware of the impending attack and prepared for it, and he was not about to risk his life finding out the truth. 'Return to the horses,' he called to the knight, as he began to move back up the slope. 'We have lost the advantage here.'

He glanced back to see if the man was following and noticed large bubbles bursting on the surface of a pool in the bog. The knight turned just as a figure rose up from the depths, black slurry streaming off him. White eyes appeared in the mud-dark face, and then white teeth in a triumphant grin.

Rooted, the knight could only stare as Hereward's blade flashed towards his neck.

CHAPTER FIFTY-FIVE

The barked orders of the Norman commander echoed through the fog. Redwald grinned. Though he could not understand the words, he could hear the uncertainty in the man's voice. Another scream tore out nearby. Hereward's plan was working perfectly.

Leaning against the damp trunk of an ash tree, he listened to the sound of feet running in confusion. When heavy footsteps drew near, he cupped his hands to his mouth and called out as though he were lost. *The Normans lumber like oxen in their armour*, he thought as the leaden footsteps moved in his direction. He waited until the figures coalesced in the fog and then turned on his heel and ran down the slope.

Branches tore at his face, but his breathing remained regular. He had not felt this alive since the days with Harold Godwinson. From the thunder at his back, he estimated he had drawn seven or eight of the knights; a good number.

Leaping over a rotting log that had been dragged across the path, he flashed a quick smile at Guthrinc who waited behind a tree beside it. The large man's face was smeared with white mud, the hair matted, charcoal ground into the skin around his eyes. He had the face of death, like many of the rebels. Redwald remembered Hereward's words: *terror strikes as sharp as any axe*. He hesitated a little further on and glanced back. As the first knight slowed near the log, the burly rebel swung his axe into his chest. The *chunk* of iron carving bone echoed down the slope. Guthrinc wrenched out the blade and had faded into the fog before the knight had slumped to his knees in a gout of blood.

Turning, Redwald continued down the slope, just slowly enough to catch the attention of the Normans who had hesitated beside their dying fellow. He allowed himself a gleeful laugh. He felt a queasy joy at seeing such vengeance for the terror the Normans had inflicted on him during William the Bastard's victorious battle for the English crown. The enemy had made him feel weak that day, and that was the harshest blow of all. He would rather lose a hand than feel that way again.

Further down the slope, he leapt across a spread of branches, yellowing turf and dry leaves. Once more he turned and glanced back at the wall of iron speeding towards him. The knight at the head crashed through the thin covering into the hidden pit. His bubbling scream rang out as the stakes embedded in the bottom rammed through his body. Unable to slow, a second knight tumbled in after him.

Redwald clenched his fist in triumph. He had doubted Hereward's assertion that the numerous pits they had dug would claim lives, but the warrior had insisted he had witnessed the tactic's lethal success on his travels on the other side of the whale road. His brother had grown during the years they had been apart, Redwald decided. Perhaps Hereward truly could lay claim to the throne.

Sprinting to the edge of the marshland, Redwald continued along the rim until he came to a green area reaching into the fog. He glanced around for the secret marker and then ran out from the treeline. The four remaining knights roared as they saw him.

Feigning panic, the rebel raced ahead. A sly smile crossed his face as he heard the pounding of the Normans' leather shoes turn to splashing. A moment later their frantic cries sounded and Redwald came to a halt. He turned and placed his hands on his hips, relishing the sight of his enemies' final breaths. The four knights thrashed thigh-deep in the sucking bog, the weight of their armour dragging them down. Redwald stood on the thin finger of solid ground reaching out into the marsh that only a fenlander would recognize. The more the Normans fought to get free, the more they sank. In desperation, they tossed aside their swords and axes, and hurled their helmets away. Redwald enjoyed that, for it meant he could see the terror in their eyes more clearly. Two of them struggled to remove their hauberks, but it was a futile task. Down they went, with gathering speed, the stinking black mud pulling at their stomachs, their chests, their necks. Their cries became childlike, their eyes filling with tears.

Redwald drew closer, dropping to his haunches to see better. His enemies pleaded with him in their tongue, but then the mud washed into their mouths, and only chokes and gurgles emerged, and then a silence broken only by the bubbles bursting on the slimy surface.

Redwald stood up, brushing the dried mud from his hands. His darkest days lay behind him now, he was sure. His heart swelled. He would never again be deflected from reaching his goal. By any means necessary, power and security would be his.

CHAPTER FIFTY-SIX

Blood streamed from the ragged neck of the severed head. His eyes burning with fierce fire, Hereward held his trophy high for Harald Redteeth to see. Hatred burned in the Viking's chest, not just for the English warrior, but for the Normans, whose many failings had denied his axe the life for which it hungered. The red-bearded mercenary fought his urge to confront the rebel leader and raced back up the slope, knowing that he was in danger of being outnumbered. He loathed fleeing from a battle, but he was wise enough to know there would be another opportunity for his axe to drink deep.

Avoiding the paths that snaked between the trees, Harald crashed through the undergrowth, hacking at any branch that fell in his way. Everywhere he looked he saw death. Knights stumbled into bogs. Bodies bristled with arrows. Weakening moans rose from gaping pits. The *alfar* had been right. There were raven harvests aplenty, but all of them Normans. The rebels had made fools of them all. The Viking glimpsed them moving through the fog like spectres. Some climbed from ditches or rose up from covered hiding places. Others called warnings from the branches above. And floating on the floodlands, two men had wielded bows from strange shell-shaped boats, the like of which

Redteeth had never seen before. All of them bore hideous masks of mud and ash and charcoal.

A battle cry resounded at his back, taken up on all sides. As the mercenary hauled himself through the willows, he heard the bellicose shouts begin to draw near. The English were not about to let their enemies escape, if they could help it. Spitting epithets, the Viking crashed through tangled branches and twining bramble.

But when he reached the lip of the downward slope, he glimpsed a shape looming on the left of his vision. A spear ripped through the flesh of his forearm. Numb to all pain, he reacted faster than his foe could have expected. Before the English rebel had a chance to dart back, the Viking whirled, crunching his axe into the man's neck and wrenching it free in a gush of blood. For a moment, the shower of red jewels gripped him in a mushroom-fed fascination.

More battle cries tore him from his reverie and he threw himself over the rim and careered down the slope. Through the folds of grey, he glimpsed other figures hurtling through the trees alongside him. The heavy thud of feet on the soft loam told him they were Normans. Crashing out of the trees, he sped on to the grassy shoulder where the fog had started to clear. The musky smell of the horses hung on the breeze, and he could hear their snorts and whinnies ahead. The beasts smelled blood and death.

When he mounted his steed, the mercenary allowed himself the luxury of glancing back. Barely twenty Normans from the fifty-strong force were racing away from the island. Behind them, shadowy figures shifted through the mist along the tree-line.

I will be back, he vowed, *and I will take your ears to hang on my mail.* He began to sing a jaunty song that ended with a peal of high-pitched laughter. The surviving Normans eyed him as if they thought the privations of the battle had driven him mad. That only made him laugh harder.

Once they had put some distance between them and the

rebels, Aldous Wyvill slowed his men to a trot. Dried blood caked the corner of his eye and a blue bruise was spreading over his cheeks. 'We will be back to avenge our fallen,' he snarled. 'Be brave. Hold fast.'

'They were taking the heads,' one of the knights gasped in horror.

'I said, be brave!' the Norman commander yelled at the man. 'We shall not be beaten by peasants armed with clubs and rocks, and warriors who trick us with traps.'

The men fell silent for the rest of the ride, but Harald could smell the sour stink of fear in their sweat.

In the enclosure, Aldous ordered the gate to be shut and barred. As the dispirited knights dismounted and led their horses away, Frederic of Warenne eased out of the hall in a flap of silk and linen. He pressed his hands together in anticipation of delight, but the thin-lipped smile fell away when he saw how few men had returned, their sagging shoulders and the wounds on show.

'What is this?' he cried in dismay.

'The English were waiting for us. It was a trap.' The Norman commander tucked his helmet under his arm.

Aghast, Frederic clutched his hand to his mouth as a dreadful future flashed before his eyes. 'The rebellion continues? Will it spread? Will the English retake their lands?'

'Your lands are safe,' Aldous snapped. 'For now. But we need reinforcements soon. Our scouts report that the ranks of the rebels are swelling by the day.'

Harald Redteeth watched the simmering tension between the two men. Neither knew how to combat this turn of events, he could see. No cavalry charge could move the rebels from their natural fortress of water, bog and mist. Stifling a giggle, he put on a grave face and announced, 'Terror is the only answer.'

The Norman commander whirled, but Frederic held up a limp hand to halt Aldous. 'Speak,' the landowner urged.

'We must make the English too scared to come here. They must know that they will face axe and fire. Starvation. They must believe that these fenlands are little more than a slaughterhouse for their kind.'

Frederic clapped his hands. 'Yes, he is right. Let us send for reinforcements. Many reinforcements.'

Aldous looked unsure, recognizing that such a course might reflect badly on his own ability to manage the fens. But it was clear that the landowner had made up his mind. 'My men are needed here,' the commander sniffed, turning to Harald. 'Ride to the garrison at Lincolne. I will give you a message for the commander there, who will send to London for what we need.'

The red-bearded mercenary nodded. Glancing round the enclosure at the ragged remains of the Norman force, he felt it was a good time to be away from Barholme yet still be able to claim his coin. The invaders had failed to respect Hereward and had paid the price. The English warrior had changed greatly since their first meeting, Redteeth now realized. He was more dangerous, cleverer, wiser, and had learned many new strategies. To treat Hereward as just another rebel was to court disaster.

As he strode towards the store to fetch supplies for his journey, Frederic's reedy voice floated back to him: 'At least we are safe here.'

Harald Redteeth laughed long and hard.

CHAPTER FIFTY-SEVEN

An owl shrieked away in the moonless night. The wind lured whispers from the reed-beds. And out of the lonely wet-lands the silent ghosts walked, dark-eyed, sallow-skinned, with murder in their hearts.

We will drench this land in blood to honour our ancestors.

The whispered exhortation rustled among the band of men as they slipped past the ebony lakes and through the wild woods; an oath that could never be broken. With his shield on his arm and his axe in his hand, Hereward led the rebels towards the old straight track. After the rout at the camp, the men had learned to follow him without question. His mail shirt jangled with the rhythm of every step, but he wore no helm. Instead he showed his ash-painted face to the enemy; in the dark the crusted, grey mask became a glowing skull, a portent of what was to come for all who saw it.

His head throbbed with the beat of his blood. The thing he carried with him at all times, shackled deep in his heart, was rising free. He welcomed it. There was no other way. Back at the camp, in the grey hour just before dark, Alric had pleaded with him to hold his true nature in check or risk losing his soul for ever. And part of him knew the monk was right; to

363

give in to the bestial bloodlust and the slaughter, where was the honour in that? But the peace of which he had always dreamed now seemed as ephemeral as the fenland mist. Alric had been a good friend to him, perhaps the best he had ever had. But Hereward Asketilson was already dead. Hereward the scourge of the invader, the feeder of ravens, demanded blood. And his devil would ensure it flowed in torrents.

Through the leafless trees, the torches glimmered round the Normans' hall, Hereward's old home. The warrior raised his hand to bring his war band to a halt. For a long moment, they waited in silence until a shadow separated from the trees and edged towards them.

'Did I do well?' it whispered.

'You did well, Hengist.'

The thin-faced man from the village ran a shaking hand through his lank blond hair. His pale eyes glistened. 'The Normans killed all the other men,' he croaked. 'Once I had told them the location of your camp, as you instructed, I thought they would leave. But they put my neighbours to the sword, while they knelt, while their women sobbed and prayed.' The words died in his throat.

Hereward rested a supportive hand on the trembling man's shoulder. 'The invaders can never be trusted. They have no honour. But through your courage, and your neighbours' sacrifice, we lured them into the fens and broke them. And soon, perhaps this night, we will be rid of them.'

Hengist nodded, wiping the back of his hand across his sticky nose. 'I will join you,' he vowed, 'and I will pay them back in kind.'

'And this night?'

'Two men upon the fence.'

'Only two?'

'The others feast in the hall, and lick their wounds.'

Hereward shook his head in disbelief. 'Then they have brought this end upon themselves.' He nodded to Redwald, who flashed a grin, and Guthrinc, who cracked the knuckles of his large hands. The two men pulled their hunting bows from their shoulders, and an arrow each from the pouch upon their backs, and then moved quietly into the willows surrounding the enclosure.

The rebels ghosted among the trees. Beyond the palisade, the Norman guards stood on their platform, their helmets agleam in the torchlight. Redwald and Guthrinc knelt on the treeline, shafts notched. Hereward knew it would take a good eye to hit their prey in the gloom, but those two men were the best archers he had. They would not fail, as he had failed Vadir.

The bow-lines creaked, held for a moment, and then snapped free. Twin arrows whistled through the dark. The shafts flew so fast Hereward didn't see them strike, but he heard them puncture flesh, and a gasp of shock and a gurgle. Both knights fell from their platform.

For a long moment, the warrior listened for any sign that the Normans in the hall had heard the falling bodies. When no sound came, he waved the rebels on. Clambering over the newly dug ramparts, the men gathered at the foot of the fence. Dropping to his hands and knees, Hengist felt around the base of the timber palisade until he came to an area that had been padded with loose chips of wood under a thin covering of soil. Hereward felt his heart swell at the risks the English farmers had taken to meet his strict instructions during their labours. At his nod, four men fell to the ground and scrabbled out the padding until there was space enough for a slight man to crawl under the fence.

'Let me,' Redwald whispered.

'Take care,' Hereward said. 'The guards may still be alive. The knights could leave the hall at any time—'

'Brother,' Redwald interrupted with a grin, 'trust me.'

'I trust you,' the warrior replied. He felt a burst of pride at the other man's bravery.

Redwald wriggled through the narrow gap, and a few moments later the rebels heard the groan of the bar lifting from the gate. Once the way swung open, the men flooded inside the enclosure. Hengist padded around to the rear of the hall, Hereward and Alric darting behind. From within came the sound of drunken singing and laughter. Fools, Hereward thought. The Normans had too quickly drowned their misery at the day's dismal outcome. But then they did not understand the English, and the fire that burned in their hearts, or the weight of their hatred.

Edging past the pit where the waste and rotting food was tossed, along the side of the chicken hut, Hengist ducked down at the hall's rear wall and moved a pile of wood. A hole had been dug behind it, just big enough for a man to squeeze into the space beneath the hall's timber floor where the straw had been stuffed to keep out the winter cold. Hereward nodded approvingly. Once again he felt impressed by the risks that had been taken by the men the Normans had put to work. He found a grim humour in the thought that the invaders had turned good men into their slaves and thereby brought about their own demise.

The warrior sent Alric to fetch one of the torches. When the monk returned with the sputtering brand, Hereward handed it to Hengist and whispered, 'You know what to do.'

'Aye. With joy in my heart,' the other man replied, his face cold.

As they made their way back to the front of the hall, Alric caught Hereward's arm. 'You are not alone. I will pray for your soul.' The monk's face looked like stone, but his eyes swam with passion.

'Then pray hard, monk.' Clapping his arms around his friend, Hereward squeezed tightly. He held the embrace for a moment, and then, without a word or a look, turned and loped to the front of the hall where the rebels waited in the shadows along the palisade.

Grasping his axe with both hands, Hereward strode to the side of the door and waited. His men darted into a tight semi-circle around him. The warrior looked across the row of faces, seeing courage and fear, the iron of defiance and the fire of righteous fury. The English were ready. And now there would be blood.

Hereward closed his eyes. In his mind, he pictured Asketil within the hall, his father's fists beating his mother to death. The warrior remembered the way her blood had drained along the lines of the timber boards, creating an indelible stain that had haunted him every day he had spent there. He recalled the deep wound of his grief and his long belief that it would never heal. And then he felt his rage, his old companion, begin to simmer, and then boil, and then rise up through him. With a whisper, he summoned his devil.

The acrid scent of burning whipped in on the breeze. Wisps of grey smoke began to curl out from under the mud-coloured wattle-and-daub walls of the hall. And then the night filled with a roaring as if a great beast had been woken. Orange sparks glowed, whisking up towards the starless sky. Tongues of flame licked out from the base of the walls. Within the hall, a panicked din erupted. Feet thundered towards the door.

Coughing and spluttering, the first man burst out into the night. Hereward swung his axe. The head spun through the air and bounced across the mud and wet leaves. Blood drenched the warrior, but he barely recognized the sensation. His thoughts had washed away on a tranquil sea, his vision narrowing to that small doorway. Things emerged, familiar shapes that could have been shadows or monsters or memories, and each time he swung his axe. The bodies piled around his feet in the growing red pool. When the commander, Aldous Wyvill, lurched out, his gaze locked on the warrior's face for a moment and his lips curled back from his teeth in horror at what he saw before the axe fell.

As the smoke billowed out in clouds, the warrior stepped back to give the others a chance. They lunged in one after the other, hacking with their axes or thrusting with their spears, their faces dark and emotionless. The only utterances were the prayers and screams of the Normans.

When the landowner staggered out, Hereward recognized the expensive clothes and the soft body and dragged him to one side before he could be cut down. Frederic fell to his knees, sobbing in fear.

Flames tore through the hall, cleansing it of its ghosts, and soon the intense heat drove the rebels to the edges of the enclosure. No other Normans emerged. When the roof fell in with a resounding crash, the fire whirled up towards the black sky in a gush of golden sparks. And the beast roared on. Hereward flashed back to the night Gedley had burned, the moment when the trajectory of his life had changed. A fleeting thought of Harald Redteeth whistled through his head, and he wondered where his hated enemy had gone. The red-bearded mercenary would never have allowed himself to die in the conflagration. But they would meet again, he knew, and then he would take his revenge for Vadir's death.

But this was a night for a bonfire of the Normans' vanity. They thought they could hold England in their fist and slowly choke the life from it. Now, as they felt the first cold fingers of terror on their spines, they would have to accept that the war had not yet ended.

Frederic of Warenne lurched to his feet, searching for a way of escape. Seeing none, he covered his mouth with his hands and began to shake. His fine clothes were smeared with ash. Hereward stood before the landowner and peered deep into his face. For a moment, the warrior thought he was looking at his father, the pull of deep tides inside him growing stronger and more violent.

'Who are you?' Frederic croaked, his gaze fixed on the skull of ash.

'You know.'

Frederic began to cry.

'Some say war turns us into beasts,' the warrior continued, refusing to lower his coruscating gaze. 'But men do it to themselves. Are we all devils? Is this hell?' He shook his head, not knowing the answer, nor caring. 'Know this: I see no angels anywhere, though the churchmen tell us we were all made in God's form. Prove me wrong. Renounce your lands. Return to William of Normandy and tell him he should leave England before judgement is pronounced upon him. For these are the End-Times. The last days. His. Yours. Mine.'

Frederic's eyes flickered to one side, his cunning thoughts clear.

Hereward smiled. 'No, that would never happen. For men never give up power unless it is taken from their dead hands.' He beckoned to Guthrinc.

'Aye?' the rebel answered.

'Give the thief of land your axe.'

Frederic's brow knitted. When his fingers closed around the haft, he looked at the weapon as if he had never seen one before. 'What is the meaning of this?'

'I am a knight now. An honourable man.' Hereward could see in Frederic's eyes that the landowner already knew what had happened at Burgh. As the warrior had anticipated, his uncle had informed the Normans. 'No murderer, despised by all who hear his name. No common outlaw. A knight. I walk shoulder to shoulder with you, and all the Norman invaders.' He nodded towards the axe. 'We shall have a wager of battle.'

Frederic's mouth fell open. 'A trial by combat?'

'And thereby solve this dispute between us, as the law demands.'

The landowner shook his head. 'No.' He tried to hand the axe back to Guthrinc. 'I . . . I do not recognize your knight-hood. It was conferred by a spiritual lord. Not by the king.'

'Raise the axe,' the warrior said.

Frederic threw the weapon to the ground as if it had burned him.

'Pick up the weapon and fight. You have no choice.'

Dropping to his knees, Frederic clasped his hands together. 'Have mercy.'

Hereward could feel Alric's eyes upon his back. As the warrior raised his axe over his head, the landowner's sobs cut through the roaring of the conflagration. 'Is this hell?' Hereward asked.

The axe drove down.

CHAPTER FIFTY-EIGHT

Blades of ice hung from the branches, glittering in the early morning sun. After the first hard frost of the winter, the wetlands shimmered white as the column of riders made their way along the frozen track from the direction of Lincolne. At the head of the band, Harald Redteeth looked up into the clear blue sky and knew that soon the snows would begin. He already wore his greased furs over his mail shirt, and his beard and hair had been freshly dyed red in anticipation of what was to come.

Beside him, Ivo Taillebois scanned the empty landscape for signs of life. His swarthy features had the heavy bone structure of mud-grubbing stock, but beneath his low brow his eyes gleamed with animal cunning. The Viking mercenary had heard the new Norman commander's nickname whispered throughout Lincolne and it was rumoured that King William himself had dubbed the man the Butcher. It was a title Taillebois had earned in earnest with his axe during the fateful battle at Hastings, Redteeth knew. And William the Bastard had rewarded the adventurer from Anjou well, in land, for the ship, horses and supplies Ivo had provided for the invasion. The Normans believed that if any man could crush the fenland uprising, it would be the Butcher. Harald remained to be convinced.

'How will the rebels survive the winter?' Ivo said in emotion-less, heavily accented English. He wore a black woollen cloak over his mail shirt, and brown leather gauntlets against the cold.

'Hereward celebrated a great victory against your men, and for that reason alone the fenlanders will be behind the rebels, for now. They will get the food they need, make no doubt of that.'

Taillebois grunted. 'If the people are afraid, they will offer no support.'

Galloping hoofbeats rumbled ahead. The commander brought the column of helmeted soldiers to a halt, and a moment later a black-capped scout rode hard towards them. He pulled his mount up sharply and said, 'The camp you described is empty. The rebels have moved on.'

Harald stifled a giggle at the voices in the willows that only he heard. Sweeping his hand in an arc, he said, 'This is their fortress. Water their ramparts, mist their walls, and every step a stranger takes through this land is one closer to death. Wherever their new camp is, you can be sure it will be more heavily defended and more lethal to approach.'

'You give them too much respect,' the Butcher sniffed. 'We have crushed English rebels time and again, from the south to the cold north.'

'Not rebels like these.'

The iron serpent of soldiers crawled on. By midday they had reached Barholme, where the Viking thought he could still smell burnt wood in the air. The frost had melted under the warm sun, but the wind stayed cold. Nothing remained of the old thegn's hall but a charred circle on the brown earth and heaps of wet ashes around black bones of wood. In other circumstances that would have been enough to hold the attention of the new arrivals, but all eyes were caught by a row of poles torn from the enclosure fence, fourteen in all. On each one hung a rotting head, the eyes long gone, the jaws gaping in a silent, never-ending scream. Hereward had taken his revenge on the men who had slain his brother, the Viking thought, and in the process had left a stark message for anyone who ventured to this place.

Taillebois remained silent, seemingly unmoved, as he stared into each face in turn.

A grey-haired man lurched from the surrounding willows, leaning on a tall staff. Redteeth recognized the old thegn, Asketil, who had spent so long inveigling himself into the favour of Aldous Wyvill, much good did it do him. The Viking didn't like the man. How could he betray his own kin? But he put on a broad smile and hailed the thegn.

'You are the new commander?' Asketil asked. When Ivo gave a curt nod, the older man said, 'Then I greet you. We have much to discuss, you and I, for it is my son who leads the rebels.'

'Your son?' Taillebois's eyes narrowed.

'He is a wicked man who cares only for himself, and has brought much pain and suffering to all who know him. This vanity of his will be the bane of the English, and he must be stopped before he leads all our people to disaster.'

'And you offer your services to this end?'

'The commander before you ignored my advice. But if you are wiser you will heed me, and Hereward will be crushed before you meet the fate of these men.' Asketil waved his hand towards the rotting heads.

Harald Redteeth grinned. He saw a near endless supply of coin in this, and, at the end of the road, joyful revenge upon his enemy. The ravens would be fed, the gods and his ancestors honoured. It was a good time to be alive.

'Very well,' Taillebois said, looking out across the inhospitable fens. 'This Hereward has met his match. We shall have such war as the English have never seen before.'

CHAPTER FIFTY-NINE

The sweet scent of fresh-cut wood hung over the hillside. Already the camp was taking shape. Wherever Alric looked, he saw timber frames rising among the dense ash and willow, woven wattle panels and wooden pails of daub. Each hut was half buried in the hillside, straw-packed under the boards for warmth, the roofs covered with turf; from even an arrow's flight away the shelters couldn't be seen.

Stamping his leather shoes for warmth, the monk rested one hand on rough bark and looked out across the wetlands, afire in the morning sun. An elusive peace settled on him for the first time in days. He found it a surprising sensation, with the weather of weapons blowing up on the horizon and the scent of blood in the wind. But he had the weight of purpose in his heart. The stain of his sin could be washed away, he felt sure. The murder of an innocent woman could be balanced by the saving of a wayward soul.

Turning, he watched Hereward, his friend, moving among the rebels, giving orders, offering guidance, wisdom even, encouraging, congratulating. A true leader. Alric nodded and smiled to himself. God's strange plan never failed to amaze him. Yet in the warrior's black eyes the monk saw his devil rising. The love of violence and death had been reawakened. Alric knew it numbed his friend's pain while at the same time destroying him by degrees. Hereward had filled the space in his heart carved out by his father with the need for blood.

Some say war turns us into beasts. But men do it to themselves.

This was his life now, Alric accepted. He would not stray from the path. Hereward would never be abandoned again, and though the monk had to wrestle with the Devil himself, he would bring that soul to heaven and grant his friend the peace he deserved. He was building a monument to God, a cathedral of the heart, and he would not falter.

The monk allowed his gaze to drift across the rich stew of humanity at work on the hillside: familiar faces, new friends, men with blood under their nails and unblinking stares, men filled with life and laughter, some cold and brooding and seeing only misery ahead. Redwald whistled as he hammered pegs into a joint, flashing occasional glances at his brother, looks which Alric felt were not brotherly at all. Redwald would need watching, he though. There was Guthrinc, uttering sardonic words that baffled all who passed, and Kraki, fierce and strong and passionate. And there was Acha bringing a cup of ale to Hereward, and turning the power of her dark eyes upon him. She smiled in the manner of a merchant haggling over a gold ring. All of them united in common cause; all of them driven by their own demons.

Dappled by the sun breaking through the branches, Hereward strode over. He eyed the monk with suspicion, as if he felt he were being judged. 'They work well,' he said. 'We will have a camp here that will keep them through the hard months.'

'Them?'

'I return to Flanders tomorrow. Turfrida waits for me and I would bring her back to be by my side, and the two Siwards who guard her. They will make a fine addition to this rebel band.'

'And then?'

Hereward smiled without humour. 'You know what then.' He looked past the monk to the sheet of shimmering water and the wooded islands rising from it, green ships asail upon a sea of glass. 'The scouts have returned. The Norman reinforcements have arrived, and Harald Redteeth is among them. We will be ready for them. Our stock of spears and axes grows by the day. And every man and woman here will be trained in the bow, so that we can match the invaders shaft for shaft.' A shadow crossed his face; a memory. 'And then we will sweep out of the marshes, and strike like serpents, gone before our enemies even know we are there. We will scourge them with fire. We will take heads as prizes, and hearts and fingers, and over time they will know the dread that comes with the night, and they will know they can never escape its cold grasp. There will be terror, and I will be the king of it.'

Alric saw his friend's eyes take on a strange cast, and heard his voice become like stone. The monk felt a wave of pity, and fear too, but he would not show it in his face. 'God watches over you, my friend.' *And I do, too.*

Under the swaying branches of the ash tree, they embraced as brothers. And then Hereward walked through the milling crowd, oblivious of the hopeful eyes laid upon him, and into the trees. Alric watched until his friend was gone. But the monk knew it would not be long until the wetlands ran red with blood again. He would return.

The Devil of the Fens.

The Ghost who comes from the Mist.

Hereward, the greatest of the English. The King of Terror.

A NOTE FROM THE AUTHOR

History is like an old movie with a degraded print. Scratches and crackling incomprehensible dialogue mar even the earliest scenes, and the further back you go, frames are burned out and sometimes whole reels are missing. Characters walk on and disappear a moment later, their story untold. Narrative jumps challenge even the most careful viewer, and meaning is lost or warped in the whirr of seemingly unrelated scenes.

Frustrating as this is for the historian, it provides an exciting opportunity for the novelist. The author can polish up what remains and fill in the gaps where something is missing, draw connections, perhaps, or search for that elusive meaning.

Decades of remarkable academic research has filled in a great deal of our understanding of the eleventh century, but so much of that era is still ambiguous or intangible. Heated debate rolls on about the politics and the motivations of the central figures; hardly surprising when the sources are so few and the propaganda so great. One thing we do know is that the men and women of those days were the same as us. The same drives, the same hungers, loves, flaws, ambitions and failings. We don't need narrative sources to understand that. We know men who seek power sometimes do terrible things. We know that there are few heroes, few villains, but lots of people trying to get by as they become swept up in events beyond their control.

Our protagonist in this novel, Hereward, is an intriguing prospect. Few today know of him, although his exploits have attained a mythic power that make him one of the three great heroes of Britain, alongside King Arthur and Robin Hood. He shares many qualities of those other two legends, but Hereward is rooted in a harder reality. The archetypal warrior's story is told in *De Gestis Herewardi Saxonis* and touched on in various monastic chronicles, and we are aware, in general terms, of the part he played in the English resistance to William the Conqueror. But even then the 'truth' – whatever that might be – is hidden by what appears to be fabulous invention as the writers of the time attempted to cast a mythic sheen on Hereward within years of his death. How much can be trusted? Certainly, the account in *De Gestis* is based in part upon an older version, and extracted from only a few surviving leaves, all of them mildewed and torn, so a great deal is missing. Timelines are confused, narratives conflicting. Yet it appears that Hereward's story was part of a popular tradition and that he was regarded, even within years of his death, as a legendary hero.

The missing reels of the film of Hereward's life are many. Historians have attempted to build a family background for the warrior from fragmentary evidence. Many accounts have veered towards the romantic and were common currency until recent times. But a detailed investigation by Peter Rex in his book *Hereward: The Last Englishman* demands a reassessment of much that was accepted about the warrior's life, and it is this more convincing work that I have decided to use as the basis for 'my' Hereward. I am also particularly indebted to Elizabeth Van Houts, whose essay 'Hereward and Flanders' in *Anglo-Saxon England* 28 (1999) provided the historical background for some of my account of the hero's time in exile.

Two other notes: the dates used at the beginning of several chapters correspond to our modern calendar, for the sake of clarity. And while Hereward calls himself a Mercian, at the time of this story the old Kingdom of Mercia had become a part of England during the political unification of the country in the previous century. Hereward's claim is purely a matter of cultural identity, based on the area where his father had his major landholding (even though he spent much of his childhood in the Fens). There was still a great deal of rivalry among residents of the old kingdoms, in the manner of the long-standing enmity between people of Lancashire and Yorkshire today.

In the end, Hereward remains only a ghost-image on the screen of history. His life story is fragmented and distorted. But the essence remains: a bloody warrior who used terror as a weapon; a flawed man, but a hero, perhaps, as great as any we have known.

James Wilde is a Man of Mercia. Raised in a world of books, he went on to study economic history at university before travelling the world in search of adventure. Unable to forget a childhood encounter – in the pages of a comic – with the great English warrior Hereward, Wilde returned to the haunted fenlands of eastern England, Hereward's ancestral home, where he became convinced that this legendary hero should be the subject of his first novel. Wilde now indulges his love of history and the high life in the home his family have owned for several generations in the heart of a Mercian forest.